MW01590846

The Queen's Garden Mage

Briana Bates

Copyright

Copyright 2016 by Briana Bates.

All rights reserved. No parts of this publication may be reproduced, distributed, or transmitted in any form or by any means, including photocopying, recording, or other electronic or mechanical means, without the prior written consent.

This is a work of fiction. Names, characters, places, events and incidents are either the product of the author's imagination or are used in a fictional manner. Any resemblance to actual persons, living or dead is purely coincidental.

DEDICATION

TO MY MOTHER
VERNICE LYNN BATES

I MISS YOU MORE THAN
WORDS CAN SAY

Characters

Adri Averell- Heir Apparent, second child to Servasli

Alia Averell - the first Queen of Angileri

Arely-Leader of the Queen's entire army, the Head of Heads

Arian- the cook's daughter

Carina- Rhyme's mare

Dahni Bluar- hails from the land of Raleli, a kind hearted water mage small in stature

Donta- A recruit, the Guard Captain's son

Eden Senchi- Queen's Gardener, large but gentle

Emery Randell-Queen's Gardener, shy and yet intelligent

Eris Rayon- Heir Apparent to the nation Ierilo

Fletcher- Lead centaur

Fawlin- Fletcher's Second

Kiyen- maidservant in service to the Queen

Lady Dai- Lady in waiting to the Queen

Leaf- green knight formed from Rhyme's magic

Lialey- Owner of one of the most famous Inn's in the capitol

Libeth Leair- Queen's Gardener, overly chipper and vibrant

Mariel Averell - Princess of Angileri, third child to Servasli

Neola- Guard Captain to the Queen

Resli- maidservant in the service of the Queen

Reason Denarii - twin brother to Rhyme, Horse Master

Renka- an enslaved Marr

Rhea- Rhyme's daughter

Rhyme Denarii - main character, one of the Queen's gardeners

Rosen Len- The Queen's Head Gardener

Santi- Merchant

Sir Zeron- Knight Protector to Prince Eris

Sorel Averell - Prince of Angileri, first born to Servasli

Servasli Averell- Current Queen of Angileri

Sowin- Captain of King of Dangilere's guard

Tailaan Kenta- Pretty boy from Erangi

Taeli- Childhood friend, adoptive daughter of the King of Dangilere

Teaon- King of Dangilere, adoptive father to Taeli

Zayez- brother to Lialey

Glossary

Alia Rose- named in honor of the first queen's beauty

Anear- capitol city of Angileri

Angileri- the country in which they live

Blue Bell- less potent than child's slumber

Child's Slumber- a flower that only carries one seed, it can make a grown man sleep like a child

Dangilere- a kingdom bordering Angileri

Death's Door- poison that is harder to detect, less well known but just as effective, no known cure

Dragon's Breath- a flower resembling flames

Dragon's Tongue- well-known poison which causes a painful death

Erangi- a nation across the ocean known for the beauty of its men and its architecture

Eternal Firefly- a stalk like plant with a bud at its topmost part that glows in the night and never dies

Fae Grape- a flavorful fruit only grown on the palace grounds

Fifth Day- Friday

First Day- Monday

Forth Day-Thursday

Giant's Spine- a tree taller than all others in existence said to be planted by the fabled giants

Green Sprout-Tavern

Hornets' Nest- a plant that when touched makes you feel as if you've been stung by hornets

Ierilo- a nation found in the mountains

Kantari- Island natation, covered by a jungle/rain forest

Last Garden- The haven that lies in the heart of Griffin Forest

Lialey's Inn- one of the most famous Inn's in the capitol

Limp Limb- Causes the limb you touch the plant with to go limp for no discernable reason

Marr- cousin to the centaur, can turn into horses

Pleasure's Curse- a plant which induces pleasure once ingested

Pleasure Garden- garden meant for the pleasure of all

Queen's Garden- garden meant for the Queen alone and those she allows to enter

Rahshi- capitol city of Raleli

Raleli- a land to the south, a desert oasis ruled by council

Raptor Vines- a hardy vine often used to replace rope for its flexibility, less likely to wear or snap

Samere- a land that keeps to themselves often forgotten

Second Day- Tuesday

Seven Day- a week

Seventh Day- Saturday

Shadow Garden- garden that holds many exotic, poisonous plants

Sixth- Day- Saturday

Slither of the sun's span/moon's- an hour

Sol-Lea-Leader of Leaders

Sun's span- a day

Sweet Grass- grass that's sweet in nature and can be eaten raw or cooked

Vipers Wrath- a thorny bramble that grows in excess on the edge of the Void

Were Lily- flower that blooms only during the full moon

The Heart Garden- the garden at the center of the palace

The Void- a place covered by vipers' wrath slowly eating away at the borders of surrounding nations

Third Day- Wednesday

Training Fields- Where the recruits and soldiers train

Twilight peony- peony made in the color of the Heir's eyes

Table of Contents

Chapter 1
Garden Mage

"Did you hear?!" My brother burst into the Queen's Garden as if a battalion of Royal Guards were chasing him. Not putting it past him, I glanced behind him to make sure no one followed. I relaxed, glad that I didn't have to aid him in getting out of yet another situation.

"Hear what?" I stroked my finger lightly along an Alia rose, named after the first Queen to rule this land, the most stunning woman alive during her time, Alia took the world by storm stepping into her father's shoes and ruling the land with an iron fist and gentle heart, loved and renowned by all, Alia was the first in a long succession of Queens. She opened doors for women, doors that once took centuries to even find, flew open as the land flourished under her reign and so it was that the dragons made peace with the land of Angileri and a law was passed that every ruler there after must have a strong bond not just with their ruler but the entire race, our strength shared through generations to come.

Our ruler was not based on gender, but by some luck of the draw we'd been ruled by Queens for as far back as man could remember, the history books could remember further. No one understood the anomaly of it, and no one questioned it for every Queen was a good one. The Trials ensured it. The princess having just reached her twenty first year of life had gone through the Trials the night before, Trials that would decide if she succeeded her mother or if she'd remain a princess until married to some foreign dignitary. Everyone had an opinion on the matter, everyone but me it seemed, my brother found it immensely frustrating. I was his sister and should be willing to gossip with him or at least help him gain a bit of dirt on his many…many enemies.

"Rhyme!" He growled as I smiled down at the tittering roses completely ignoring his excitement.

"What?" I snapped back impatient to get on with my grooming. These roses would bring forth faeries. I could tell by the glow in the center of their buds, my mother often told me all the flowers I spoke to bloomed Fae. I told her not to mention that where others could hear, to most I was a gardener, to a select few a healer. Not many knew that I could see the spirits within the plants, from the small blades of grass to the most ancient of trees. I saw them, and sometimes they spoke to me. The faeries were the only ones that could be made visible to others. With a little coxing that is…

"Are you even listening to me?" Reason grumbled in exasperation. I listened to the whispering of flowers eager to bloom and I smiled broader still sure that the news they shared is what my brother wished to tell me, I decided I would not ruin it for him. I sat back on my heels and gave him my full attention, letting the murmur of the plants surrounding us fade into background noise.

"What news has you so excited that you've left your duties for the other stable hands to finish." Reason snorted at the insult to his character. I chuckled as he puffed up with pride.

"You know damn well I would never be slack in my work; the horses love me as I love them. I'd never leave my duties to be finished by those I'm not sure could get the job done, no, the Guard Captain cut us loose a bit early today due to the news. Great for some and not so great for others."

"The news brother before I die of old age," he gave me a withering stare at my impatience, which I ignored easily. We'd known each other all our lives, that look hadn't worked when we were but children, it certainly didn't work now.

Reason heaved a heartfelt sigh, "I'll never understand how you can be a gardener, dithering your days away in the dirt, but as soon as people come into your presence all that serenity goes out the window."

"Plants know the sun, they know peace, they're free of stress, lacking in the need to gain power. Plants are simple, their spirits are simple, people on the other hand, are complicated." I countered without hesitation. "Also I do not have to deal with stupidity when gardening."

"I'm going to ignore the fact that you just subtly called me stupid…"

"Well if the boot fits," I watched his nostrils flare in frustration, it was so easy to rile him up. I smiled softly waiting for him to tell me the news I already knew.

"Are you done now?" He questioned once he'd calmed down.

"I've been quite ready since you burst into the Queen's Garden as if Royal Guards were chasing you. I haven't been able to focus on anything since." I stood dusting off my knees.

"You have a funny way of showing it," I just smiled until he gave up and told me the news he was clearly still very excited about. "Her Highness will succeed her mother." My lips curled into a grin as he deflated at my lack of shock or excitement.

"You knew!" Reason huffed crossing his arms over his chest petulantly. "You knew this entire time?"

"No. Not before you arrived. Sorry brother but the wind travels just a tad faster than you do and the flowers are even worse gossips." I patted his arm consolingly.

"Well do you know that not everyone among the Council is rejoicing?" He asked after a moment of silence.

"There are those that oppose the Princess' succession? Why?" I questioned brow furrowed in confusion. "She is kind, benevolent and hardworking…"

"Her image Rhyme, she is...on the larger side and some don't think it becoming of a queen to be...fat." He exhaled the last word seeing that I did not understand. The confusion cleared.

"Her Highness is not fat," Reason looked at me as if I were speaking a blatant lie in respects to our future monarch.

I shook my head, "Reason to oppose the Princess for image alone is very..."

"Shallow minded." He supplied.

"Human," I finished dryly reiterating why I preferred plants to human company.

"Well yes that is a very human trait, but I'm sure the Fae could be said to have their fair share." I did not disagree. It could be argued that the Fae had more than their fair share of shallow minded people. "Then you have those who hoped that the Prince would follow his mother."

"He failed his Trials, he has not even the hint of a connection with the dragon ruler let alone the entire race. Sorel is hot headed and rash and yes he is young, but I do not believe he will grow out of it anytime soon. We three are of the same year, just two older than the Princess herself and despite the fact that you are somehow always found in the midst of trouble I do not doubt your maturity for I know it is of a level with mine when you wish it to be." Reason stared at me as if I'd grown a second head. "Why are you looking at me like that?"

"You actually know things." I gave him the look those words deserved. "What? As I said you're always dithering away in your garden, not bothering with the outside world, of course I'm surprised you actually know about Prince Sorel and how he failed his Trials."

"The flowers gossip worse than you do, the trees hold many secrets and the grass converses with the wind, all I need do is but ask and I'd know it." I countered dryly.

"You could be truly powerful if you wished." Reason gazed at me with new respect in his eyes.

"Yes, but I have never craved power." I shrugged letting the moment of seriousness fall away, we did not often speak of our gifts, for both our sakes. It wouldn't do to have others ask questions.

"Part of the Council is still in full support of the Prince; they want a male ruler back on the throne." Reason snorted in disgust. "Those misogynistic idiots are living centuries in the past."

"Why have they not been eradicated from the Council? Do they have any real power?" I asked in disbelief.

"Her Majesty keeps her enemies close. She has always been a very intelligent woman." I nodded in understanding before he continued. "Those men are few and far between and not enough sit the Council to have real power. There are those other select few that support the youngest of the royal line, a year junior to Princess Adri, Princess Mariel who is the spitting image of her mother after all. Those members of the Council do not personally have qualms with Adri's succession per say they just dislike the fact that she's..."

"Her Highness isn't fat." My brother once more looked at me as if I were going above and beyond what was expected of a subject, even one whom worked in the Queen's Garden, closer to royalty than most dreamed of experiencing in their lifetime.

"I take that back, you know nothing beyond your gardens and your flowers." Reason shook his head at me in exasperation and I wasn't up to arguing with him about something I didn't fully understand.

"Do we know her connection? Has she accepted the crown? Have any suitors come forward?" I asked instead changing the subject to something different but no less important.

"I believe her connection is a secret, though there is talk that it's stronger than her mother's," Reason gazed at me thoughtfully, glancing briefly around the Queen's Garden before speaking. "Though probably not stronger than yours." I didn't acknowledge his words, he continued as if he'd said nothing at all out of the ordinary. "We'll know if she's accepted the crown this evening, who knows she might choose otherwise and then we'll have to wait another year hoping and praying that Princess Mariel passes her Trials."

"The land is tense Reason, I do not think another year of waiting and hoping would be good for us. As well Mariel may be the spitting image of her mother, but her work ethic is lacking. She is not one to get dirty. I haven't ever found her in the Queen's Garden." My brother didn't question me, after all I knew plants and dirt and he knew horses and tricks.

"Truly the biggest problem most people have with Princess Adri is that she's fat." Reason didn't hesitate simply stating the facts he'd heard as he'd heard them. "As for suitors none worth mentioning. The ones who have are after power and not truly interested in the Princess. It would be a sad day in history to not have a Queen's Tournament soon after a Princess passing the Trials."

I shook my head at the absurdity of it all turning back to my gardening, "Leave me to my flowers brother, though I had not mentioned it. I'm sure you could guess that flowers do not judge. After all every plant has a purpose."

"For what it's worth despite her size, I'm sure she'll make a great Queen." He mumbled softly after a moment of silence.

I listened to the flowers smiling softly as they rejoiced in discovering their most common visitor second only to the Queen herself would one day walk their paths carrying the title of Majesty. They could not think of one more fitting to rule than the Queen's eldest daughter and neither could I. "She'll surpass her mother by far and someone worthy of her hand will come forward regardless if it's one or many, someone will come." Reason bowed his head in agreement.

Reason opened his mouth to speak only to freeze at my up raised hand, I took in the excitement, the cadence of soft voices growing louder as we stood in silence. "We must go; her Highness Adri is coming."

I turned from the path my brother had taken to arrive in the heart of the Queen's Garden and I asked the flowers to part for me as I raced with the lightest of footsteps to the stone wall meant to keep out prying eyes. I ran up its face catching the edge with the use of long arms and slung myself over. "Hurry Reason, none should be caught in the Queen's Garden save the Queen, or her children." I breathed urgently while my brother stared in awe at the soil now free of roses.

He started from his stupor before racing forward running up the wall and catching the edge beside me, hefting himself up with a grunt of effort. We both dropped to the other side as the Princess raced into the Queen's Garden like my brother had not long ago. Though I'm sure her haste was for entirely different reasons. I thanked the Alia roses for their aid patting the stone wall covered in slow growing moss soothingly in apology for disrupting its slumber. "When did that become a law?"

I turned to my brother as we strolled away from the wall following a path that would lead us to the Training Fields and the stables where Reason was usually found when not in some form of trouble or another. "It's not, of course any Gardener can be found in the Queen's Garden it's our profession after all. I simply make it a point to not be found there."

"Is there a reason for this?" We stopped by the Training Fields watching the Guard Captain and his Second as they instructed new recruits on fighting techniques.

"When we first arrived here," I leaned on the wooden fence observing the lithe combative dance that would help them prevail in combat. "It was a game, to test my gift. I would do my work and listen to the green while trying not to become overwhelmed or distracted because unlike you I cannot turn it off. The plants, the trees, the flowers they never stop talking, there are sleepy murmurs even in the depths of winter, and even in the silence of night the trees sing to the moon. So I practiced. I practiced every day since the first day of arriving in the palace. I practiced until I could speak with them individually, until I could distinguish voices, until the slow drawl of the most ancient of trees became second nature. I practiced and I listened so that when the Queen arrived I was nowhere to be found and in the beginning it was but a game to help me practice. Now it's a way to preserve their privacy, after all only the Queen may enter the Garden and those who have permission, her children and her Gardeners. They go there to escape from prying eyes and I do not want it ever said that my presence disturbed them." I smiled as a young recruit was swept from his feet, the grass beneath our feet laughing merrily at his expense. "The Head Gardener often wonders if I actually do my job because save for you none have ever found me in the Queen's Garden."

"The plants do not warn you of my approach?" Reason leaned on the fence beside me our long hair mingling together between us his dark waves cascading into mine. Somehow despite that I often wore it up, my hair always somehow found a way to escape it's leather binding. I caught the leather thong still wrapped in bits of my hair and tucked it into a pocket for later, it didn't matter now. My work was done for the day. Though perhaps I would go back in the evening to see about my Were Lilies, named so because they were only found when the moon shone its full face…

"They speak of everything brother, but you are my blood and so why would I hide from you," I gave him a look that justly questioned his intelligence.

He laughed loud and long before pulling me into a one-armed hug, "Never change sister. Never change."

I wrapped my arm around his waist hugging him back, "I had not planned on it brother, not in the slightest." He snorted softly trying to contain his amusement, but I could see the glimmer of it shinning in eyes.

"There will be a feast in her honor tonight." My brother chuckled, "I get the feeling you'll be nowhere to be found throughout the entirety of it." I gazed at Reason through dark raven locks before turning back to the Training Fields deciding that observing my Were Lilies had suddenly become a priority.

"I have no idea what you're talking about brother." Reason snorted again squeezing me one final time before releasing me.

"I'll see you at the celebration, it starts this evening and if Princess Adri chooses to succeed her mother there will be a greater one held in her honor a seven day from now." I grimaced at the thought. "Do try to at least make an appearance." He tossed over his shoulder as he walked away likely to find some form of trouble or another.

I drifted away from the fence bordering the Training Fields disappearing into a copse of trees that lined the wall shielding my beloved garden. I'm sure it looked a lot like magic as I asked the trees to aid in my escape from prying eyes. More than one servant around the palace thought me more than a little strange. I tried my best to encourage them, with the color of my skin and the magic so very different than any had experienced in this land my brother and I were never going to fit in. From the start we'd decided to stand out, and yet at the same time hiding the most important parts of our gifts from unlikely enemies and even each other at times. I was sure that was genuine awe on Reason's face when he'd witnessed the roses part for us with nary a word spoken. I grinned as I scaled the stone wall covered in slumbering moss trying to decide how much trouble I'd get in if I failed to make an appearance at her Highness Adri's celebration.

I gazed down on my pride and joy, my whole world now filled with more flowers and plants than any normal person could think to imagine. My smile faded slightly as I took in the Princess sitting in the center of a place I considered a sanctuary weeping softly. I took in her appearance larger than her sister, but taller as well, though shorter than my near six-foot height she was not a short woman. Her hair was rich earth mixed with sand, if it were soil palm trees would grow there. It was messy more curls than waves, her skin was fair, palm cream to my tan. Her eyes were blue and purple an eternal twilight that could fascinate when filled with happiness or mirth and frighten when filled with frustration or rage. Some would argue it was her most notable feature. Others would disagree…

I took in her size, her face was free of baby fat, her jaw was a stubborn one, given to a woman used to fighting for what she wanted. Her fingers thick and long made for strong hands easily able to hold any weapon, though I knew she favored the bow, she was not afraid to get dirty. Her figure was all curves, I traced my eyes over the trim of her waist which would never be small, her wide hips meant for bearing children and enticing anyone willing to look below the waist, over thighs that could perhaps kill a man or draw him closer in the heat of passion. I took in her Highness, and decided that no she was not small, but nor was she fat. She was a healthy woman who enjoyed food, but I knew she ran with the guards, I knew she practiced on their training fields, bleeding, sweating, crying and laughing with the lot of them. I had seen her cooking in the kitchens, I had seen her mucking the stalls with the stable hands and washing clothes with the maids. I had seen her tenderly tend to my garden and talk politics with her mother. I had seen more of Adri than I had of either of her siblings and I knew more than anyone that she would be the best to seat the throne…if she accepted it.

I watched her Highness belt out her sorrows in the center of a garden that would one day be hers and I let the voices fade to indistinguishable murmurs around me. The flowers spoke of everything, indeed the lot were worst gossips than my brother, but unless requested, and I rarely made the request, their memories were short. I'd been giving the royal family their privacy for this long, not even such astounding news would change that. After a time, the Princess dried her tears, though she wore sadness like a mask etched into her features.

I glanced up at the sky slowly fading to darkness, before waving my fingers slightly at the patch of land where the Were Lilies would bloom, using my magic to coax them forth just a bit early. Her Highness Adri watched awe sparkling in her eyes as the flowers unfurled their leaves and white lilies bloomed, each of their hearts holding a different color, glowing softly in the growing light of the moon. She moved from her perch on the fountain, covered in vines growing in a spiraling pattern enhancing its beauty, to the patch of soil once covered in green sprouts now blooming a small army of one of the most sought after flowers in Angileri.

She kneeled on the ground not worried in the least about dirtying her trousers as she traced her fingers along each and every lily leaning into to breathe in a scent more heavenly than any rose. Her Highness sat in my garden for a long time after that, finding peace in the feel of soil crumbling between her fingers and the scent of flowers filling the air. I watched her for a while before quietly climbing back down the opposite side of the wall. While a princess could afford to be late to her own celebration. I do not believe anyone else on the guest list was able to do the same. Unless of course it was the Queen her own self. Though as long as I'd lived in the palace Queen Servasli had never been late to any celebration held in her honor. There was her coronation, but that was long before I had come to live here.

I raced past the Training Fields hoping that my brother had thought to prepare my dress uniform, thankful in that moment that any servant to the Queen herself had the privilege to don the colors specific to their job title. It was considered an honor that I did not honestly care for, but it made it easier for one to get ready in a rush. I sprinted into the courtyard slipping and sliding through the procession of people whom had likely received their invitations months in advance to this monumental event to the servant's door hidden around the corner. I ducked passed a tray piled high with food, before speed walking down a corridor lined with Royal Guards each giving me a curious look as I passed the throne room without so much as a by your leave. I was just rounding the corner leading to my quarters when my brother appeared eyes wide with panic.

He relaxed instantly upon catching sight of me, "Hurry Rhyme there are foreign monarchs and the Queen wishes to show case her garden." I let him pull me into our shared suite getting ready with the haste born of long practice.

"Why must I hurry I am not the Queen's Head Gardener; in all honesty I am not even sure she knows I exist." I pulled on a pale green undershirt while my brother laced up my trousers, as green as the grass grows, embroidered with leaves formed from golden thread.

"She wants you all there, Rosen impressed upon me that if she did not find you mingling among the guests that she would murder you with the raptor vines cascading from your window sill and then bury your body in your beloved garden where nary a soul would dare to look." I allowed my brother to help me into my shirt which laced up in the front much as the trousers did. He helped me settle the heavy fabric while I fussed with the cuffs of my sleeves.

"That's a very graphic description," I offered brow furrowed.

Reason stroked my hair from my face catching my eye with a serious look of his own, "She was very angry Rhyme, do not slip away until the Queen her own self has seen you among company. I'm sure Rosen will be one of the first to find you."

"I am not looking forward to that conversation," I grumbled turning my back to him so that he could do my hair up in the intricate warrior style bun he now wore his in. My brother would never admit it but he was almost as good as any Lady's maid at doing hair.

"Yes well I did not enjoy her threat to my manhood if I failed to locate you in time, but I dealt with it and you will too. Likely with more grace than I." He finished softly the playful tug of my hair the signal that he'd finished.

"Likely," I agreed turning to face him. He looked dashing in the military standard of green and black, though not a part of the Royal Guard he trained the horses and the soldiers that rode them into battle not as horse and rider separately but as a whole, one unit. His training had spurred the rumors that we had centaurs in our midst. My brother was second to none in the stables, though he often played the part of a stable hand, for he would never shriek his duty, he was his Majesty's Horse Master and would likely hold the title for the entirety of his life…if he could stand clear of trouble that is.

I straightened the broach pinned over his heart, a stallion in full rampant, a grin filled with pride stealing across my features. "That would be a great feat considering no flower I have ever handled would dare to harm me and I have handled near about all of them, though I would enjoy being buried in the Queen's Garden when I am finally laid to rest." I added as an afterthought as he pinned a golden Alia rose just over my heart.

While his dress uniform resembled the Royal Guard's mine was newer created in rein of our current Queen, beneath her the Queen's Gardeners had become less of a joke and more of an honor. We donned the deep green of the forest and the yellow gold of the sun, with leaves of shimmering golden brown mixed with hints of jade embroidered in random patterns throughout the fabric. Many thought the Queen's uniforms flashy, but anyone of her soldiers could easily tell you how practical it was to wear green, black and near golden brown when living in a country renowned for its forest and greenery. There was many a war that had be won simply because the enemy had failed to see us coming.

"Only you could counter a threat with cheek without so much as a change in expression," I gazed back at him brow raised.

"Was I supposed to feel frightened?" Reason shook his head before turning me around and shoving me towards the door.

"Move along sister, my manhood and your life lay on the line. Though more importantly my manhood." He ensured that our pace was anything but slow. I hooked my arm in his as we drew closer to the ballroom the cadence of voices quickly growing louder, unlike the voices of the flowers often soft and soothing besides. I could not let them fade to the background and ignore that they existed.

"Your manhood is more important than my life?" I asked after I finally realized what he'd said. I'd have given him the look that comment rightly deserved but we soon stood at the top of a wide staircase lined with green and black carpet used only for special occasions any other time it was red…any other time no one was announced into the room save for the Queen and her children. Important night indeed…

"As you said the plants would never lay harm to you making Rosen's threat moot. Her threat to my manhood on the other hand, still stands and I would very much enjoy being able to have children in the distant future."

I snorted softly rolling my eyes as our names and titles were shouted for the entire Queendom to hear and process. "You are lucky that we have a celebration we have no choice in attending or I'd make Rosen's threat to your manhood seem like a child's whimsical mocking session on the playground."

Reason chuckled at my underlining threat whispered as we walked in time with the music down the staircase while everyone took us in murmuring about our unique features. "I am quite glad for this celebration actually it ensures that I will make it through the night alive."

"Sometimes brother I wish you had been born a girl," I offered back voice filled with mock exasperation.

"You say that but we both know you wouldn't trade me for the world. We're twins and that means something…to both of us." I silently agreed though I didn't give him the satisfaction of hearing it aloud.

"Ahh, I think I see the cook's daughter Arian, and perhaps she'd be interested in bearing my children." Before I could warn him of the danger my brother was off in pursuit of a woman he would never get, at least not beneath the watchful eye of her mother. I grabbed a flute of wine from a passing servant and took a carful sip while I watched the festivities around me waiting for the best opportunity to slip away.

Chapter 2
Twilight Peonies

"Rhyme if your dress uniform did not fit you as it did you would be the spitting image of your brother from behind." I smiled turning to find Rosen glaring at me in all her aging glory, despite the fact that she was well into her fiftieth year she could easily pass for thirty. She was the Head Gardener, the Queen instructed her in what she wanted done and she instructed us. Well she instructed the other Gardeners. Rosen had trouble locating me at the best of times, though she would never admit that to our Lady Queen, but then again nor would I.

"Why Rosen, you flatter me insinuating that I actually have a figure buried beneath all this fabric," Her simmering glare settled into a look of bemusement and I smiled more brightly for getting her to break her steely resolve. Though Rosen could rarely find me actually dallying away in the gardens, she knew my work, she knew the taste of my magic. As well she knew that I could easily steal her position from beneath her, but we both knew that though my magic was strong I did not want a high position or the power that came with it. We had an understanding Rosen and I. So long as she left me be I would do my share of the work nothing more or less than that. After all, if I did everything where would that leave my fellow Gardeners. No we rotated through the gardens littering the palace grounds. There were four gardens and five gardeners Rosen at the Head instructing us. Every one of us had some sort of plant magic after all the Queen had wanted the best.

"You clean up quite nicely when you choose to," She stroked a streak of soil from my cheek that I had missed in my haste to be here on time. "I see your brother delivered my message."

"Yes, he was quite adamant in my attendance." I raised my glass smiling softly as I took another teasing sip, the taste of Fae grapes singing across my taste buds. I knew they were ready to harvest. My gentle smile turned into a full blown grin, "You did threaten his manhood after all."

"Yes but I threatened your death, you'd think that would be of priority." She countered wryly.

"I love my brother, he is a hard worker, a great stable hand and the best Horse Master in the entire history of Angileri…"

"Bragging much," Rosen added though she raised her glass in full agreement of everything I'd said.

"He also finds himself in more trouble than a grown man has a right to," Rosen choked on her drink in startled amusement, turning away to clean herself up and regain her composure. I waited patiently.

"Sometimes I forget how harshly honest you can be; after all you so rarely grace me with your presence." She said by way of explanation tucking her handkerchief back into her pocket setting her empty glass on a passing tray.

"Yes, it's quite unfortunate." I set my half empty flute on another passing tray.

"Quite," Rosen agreed lips curling slightly.

"All that aside at the end of the day my brother is a man, despite how much he loves me his manhood will always come first. As it does with every man it is often times their down fall." I waved my hand in my brother's direction just in time for him to get a drink thrown in his face.

Rosen laughed heartily unable to contain her mirth at my choice words and perfect timing. Once she'd calmed and wiped the tears from her eyes she gave me a friendly pat on the shoulder. "I know that celebrations of this nature make you feel right uncomfortable but stick around for this one Rhyme it's important to the Queen and the Heir Apparent as well."

I bowed my head slightly deciding to stick around longer than I'd first planned if only to appease her Majesty. Rosen left me as my brother had without so much as a backwards glance. I watched another tray pass me by before trying to find the buffet table littered with foods that would no doubt wet our appetites without actually sating them no matter how much we ate.

"Rhyme!" Slim fingers wrapped around my arm pulling me around and deterring me from the ultimate goal of filling my belly.

"Lady Dai," I offered by way of politeness more than anything. Technically speaking when showing respect one would refer to me by my title followed by my last name if we were but strangers or my first if we were close friends. As my brother called me Gardener Rhyme in the company of nobles and I referred to him as Horse Master Reason. Lady Dai lacked such decorum honestly there were days I wondered if she was house broken, though that could just be my lack of social grace showing through as my brother often told me in good company. Actually usually he just told me not to speak at all when I wore a certain look on my face, a look I'm quite sure I was wearing in that moment as the Lady went on and on about one thing or another that had nothing to do with me, my brother or any garden spanning the entirety of the palace grounds.

"Rhyme can you believe that such a…such a pig might one day sit the throne?" Lady Dai questioned with an undignified snort that quickly drew me back to the conversation at hand.

"Whom do you mean Lady Dai?" I knew exactly who she meant but I wanted her to say it. If my brother were here he'd probably be ushering the good Lady away from the very volatile situation she found herself in.

"Why the Heir Apparent, Princess Adri her own self," She spoke as if I were a few plants short of a full garden.

"I believe that Princess Adri will make a fine Queen, she is beautiful, just and kind. Certainly not a pig, unlike others I know." I gave a dismissive once over to show her exactly who the comment was meant for, "and Lady Dai." I waited until she looked me in the eyes. "My name is Gardener Denarii to you, try to remember it this time." With those words I walked away once more in search of the buffet table completely forgetting Lady Dai in my quest to find food.

I came across two servants I recognized, as servants they had given up the rights to a title for a life off the streets, though it wasn't unheard of to give servants you associated with often titles of their own. "Maidservant Resli, Maidservant Kiyen," I addressed them each respectfully drawing their attention.

"Do either of you happen to know where I can find the buffet table I am quite hungry," I said rubbing my aching belly to prove a point.

Kiyen smiled at me ever the exuberant one of the two, "Forgot to eat again in your dalliance with the Queen's Garden?" she asked overly suggestive.

Resli blushed on my behalf, "Excuse her Gardener Rhyme, her parents were heathens."

Kiyen rolled her eyes, "My parents are farmers, and still very much alive Resli. Gardener Rhyme knows what I meant."

"I did, just the way she went about saying it was quite amusing. Now the buffet table," I prompted before they could start bickering as they were wont to do when paired together.

"It'll be towards the back of the ballroom closer to the doors leading into the heart of the Pleasure Garden and without a doubt where the Queen has the foreign dignitaries enthralled with one tale or another." Resli supplied before Kiyen could open her mouth shoving her away before she could think to say another word.

I watched them go, smiling softly as they bickered like siblings do, though they weren't at all related they'd found family in the most unlikely of places and were all the better for it. I turned and made my way to the buffet table. I lamented the fact that they did not have bigger plates, I could not in good consciousness pile a small one high with food knowing how poorly it would reflect on her Majesty. I signed resigning myself to feeling hungry until dinner later in the evening.

I reviewed the selection of fruit and grabbed two of each before I decided I was pushing the limitations of how much I could fit within the confines of such a small circumference. I popped a grape into my mouth enjoying it far more than I had enjoyed the wine. Fae grapes were tarnished when someone decided they would make a lovely wine.

"Gardener Denarii?" It was a question more than a statement spoken by a voice I'd heard only at a distance for my entire life here. Save that first time, still a bittersweet memory of loss and freedom.

"Your Majesty," I turned to face the Queen bowing but slightly to acknowledge her station above me, I would give her that respect because she had saved me from poverty, she had given me a chance I would not otherwise have. She had educated me and fed me and allowed me to perfect my gift in a place meant specifically for those like me and so I bowed to her, but she had taken me from my people. From a life of poverty that I would have struggled in yes but I'd have made it out of on my own. My gifts ensured it. She had taken me from a loving family, from a place where I was not the dark haired tanned skin foreigner. She had taken me against my will to give me a better life and though I could appreciate all that her decision had wrought me I could not forgive her. I bowed just low enough to acknowledge that she was my ruling sovereign, but no lower unwilling to bow my head past the point where I could no longer look her in the eyes the true respect you showed a Queen.

She acknowledged my bow with a head tilt of her own, a question shinning in her eyes. Prince Sorel choked on his drink, Princess Mariel having her head turned missed the entire affair and Princess Adri as composed as her mother simply looked at the

Queen curiously. The foreign dignitaries did not understand our customs and so were lost as to what had caused such an extreme reaction in the Prince now slowly growing red with embarrassment.

"I do not think I've seen head nor tale of you since you arrived here all those years ago," The Queen said after a moment of uncomfortable silence.

"I have been very busy your Majesty," I offered taking in whom I believed to be a foreign King and his son both were quite dashing though neither appealed to me.

"As you should be, Head Gardener Rosen often tells me I am a hard task master." Everyone laughed softly as she meant them to, I simply smiled down at my plate.

"Not everyone is equipped to make the hard decisions your Majesty, you do what you must for the good of all," Everyone raised their glass in acknowledgement of that stated truth, save your Majesty and I. I held a plate and the Queen stood observing me with intelligent eyes smiling softly.

"Thank you for such high praise," I tipped my head respectfully her words were sincere. "Sir Zeron, Prince Eris," Queen Servasli turned to her guests. "This is one of my Gardeners. I think of them all very highly and treat them with the respect of any well favored noble." Prince Eris raised his brow slightly at that but did not question the respect shown to one he no doubt considered quite low as he shook my hand. I clasped arms with Sir Zeron one warrior to another, I saw a glimmer of respect spark in his eyes I tipped my head and he hesitantly did the same the gesture far more awkward in someone who only half understood our customs no doubt.

The fact that the Prince knew nothing of them brought him lower in my eyes, I decided that he'd be perfect for Princess Mariel who seemed quite bored with what was going on before her. I ate another piece of my fruit while the Queen explained the workings of her four gardens talking about how if one knew the workings of each they were all connected. Of course she did not explain how but it kept the Prince and Knight absorbed nonetheless.

"Do you enjoy your work?" I blinked at the delicate voice I'd never held the pleasure of hearing so close, it was like sunlight peeking through the clouds on a rainy day a small but pleasant shock you weren't the least bit expecting.

"I am a plant mage, the gardens are my life," I replied turning my attention to the Heir for whom everyone had an opinion nary a one of them good.

She smiled a smile that did not at all reach her eyes. A practiced smile, one for courtly affairs and polite conversation. It did not fit her face, oh not to say it wasn't a lovely smile it was but it wasn't real, I could see in her eyes that she wanted to be anywhere but where she was in the midst of a party where everyone had something to say about her. Of course they wouldn't say the half of it to her face, she was a Princess after all but all you need do was watch out of the corner of your eye at how they pointed, how they stared and laughed at the most unlikely Heir that could be chosen. I'm sure more than half the room hoped she would decline, step down and move to some distant land out of sight and out of mind.

My brother often said that I was horrible at social niceties, until I wasn't that is. "Your Highness gossip tells me that congratulations are in order for passing your Trials." The Princess started slightly at the word gossip. I smiled softly. "I know that none truly know the news on whether you've chosen to succeed your mother despite passing your Trials but I hope your answer is a resounding yes."

The smile stealing across her features shone brightly in the blue violet that was her eyes, Prince Sorel of course had to ruin the moment. "Gardener Denderi was it?"

"Denarii," I enunciated with the accent of my homeland.

The expression on his face resembled more of a grimace than a smile, I decided that Prince Sorel was more suited to Prince Eris at least his sister had the social grace to be embarrassed at his purposeful insult. "Of course my apologies," he didn't sound in the least apologetic. "I was just wondering if you would show us a bit of what a plant mage does?"

I narrowed my eyes at him, "There are no plants in the room fair Prince," insulting his masculinity subtly. Princess Mariel stepped closer to her sister suddenly fascinated with the conversation. The Queen watched us over the shoulder of her company keeping them engaged and out of the fray, no need to make this bigger than it was. I could almost hear Reason arguing about how I was meant to be the cool headed one as I was always getting him out of trouble.

"There is fruit on your plate and a wilting flower in Princess Mariel's hair, surely one or the other is something you can work with." He sniffed, a sneer of disdain plastered across his features.

"Brother," Princess Mariel warned, my estimation of the Queen's third child rose in that moment, "You over step your bounds."

"I am a Prince," he shot back smartly.

"Yes," Princess Adri replied calmly, "But she is the 'Queen's' Gardener" she emphasized the word Queen's.

"No one asked you to speak," the Prince snarled, the Heir closed her mouth turning her face away.

"She has every right to say as she pleases." I countered as Princess Mariel opened her mouth to admonish him. "More right to command me than you ever will, after all she passed her Trials, she bonded with the dragons and she will one day be your Queen if she so chooses. You will do well to remember that." I finished sharply wanting nothing more than to smash my plate it to his face.

Princess Mariel covered her mouth a look of approval • shinning in her eyes as she hid the smile spreading across her features at her brother's speechlessness. I offered my plate to the Heir, "Hold this please your Highness," Princess Adri took my plate a look of amused shock brining out bright specks of lavender in the violet blue of her eyes.

"Princess Mariel if I may?" I raised my hand slowly to her hair, she ducked slightly allowing me to take the dying flower. "A peony," I smiled softly at the slowly dying flower as it sung softly about a life of sunlight and camaraderie. "Fitting for you Princess," she smiled softly at the compliment. I cupped the peony in my hands while the three royal children watched with varying looks of curiosity. I released a trickle of my magic and the peony began to wither and die.

"You're killing it," Princess Mariel murmured face saddened at the display.

"Yes," I glanced up at her briefly. "All flowers die, all the flowers at the palace bloom again. Such is the point of our magic. Any plant mage can make a flower grow given enough time, it's nature's way." They gazed at the shriveled husk now laying in my hand. "Peonies bloom in nearly every color except blue." Slowly the pods that remained began to crack open revealing their seeds, "Growing the flowers from seed can sometimes take up to five years, but it is rewarding because the blooms from these seeds will be new, a completely different variety of peony than their mother plant. Rosen has tried for years to grow blue peonies; she has told me it is nigh impossible despite cross breeding."

Once the husk of the old plant became nearly nothing in my palms and all that remained were the seeds I murmured a request only the shivering seeds could hear, they heard but could not yet speak. All I felt was a glimmer of excitement at the opportunity to be more than they ever thought they would be. I smiled softly blowing the seeds from my hands and watching them float on a perfectly timed breeze that had nothing to do with my magic and everything to do with luck. "Is that it?" Prince Sorel asked expecting something more.

Princess Mariel was becoming my new favorite royal with her utter disdain for her brother's incompetence, though I could see the disappoint in her eyes that there wasn't anything more. "I am not the Head Gardener, no two gifts are the same and so I may never know how she coaxes the sprouts from the soil, how she convinces the trees to bloom different blossoms every year or if she convinces them at all. Perhaps she demands it and her power is so great that the flowers bow before her and the trees listen without question. I do not know how she went about getting blue peonies to grow save the fact that she has tried for many years." I grinned letting my magic touch upon every seed still floating in the air. Slowly but surely gasps of startled delight filled the room as violet blue peonies bloomed in the air drifting about on a breeze that came from the large open doors leading out into the Pleasure Garden. One slowly fell into my up raised hand.

A second one bloomed beside it and I gazed down into the perfect imitation of Princess Adri's eyes, violet blue, twilight with hints of lavender specks in the mix. "If I may?" I leaned towards Princess Mariel whose eyes shown with untold delight in seeing something so magical. She bent forward allowing me to place the flower in her hair. I offered the second more vibrant flower to the Heir, "A gift Highness to the future Queen of Angileri." Princess Adri took it gently while I stole back my plate, she raised the flower to her nose taking in the scent of the delicate bloom. All around us the ballroom was in an uproar as others reached their hands into the sky taking hold of the floating blooms.

Rosen stood on a cleared section of the buffet table to the horror of many a maid servant and quickly calmed the crowd with a speech about beauty, honor and the blessing of the Gods that allowed her to finally have her years of research and cross breeding come to fruition on the eve of the Princesses feast for which she would hopefully announce that she would be succeeding her mother the Queen. Rosen went on to describe all the hard work that had gone into such a display stressing how it had taken every Gardener in the Queen's arsenal to set it up in time. Tears of joy shown in the Head

Gardener's eyes at the beautiful display that many no doubt would remember for the rest of their lives. Rosen raised her glass dubbing the blooms Twilight Peonies in honor of the Heir's unique eyes and even though not everyone supported the succession everyone cheered filling the large room as they applauded Rosen's perfectly timed speech raising their glasses in shared respect of the woman who had managed such a phenomenal feat with only four plant mages and none the wiser besides.

"She took credit for your work?" Were the first words spoken as the three siblings slowly collected themselves still reeling from the display and the perfectly timed speech.

I gazed at Princess Mariel smiling softly, "Who's to say it was me at all?" I countered.

"We saw…" Princess Adri paused in her words unable to complete her sentence.

"You saw me help a flower die and then blow the seeds away," I finished for her.

The Prince stood speechless, "You're good," Princess Mariel said after a long moment of silence in which no one could think of anything to say. Respect shown in the oceans of blue that made up her eyes. "You abided my brother's request, you showed him your magic by speeding along the peony's death. You gave a gift to the Head Gardener who has, as you said been trying for years to produce blue peonies. I'm sure those were tears of joy shinning in her eyes. Her speech though not planned was inspiring, anyone would be quite hard pressed to question my sister's succession for the remainder of the night after such a display of devotion from the Queen's Gardeners. The Head Garden basically said you all support her and near about see her as Queen. You have also given my sister a flower that no doubt will be just a renowned as the Alia rose, though it doesn't carry her name no one can mistake the fact that it resembles the quite memorable violet blue of her eyes. You have showed us magic, more magic than we have ever seen in a plant mage and we cannot in good conscious prove it was you. As you said you blew away the seeds, we saw no murmured incantations no hand motions, nothing save that final bit where you took a peony from the air and caused a second to bloom from nothing. That is all we can claim you have done and so I tip my head to you Gardener Denarii," She did so then as well raising her glass high along with her sister. Her brother grimaced but did the same all while the Queen looked on curiously questions sparkling in her eyes.

"Everyone is quite wrong about you Princess Mariel," I said as they dropped their glasses while several guests murmured curiously around us wondering what had caused such high regard. "You are as beautiful as your mother, the spitting image in fact but you are just as intelligent and people fail to realize you are more than your face. If I had a glass I would raise it to you," I raised my plate instead and the Princess blushed prettily while Princess Adri raised her glass in her honor.

"Thank you," I tipped my head in respect.

"Have a blessed evening," I bowed to Princess Mariel as low as I bowed to the Queen, I gave the Heir the respect I should have given her mother and bowed low enough that I could no longer see her eyes and I stared at the Prince bowing not at all before turning and taking my leave.

"Gardener Denarii," I glanced over my shoulder at the red faced Prince, while his sisters gazed on once more shocked at my very deliberate display of respect. "I am still a Prince; you'll do well to show me the proper respects."

I grabbed a passing glass of wine, raising it mockingly in his honor. "For you fair Prince." I tipped the glass spilling it all on the pristine wooden floorboards. His face grew even more red while the Heir and her sister raised their hands to their mouths in startled disbelief. "To you and all the men like you." I finished setting my glass down on the buffet table before strolling away.

I disappeared from view before the Prince could think of a form of retaliation deciding to wander in the Pleasure Garden until the feasting began, least I get myself hung at the next opportune moment for speaking too honestly. I knew if I found myself with the noose around my neck, despite the solemn occasion my brother would somehow find a way to mock me for always teasing him about getting into trouble.

I shook my head as I pulled myself up onto a low hanging branch slowly climbing into the canopy as I listened to the ancient oak tell me of the kingdom that had once flourished where Angileri now sat. I listened to the slow drawl that made up its speech as it encompassed centuries in the passing of hours feeding me images of all that came before. I sighed resting my cheek against rough bark cradled in its delicate branches as I took in its story all the while gazing out onto a night filled with the brightest stars I'd ever seen.

This is what I lived for, not the power or prestige my gift could bring me, but the peace, the calm before the inevitable storm. The stories of time long past, the secrets that make you laugh with untold joy for those involved. I lived to experience the happiness every bloom felt at the touch of the sun, a simple happiness, unfiltered and raw. As innocent as children for all eternity and just as heartwarmingly beautiful. Forever changing, forever striving to grow, sprouting, budding, blooming, dying only to start the process all over again. The voices were many and despite the death of all things the voices returned, again and again they found their way back to me. A similar flower, but different, individually unique from the one before it. Perhaps they held the same spirits, perhaps not. I did not question it. I never had, I just knew that regardless of how they faded and died with the seasons in time my flowers would come back to me. A cycle that soothed my soul more than I was willing to admit. The ancient oak finished its life story ending with me climbing into its branches, I placed my hand soothingly against its bark sending out some of my magic, in thanks healing old scars and causing new leaves to grow before climbing down and heading back to the party hoping that the Prince had calmed a little in my absence.

At least enough to not want my head on a silver platter. I would hate to give my brother the satisfaction of proving me wrong.

Chapter 3
Poison

"Gardener Rhyme?" I glanced up from dusting off my trousers to find Kiyen and Resli standing in the shadows of the double doors leading into the ballroom. I straightened my sleeves waiting for one of them to explain the solemnness of their expressions. They shared a look before Resli stepped forward. "Gardener Rhyme, her Majesty would like to speak with you in private before the feast begins."

"Of course," I followed them through the palace until we reached a door I had never considered opening, after all one did not enter the Queen's study without her permission. Resli knocked, three than two than three again. I noted it but did not comment.

"Come in," Kiyen twisted the doorknob and pushed waving me forward, I entered without preamble and Kiyen closed the door behind me.

"Gardener Denarii," The Queen stood facing the window on the left side of the room, the cool night air gently caressed her dark locks of hair, causing her gown to billow around her ankles as if she were dancing despite the fact that she stood motionless. It was a transfixing sight.

"Majesty," I countered from where I stood just inside the door.

The Queen chuckled softly before turning to face me with eyes even more shockingly blue than her daughter's. "Anyone else called to a meeting with the Queen so late, just after insulting her own son, the Prince, would be afraid and yet you stand here

Gardener Denarii and you challenge me. You challenge me with a word. My own title no less."

"I gave your son the respect he deserves, the same respect all men like him deserve." Her Majesty stared at me then for a long moment, face a solemn mask, she stared into my eyes looking for something I could not name. Perhaps she found it perhaps not, she closed her eyes sighing softly.

"You're suggesting that my son, a man that could have, if the Gods willed it, one day have sat the throne, deserves less than no respect. You poured out an entire glass of the most expensive wine in all of Angileri." The Queen's voice while filled with exasperation, and I think not directed at me but her son, held no true malice.

"Let us thank the Gods then that he will never sit the throne," the Queen gazed at me shocked that I had the audacity to speak so plainly and then she laughed startling me slightly at the completely unexpected sound. Much like her daughter's voice had when I first heard it, the Queen's laugh was a pleasant shock to the system. I smiled softly while she covered her mouth eyes crinkling with mirth as she laughed heartily before turning away to calm herself.

"I should not find it so amusing," Her Majesty said by way of apology, "But your words conjured up the look of frustration on his face that he could do nothing because in essence you had done exactly what he'd asked, from showing him your magic to giving him the respect he'd requested." The Queen turned back to me, "You put my son in his place and I do not plan on punishing you for doing it in the most respectful and yet blatantly disrespectful way possible. Truly if I had a glass I'd raise it in your honor." She tipped her head in respect by way of compensating for the lost opportunity. I tipped mine in turn acknowledging her respect.

"If I am not to be punished, then why am I here?" I questioned finally getting to the point of this impromptu meeting.

"I wanted to meet the woman who inspired such awe in my people in just a matter of moments no less." She gazed at me with smiling eyes though her face remained serious.

"What happened in the ballroom was a team effort..."

"Rosen's speech was very heart warming and perfectly timed but I know the feel of her magic. I know the feel of Eden's, of Libeth's and Emery's..." She stepped towards her desk removing the crown that I knew sat heavily upon her brow despite the lightness of the metal it was created from. "Once upon a time I could walk into one of the palace gardens and name whom had worked there that day simply by the feel of their magic. I still can, Rosen's is strongest, Eden's despite his large stature is gentle, Libeth's is vibrant like she is and Emery's is delicate as if it will break at the most opportune moment and reveal something startling but wonderful."

"You have failed to indicate the feel of my magic your highness," she smiled wryly setting her crown in the center of her desk. It was a beautiful work of art meant for a beautiful woman.

"Yours has changed, at one point yours was achingly beautiful a small strike to the heart. Over time it has faded until now I can hardly feel it all if I'm not concentrating and so I cannot feel your gift but none the less I can identify whom has worked my garden by the lack of that feeling." Her gaze was penetrating, mine did not falter despite how it felt, as if she were looking into my soul and measuring my worth.

"I know when you work the Queen's Garden Denarii," I started at hearing my name without the title from one so high as she, even if it was only my family name it was a level of familiarity I wasn't expecting. The Queen noticed. "I know that you somehow slip away before nary a royal knows of your presence. I know how you hide from Rosen, and how she often asks for your assistance in the large things in the most creative of ways because of this fact. I know that you do not wish to take her position... I know all these things but I don't know you. I know nothing about you save what I've heard and that is hardly anything at all save the fact that you love every one of the gardens, you tend to them as if they are your life. Most especially the Queen's Garden. When you can be found, it is in one of the garden's lost in your work. I have heard that you are loyal, you speak with the servants as if they are equals, you love your brother and you are honest." She chuckled leaning back against her desk covering the beauty of her crown while I stood listening to her words. "Brutally honest in some cases but respectful, calm, clear headed even in your anger and fierce in your protection of those you care about...I know the things that matter in this moment."

"You are an intelligent woman," I acknowledged as she pulled forth a bucket of ice that held a bottle of Fae wine.

"Yes a bundle of beauty and intellect," Her Majesty grinned, gazing off into a memory I wasn't a part of. I let her have her moment. "Beauty helps many a deception with men, they do not often associate beauty with intelligence and many have fallen beneath the blades of my men because of it."

"I have heard the stories," I continued.

"There are many, not all of them true." She countered.

"But the brunt of them are," The Queen bowed her head in recognition of the truth in my words.

"My daughter, Princess Adri wishes to succeed me, I could not be more proud of her decision," Her words were sincere but her features were grave. "She can be so kind and yet so strong at the same time and though I thought it would be Mariel I think Adri will be better for Angileri." She breathed a heartfelt sigh, "I simply wished that others looked beyond her image and saw that as well..." The Queen shook her head before turning back to me. "My request is quite simple Denarii, befriend my daughter be the honesty that she does not believe coming from her family."

"You called me here, before the feast to tell me all these things that you know, proving that you were not as in the dark as I once thought, laughing at the injustice to your son and calling me by my family name with a familiarity I had not expected simply to ask me to befriend your daughter?" I asked for clarification.

The Queen poured herself a glass of Fae wine as she listened to me speak before bowing her head. "Yes is that too straight forward?"

I stared eyes narrowed as she raised the glass to her lips, I started heart racing, "Don't!" I exclaimed causing her to flinch and spill the wine all over her gown, as green as my own trousers, the crimson wine stained the fabric but that was of no matter. I took the glass of wine from her loosened grip before chucking the entirety of it glass and wine out the opened window.

The Queen stared at me waiting for an explanation, I straightened my sleeves trying to calm my racing heart at the near fatal incident. "There was poison in your wine." I stated after a moment of silence.

Her Highness nodded, "Rosen said you could detect poison, I was hesitant to believe her after all it was my life on the line if she were wrong." I gazed at the Queen truly shocked for the first time since I'd entered the room.

"You'd have poisoned yourself," I murmured in astonishment.

"I had hoped it wouldn't come to that." She countered wryly. "Rosen informed me that you could detect any poison made from a plant, the deadliest being dragon's tongue. This was not that no, this was something a strong abled bodied woman could easily overcome given enough rest and time it induces a feverish like state and of course if someone were to die under feverish conditions well it was the sickness itself, which could have come from anything or anyone. Death's door, it's very hard to track and once you fall beneath its spell there's no escaping it."

"How did you acquire it?" I asked after a moment of uninterrupted silence.

"The Shadow Garden," I blanched upon hearing the name of the garden no one knew existed except Rosen, myself and the Queen her own self. It was a garden made up of the deadliest plants in existence, a garden only the Head Gardener could enter it took skill to cultivate plants that could destroy entire nations without succumbing to their fatal embrace. Any lesser plant mage would quickly die trying.

"You could have died today, to what end? What if Rosen had been wrong? What if she had wanted you dead? What if I weren't fast enough?" I shook my head unable to comprehend the reason for such a life threatening maneuver.

"I could have died yes, but I am healthy and strong I knew what I was getting myself into if you failed. Rosen knows her Gardeners, she knows you and so I trusted her. She has known me from a young age, if she wanted me dead so that my daughter may sit the throne without opposition well…I know it would take years for her to forgive herself if she ever did. As for being fast enough…we'll never know because you were. I did this for my daughter Denarii, I want you to be her friend, and I want her friend to be able to protect her from what she cannot see." The Queen and I gazed at each other unwaveringly neither of us willing to look away.

"I do not like politics your Majesty and what you're asking of me is to submerge myself in it until I feel as if I am drowning. Not every noble will be as understanding as you have been in my disrespect of their children or themselves." I countered already knowing my answer.

"Your brother tells me you are horrible at social niceties until you aren't…" The Queen gave me a look. "The answer is yes or no Denarii? This conversation never leaves this room no matter the outcome."

"The thing about secrets your Majesty is that somewhere down the line they always come to light." The Queen turned her face away, lips curling wryly.

"It was a delight your Majesty," I bowed until I could no longer see her eyes but still not as low as I bowed to her daughter. "I hope you enjoy the feast as much as I will."

"I don't regret it…" I had turned to leave hand resting lightly on the knob when she'd spoken. I paused gazing over my shoulder waiting for her to finish her sentence. "I don't regret taking you away from the jungle, from your family. I did at the time, even knowing that you'd live a hard life and perhaps would never be educated, never know the full potential of your gift. I regretted my actions because I could see that she loved you, your mother loved you and I took you away from her and for that I'm sorry. I truly am but I don't regret it anymore because I know that she'd be proud Rhyme, she'd be proud of the woman and man you and your brother have become." I gazed back into the Queen's eyes heart aching for the mother I'd lost and I forgave her.

"Thank you," I murmured softly unable to see her bow her head in respect as I left the room slightly overcome with emotions I hadn't felt for quite some time.

"You're an honorable woman," I finished closing the Queen's study looking up to find Princess Mariel standing not even two feet away.

"Highness?" I questioned brow raised slightly waiting for her to elaborate.

Indent

"For forgiving my mother, for not doing what she asked because my sister might one day find out in the distant future. It would devastate Adri by the way, to know that my mother is the reason for one of her closest friends." I stared at the Princess much as I had stared at her mother, as if I had seen her for the first time.

"If your brother show's a more enlightened side…"

Princess Mariel laughed softly, "I don't believe he has one Gardener Denarii." I smiled, silently agreeing with that statement.

"Can I help you Highness?" I asked stomach aching with hunger.

"I thought perhaps you'd like to avoid the feast and enjoy a dinner alone with my sister and I. We'd love to hear more about your work, no politics what so ever."

"I'd love that Highness," She offered her arm and I hooked mine with hers allowing her to guide me through the palace to her private quarters.

I stepped into her private rooms briefly taking in the splendor before following her to a small dining table. I pulled out a chair offering her the seat. "Thank you."

A knock sounded at the door before the Heir entered looking a little ruffled.

"Goodness I'm glad to escape after such an announcement, Mari you should have heard the uproar. I do not believe anyone thought I'd say yes." Princess Adri shook her head as she closed the door behind her turning around and stopping short upon seeing someone standing beside her sister.

"Your Highness," I said by way of greeting, "I'm glad you said yes."

Princess Mariel smiled into her drink as her sister stood blushing prettily before us. "Sister this is Gardener Denarii; we've decided to cut the politics."

"It's a pleasure to meet you…" She hesitated for a moment before relaxing slightly speaking my name with confidence. "Gardener Denarii."

"The pleasure is mine Highness," I pulled out another chair offering it to the Heir much as I had her sister. She took it smiling in thanks before I uncovered the dishes littering the table taking the final chair seated at the table. We served ourselves, I took more greens and fruit than anything else, while each Princess looked on curiously without trying to make it appear they were doing so.

"Are my eating habits overly interesting?" I asked after taking a bite of my salad.

Princess Adri looked down taking a bite from her plate while her sister smiled at me unabashed. "We are simply curious, those who have the gift to speak with animals cannot bring themselves to eat them and so we wondered if your gift made you feel the same. Except your plate is more green than anything else."

"The fruits, the greens, all these vegetables on my plate do not call to me as the gardens do. They are flavorful though and so I eat them, I thank them for their nourishment. They have served their purpose and so they are happy, plants are simple that way." I offered easily.

"It's a relief to know my salad is not silently screaming murder with every bite," Princess Adri said seriously no longer hesitating to eat her greens.

I laughed softly at the relief on her face, "Princess if the plants screamed every time you ate them I'd have gone mad long ago." Princess Adri and her sister laughed with me no doubt picturing the silliness my words had conjured up.

"No thankfully plants do not scream when you eat them. They sing lovely notes that linger on your tongue, makes it ten times more enjoyable." I ate a Fae grape while they watched once more fascinated.

"I do not know if you are attempting to fool us or not?" Princess Adri said after a moment while we all sat enjoying our food.

"No it is true, it is why plant mages are known to be vegetarians it strengthens our gift. Here," I offered Princess Adri a bite of my greens, she stared at my fork blushing softly while Princess Mariel looked on without murmuring a word.

"I fail to see how your salad will taste any different than mine Gardener," Her Highness said stiffly shifting in her chair.

"Magic," I countered not unkindly hand unwavering as I waited for her to take a bite. The Heir stared at me for a moment before leaning forward slowly and wrapping her mouth around my fork sitting back and chewing slowly eyes widening no doubt at the sudden burst of flavor on her tongue.

I smiled softly before continuing to eat my food, "How is that possible?" She asked once she'd composed herself.

"Magic your Highness," I offered with a shrug unable to explain it further. Each sister nodded in turn before returning to their food. The rest of the evening passed in companionable silence broken by light conversation that had more to do with each other and nothing to do with politics. It was absolutely lovely, if a bit surreal to be dining with two of the most powerful people in all of Angileri. My brother would never believe me, I smiled at the thought.

"How strong are you?" Princess Adri asked during a lull in the conversation, from the look on her face it seemed that was a thought that just so happened to slip out of her mouth.

Though Princess Mariel didn't ask the question I could quite clearly see that she was interested in the question. I thought back to the moment when the Queen raised that glass to her lips, thought about the near indistinguishable note of triumph that wavered in the air from a plant that nearly achieved its purpose, and how if it had no matter what the Queen said she'd not have lived to see tomorrow. I gazed into the eyes of her daughters and I smiled a smile that likely did not reach my eyes. "Strong enough to be one of the Queen's Gardeners," both Princesses laughed softly at my cheek but didn't question me further knowing it was rude to have asked in the first place.

"I should take my leave," I said after a few moments more standing slowly setting my napkin on my empty plate. "I have work to finish yet in the Queen's Garden."

"I will see you out."

"Have fun."

Both royals spoke simultaneously with Princess Adri standing to walk me to the door, while Princess Mariel remained seated enjoying the last of her meal.

"I had a nice evening," I gazed over at the Princess as we walked through the corridors of the palace side by side.

"It was an interesting night for sure," I countered wryly. She chuckled softly unwilling to disagree.

"What work remains in my mother's Garden?" Her Highness asked after a moment spent walking in silence.

"I am trying to cultivate Were Lilies so that they bloom every full moon without the existence of magic in the same exact location. People do not realize that the only places they bloom are all strong in magic." I sighed softly as we left the palace via the servant's wing avoiding all the guards. I do not think the Princess noticed. "It's harder than I had first thought, I can only test my theories just a few days out of the month."

"I am glad there are those here with magic enough to make them bloom Gardener. They are a rarity that should be cherished and remembered, because no two lilies are exactly the same. As well you may never have the opportunity to see them again. I've only had the pleasure of seeing them once in my entire life. They bloomed early today," The Princess gazed up at me with smiling eyes. "At first I thought it was happenstance that I was there in that moment, but now I am not so sure."

I smiled softly, neither confirming nor denying her assumption. "I suppose you'll never know Princess."

"I know it was you Gardener," she bumped me with her hip playfully causing me to laugh. "As well I know you aren't willing to admit it."

"Why does it matter?" I asked as we strolled along the moonlit path the voices of the flowers soothing my soul as they always did when I was near.

"I wish to thank them. You do not know how hard it was for me to stand up in front of all those people and tell them that I wish to be Queen. It is my birthright yes, I have passed the Trials and proven myself and yet still more than half of them do not respect me and why? Because I am not as small or feminine as my mother and sister." I snorted unable to help myself and the Princess turned on me hurt and anger flashing in the violet blue twilight that made up her eyes. I blinked several times turning away slightly to compose myself. I felt slightly dazed for some unknown reason. "You're laughing at me."

"I am amused yes but at your words not at you. You are not small," I looked at her slowly from her head to her toes. "But that gives you an advantage on the battle field, as for being feminine," I placed my hands on her waist quite trim for a woman everyone considered large, tracing them down to her hips. "You are the embodiment of every fertility Goddess in existence." I murmured softly suddenly finding it difficult to speak.

The Princess gazed up at me for a moment letting my words seep in, "Has anyone ever told you that you are very tall for a woman?" She questioned shattering the moment with a well-placed smile and a hint of tinkling laughter.

I chuckled letting my hands fall to my sides, "Yes many times. For my brother to be tall it is normal, my tallness is considered an abnormality but where we come from everyone is as tall as we are. It is said that those in the jungle have just a wee bit of Fae blood in them." We rounded the corner into the Queen's Garden with the Princess shaking her head in disbelief. "I never said it was true Highness, simply what has been said."

I knelt before the patch of glowing Were Lilies, pulling several vials from a pouch I kept tied to my belt, and snipped off a few petals from each bloom seeing which ones continued to glow in their vials and which ones instantly faded once cut from the mother plant. I marked each with a letter indicating the outcome. While across from me the Princess practically lay on the ground smelling each bloom and tracing her fingers along their petals laughing softly as the evening breeze caused the lilies to stroke her face. I finished my work quickly sitting back on my heels to watch her enjoy my garden.

She gazed up at me through the pale blooms, eyes sparkling with mirth. "Did you know long before, when the Queendom was young, when the dragons had first made peace, plant mages were revered. The Queen ensured that one lived in every major city as well as the larger towns so that crops could flourish. It was needed then, when we were fresh from war and did not know if the dragons would turn on us. Alia said, "If we are to die the summer after the next we will do it with sated bellies and souls filled with the beauty of the land.' The Queen's Gardeners just two at the time came to be and over the years as the Queendom grew and expanded so too did the palace, the gardens and the Queen's Gardeners. The Queen dictates how much respect her Gardeners should be given…for the last few generations they haven't been given the proper respect they deserve. My mother changed that…"

The Princess shifted slightly never turning her gaze from mine, simply getting more comfortable on the ground resting her chin upon her arms, "The plant mages help supply the land with food, as well they fill our souls with beauty of a land we sometimes forget to appreciate and all they ask is that we let them tend our lands as they see fit. It should not be a struggle to give them the proper respect and yet it happens, memories are short and our people forget and so each Queen need remind the people that before the soldiers, walks the Queen's Gardeners, for they ensure we are fed long after the war is over and the land lay healing with their helping hands."

"I plan to make sure that my plant mages are well rewarded for their troubles Gardener," the Princess finished after a small moment of silence.

I smiled softly gazing down upon the Princess in all her glory, "Highness it is said among plant mages that once you are strong enough to tend an entire field alone for a week without help and yield something beautiful or edible by the eve of the seventh day that you are no longer simply a plant mage."

"What have you become at that point?" She asked the question I knew she would and I smiled more fully.

"You become a garden mage, and so the Queen does not simply have the best plant mages in all of Angileri. No, she has the best garden mages in all of Angileri and one is entirely different than the other." Slowly but surely the entire garden came to full bloom with the help of my magic glowing softly in the moonlight. The Princess pushed herself up and gazed around her with an awe she had no chance of hiding.

"Different indeed," She murmured softly unable to keep her eyes from exploring all the exotic blooms that had never, bloomed all at once let alone in the same season. "Emery tried this once, I told him to never do it again because once he'd forced the flowers to bloom half of the garden died and took days to regrow." I grimaced remembering that moment quite well, thankfully the Queen had been away and Rosen and I had been able to fix it before her return or else we'd be short a Gardener.

Slowly my magic faded and the blooms slowly went back to their previous states. "He did it wrong, when causing a field to bloom unless your purpose is to destroy said field for planting purposes you simply fill the flowers with enough magic to bloom, and then you stop, you hold it for a few moments and no longer so that when the magic fades they simply return to how they once were. It's a trick that takes skill and concentration."

"Which was Emery lacking?" the Princess asked after a moment of thought.

I chuckled softly thinking about Emery trying to concentrate with Princess Adri gazing at him with those twilight eyes, smiling softly and perhaps laughing at his jokes while he puffed with pride filling the flowers with too much magic without realizing the delicate balance of the entire garden lay in his hands. "Likely both, even if one reaches the level of a garden mage it doesn't necessarily mean that they will progress further than that."

"There is a progression?" Her Highness gazed at me with wide eyes.

"I have shared too much Princess, if I say more I'm sure we'll be talking until the sun lightens the sky." I deflected standing quickly offering her my hands.

She took them easily allowing me to pull her to her feet, an easier task than I'd expected and so I pulled harder then I meant causing us to stumble slightly, the Princess falling to rest against me. I caught her easily holding her until she was able to steady herself. "My apologies Princess I did not take you to be so light."

"Are you calling me fat?" She questioned poking me in the chest a playful glint in her eyes.

"No but I did expect you to be just a bit heavier than a feather," Her Highness snorted rolling her eyes before shoving me away gently. I caught her hands pulling her close again wondering why I continuously found myself lost in her eyes, or why it was that I struggled to breathe or even speak when she was just a little too close. I never had this problem when Kiyen was around. "You should eat more, it's not healthy to be so light." Adri laughed a genuine sound that made me smile to hear it before pulling her hands away.

"You're silly Gardener Denarii," She tipped her head to me. "Have a blessed evening," She raised her finger, "Do not think I forgot about how you avoided my question."

"I have no idea what you're talking about Highness, no idea at all." Adri snorted again before waving her fair well and turning to walk away. I watched the enthralling sway of her hips in the moonlight unable to look away. I shook my head once she was gone not entirely sure what was wrong with me.

I rubbed my tummy soothingly not sure if it would be best to ask my brother or Kiyen about the strange sensation filling my guts. It felt as if small saplings were taking root and struggling to grow all at the same time. It faded soon after and I decided that since it was gone there was no need to share it with my brother only to have him mock me for the rest of the day. No if it came back I'd find Kiyen and have her explain it to me, she at least would be more understanding. I dusted off my trousers ensuring that all my vials were tucked safely in their pouches before making my way from the Queen's Garden hoping that the strange sensation did not return. I wasn't sure how to explain it in my own mind, explaining it to another person would surely be ten times harder.

Chapter 4
Queen's Request

"You are a hard woman to find." I glanced up to find the Heir walking towards me donned in the guard's practice uniform a green tunic and brown trousers, hair pleasantly mussed sticking to her neck and brow. She had a streak of dirt on her cheek I was sure she was unaware of.

"Training with your guards Highness?" I questioned smiling softly as I set the horse brush back in the bin I'd taken it from.

"Yes, it motivates them to see me fall on my... behind." She finished after seeing my upraised brow.

"I'm sure they're motivated because their future Queen takes the time from her busy day to spar with them, not because you fall on your behind. As well I'm sure you don't fall half as often as they think you should, being a woman and all." Her grin could probably make the flowers bloom in that moment, it certainly took my breath away.

"They underestimate me and I always use it to my advantage," I chuckled softly shifting closer to the mare feeling slightly uncomfortable in her Highness' presence and not knowing why.

"How do you use it to your advantage Princess?" I asked curiously.

"Well most of them are men and so when I fight them I," She leaned close looking at me with sparkling eyes. "I just make sure that my tunic is just a little looser than normal." I gazed down into the valley between her breasts before tossing my head back and laughing fully for the first time in a very long time.

"Princess, the Queen has raised very intelligent daughters...I have no idea what happened to her son," I finished brow furrowed.

"He craves power and he will never have it. Not truly anyway..." Adri sighed softly fixing her attire. "We were close once..."

"What happened?" I questioned softly seeing the need to share in her eyes.

"We grew up and he wanted to be King, he wanted to be remembered as the one who broke the succession of Queens and I, I wanted that for him as well because if Sorel was King then I could stay here and spend my days in the gardens. Then reality set in, he failed his Trials and I...I didn't." The Princess traced her fingers along my mare's muzzle allowing her to nip at her palm. "He's bitter, when our mother took me beneath her wing and taught me the things a monarch should know it became worse." The Princess shook her head; tears that she was unwilling to shed shimmering in her eyes. "I would give it all up if I could just have my brother back."

I hesitantly placed my hand on her shoulder, "Your Highness, if your brother were half the royal you or your sister are he'd be happy for you. He would gaze on you with pride in his eyes and try in his own way to better the Queendom, to better himself and his people. Instead he uses his title to get what he wants and grows angry when it doesn't work. That is no fault of yours."

Adri took a deep breath before wiping her face. "I apologize, you are but a commoner and here I am practically weeping my sorrows away on your shoulder."

I laughed good naturedly taking no offense to her unintended slight. "Princess, my people are said to be descendants of the Fae and Gods alike and so who would be considered the commoner among us?" She blinked at my gentle rebuke before chuckling softly.

"You are good with words Denarii," Her Highness countered smiling softly.

I shrugged but chose not to reply. "Rhyme, I need you to leave the stables you have my stable hands wandering around like ninnies wondering what to do with themselves…Oh," Reason stopped in his rant upon casting eyes on the Queen to be. "Your Highness," He bowed until he could no longer look her in the eyes. "It's a pleasure to have you grace us with your presence."

The Princess tipped her head in respect, stepping forward to take his arm in a warrior clasp, catching my brother by surprise. "The pleasure is mine Horse Master. I had hoped to see the men in action upon their mounts but alas all I had time for was a few light sparring sessions."

"Perhaps another time?" Reason offered without hesitation as they let their arms drop to their sides.

"I would like that," the Princess smiled brightly stealing my breath once more, and this time my brother's as well judging by the slight widening of his eyes. I smiled softly turning to trace my fingers through my mare's mane. "Gardener?" I glanced up to find the Princess looking at me with serious eyes. A word?" She beckoned me away, leaving no room to question or argue. I followed without hesitation while my brother looked on with curious eyes.

"You do realize the next time he sees me he'll try to pump me for information?" I walked towards the Training Fields, stopping by the fence to watch the recruits train.

"Yes but unlike the Horse Master you aren't known to be a gossip, you aren't well known at all actually and you are very hard to find when you're working. The only person said to be able to find you in one of the palace gardens is your brother and considering how rare it is he actually looks for you, one could say that was luck more than anything else." Adri shook her head, "It's very frustrating and fascinating at the same time."

I leaned on the fence strands of hair falling into my face, I ignored them not sure where I'd lost the leather thong that held it back this time. I was starting to wonder if I tied it right, Reason never had this problem and he moved around more than I did training the recruits, the guards and soldiers alike. "The Queen's Gardeners work four days on and then have two off. Libeth and I work the same shift from first day to fourth day, off fifth and sixth day and then working seventh day to third day. Emery and Eden have off first day and second day and work third day to sixth day and then have off seventh and first day and so when two of us have off there are still two Gardeners working at the same time. Rosen's schedule is more random she works the gardens as she pleases and rarely if ever takes off. Then the schedule is compounded by the fact that we rotate through the four gardens spanning the palace grounds. It makes it nigh impossible to know for sure where the Queen's Gardeners are at any given moment in time."

"I've noticed," I chuckled at the Princess's wry tone.

"It protects us Princess crazy though it may seem, there are many people out there who would kill to have the power your mother has at her fingertips after all plants can be dangerous too…"

"Indeed," Adri flinched at Rosen's sudden appearance, I smiled having seen her coming over her Highness' shoulder. "Every poison in existence can be traced back to a plant of some kind. Some can destroy entire armies; the worst are the kinds that poison the land. The Void is a byproduct of such a poison. It sits on the edge of our Queendom and reminds us of the evil that mankind can commit."

The Void was created long before any of us were even the inkling of a thought in our parents' minds, it was not the cause of any of our wars but its existence affected us all. After all it took the work of many a plant mage to keep it from spreading. Angileri was at war with the Void and we'd been at a standstill for generations, neither eradicating it nor losing land to the ever expanding wasteland. Other countries weren't so lucky as ours, they hadn't realized the importance of plant mages until it was nearly too late and they suffered, while we flourished. "What brings you to the Training Fields Head Gardener?" I questioned breaking the sullen silence that had fallen over us.

"The Queen has a re…"

"Watch out!" We all looked up at the shouted warning to see an arrowing speeding straight for us. Rosen raised her hand as I whispered a request. Long before the bolt reached us it split in two and fell to the ground sprouting leaves. Rosen furrowed her brow lowering her hand.

"Such an amazing display of power Head Gardener you stopped an arrow with the raise of your hand." The Princess smiled softly before continuing. "I can see why my mother holds you in such high regard."

"The Queen respects my wisdom more than my power after all power can fade over time. Wisdom only grows," The Princess and I tipped our head in mutual respect of that statement while watching Rosen leap the fence to retrieve the arrowhead, the shaft itself had become a small plant billowing in the wind. She came back to us twirling the perfectly shaped arrowhead between her fingers. "It was impossible to avoid, but well the wood was once a part of a tree." Rosen caught my eye as she finished her sentence. "It took no power at all to do what it was meant to do." She turned back to the Princess smiling softly as she pocketed the arrowhead.

"I hope you serve me half as well as you serve my mother Head Gardener Rosen, with great wisdom and unfailing grace." Her Highness said bowing slightly, about the respect you'd give a well favored noble. Adri took her mother's words to heart.

Rosen smiled more fully, "Highness I'm old and gray now, surely I will be dead and gone long before you sit the throne."

I snorted softly and the Princess laughed. "Yes, you must have missed my mother talking about how she plans to enjoy her later years in retirement only keeping a seat on the Council so that she may keep up with the going ons of the Queendom. There is more than one reason my mother did not allow my brother to inherit, passing the Trials being the largest one."

Rosen chuckled shaking her head. "I can hear the shock sweeping the land as we speak."

"Adri?!" We all looked up to see Prince Sorel racing toward us, Rosen grimaced, the Princess deflated and I just stared at the blatant disrespect he'd just given his sister.

He reached us a few moments later none of us willing to make it easier by meeting him halfway. "Brother." Adri acknowledged his presence with a tip of her head, neither Rosen or I were willing to give him the courtesy.

"Your suitor is waiting for you," He offered smiling graciously, it looked uglier than the sneer he wore last night, at least that expression had been genuine.

Her Highness made a face of distain while her brother grinned more broadly, "Prince Eris may be my only suitor but that does not mean I will sink low enough to marry him."

"It goes against custom…"

"Does the Queen not dictate what custom demands." I countered before he could begin his argument. The Princess smiled behind the cover of her up raised hand while the Prince stared at me with open hostility, Rosen simply observed without comment.

"One day I will show you your place," He growled threateningly.

I swept my hand towards the Training Fields, "Why not let that day be today fair Prince?" I asked calmly waiting for him to refuse as I knew he would. He continued to glare no longer willing to speak. I nodded slightly letting my hand fall. "As I thought, there is a reason you failed your Trials."

Rosen caught Sorel's fist before it could connect with my face, Adri started at the show of violence I didn't so much as flinch. "Quick to anger," I tsked while Rosen shoved him away. "Not a trait befitting a ruler, much less a noble of such high stature. Every time I see you Highness you prove me right." He stood up straight dusting off his clothing while Rosen gazed at him with open disdain, Adri took hold of her brother pulling him away.

"Let us go brother before you embarrass yourself more in front of the Queen's Head Gardener and her successor." The Princess shook her head confidence growing in the face of his small dishonor.

Sorel tore his arm away from his sister before marching down the path fuming. "I can protect myself," I said without turning from the path after the Heir and her unruly brother was long gone.

"As well I know it but I did not want to you to so openly disgrace, the soft handed man. He's a snake if I've ever seen one and I couldn't tell you if he's poisonous or not." Rosen replied gaining my attention.

"Poisonous for sure, I do not need to feel his bite to know it." Rosen bobbed her head in agreement. "What did you want of me?" I asked changing the subject to more important things.

"The Queen requested that we somehow insert more greenery inside the palace." Rosen sighed softly.

"Are the five gardens not enough for her?" I questioned brow furrowed.

"Well no one, save we three, know that the Shadow Garden exists, and possibly soon the Heir, but that is beside the point. Regardless of the fact that most do not think that Adri should sit the throne, royalty will come, nobles, sons and daughters alike will come and a tournament will be held in the Princess's honor in the hopes that the winner will take her hand." Rosen's face showed the unlikelihood of that happening. Everyone knew that the Queen's Tournament was a way to foster good relations with the people and the neighboring lands, it was a way to form new alliances and perhaps a way to find new love. Though many a consort had been found via the Queen's Tournament it was not always a participant and just as many had not been found at all. No, the Heir did not have to marry the winner but it was seen as a sign of good fortune for her to at least give him or her a chance if she'd not already found a likely match by then.

"If Prince Eris is any indication of the suitors that will come forth well…" Rosen heaved a heartfelt sigh at my words.

"I hope her Highness will not settle for less than what she deserves, someone equal to her in all things." I patted Rosen lightly on the arm consolingly. "Amazing work by the way." I raised my brow waiting for her to explain. "You dropped that arrow with no more than a look and an inkling of power, I simply supplied the perfect cover." Rosen looked at me respect shinning in her eyes. "Truly each time I see you in action I know it's only by your grace alone that I retain my position. You are one of the strongest mages I've ever known and I have known many and seen more spanning all crafts, countries and continents in my years of living. It is an honor to work with you."

"I have practiced nearly the whole of my life…"

"Yes," Rosen bowed her head slightly in acknowledgment of my words, "As have I and I am near about thirty years your senior, while I have reached the peak of my power yours is still growing. After all I can cultivate poison without coming to harm, you can detect it in any food or drink man can imagine and then eat it without any adverse effects."

"I still haven't forgiven you for that," I murmured referring to the time she'd fed me a poison most well-known for inducing stomach sickness often used when someone had ingested something fatal. Given randomly it could have you bedridden for weeks depending on the dosage, a drop was enough to throw up for hours, she'd given me an entire vial. Thankfully I'd been fine, in fact I hadn't even been aware until she'd told me later that week. I had quickly learned to detect poisons soon after, if I didn't know her I'd have thought Rosen was trying to kill me not help me. I had ingested more poison than I cared to admit in the name of Healing.

"I know," She smiled softly remembering what I'd done, how the Pleasure Garden had bloomed red for an entire week and not a one of her Gardeners could fix it. Rosen had seen the glint in my eye and had come up with a very good explanation when questioned by her Majesty. Now every year during the summer months, a seven day is chosen and whatever garden Rosen happens to be working at the time blooms red in honor of that seven day where my rage simmered. And on the eve of the seventh day, the night she apologized, we share dinner together. No one knows the why of it and everyone assumes it's the Head Gardener's doing, we've told no one differently. People come from all over to see the strange yet beautiful anomaly.

"The Queen wants to display her power by having greenery placed strategically throughout the palace. The Queen's Tournament will be announced during this coming seventh day, and will start a fortnight after that, lasting seven to ten days depending on how many suitors actually decide to participate. Near about the entirety of it will be held on the Training Fields, all hunting parties will of course be held in the forest. We have three seven days to get this done. Do you think we can manage it?" Rosen gazed at me while I calculated all the things that must be done each day to ensure that the Queen had what she desired in the amount of time she'd allotted us.

"Will we build the seating?" I questioned referring to the tiered benches that the audience would sit on to observe the tournament. There were two built already but they would not be able to hold the captivity of people that were sure to arrive for this event. The last had been nearly thirty years ago after all. It had taken three months to build temporary seating, it would take all of Angileri's carpenters to do it on such short notice now and still they may not be finished in time.

Rosen gazed across the entirety of the Training Fields ignoring the recruits and taking in the space, it was large, nearly as large as the ground the palace sat on but not quite. "How long would it take?"

"A seven day," I offered without hesitation. "A hundred saplings evenly spaced spanning the circumference of the entirety of the Training Fields. I'd give it a seven if we all worked together towards a common goal. It would exhaust near about all our reserves so I would do this last."

"Could you do it alone?" Rosen gazed at me face a mask of indifference, the answer lay hovering in the glint I saw shimmering in her eyes.

"It would take a lot of power…"

"That's not what I asked," She countered not unkindly simply unwilling to take my nonsense.

I heaved a sigh rolling my shoulders as I once more took in the space, after a slight hesitation I nodded firmly. "I could…"

"Will it exhaust your reserves?" Rosen questioned brow raised curiously.

"So long as I do not have to do anything of that magnitude again before the tournament is

over I should be alright." I offered slowly thinking it over.

"How long will it take you?" I sighed considering all the other things still to be done.

"A seven day to do it right, but regardless it's up to the Queen to make the decision." I countered trying to end this conversation.

Rosen laughed, "Yes and it will be a hard decision indeed, pay near every carpenter in Angileri and hope that they will finish before the start of the Queen's Tournament or simply have her Gardeners whom she need not pay more, build it and be assured that it's done on time."

"When you put it that way there doesn't really seem to be a choice," I murmured softly.

"Exactly, the stands will be the last thing done a seventh day prior to the beginning of the Tournament. Every day of that last seven day we will stand here leaning against this fence and you will use your magic to grow the stands. It will seem as if we are working together, when in reality you will be doing it alone and once more I will be taking credit for your work." Rosen looked at me a question in her eyes, it took her but a moment to ask it. "How do you feel about that."

I gazed out across the recruits training now with the more seasoned guards and soldiers to give them a feel for different styles, builds and ages. "If I wanted your position Rosen perhaps I would be upset but you will always be the better politician, your wisdom will always be greater than mine and you guide us all with a gentle hand. Without you I would not be here, able to do what you ask of me. You sit here and tell me I am more powerful and yet in my mind you will always be the greater mage…" I let her take in my words before finishing. "I feel thankful that you would do this for me, knowing it causes you no small guilt to claim work that is not your own."

"You are going to be the greatest Head Gardener Angileri has ever known, that is, when you decide you're ready for it." Rosen chuckled. "Let it not be when I am too old to enjoy the stir you'll cause among court with your blunt honesty, and very accurate displays of respect."

I laughed with her, thinking about the look on the Prince's face, "I make no promises I don't intend to keep."

Rosen bowed her head in acknowledgement, "A good trait to have."

"Are we starting today?" I questioned referring back to the Queen's request.

Rosen smiled, "I know how much you miss your gardens on your days off, but I felt we could make an exception just this once. You have the royal wing, the ballroom, the dining hall and the throne room. I will task Emery, Eden and Libeth as I cross their paths today. Try not to finish too quickly, wouldn't want to make your fellow Gardeners look bad."

"I will try to remember that sound advice," I countered wryly.

"And stay out of trouble." Rosen warned turning to head towards the Queen's Garden where either Emery or Eden would be found covering for me that day. Libeth was probably hovering close to the kitchens, that woman was always hungry.

"Trouble is my brother's middle name not mine, I am a saint among the masses!" I called as Rosen walked away, easily able to hear her snort of disbelief despite the distance.

The grass beneath my feet chuckled gaily in amusement at my antics and I smiled before racing towards the palace, excitement building with every frantic step, not for the Tournament, not for the many feasts, nor for the royalty. No I was excited that I would get to test my magic, that I would get to create something truly magnificent, I raced through the servant's entrance laughing with delight. My work would hold for generations to come and none would be the wiser that I was anything but an ordinary plant mage. I burst into my rooms falling onto the couch that sat in our foyer. I leaned back and closed my eyes listening for the murmured voices of the raptor vines that adorned my windows. Three seven days of arriving suitors and royals alike. I opened my eyes gazing up at the ceiling as I thought about all that the Heir must endure even before the Queen's Tournament has begun. I thought about those saplings growing in the pit of my stomach, about the difficulty to draw air when she smiled at me, about the sensation of drowning in the twilight wonder that was her eyes. I thought about all these things and wondered what it was about Adri that made me not mind sharing my gardens with her.

A knock sounded on the door drawing me from my thoughts. "Come in!" I called pushing myself up into a proper sitting position.

"Every time I come to your rooms I dread actually knocking on your door, not knowing if it'll be you or your brother that responds." Libeth sighed in relief stepping into the room and closing the door before coming to join me on the couch.

"Is my brother trying to court you still?" I asked curious about her reaction.

"It is not so much that he wishes to court me, I would be alright with that, it's that he also wishes to court every other female he can think to get his hands on at the same time." Libeth offered clearly exasperated.

"My brother can be foolish sometimes," I nodded sympathetic to her plight.

"An idiot is more accurate." I laughed softly at the look on Libeth's face.

"Well I have been making fun of him quite a bit of late and I did not want to be the one to say it." I shrugged. "I will simply agree with the honesty of your statement. Now what brings you to our shared quarters if you're not looking for my brother to give him a piece of your mind."

"Rosen has informed me that we have a lot of work to do in the three seven days leading up to the Queen's Tournament, she asked me if I wanted to partner you and of course I agreed. It's not every day that you get to work with the most skilled garden mage in the palace second to the Head Gardener her own self…though that could be debated." A spark shown in Libeth's eyes. "I've had the pleasure of talking to your brother while he's deep in his cups, he speaks very highly of you when asked despite the insults passed between you by the way."

"Considering my brother does not actually know the half of what we do I would take everything he says with a grain of salt," I replied with unwavering eye contact.

"So his assumption that you are a bit backwards in your loving affairs is completely untrue?" Her questioned sounded more like clarification more than anything.

I looked at her with narrowed eyes, "He insinuated that I preferred women to men?"

"Insinuated," Libeth clucked her tongue, "Outright stated as fact more like, I decided I should hear it from the mother plant herself."

I furrowed my brow, "I have been courted by both and slept with neither…"

"So you're still unbroken?" Libeth's eyes were wide with disbelief.

"Is it so hard to believe?" I felt a bit insulted at what she was implying.

"Excuse the insult to your character but yes, you're magnificent, a gem among stones, more honest than any truth sayer, more loyal than the most loyal steed walking the palace grounds, a hard worker and strong in your magic. You would make the perfect partner to any woman or man alike. I would think that many would try to claim your heart if even for a short time. I know I would if I'd even thought for a moment that you considered me in that way." Libeth blushed softly as she finished her small yet passionate speech and found me staring.

"You think that of me?" She nodded no longer able to speak. I leaned forward gently resting my brow against hers. "My brother does not deserve you." I murmured softly before leaning forward to kiss her softly on the lips, a gentle kiss, soft and lingering an apology more than anything else. I pulled away first as was prudent.

Libeth sighed softly, "Only you could break someone's heart with a kiss," we both laughed at the sardonically spoken comment.

"Is it not proper to let your suitor down with a chaste kiss?" I questioned not sure if the custom had changed.

"Only to those you like and wish to remain friends with," Libeth traced her fingers lightly over her lips still a little flushed in the cheeks. "I will tell my children of the Head Gardener and how she kissed me, long before the world knew her name."

I smiled for her words were sincere, "You think too highly of me…"

"No," Libeth shook her head, "You don't think highly enough of yourself. I know you don't think it but you are fit for royalty regardless if you were born to it or not."

"Thank you." I accepted her words and Libeth tipped her head in respect.

"Now let us get back to work so I can sooth my broken heart with manual labor," I chuckled knowing she wasn't serious but thankful for the change of subject.

We talked about where we would start and what flowers and plants we would use well into the evening. My brother didn't understand how we could have so much fun talking about what basically amounted to flower arrangements. Libeth scoffed and before I could throw something at him for such an insult to our profession, after all we catered to the land and understood the earth far more than he could think to image, all he did was instruct a few animals that graced the surface of this land, our work did not compare. Libeth put him in his place while I sat laughing softly. It had been a long eventful day; I just knew that there would only be more of the same to come. I hoped the Heir was ready…I hoped I was ready because I felt that we'd all be tested in one way or another. Let us hope that the other lands did not find us lacking…

Chapter 5
No Fault of Yours

I stood at the base of a great oak still young in its thinking, as it should be, it had grown to full height and beyond just that morning while Libeth looked on in awe. Libeth had climbed to the top most part of the oak in perhaps half the span of an hour and now she sat somewhere beyond my sight dismantling the chandelier as I had requested so that we may distribute the magic imbued stones throughout the leafy canopy. "Are you sure that we're allowed to take this apart?!" She exclaimed for nearly the hundredth time.

"Not particularly, but if asked we'll say Rosen allowed it!" I called back, I could hear her laughter echo through the trunk of the tree, something I'm sure she did on purpose with the use of her magic, no way I'd hear her otherwise.

"Ahh look, the Head Gardener's pet," I turned from the trunk my hand rested upon to see Prince Sorel and Prince Eris strolling towards me.

"I see but one animal in this room fair Prince and it isn't me," Sir Zeron trailing behind the two chuckled softly. "It is good to see you again Sir Knight," I raised my hand in greeting to him.

He returned the gesture, "Same to you Gardener Denarii, I am awed to see you in action. Is this great oak your creation?"

"It is, with the aid of my fellow Gardener," I gazed up high into the canopy unable to see her, "She is a bit busy at the moment."

"Afraid of heights Denarii?" Prince Sorel taunted stepping closer.

"You are asking a plant mage if she fears heights, when she stands before a great oak she has helped grow…" I gazed at him allowing him to become a bit uncomfortable in the silence. "No tree I have touched would dare let me fall and so the answer to your poorly asked question is no."

"You don't know how to speak to your betters do you?" Prince Eris asked not unkindly.

I smiled softly, "I see no one better than me here Highness and only one that may be counted as my equal," I looked to Sir Zeron as I spoke, he tipped his head in respect better than he had the first time, showing that he had practiced. "If you think that your title makes you better than I, then you are mistaken, a title is just a word after all, a word created to separate the masses, and that word to some equals power, but not to me. And so I will treat you with the respect I feel you deserve regardless of the word that comes before your name just as you do me. It is the way Angileri works does it not?"

"I am a Prince…"

"And yet I have yet to see you show it, ask any servant, a title is earned…" I watched his face grow red with rage while Prince Eris looked on not knowing how to respond, "And you have not earned yours."

He stepped into my personal space, I did not move nor lower my eyes, "I am going to destroy you." He breathed silently through his rage.

"Sorel, Sorel," I murmured so only he could hear. "You say all these words, you make all these threats and yet I have yet to see you actually do anything…" He struck me then with the flat of his palm, it stung a bit but I did not move. "No Prince stands before me. Just a boy crying for power that will never be his." I finished.

Sir Zeron caught his hand before he could strike me again, "Do not strike her again," He warned roughly pulling the Prince away. "She is not some tavern wench you can place your hands on when you are angered, she has the Queen behind her and as she said regardless of the title that sits before your name you can and will be punished for harming any who belong to the Queen." Zeron warned proving he had read up on our customs more than I had realized.

"I am her Majesty's son; my mother wouldn't dare." Prince Sorel tore his arm away, while I gazed on unmoved by his antics.

"Zeron," Prince Eris rebuked, "How dare you place your hands on royalty."

"The good Knight has read up on the social niceties of our Queendom, the same cannot be said for his charge, truly a disservice to your father Prince Eris, I hope word does not reach him of the ignorance you display so openly." I shook my head at the pair of them.

"I apologize," Zeron bowed slightly, after all Sorel was not the Queen and did not deserve such respect. "Be that as it may, nothing that has transpired in this moment is befitting a Prince and I am ashamed on behalf of the House of Rayon, your father…"

"Do not speak of my father!" Eris snarled breathing heavily.

"The King of Water would not approve of your conduct, I had thought this trip would change you for the better," Zeron gazed at Prince Sorel with disdain in his eyes, "I can see that I was wrong. I serve your father first and our Kingdom second…find me when you choose to show respect befitting both." Sir Zeron tipped his head in respect to me before turning and marching away.

"This is your fault." I gazed at the foreign Prince with a look those words deserved.

"You are a grown man standing here, blaming another because you do not wish to deal with the repercussions of your actions." I scoffed at the audacity.

"You are little more than dirt and you dare speak to me this way," Prince Sorel stood behind his partner, they matched each other in attitude so well, I could not think as them as anything but, with a near about permanent sneer on his face.

"Dirt," I cocked my head thoughtfully, "Soil, sand, earth...where the plants grow, where the flowers bloom, earth makes up the bottom of every ocean, sand and stones line every stream and river bed, muddy clay settles slowly upon the lowest point of every lake and so it could be said that earth is every starting point that man can think of, every foundation in existence. It is needed as much as water, for without earth where would water lie, where would the grass grow. Where in fact would man thrive... You stand here and call me dirt as if that is some insult, no, to a plant mage it is the highest form of a compliment..."

Each Prince stood before me speechless, unable to counter my intellect, every sparring match of words between us ending in their rage, which they could not control. "Both of you were born to royalty and yet that does not make you great, no, it has simply given you an inflated sense of entitlement. Perhaps one day you two will see the error of your ways but that day is not today. I can tell by the glimmer of frustration now sparking in your eyes, that I have won yet again. It would be prudent to walk away, nothing good will come of lingering." This once Prince Sorel took my words to heart turning to walk back the way he had come, the hatred in his eyes, a chill raced down my spine as Prince Eris turned to follow in his wake, hatred such as that had started wars...

"Gods and Goddesses Rhyme why was the palace ceiling built so high," Libeth gasped slowly sliding down the massive tree trunk.

I removed my hand from where it lay against bark, it had been our only means of communication and moving might have meant disaster if she'd needed me, I would never forgive myself if she came to harm because I had failed to be vigilant. "The palace is meant to be magnificent Libeth, I'm sure it's dimensions were made to ensure that it was, and so it is an architect, long dead is remembered for this very master piece she has created."

"Did not a King's daughter create the plans for this very foundation?" Libeth murmured thoughtfully taking a long drink from the water skin she had slung across her chest.

"It has been written in more than one history book and so I believe it to be true," Libeth nodded at my confirmation pushing her sweat dampened hair out of her eyes.

"I do not know how you survive with hair as long as the river flows, when I am barely managing with this short mop on my own head." Libeth pulled a dry cloth from her pocket to wipe the sweat and leaf particles from her face and neck. "I feel right itchy, it seemed as if every branch wanted to hug my face." She grumbled before turning to me flinching slightly, "What the hell happened to your face while I was gallivanting around up there!?"

I stroked my cheek no longer aware of any pain, "I feared if I moved my hand from the oak that you might need me and I would not sense it and so I did not move when struck for my perceived insolence. It was by a weak handed man, with nary a scar to mar his fingers." I chuckled softly patting the trunk lightly. "I'm sure it won't even bruise."

Libeth sighed softly deflating, "I wish I'd seen it at least you have a way with words, so eloquent you could make a grown man weep."

"You are a true poet, have you never thought to become a bard?" I questioned as she hefted a much larger bag over her head letting it fall to the stone floor beneath us wincing slightly at the loud clinking noises that it produced. "If any of them are broken the blame is on you." I warned crouching down to examine the stones.

Libeth snorted, "The earth calls to me more than mere song and I will simply do what you asked of me and blame it on Rosen," she countered crouching next to me.

"Rosen will forgive us for using her name is such a display as we wish to create, she will not forgive us for using her name to get us out of trouble we rightly deserve for not being careful and I will not incur her wrath by doing so." I opened the large cloth sack examining every shard for fractures or cracks sighing softly in relief when I found none. "Luckily it's not something we have to think about, do try to be more careful." I finished with a pointed look.

Libeth nodded sheepishly, "It has been a bit of a tiring morning. My apologizes." I accepted her apology with a nod before removing one of the now dormant shards.

"Did you disrupt the magic or destroy it?" The look I shot her told her that I was only willing to hear one answer.

"Disrupted, I enjoy living thank you very much. An enchantment of this magnitude, Libeth shook her head, "surely took a bit more than a decade. I'd not to be the one to break it just a little under a fortnight from an event that will change lives and history if my mother can be believed."

"Did you capture the inscription at its heart, we cannot light them again without it?" I wasn't willing to let her off the hook so easily.

She grinned offering me a glowing acorn, "I could not for the life of me remember it all or write it correctly, but well this guy was ready and willing to help me." I laughed softly at her genius. "You feel less like you regret allowing me to be your partner now that you know I'm not an idiot?" Libeth asked smiling softly now.

"Just a bit," I offered taking the acorn and tucking it into the pouch at my hip, inside a pocket that did not allow the light to bleed through.

"What do you think her Majesty will say when she finds a giant tree has grown in the center of her ballroom?" I helped Libeth close the sack holding the shards we'd place after we'd broken for our afternoon meal.

"Thankfully, that is not for us to know, after all that is what the Head Gardener is for, let us just try to finish before the day is out so that Rosen does not have to explain the missing stones, that cost more than our families combined, and the large tree." Libeth readily agreed once more slinging the bag over her head to rest opposite the water skin she still carried.

"Where should we keep the stones until then?" The look in her eyes said the decision was on me.

It took me a moment to supply an answer that wouldn't have us exiled by morning. "The stables, for sure, annoying though my brother may be at times, no one enters the stables without his say so, especially the Prince."

Libeth chuckled softly. "Smart idea, your brother's stubbornness concerning Prince Sorel entering his domain is legendary."

"My brother does not like the way the fair Prince treats his horses and so Reason monitors him every time he rides. My brother calls it special training," I offered by way of explanation as we strolled towards the double doors that would lead us out into the Pleasure Garden. "Though all the guards, soldiers and recruits alike know the real reason behind it."

Libeth shoved the doors open waiting for me to step clear before allowing them to close behind us. They could not be opened from the outside by normal means, only a plant mage could open them from the outside, a plant mage or the Queen. "Do you think the Prince is the way he is because he grew up without a father?" Libeth asked quite randomly, more than likely thinking outloud.

"Her Majesty's Consort died before the Prince was old enough to remotely understand death, indeed I haven't heard many stories about him, all I know is that he was a gentle, loving man that did not deserve the death that took him." I traced my fingers through a bunch of flowers smiling softly at their whispered greeting, relaxing slowly in the presence of their voices.

"More than one person has claimed that his death was not of natural causes." Libeth spoke softly so that others might not hear, I did not tell her to do differently the flowers would have warned me if others were about but they were but plants and they could sometimes be fooled by magic. I did not work the Pleasure Garden often enough to ensure that not even magic could slip past them too many were often found walking these paths.

"Rosen spoke of poison and I agree," it was not my place to speak of the Shadow Garden it had been a small thing before the Queen's Consort had passed, with his passing came the demand for knowledge, the need for closure and the proof that she wasn't wrong. The Queen was proven right I do not know if Rosen ever informed her of this fact and I did not ask. It was not my place to know. "Though that is not what you asked, and the answer to your question is no. Princess Adri and her sister Princess Mariel alike grew up without their father and turned out to be intelligent self-sufficient women."

We exited the Pleasure Garden through an archway made of two connecting trees, moving quickly across the grounds towards the Training Fields and the stables beyond, Eden and Emery could be seen on the other side of the large expanse of land digging holes, a cart of varying kinds of saplings close at hand. I was glad that Rosen hadn't given us that task, I stepped over a long curving log no doubt used to measure the circumference of the entire field and how the saplings would be spaced.

Libeth whistled at the task before them. I silently agreed before coming back to the conversation at hand, "I believe that the Queen spoiled her son, perhaps for a long time they both thought he would be King. He grew up thinking that he would be great and that one thought shaped his every action. He feels entitled, untouchable…his world shattered when he failed his Trials. He has no power, perhaps only an inkling of magic so far as I can tell and he will never truly amount to anything, not because of his lack of magic but because of his unwillingness to try. The Prince has shaped himself and everything that befalls him from this point on will be his own fault. I feel that given enough time he will be his own undoing."

"Yes but what destruction will befall the land in the time it takes for that to happen…" Libeth questioned as we entered the stables.

"Let us hope none at all." Libeth hid the sack of dormant stone shards in the loft where nary a stable hand went unless absolutely necessary and we went our separate ways to enjoy our midmorning meal.

*****

"Truly it is a wonder to finally find you in the Queen's Garden," I smiled softly turning to gaze through the water pouring from the fountain to find Adri gazing at me practically beaming in delight.

"I had decided that perhaps you were looking for me and not privacy and so just this once I stayed," I raised my meager lunch of water and a cold meat pastry. "Besides I did not know what to do with my meal."

"I'm sure you'd have thought of something as clever as you are," the Princess countered taking a seat beside me on the fountain, she looked lovely clade in her full royal robes. Green as the grass grows with accents of golden brown and embroidered vines, much like the Gardener's dress uniform. I smiled at the veiled support.

"Is there a special occasion I'm unaware of?" I waved my hand at her attire. "You're stunning in your beauty, while I sit here before you covered in garden soil and tree sap, surely I shame you with my mere presence."

Her Highness blushed prettily bowing her head in the face of my compliment, "No occasion, my mother had robes made for me, something befitting a queen, anything my heart desired she said and I could not think of anything I loved more than these gardens." She gazed at me through the curtain of her hair eyes shining with happiness, "and so I had robes made similar to the Gardener uniform with a few small differences. I was so excited I put them on as soon as they arrived."

"Well I am honored on the behalf of us all, they are perfect," I traced my finger along an intricately embroidered vine, "Well nearly perfect," I murmured softly dipping my hand into the bubbling pool of the fountain and pulling free a water lily that had just begun to bloom. "If I may?" The Princess ducked her head slightly allowing me to tuck the flower into her hair. "Now it's perfect."

"Thank you," I dried my hands on my trousers before finishing off my lunch.

"It's no trouble Highness…"

"Not for the flower," She said abruptly. "I'm not thanking you for the flower, but for the compliment, for calling me stunning and beautiful. I've heard it before, from Prince Eris, from a few of the Councilor's sons and daughter's alike and their words always ring hallow in my ears. When you say it I hear the sincerity of your words and know you mean what you say."

"If being a plant mage has taught me anything it is honesty," I offered by way of explanation, "though the flowers do not dictate what I say or how I say it they've taught me many things. One being to never say anything you don't mean."

Adri smiled softly, "I'm learning that Gardener, one meeting at a time I'm learning."

"There is much to be done before the start of the Tournament and so I should take my leave to complete the task before me." Her

Highness stood with me tracing her hand down my arm in a friendly gesture squeezing my fingers when her hand found mine.

"Do not work too hard Denarii," I nodded squeezing her fingertips before allowing her hand to fall from mine.

"I will try not to Highness," I went to bow only to have her catch me by the shoulders startling me into standing again.

"Please, when we are alone, do not bow to me, friends do not bow to each other and I would like to consider you a friend." I bowed my head in understanding.

"Good day to you Highness, I am glad that we are on our way to friendship." I waved in parting and she waved back once more taking a seat at the fountain.

I stood gazing at her from a distance. The way the sun shone through curls of her hair it looked as if earth and sand were mixed, glowing in the afternoon light, I watched as she traced her fingers through the water of the fountain smiling softly at some stray thought that crossed her mind. I shook my head continuing on my way unable to understand how anyone could see her as anything but beautiful despite her size.

I retraced my path back to the Pleasure Garden asking the doors to open for me, which they did without hesitation, Libeth sat at the base of the great oak separating the dormant shards into a separate cloth bag. "Ahh you've arrived; I was beginning to think that you would leave me to finish alone."

"Surely you know I would never do such a thing." I took the bag she handed me slinging it over my head.

"I know," Libeth smiled softly offering me the second water skin she had slung over her chest, "I jest of course, now let's get to work. I want to finish long before the sun sets." I agreed whole heartedly not wanting to experience the act of climbing down in near darkness, the shards could not be activated while we placed them, their brilliance would surely blind us and make getting down from such a height more dangerous in the end.

Libeth climbed one side of the great oak while I climbed the other and we both set about placing the shards. I do not know how she set hers, perhaps she had rope, I simply asked each branch I chose to make a home for it and they readily agree allowing small divots to appear in their surface where I placed each shard and then growing around them. It took longer than expected, though no tree I helped grow would ever let me fall not every limb was strong enough to hold me easily, more than once I found myself shimmying along a leafy appendage praying to the Gods that my magic would hold and that it wouldn't snap midway through.

Several times I heard Libeth cursing the day she discovered she had plant magic, I was glad she could not see me while I laughed. I ensured she could hear me through every tree limb she touched, of course more cursing followed. Once I'd finished I made my way out of the tree, feeling as tired and itchy as Libeth had no doubt felt the first time.

I leaned back against the trunk allowing the great oak to sooth me with its murmured excitement for what was to come, I waited for Libeth to join me before pushing myself away from the tree. "Now?" I asked to be sure.

The sun disappeared beyond the point where it was useful, "Yes," Libeth murmured catching her breath.

I pulled the acorn from the hidden pocket in the pouch at my hip and smashing it against the trunk leaving behind a glowing imprint of an acorn on the rough bark. Slowly but surely the throne room lightened and Libeth and I both breathed a sigh of relief. "For a moment I thought it wasn't going to work." Libeth breathed shakily patting her heart.

"I felt the same sense of panic," I closed my eyes taking a deep calming breath.

"We deserve a hot meal and a good rest," Libeth clapped me on the back laughing happily. "Goddess I wished to have children simply so that I can tell them I was a part of this moment, I cannot believe we did it…"

We moved back to gaze at our handiwork, "It is something to be proud of for sure." Libeth nodded her agreement. After admiring the final product of our hard work we gathered up our belongings and left the ballroom

"Sleep well!" Libeth called once we entered the Gardener's Wing of the palace.

"I will for sure!" I called back waving her off before heading to the rooms I shared with my brother. I cleaned up thankful we had our own little private bathing room and changed my clothes braiding my hair down my back so that the entirety of my clothing wouldn't become soaked again.

Reason walked in just as I moved to leave, "Where are you going so late in the evening?" He asked brow raised curiously.

"I'm off to find something to eat, I have not had anything since my midmorning meal." I tossed back over my shoulder as I pulled on my boots.

"Resist the urge to wake me with the noise you'll make coming back here, I have an early start in the morning." He grumbled as he often does.

I glanced back at him, "You say that as if I don't."

"Yes but you don't struggle dragging yourself out of bed as much as I do." I nodded in agreement.

"Completely true," I stood from my seat on the couch. "I will try to be quiet."

"Thank you." I watched my brother enter his room before leaving taking the servant's passages to the kitchen so as not to be questioned, it was impossible not to pass a battalion of guards otherwise. They were near about everywhere patrolling the palace and I did not feel like answering the same question a thousand times.

Cook allowed me to have a bit of left overs knowing how hard I worked. I was leaving the kitchens with my meal of roast chicken and greens when a servant walked in with a pitcher of wine and two cups one singing of pleasure. I dropped my plate and cup on the counter before gripping the servant, taking the cup of treated wine. "Where did you get this?" I asked urgently.

The young man gazed at me startled, "Her Highness' quarters, she was having a private dinner with the foreign Prince…Eris is his name I believe. The meal was coming to a close and I was requested to take the drinks and make my departure. Her Highness and the Prince were saying their goodbyes for the evening." The young servant shook his head, "Her Highness looked right relieved. I do not think she cares for him much."

"Thank you," I left by way of the servants' quarters and used several secret passages Rosen had shown me in the past to sneak into the Royal wing of the palace. I marched straight to the door with all the guards.

"Halt…" I pulled a dried pod from my pouch and tossed it at the guards, it bloomed long before it reached them gently floating before them, every one of them dropped like a collective sack of potatoes as the scent of Child's Slumber filled the air. The flower withered and died once more turning into a pod that fell into my out stretched hand, I tucked it away stepping over the sleeping guards and pushed open the door.

I glanced around spotting the half open door on the other side of the small receiving area, I leapt over the couch and burst through the door racing towards the bed a bit blinded by my rage, I grabbed the Prince and threw him clear across the room. "What in the Gods!"

I slammed him against the wall, "What have you done?!" I breathed heavily quivering with anger.

He chuckled, "She wanted it." I slugged him in the mouth allowing him to slump to the floor in his pain.

"You drugged her," I unsheathed a knife made of the hardest material in existence, Vipers Wrath, a thorny bramble that grew on the edge of the Void, it was impenetrable by anything but magic. I held the sharply curved, blackened blade to his throat. "Give me one good reason why I shouldn't end your miserable existence?" I questioned wanting to gut him through like the animal he was.

"If you kill me," he gloated, "You'll start a war."

"And what do you think you've done by attempting to rape the Heir to Angileri?" The picture frames beside our heads shattered, Eris flinched when I stood back watching leafy branches encase his entire form. He stood trapped against the wall struggling to escape.

"She wanted it, and that's all she'll remember in the morning with the shame of what she's done, of how she ached for me to fill her." He laughed blood trickling from his mouth attributed to the blow I'd struck him earlier. I punched him so hard his head whipped back against the wall before hanging forward. He groaned eyes rolling in his head as he struggled to stay conscious. I clenched and unclenched my fist around my blade, badly wanting to end his life.

"What good would come of this…" I asked speaking as calmly as I could.

"I would get her pregnant and she would marry me, I would be assured a seat on the throne," He mumbled only half aware.

I laughed at the audacity before tracing my blade quickly along every one of his limbs. "I cannot kill you, as you said but I can let you sit here trapped against this wall wondering if you'll ever regain the use of your limbs…wondering" I lowered my blade to his manhood, "If I actually cut it off or not." He attempted to struggle but the branches were growing, sprouting, twinning to make a more secure prison. I watched as they sealed over his face leaving a small space to draw air and nothing more.

"You will pay for this!" He screamed in his rage.

"Be silent," I murmured as I nicked his throat through a small opening in the foliage, paralyzing his vocal cords and making him struggle to breathe. "I hope it takes a very long time for people to find you."

I turned sheathing my blade as I approached the bed, Adri's shirt lay open, her breasts on display, her trousers were undone slightly but not enough for him to have penetrated her. I could see the cloth of her underwear through the opening he'd created. Sweat glistened on her skin, while tears streamed from eyes now filled with shame. I gathered her up in my arms, "All will be well Highness, all will be well." I soothed carrying her from her room and taking as many servant's passages as need be to make it back to my room undetected. Of course many a servant saw me and wondered but none asked knowing it was not their place.

"I wanted this…" Adri finally spoke as I laid her gently on my bed climbing in next to her.

"No, he drugged you Highness, he attempted to take you against your will and I know you will not remember this in the morning but I need you to go to sleep knowing that nothing that happened this evening was your fault. Do you understand?"

The Princess turned from me, I tugged her back. "Adri…" The use of her name got her attention. "Tonight wasn't your fault…"

"Then why did I want it…want him?" She asked confusion clear on her face and it broke my heart to see such a usually strong woman brought so low.

"It was the drug Adri, that's what it does. It makes you want pleasure, makes you ached to be filled, to be touched and you can say no all you like but your body keeps saying yes. That doesn't make it your fault." I stroked her hair from her sweat slicked face. Her Highness gazed into my eyes for a long time before accepting my words.

I offered her a mint leaf, the antidote to the drug knowing that she wouldn't remember much if anything from this night save the fact that what happened, the little that she retained, was no fault of hers. Her Highness slept soon after, the fight between what her mind wanted and what her body demanded against her will taking its toll at last. I held her close stroking her hair soothingly as my mother had done when I was but a child murmuring words of comfort that she could no longer truly hear. I closed my eyes to rest them and found myself drifting off to sleep…if only for a moment I thought before darkness claimed me completely.

Chapter 6
All In

I woke to find Libeth gazing down at me with a large cup of my favorite tea steaming in her hand, the brew was dangerous to consume for most if made wrong, no plant mage had ever made it wrong. "Now I know I said that you were fit for royalty, but that did not mean that I wanted you to break the Heir's innocence and be murdered or exiled in consequence."

I gazed at her brow furrowed in confusion shifting to find that her Highness' breasts were peeking through the vee formed by the loosely tied laces at the top of her tunic and that somewhere in the night she had curled against me slipping her hands beneath the fabric of my shirt causing it to ride up revealing part of a tattoo that near about spanned across every limb of my body. "Fully clothed no less she didn't even get the pleasure of breaking your innocence or seeing the rest of that tattoo that I don't think even Reason knows you have." Libeth stared at the vibrantly green stem covered in thorns curling across my ribs down towards the apex of my thighs. "Does that end where I think it ends?" She questioned softly taking a sip of her own drink.

I sat up slowly gently taking her Highness' hands from my body and placing them on my bed, pulling my tunic down before standing up and straightening my clothes. "That is none of your concern. As for the Princess…" I took in her now peaceful expression as she snuggled into the warmth my body had left behind. "She's had a rough night."

A knock sounded on the door before I could explain further, I swept the blanket up and over the Princess and Libeth stood beside me allowing us to cover the view of the bed as the door opened revealing Reason a little worse for wear. "Rhyme," he murmured voice still a bit rough from sleep, hair a rat's nest, telling me he'd forgotten to braid it last night. He rubbed his face trying to wake up a little more, Libeth went to offer him her tea before thinking better of it. He sighed softly before standing a little straighter, his shirt fell open; he'd forgotten to button it in his haste to answer the door. "There are Royal Guards standing at the door led by the Guard Captain himself, you are to report to the Queen's Study..." he glanced back and forth between us. "The both of you." He finished before stumbling away mumbling about how he hated mornings.

Libeth and I shared a look before she offered me my cup, I took it nodding my head gently in appreciation. "I have no idea what happened last night." She glanced at the bundle of blankets now hiding the Princess, "But I am sure we are about to find out."

I straightened my clothes thankful that I'd changed the night before into something decent, I unbraided my hair stroking my fingers through it gently before tying it up with a leather thong. "Why don't you just keep it braided all the time?" Libeth asked as we left my room.

I dropped a mint left in my tea taking a long drink as we approached the door behind which Royal Guards waited, "If I braided it, I would not know how to fight with it unbraided, I would trip and stumble and it would be my down fall and so I leave it free save to tie it back from my face. In the jungle not many children grow their hair, those that do grow into warriors because it is in all honesty a weakness an enemy can exploit, but they make it into a strength. My mother had but one request of me when I left, of course she knew I would choose to heal over all else, but she wanted me to be able to protect myself, to protect my brother if need be. And so I grew my hair and though I am a Gardener to the Queen, and sometimes a healer in her infirmary. I am also a warrior...for my mother." I finished opening the door before Libeth could speak again.

I tipped my head in respect to the Guard Captain Neola, he tipped his head in turn, "I do not know what has transpired Gardeners, I simply know that the Queen wishes to hold a small council...without her Councilors." For the remainder of the journey to the Queen's Study all was silent, those that passed did not speak, instead bowing their heads solemnly and moving along more quickly. "Whatever comes, I wish you good fortune." Neola clapped us both on the back before turning to guard the door with his men.

Libeth and I entered without knocking to find Emery, Rosen, the Queen and her Highness Mariel already in attendance. The only Gardener we were missing was Eden, and he arrived a few moments later, clothing in disarray and confusion clear on his face. There were seats enough for all of us surrounding her desk in a half circle, her Highness stood behind the Queen, an observer. Once Eden had taken his seat the Queen stood and began to speak. "Last night and into the early morning Sir Zeron, worried about the lack of his charge's appearance in his rooms went in search of him where he'd last left him. He found several unconscious royal guards, a broken door, shattered picture frames, disarrayed furniture and at last his Prince curled on the floor of my daughter's bedroom, half naked, bleeding from several cuts and unable to move." I brushed a strand of hair from my face, he'd been there for so long that my magic had worn off. "He was paralyzed, struggling to breathe and unable of course to speak. He has just fully recovered and the picture he has painted in my mind is a disturbing one."

Her Majesty took off her crown as she had done near about a seventh day prior in her study the night of the feast, once more she placed it on her desk before coming to stand in front of it leaning heavily on sturdy wood. "He claims he was attacked by one of my Gardeners', he could not tell me why he was half naked, where my daughter was or why he'd been found in her bedroom no less. He said he did not remember," She scoffed shaking her head. "I have been Queen for nearly thirty years and this is the excuse he gives me. Of course I do not believe a word. I did not call any of you here to offer blame or punishment, no I simply wish to thank you for saving my daughter." Her Majesty turned from us then, tears glimmering in her eyes.

"I had spoken with the Council before calling this meeting, I had wished to prosecute the Prince, but there is no evidence, he claims he does not remember much of the events prior to him being found. The drug found in the cup given to my daughter causes pleasure but steals the memory and the Council is not behind her, they believed it was her doing so that she may claim a husband because no one would dare want her for who she is." The Queen quivered with her rage struggling to control herself repeating those words. "You can image my anger, as a mother and a Queen when my people, her people failed to protect her. I have never been more ashamed. Every woman of course was behind me but again we lack the evidence."

I sipped my tea remembering the look of triumph in Prince Eris' eyes when I'd slammed him into the wall, I thought of the guards outside the door keeping watch of how much planning had gone into what he'd done. I wondered how many Counselors had known… "I have hired every one of you save Rosen who has stayed on from when my mother was Queen, I have seen you grow from children and I would trust every one of you with my life, with my daughters' lives." She took her crown in her hands and held it before her. "I have removed my crown because I stand before you not as your Queen but as a mother willing to protect her daughter and I ask of you a favor of which you may refuse."

We all sat waiting, I looked at my fellow Gardener's each of us from a different country, a different culture and I could see that no matter the request they would agree, not for the Queen but for a mother because if any one of our mothers' had but asked us to protect another one of her children we would for that is our blood. And the Princess was not our blood by any means, none of us could claim to be of royal ancestry, but she was a daughter of a mother whom had the means to ask children that she had raised as her own for fifteen to twenty years. "I ask that you enter the Queen's

Tournament?" I sat back in my chair not having expected that in the least.

"Your Majesty…" Emery hesitantly broke the silence that had settled over us. "You're giving each and every one of us permission to court your daughter, to perhaps one day sit the throne in your stead. We truly feel honored that you trust us that much, but none of us are warriors, we are but plant mages dillydallying in the most extraordinary gardens in the known world."

Rosen stood from her seat turning to face us, placing herself beside the Queen. "I was just as shocked by this meeting as all four of you and I know that none of you are true warriors, you did not spend the entirety of the little childhood that you had on these grounds training with the Royal Guards and the soldiers, but I know you can all fight. You can all protect yourselves as well as any friends or family if need be. The Queen…no, Servasli is placing the utmost trust in each and every one of you. Yes, perhaps one of you will win, but that is not what her Majesty cares about, protecting the future Queen of Angileri is the goal. You are doing this to ensure that those that do not deserve to even grace the Princess' presence do not remotely stand a chance. You are doing this to weed out people like Prince Eris who come here and think that they can do as they please without consequence."

Libeth stood first, "I may not be a warrior but I have a few tricks up my sleeve. I stand no chance of winning but if me doing this helps her Highness in the long run well I'm in."

Eden followed, "I do not mind smashing a few heads together in the name of justice."

Emery stood sighing as if it were some great struggle on his part. "I suppose I can't leave you two to do this without me."

I sipped my tea watching them all while they in turn watched me, "If you think I will join you because of some insane sense of comradery then you are mistaken." I stood finishing my tea. "There are now three of you to protect the Princess where before there were none and you do not need me."

"I would think you'd be the first to stand," her Majesty said without anger or reproach.

"I said you do not need me, not that I would not join you." Libeth grinned raising her hand to touch the pin on her chest.

"All in then?" She asked as I stepped forward raising my hand to the broach resting over my heart.

"All in." We said as one allowing our hands to fall into the open space between us, an Alia rose coming to full bloom in each of our palms.

"Goddess above and below, I did not think we'd actually use that binding agreement in the entirety of our adult lives." Emery murmured smiling softly.

"Neither did I," Eden withdrew his hand first and the rest of us followed I closed my hand around the dying flower before tucking the seeds into the pouch at my hip.

"I will see you all on the start of the Tournament, good fortune to the lot of you." Her Majesty replaced her crown in a clear sign of dismissal.

"Is it wrong that I hope I fail out of the first competition?" Emery questioned softly as we moved as one to exit her Majesty's study.

"We'll ensure you're with us for the long haul Emery don't you worry," Libeth chirped excitedly slapping him on the back.

"Gardener Rhyme," I allowed the others to flow past me out the door, Libeth stood lingering curiosity burning brightly in her eyes. She motioned that she'd wait for me and I bowed my head in understanding before turning around, the door was once more pulled shut, leaving me alone with Rosen, Princess Mariel and her Majesty.

Silence stretched between us for a long time Rosen had moved to
gaze out her Majesty's window, the Queen had once more taken a
seat at her desk, her daughter a silent observer still. "I know that you
will not admit that you've done anything. Which is why I will not
ask you to explain. I just want to thank you personally and you can
fill in for what. Good day Gardener." Her Majesty smiled a smile I'd
only seen on her daughter's face a few times; it was just as beautiful.
Though it did not steal my breath away I smiled back.

"Good day your Majesty," I tipped my head in respect before
turning and marching from the room, nearly running into Libeth on
my way out. It seemed, done with their duties, the Guard Captain
and his men had dispersed. "Is there a reason your face was
practically glued to the door?" I asked Libeth brushing a stray lock
of hair from my face.

"I wanted to know if you were finally going to fill someone
in on what happened last night, but I was mistaken. Clearly the
Queen knows about your penchant for stubbornness when it comes
to all things magical and personal in your life." My lips twitched in
amusement at Libeth's exasperation.

"I have no problem speaking on the subject of magic or
sharing bits of personal details with those I trust." I countered as we
headed back to my rooms passing several servants and countless
guards on our stroll through the corridors. I grimaced at all the
traffic, there was a reason I took secret passageways and servant's
hallways. There was rarely a soul in sight along them.

"Yes, the problem is gaining your trust." I shrugged
unwilling to argue on the matter. Libeth, reaching a dead end,
changed the subject. "I wonder what the Princess thought when she
woke up in your bed alone clothes all rumpled and open…"

Libeth trailed off slowing to a stop as she caught my eye, we
ran the rest of the way to my shared rooms. Slowing as we
approached the door. I opened it without knocking, Reason always
forgot to lock up in the mornings when he left. "Do you always leave

the door to your living quarters unlocked?" Libeth questioned eyes wide with shock.

"Reason has a bad habit of forgetting to lock up when he leaves half asleep in the morning, hence why I usually leave after him. Her Majesty's unplanned meeting was…"

"Unexpected." Libeth finished cheekily.

I shook my head before rounding the couch and heading towards my own private room. I pushed the door open slowly not really sure what to expect, but it wasn't my bed completely made and her Highness nowhere in sight. "You're missing a Princess." Libeth murmured from behind me having glimpsed the empty room just passed my shoulder.

"I have noticed." I countered in a dry tone.

"Should we look for her?" I cocked my head listening to the murmured voices of the raptor vines hanging from my window. I smiled softly.

"No need." I closed my door while Libeth looked on confused. "We have work to do."

"Are you going to tell me anything pertaining to her Highness, and where she is or what at all happened last night?" Libeth queried as we left my shared rooms locking the door behind us.

"If I told you Libeth where would the mystery lie?" Libeth huffed while I chuckled softly thinking about what the vines had told me of her Highness of how she'd woken, dressed in spare clothes and run off to her room once she was sure my brother had gone. I knew as sure as the wind blows and the flowers bloom that no matter what time I looked, that I'd find Adri somewhere in the Queen's Garden. It was her haven after all. My laughter faded, I just wished she had no need to hide…

Later that day after Libeth and I had finished placing small shoots of growing vines around every scone, torch and light fixture we could see throughout the palace, I found myself seated atop the wall surrounding the Queen's Garden watching the Heir to Angileri.

Instead of her practice uniform, or royal robes today she wore riding gear. Clothing that would snap any man's head to attention…and I'm not talking about the one holding their brain. Dark green leather breeches stretched taut over thick thighs, black boots incased strong calves, the tunic she wore a mixture of creamy gold was form fitting without being restricting I could see the flatness of her stomach through the fabric. Her outfit was all sin, a Goddess tempting the Gods to fall at her feet and worship every inch of her. I shivered and yet there was no breeze. I could not for the world of me understand why no one could see in her what I saw. A woman beautiful inside and out regardless of her size.

"Are you going to sit up there all day Gardener?" The Princess asked after what felt like hours of me watching her explore the garden one flower, one bloom, one green shoot at a time, resting every now and again at the fountain.

I leapt from the wall as the flowers parted for me dropping onto damp soil and moving quickly until I was on the path not wishing to disrupt their home. They swayed back into position as if they'd never moved in the first place. "What gave me away?" I asked curiously knowing how silent I could be at times.

Her Highness smiled tracing her fingers lightly through the water before looking up at me with a sparkle in her eyes. "Your shadow," she laughed softly as I shook my head. "You should have picked a different perch Gardener one not so obviously in the sun. I went to gaze upon the flowers near there and your shadow blotted out the light. And then I watched it unmoving as it was for quite some time…" Her laughter faded, her eyes grew more serious. "What has brought you here Gardener Denarii, to watch me so?"

I sat down on the fountain beside her, rarely if ever did she wear her hair up, rarer still did she actually wear her circlet. When did she you had the pleasure of seeing her entire face unobscured, she had a small scar curving just beneath her jaw usually hidden by the fall of her hair now worn up in the traditional warrior bun. A knot centered near the top of the head allowing the rest of the hair to fall naturally down your back. Her Highness' bun was more intricate than mine or my brother's might have been with braids twinned in and jade sparkling like small raindrops throughout. A comb in resemblance to an Alia rose kept it in place, if she were running into battle it would be something far more sturdy than that. "I had wished to speak with you." I offered after what felt like another small eternity of staring. "I grew distracted…" my gaze once more wandered along the sinful outfit she wore.

Her Highness shifted slightly with a sigh, "I went riding today with several more suitors, my brother suggested I wear something more appealing to catch the men's attention."

"The men's attention you gain surely aren't the marrying kind." I countered brow furrowed.

"Yes well, none I've seen so far spark an interest and the Queen's Tournament starts in as little as two seventh days from now." Adri shook her head shoulders sagging.

"More will come. Those better suited to you I'm sure, they cannot all be bad." The Princess took a deep breath once more squaring her shoulders looking like the royalty I knew she was.

"I will hope up until the very last moment that the person who wins is bearable to talk to at least, it's a sign of good will to at least give them a chance." I grimaced at that but did not argue that small truth.

"I know you said you had wished to speak with me but I am curious about what transpired last night, I woke in your bed with no recollection, clothing all asunder and completely confused. I know I'd only had one glass of wine and not even a full one at that?" Adri inquired suddenly as if working up the courage to ask and finally finding it in the midst of our conversation.

I thought over what I could say and found myself at a loss, no one but Prince Eris and I knew what had happened and he claimed amnesia. "Someone thought to drug you…I caught them and brought you back to my quarters to rest." Her Highness stared at me for a long time willing me to say more but I stayed silent, I was sure Prince Eris would not dare try such a thing again for I had passed him in the corridors of the palace and seen the fear in his eyes of what I could do to him. I did not feel the need to make the Princess remember such a vulnerable moment.

She narrowed her eyes at me cheeks reddening slightly at the thought that entered her mind, "You would tell me if we…" I watched her face redden more as she struggled to find the words. She motioned with her hands trying to get me to understand without saying the words but I only grew more confused. "If we'd lain with each other," she finished breathlessly as if that one sentence had taken all of her energy.

My brows shot into my hair at her drawn conclusion which made every bit of sense now that I had time to think about it. "Highness I would not disgrace myself in such a way," she blanched at the perceived insult. I raised my hands quickly to forestall any words of rebuke. "I would not sleep with a woman with pleasure's curse in her system, unless drunken willingly, regardless of rulings otherwise, it is considered rape to me. I would rather have any woman or man I choose to lay with be willing participants."

The Princess relaxed as I finished my explanation, "As well any woman or man that you choose to sleep with would be lucky to have you for but one night…" I hesitated for a moment before continuing in a softer tone. "They would be blessed to have you for a lifetime." Adri blushed turning away from me to compose herself, I could see the scar curving beneath her jaw more fully now.

"You had wished to speak with me on something Gardener?" I blinked at her suddenly serious tone and change of conversation.

I bowed my head in acknowledgement, "Her Majesty, the Queen called a small council of her Gardeners this morning, she asked of us that we participate in the Queen's Tournament," I placed my fingers upon her lips as she moved to speak. "For your protection from men that wished to do you harm. I do not for a moment doubt that you can protect yourself, nor do I doubt that your guards can protect you, but we are not seen as threats. We can weed out as many as the unwilling suitors as we must until the last few standing are us and the select few we hope are good enough. Do not be angry she asked not as the Queen but as a mother wishing to protect her daughter." I allowed my fingers to fall, "My fellow Gardeners did it for that reason and did not need me. I chose to help because as you said yesterday you are my friend Highness and friends protect each other."

Her Highness sighed, "I did not even have the chance to grow truly angry before you had combated every argument I could think of." She smiled softly. "You are good with words Gardener Denarii."

"I have been told that before," I smiled back. "Though not by one quite so..."

"Royal," Adri supplied good naturedly.

"Heavenly..." I countered causing her smile to wane slightly.

Her Highness searched my eyes for a long time, "I wonder if you speak to all your friends the way you do to me..." Her words were filled with sorrow and I could not understand why. Once more she turned from me. "Thank you for sharing your words with me Gardener... I would enjoy being alone for a while if you please." I stood taking in the courtly dismissal.

I bowed and knew that she saw it from the corner of her eyes, tears streamed her face but I turned away with regret. I raced towards the wall running up its face and straddling the top turning for a moment to look back. Her Highness was still turned away gazing into the pool of the fountain. Somehow for the first time my garden seemed less vibrant despite the flowers blooming brightly beneath the light of the sun. I fell from the wall and left the Princess to her tears. We may have been friends but I was a Gardener and she was the next Queen to Angileri I knew there would be times I would not understand her pain and she would not understand mine.

Chapter 7
Spirits of the Green

"I hope we never have an event of this magnitude for the rest of my life," Emery grumbled sweat beading on his brow as he grunted with effort shoveling yet another hole for yet another sapling. I stuck my shovel in the dirt glad that my hair had decided to stay back for once.

"Just think after this we'll be done, no more digging, no more running around the palace with baby whatever you care to name, helping them flourish hoping they stay without dying by the Morrow least you have to go back and do it all over again." I breathed heaving another shovel full of dirt over my shoulder.

"I hate to kill your dreams," Libeth huffed leaning on her shovel briefly watching the recruits train, though it seemed that they were actually watching us work more than actually training. "But eventually the Princess will become Queen, surely the dragons will visit one of these days, as well Her Highness likely her Majesty at that point will get married. All these things are just as grand, if not more grand than the Queen's Tournament and you will live through every one." Emery groaned wiping sweat from his face.

Eden laughed softly placing yet another sapling in a hole, we had roughly ten more to place and little more than a seventh day to finish planting and then growing the stadium. Though my fellow Gardeners would be done after the planting and I could tell they would be glad, even Libeth always vibrant and happy was worn thin. "We'll be finished planting before the sun touches the horizon and then we can rest, even go celebrate if we want for a job well done. Have a drink at the Green Sprout if we're feeling up to it."

"Yes!" Libeth exclaimed digging a little faster. Emery grunted again brow furrowed in concentration. I placed another sapling before moving onto digging the next hole, muscles straining.

"I think I'm just going to enjoy a long soak in the bathing room allotted to us." I heaved out, knowing that if I did otherwise everything would be aching in the morning.

"I'm in full agreement," Emery said a little breathless. Libeth for once didn't fight us on going out with them. I'm sure Emery felt just as grateful as I did in that moment.

As Eden predicted we finished just a little before the sun touched the horizon and I could not have been more relieved though my magic was still going strong unlike my fellow Gardeners, though my body was tired. The recruits took pity on us and cleaned up in our steed allowing us to go our separate ways. I trudged my way back to my shared rooms letting myself in before taking a seat on the couch sighing softly in relief.

Nearly done, I closed my eyes listening for all the new plants spread throughout the palace, from the great oak to the green shooting vines on every light fixture I could hear them all. I relaxed drifting between sleep and wakefulness on a sea of voices, whispering, murmuring, singing all together in growing excitement. Sharing with me the gossip of the palace, noting everyone's location and what they were doing. Her Majesty and her daughter Princess Mariel sharing a meal in her study laughing good naturedly at a story shared between them.

Reason waking in a bed not his own confused but sated, Kiyen and Resli bickering in the corridor leading to the kitchens smiling through the banter. Prince Eris and Prince Sorel speaking in a dark corner voices too low to understand but perking a flower's interest none the less. The Heir of Angileri in her rooms lightly tracing her fingers along the Twilight peonies in a pot beside her bed smiling softly in delight. Despite the distance, despite the fact that flowers did not have eyes as we did I smiled feeling a little breathless because her expression was radiant. I opened my eyes still smiling allowing the voices to fade away from me, lower now but never truly gone, gentle waves lapping in the background of my mind.

I stood, groaning softly at all the new aches that had found me in my moment of rest. I went to my room grabbing a pair of dark trousers, soft tunic and under things before leaving my rooms. Though I loved the fact that my brother and I had our own private bathing room sometimes it just wasn't big enough.

I entered the servant's bathing room and took in the large pool of steaming hot water, I'd come early enough to have the entire room to myself. I stripped quickly placing my belongings in a small nook with my name on it before grabbing a bathing cloth and towel, I entered the pool with a sigh setting both on the edge as I allowed the heat to seep into my aching muscles soothing away the pain. I swam a little eyes closed against the heat before floating on my back gazing up at a scene I'd seen numerous times in history books, as well on a mural or two in the palace, and recreated in paintings you could buy at the market. Princess Alia being crowned Queen a small dragon, her constant companion, resting along her shoulders. An image captured and recaptured over time in every form of art.

"Gone for three years and I hardly recognize you," I blinked shifting to stand water cascading down my chest as I gazed on a face I thought I'd never see again. Tears formed unbidden in my eyes.

"Arely?" The Sol-Lea, leader to the entirety of the Queen's army, the Head of heads to all her men leapt into the water despite the fact that she still wore half her armor, all her knives and her sword. I swam to her and we met somewhere in the middle hugging and laughing while gazing at each other as if for the first time, this woman who had trained me as much as Rosen had, who had loved me with a passion I hadn't known in anyone since and who had hurt me like no one ever had. There would always be a small place in my heart that burned just for her, I had asked her to break my innocence, and knowing she might not return she had refused leaving me without so much as a goodbye kiss. "You never said goodbye," I murmured holding her afloat, despite that all her gear drug her down.

"I did not want you to wait for me, you were young and I did not know if I'd come back." Her voice husky with emotion, her eyes once a vibrant hazel were now dark with all the losses she'd endured. She'd changed, as had I.

"I loved you." More tears came as she held me, they mixed well with the water streaming down our faces.

Arely nodded voiced filled with no small regret, "I know."

"First I walk in on you with the Princess and now this." We both looked up to see Libeth standing on the edge of the pool fully clothed shaking her head. "I would love to hear your explanation for this…"

Arely and I parted both swimming for the edge and climbing out, Libeth started once she caught sight of the armor as well the renowned violet hair with one brilliant stroke of raven black. "Sol-Lea," she bowed. "You live…" the shock was plain to see, not a one had thought she survived, gone for three years without a whispered word or message of her whereabouts, her position had remained unfilled all this time. And now it would be filled again, by the woman meant to fill it.

"Yes and it is good to be home," She looked at me when she said that drawing Libeth's eyes to the fact that I was still very naked, her eyes instantly latched onto the vibrantly green stem lined with thorns spiraling over my shoulder forming a small circle around my heart, sharp and dangerous, something that could have resembled a flower if you looked close enough before trailing down across my ribs, through the center of my stomach and ending between my legs, on the bare patch of skin where no hair grew, lay a startlingly white dragon's breath, a flower resembling the licking flames that dragons were known to spew from their mouth when enraged. Each petal dipped in inky darkness. Libeth blushed unable to look away while I stood unashamed allowing her to look.

At last Arely cleared her throat helping her divert her gaze, Libeth snapped her eyes up to my face, "You have a lovely…" Her face burned while she stuttered not knowing how exactly to compliment me.

"I have a lovely flower." I supplied lips curling in amusement, Arely had her head bowed, shoulders shaking slightly as she fought to hide her laughter.

"Yea…Yes." Libeth stroked her fingers through the short locks of her sandy hair taking a step towards the door. "I think I…forgot something." I watched as she practically ran from the bathing room slipping slightly on titles damp from condensation.

"There's a reason that no one has seen my tattoo," Arely offered me my towel without once looking down. Respectful as she was in all things. I took it gratefully drying myself off before going to retrieve my clothes from the little nook I'd placed them in, dressing quickly I disposed of my towel as I left.

"I wished I was rude enough to stare as she had, it must be a sight for her to blush as she did." I stood braiding my hair down my back before it had a chance to tangle the both of us lingering just outside the servant's bathing room.

"Something only Libeth and my future lovers will ever have the experience of knowing." I allowed my braid to fall over my shoulder dripping water as we walked in step through the palace, Arely trailing water the entire way still soaked as she was from the pool.

"I would ask for but one more chance, but I do not think I deserve one." She offered wryly as we came to a stop before my rooms, the walk had been a short one. Too short to say all the things left unsaid between us, all the things we might not ever say.

I stroked my fingers lightly along her cheek, Arely, the only woman on palace grounds just as tall as I, with her elfin ancestry she was striking, strangely beautiful in her own way. She was five years my senior but she had always loved me like an equal despite that I'd been only nineteen summers when our relationship had started. It ended a year later when she left me in our bed without a letter or a kiss goodbye. I had hurt for a long time after that and though I had never talked much before I'd fallen more in love with my plants after she'd gone. Three years was a long time... Three years was a long time without so much as a goodbye. I let my fingers fall away smiling softly at my friend. That's all she'd ever be now, "You would be right."

"I know we can never have what we once had...but perhaps we can still spar every now and again. I am no longer sure, who is the better between us." She offered hesitantly a peace offering to sooth all the pain she knew she'd caused with her absence.

I smiled more fully jabbing her lightly in the arm ignoring the sting of my knuckles when they met the hard material of her armor. "I would like that." Arely nodded slightly before straightening her back and giving me a warrior salute eyes sparkling with mirth. I returned the gesture fist over my heart bowing slightly in respect. She left without saying anything more and for that I was grateful, my chest ached as it was, seeing the woman who could have stolen my heart if she'd but tried hard enough.

I left my rooms without opening the door and went to the one place I knew I'd find peace. The Queen's Garden...

I lay among the Were Lilies watching the spirits of the flowers dancing with each other, small and lively little beings they giggled gaily watching me watch them. It was rare that I actually had the time to see them as they were, more than green shoots sprouting from the ground, more than tiny buds struggling to bloom, more than gorgeous flowers slowly fading day by day. Hearts of the earth, they sang more beautifully than any person I'd ever known and lived more fully than any race I could name, their lives were short, but their cycles were endless. I lay among the Were Lilies with spirits dancing before my eyes and I could not be more content listening to their lovely voices sing of the sun and the moon, the sun which they'd never seen and the moon their mistress until the end of time. It was a beautiful song despite the fact that it held no words that I could truly understand, the feeling it invoked was enough. My eyes fluttered as peace washed over me, my little flowers singing me to sleep. I fought it for but a moment before darkness claimed me, their song drifting through my dreams.

When I opened my eyes the sun shone high overhead, the Were Lilies once more tucked within their cocoons though their spirits still danced their eyes were closed and it was a dance bordering on sleep. Soon they too would rest and their song would die to sleepy murmurs until the next full moon shone its face. I pushed myself into a sitting position blinking at the wreathes of still living blooms twinned around my arms and torso. I smiled softly, I suppose the spirits head done more than just dance while I slumbered. "I have no idea what I just witnessed but it was beautiful." I glanced up to find Rosen sitting on the path eyes filled with awe.

"What did you see?" I asked curiously having slept through the spectacle.

"I came into the Queen's Garden nearing dawn; the sun was just peeking over the horizon at first all I saw was the glowing white Were Lilies. It's so rare a sight that I drew closer, suddenly a form appeared and while I watched the flowers seemed to…dance twinning themselves across your form while you lay sleeping. Your hair was braided at the start and now you look a Goddess whose woken from a light doze in the forest glowing with magic, flowers blooming in your hair, wrapping around every limb calling softly to any who can hear them." Rosen shook her head while I stood moving towards the fountain slowly shedding flowers along the way.

"I helped them bloom last night, and they sang for me," I stroked my fingers through my hair finding a crown of blooming flowers, a mixture of the blossoms I'd laid sleeping beside. "I fell asleep listening to their song." I murmured pulling my hair back only to realize I had nothing to tie it up with, Rosen offered me a leather thong. "Thank you," she bowed her head in turn while I tied my hair back.

"I wish I could have heard it as you do, I hear the call but not much else beyond that." Rosen took the crown I'd worn in her hands still vibrantly alive, I blinked the spirits from my eyes as they raced up her arms finding a new playground. Rosen shivered as they settled along her body I smiled as they vanished just flowers before me now. Though I could still hear their voices, they enjoyed Rosen's magic nearly as much as they enjoyed mine. I chuckled softly at the comparison.

"I wish you could hear their voices as I do…the things they say, such innocent heartwarming things, spoken in lovely voices." I murmured softly feeling refreshed despite the fact that I'd spent the night sleeping on the ground. The flowers had kept me warm, their song bringing me peace.

Rosen smiled at the look on my face, "My gift will never be yours Rhyme, I accept that and enjoy what I have here at the palace. As well I enjoy the small bit of your gift that you share with me, it makes me feel young again." I watched her place the crown of flowers upon her head. "Now let us finish the stands so that the Queen's Tournament may begin in earnest."

I groaned at the reminder but allowed her to pull me to my feet and lead me to the Training Fields where we stood day after day talking of nothing in particular while I fed my magic to the saplings until they grew into large trees each of a height with each other and then slowly shaped them so that their limbs twinned together spanning the entire circumference of the Training Fields. Halfway through the last seventh day the stands were near about fully formed and I was beginning to feel the drain on my magic. Rosen stood rubbing my back in soothing circles while I leaned heavily against the fence feeling a little nauseous. "Do you need my help?" She questioned worried with good reason, one could die if they exhausted their magic in too quick a span of time.

"I'm good…" I breathed taking comfort in the spirits of the trees now standing with me lending me their strength once small they now stood as tall as I, though their voices were still that of young saplings. I stood straighter pointing out the Sol-Lea among the training guards and soldiers talking about her fighting style compared to theirs as I continued to feed the trees.

Rosen stopped me with a firm hand on my shoulder, "You have half of a seventh day to finish Rhyme, go find yourself a hot meal, a warm bed and rest up we'll continue tomorrow."

I opened my mouth to argue only to be given a pointed look, "It wasn't a request."

I chuckled softly shoulders slumping in relief, I bowed my head in acknowledgement lumbering away, I thought about going to the Queen's Garden knowing I would find peace in the flowers blooming brilliantly, in the sun shining just right down upon my face, in the feel of the soil crumbling soft and moist through my fingertips. I hesitated when I heard the whispering of the flowers informing me that another already resided there, my legs proceed without the command from my brain and suddenly I found myself rounding the path into the Queen's Garden to find the Heir leaning back against the fountain gazing into the sky appearing lost. Not in thought but in general as if the title she held was too big, the crown too heavy and she'd come to a place where no one could see her fall apart and yet here I was breaking my own rule.

"Strange that you find as much comfort in this place as I do," Adri said allowing her gaze to fall upon me eyes red rimmed from crying who knows how many tears.

"I feel as if I should be saying those words Highness, after all I am the plant mage." I offered moving forward on tired legs before slowly taking a seat beside her sighing softly once I could rest my weary body.

"My mother would bring me here as a baby…when I cried she said. The colors of the flowers, the burbling of the fountain, the sun on my face would calm my tears and suddenly I would be happy again. As a small child I would explore here as if it were some mystical place with untold discoveries. I would pick the blooms and weave myself crowns of flowers so much better than the weight of my circlet, so much lighter…" More tears flowed while I listened to her story. Her Highness pulled her knees to her chest tucking her face there as her shoulders shook with her sobs.

"I would dream of marrying a Prince who would take me away from this place, he would love me and we would have beautiful children, two girls because he married a girl you see and he loved her so much that he could not help but want two perfect beings in her image…and we would build another garden nearly as grand as this one."

"For the longest time I dreamed that, on my darkest days it was all that got me through and now suddenly that dream is gone. I have the gardens but I also have the crown that I never wanted and not a one of the suitors I've met, dinned with, rode with, sat with wants me for me. The little girl who would rather explore a garden of mysteries than actually sit in on a Council that playacts at accepting her for her mother's sake."

The Princess looked at me imploringly, "I never thought for a moment I would be here and now that I am it is all I can do not to crumble beneath the weight of all the disapproving stares. No one, not even I, wants me to sit the throne."

"Your mother does, Rosen, Emery, Eden and Libeth. The Queen and her Gardeners would have you, the servants every one of them would have you. The guards, and the soldiers would gladly have you as Queen Highness. You say no one wants the child exploring in the garden, perhaps they want the woman who one day thought to make her own." Adri wiped her tears away.

"Is it so wrong of me to fall in love with someone who wants them both?" She asked curiously.

I smiled softly stroking a tear from her face, "I do not think there is. I think if and when you find that person you should marry them Highness because they'll help you build that garden, in spite of the fact that you already have them they'll help you build another, not for the Queendom, not for the people of Angileri but just for you. They'll support you in all things and be strong where you are weak and they will love your children," I chuckled. "Two beautiful little girls because their mother is a girl, as much as they love you and it will seem as if the world is brighter for having them because truly they are your world." I found myself momentarily lost in Adri's eyes smile lingering on my face fatigue long gone.

"Marry someone who makes you a crown of flowers Highness because they know that sometimes flowers are lighter than the weight you bear upon your brow. Marry someone who will bear each weight with you willingly without regret…"

We sat in silence for a long time while the Princess digested my words. When she spoke her words were sincere. "I hope one day you become the Head Gardener Denarii, because I want what my mother has with Rosen, someone willing to be my friend regardless of my stature, someone willing to give their opinion without fear of reproach. I want someone like you on the Council because I know you will always be honest in your speech as well I know you will always love the palace gardens the same if not more than I."

Her Highness had somehow come to rest with her head on my shoulder, my arm around her waist resting lightly on her hip, I stroked her side soothingly while we sat leaning against the fountain gazing across the garden. "The Sol-Lea is entering the Tournament," I blinked coming back from the peaceful ambience that had settled around us. "We shared our midmorning meal together. She told me I needed someone strong by my side and that perhaps love would grow between us. I did not finish my meal…I grew tired of hearing the same words I'd heard countless times before spoken by a woman I'd once admired."

"You'll find your Prince Highness, don't lose hope just yet." Her Highness shifted pulling away from me, I allowed my arm to rest atop the fountain.

"What if my Prince is a Princess?" I gazed into the twilight wonder of her eyes watching the lavender flacks sparkle like stars in the night.

"Prince or Princess I do not think it matters Highness so long as you are happy." Adri shifted closer cheeks glowing softly as she blushed.

"And if it's neither?" I took a deep breath brow furrowed as I tried to see where exactly this conversation was going.

"Again I fail to see how their status matters so long as they love you, after all your father was a merchant before marrying your mother." I offered shaking my head.

"What if…what if I wanted to marry one of my…" I cocked my head startled by the sudden clamor of the flowers, another plant mage was near, one not belonging to the Queen.

I placed my fingers upon her lips, "Someone's listening," I murmured softly Her Highness grew still and we both sat waiting for whomever was near to pass. I relaxed dropping my hand. "It seems," I said wryly. "That someone thought to combat power with power, I felt another plant mage on the other side of the wall…they did not belong to your mother."

"Should we be worried?" Adri asked with good cause.

"I felt curiosity more than anything…but I could not measure their character, flowers usually do not know how to distinguish such things." I said absentmindedly as the garden calmed to its usual happy whispering murmurs.

"Usually?" I gazed at the Princess eyes now full of interest instead of tears.

"I do not know if other mages can do what I do, but I speak not only to the plants but to their spirits, the heart of what and, to me, who they are. They are simple, but like any being they can learn to be complicated and know the measure of a person. They know trust and deciet, kindness and love. They know more than the sun and the earth because I taught them so." The Princess listened with rapt attention. I gazed at the position of the sun, "It's getting late, I'm sure others are looking for you…I can hear them." I finished before she could protest.

Her Highness sighed once more allowing her head to fall to my shoulder. "The problem with being royalty Gardener Denarii is that you can never truly escape."

I lay my head atop hers sighing softly, "You shouldn't need to Highness."

"And yet here I am…" She pulled away and stood dusting off her robes. "Good fortune Denarii I hope you do well in the Tournament."

I watched her leave, more regal than she'd first appeared and I knew she'd be alright, for now at least. I laid my head back against the fountain and wondered at the words her Highness had left unsaid. Once the light began to wan I stood, going in search of my bed I still had a few days yet to finish the work I started. I felt tired just thinking about it…

The next day found Rosen and I back where we'd started, I leaned against the fence taking a deep breath before once more feeding the trees my magic. "The King of Dangilere had brought a plant mage with him, his daughter I believe. He hopes to win her Highness over with a suitor more in line with the Queen's Gardeners."

"Not a bad approach actually, considering how much the Heir enjoys her flowers." I murmured softly in admiration of his plan… "Weren't we at war with them but a decade ago?" I asked after a moment of thought.

"Yes, which is why I'm a bit hesitant to believe his motives are completely innocent. The Queen has ensured that a Shade or two dogs his heels for the entirety of his stay here." I furrowed my brow trying to recall where I'd heard the term.

"Shade…as in the spies that are more legend than anything?" I asked for clarification.

"As quiet as a tiger before it leaps," Was Rosen's response.

"And ten times more deadly," I finished recalling a song I'd heard not too long ago at the Green Sprout:

As quiet as a tiger before it leaps

And ten times more deadly

Coming in the night while the children sleep

You surely won't be ready

Grimmer than the grim reaper

Kiddies go run and hide

Known as the devil's soul keeper

Are you prepared to die…?

I singsonged softly tapping the beat out on the wooden fence post singing only the first two verses that I recalled from that night. Rosen chuckled softly before singing along with me. That afternoon was spent singing songs we'd heard at one time or another trying to distract me from the strain on my magic.

For the next few days Rosen would try to come up with some way to distract me, first it was songs, the following day it was naming all the flowers I'd ever grown, the day after that it was all the insults I'd thrown at Reason. Quite a bit of them were on the creative side and on the final day, I named every poison Rosen had ever fed me willingly or otherwise. I was not willing for more than half that I could think of through the fog clouding my mind. It took until the eve of that final day for the moss to grow along the benches the trees resounding a song that even Rosen could hear in my honor. I could not have named another poison if I'd tried. I lay on the grass sweaty and breathless near about having reached my limit. All the guards and recruits were long gone by then. Rosen pulled me to my feet and slung me over her shoulder with little effort.

"Tall as you are Rhyme you should weigh more than you do," was all she said on the matter as she carried me towards the palace.

"I never want to do that again in so short a span of time," I murmured into the small of her back having no energy to move, let alone walk. I grunted as Rosen climbed the servant's stairs as smoothly as she could with my entire weight on her back.

"Have you reached the limit of your reserves?" Her voice was slightly breathless but otherwise unchanged, showing that it really was no trouble to carry my entire weight through the palace.

"Just about," I groaned as she opened the door to my shared rooms, rounding the couch before entering my private room setting me gently on the bed.

"But not quite?" Rosen unlaced my boots before dragging them off my feet, then relieved me of my blade hidden by the fall of my tunic and then the pouch that held more supplies than one would think setting them both on the bedside table. The last thing she removed was my broach worn at nearly all times save on days of rest, she set that in the small case meant for it before stroking my hair from my face.

"No not quite," I murmured still able to hear the whispering of the plants, still able to see the spirit of the raptor vines growing from my window. Those vines had been growing since I'd arrived in the palace, a constant in my life, the spirit sat upon the window sill sometimes gazing out, sometimes gazing in. Her voice as clear as a perfectly struck note, for my magic more often than not sang through her veins and I pitied the fool that ever thought to climb in through my window for they would happen upon an unpleasant surprise. I sighed still able to feel the small ball of magic that lay somewhere within the center of my body, marked by the larger dragon's breath tattoo blooming on my back.

Rosen laughed softly, "Nearly but not quite, I think that's enough to know that your magic is great yes?" She wasn't expecting an answer and so I did not feel the need to give one. "Get some rest Rhyme, you deserve it." I closed my eyes as she pressed a tender kiss to my still damp brow. When I opened them again the glowing spirit of the raptor vines sat watching over me. I closed my eyes sleeping peacefully as I always did in my own bed.

Chapter 8
Archery

"Can I change my mind?" Emery asked as we stood in the center of the training field with at least thirty other suitors while the Queen gave a grand speech of what to expect in the coming Tournament. The first three days would test our skills in combat, the first day would be archery, the second a hunt requiring team work, the third sparring for points. The next three days was all politics, the three days all the noble dandies had come for, the opportunity for new alliances and trade. The final stage of the Tournament was a mystery depending on how many made it through the first two stages. It could last but one more day or extend to four. I hoped it was but one.

"It's too late for that now." Libeth countered bouncing with excitement as the crowd roared around us.

Eden nudged me slightly, "Rosen out did herself this time," he murmured his appreciation dipping his head towards the stands.

I smiled softly listening to the trees sing, "That she did Eden, that she did."

"It is with great honor that I introduce to you my Head Gardener, responsible for where you all are seated now, Rosen Len." Rosen took the stand, made from a young ash tree she'd grown just that morning and smiled brightly at the masses.

"I am thankful to be alive in this moment, the Princess has passed her Trials and we stand on the brink of another Queen's Tournament..." Rosen paused while the crowd roared anew. "This is a time of peace, a time for allies to be made, and trade to be conducted, for songs to be written and love to be found. Good fortune to each and every one of you," Rosen caught my eye bowing her head slightly. I tipped my head in acknowledgement that her fortune was meant for her Gardeners but propriety demanded that she acknowledge the entirety of us.

Princess Mariel went on to explain that the archery portion of the Tournament would start just after midmorning meal, it would be conducted in three phases, short range, long range and movement at varying ranges. There would be five groups of six suitors each since there were thirty suitors in all. Of course that number would dwindle with time after all not every noble could fire a bow.

"I almost wished the first task weren't so easy," Emery mumbled just low enough for us to hear. "Then I'd be done with the Tournament…"

"Our job is to aid her Highness," Libeth shot back hitting him in the shoulder. "The Queen's Tournament is a cover, so you're stuck with us until…until we can no longer pass the events."

"I'm looking forward to the sparring," Eden said with a maniacal grin, that was completely contradictory to his usual gentle nature.

I gazed around spotting Prince Eris chatting it up with a group of noblemen, I traced my fingers lightly along the blade hidden by the fall of my tunic. "I completely understand the sentiment."

"Now is not the time for violence." Libeth gave each of us a look in turn, "Now is the time for finding two other people we can bear to deal with to go in our group of six."

"Yes, Goddess forbid we end up with a bigoted foreigner who doesn't believe women should rule." Emery inserted, gazing around looking for a likely candidate.

"Damn, there goes the Sol-Lea stolen from us by a group of dandies." Eden chuckled at Emery's frustration.

"Let us just take who remains Em, no point in searching, we aren't like them and they see that. Regardless of the outcome we know what we're here for." Emery nodded at Eden's sage words before relaxing into himself.

We watched men and women alike drift towards one group or another while our recruits set up the archery range wheeling out a rack of bows made in every shape and size. Libeth was shaking her head. "An archery contest for a group of garden mages...I never thought it would be this easy."

Eden laughed tousling her hair, "Don't get over confident."

Libeth shook her head again as a small woman, literally half my height drifted towards us. "Me over confident..." she scoffed. "Never."

Emery nudged her into silence as the woman drew closer...she hesitated upon seeing Eden's massive frame and my overly tall stature but Libeth's smile and Emery's girlish features set her at ease giving her the courage to step forward. "Hello..."

I tipped my head in greeting supplementing it with a spoken word and a smile. "Hey."

"My name is Dahni, I come from Raleli," Libeth tipped her head more noticeably in greeting, it looked right awkward. About how it looked when Sir Zeron had done so to me, as if she didn't know exactly how it was done. Angileri's social niceties were built on subtleties. And every movement, from the tilt of the head to bowing before a monarch spoke of respect, it was a dance begun at your parent's knee and refined through schooling and social interaction. Until at one point you would know simply how one greeted you that they hated you completely or respected you more than you imagined. It was a secret language that many outside nations found hard to understand or interpret. Every Gardener save Rosen who'd been born here, had studied hard to understand it all, we'd used each other because we'd come late to this country and we were far behind the learning curve. It was frustrating in the beginning but now it was second nature.

Dahni tipped her head brow furrowed in confusion, a look more of curiosity than greeting, I smiled at its adorableness. Her skin was brown like mine, though a different kind of brown, a refined bronze to my russet tan. Her hair strangely was not black as you'd imagine it but red, a dark red that fell in light waves just past her shoulder blades, a red that made her jade eyes shine brighter in the frame of her face. Libeth asked her questions about the desert, about how they survived in such a harsh environment without aid from bordering Lands?

Dahni's smile was a crooked one, one sharp tooth peeking free every time she graced you with a closed mouth grin. "I have read that in Raleli that you do not have kings or queens but simply a council of five men and women from each major city, and they reside at times in the capitol Rahshi? I believe it is." I said after a moment of Libeth's good natured banter.

"Rahshi," Dahni bobbed her head nervously, "Yes that is the capitol, and it is true that we do not have a King or a Queen, though history states that long ago when Raleli was young and the land more unforgiving that we had a King and a Queen both. Now we have a High Council and many decisions are based on voting, as well we have a Council Head who breaks the vote if it falls evenly five instead of four. They visit their homes and rule there I suppose for a few full moons and then for the rest they reside in the Capitol and support the people. We have chosen good Councilors, I think. We vote for them every five years or so. Though they can be voted out or choose to step down before their five-year term is up and that would allow for an early voting.

"In my life time we have only voted for one new Councilor. The people have done good for themselves and the Councilors themselves are friendly people. I have met the Council Head, she sanctioned my coming here. I do not think we could pick another to replace her in the history of my life. She will probably retain a seat on Council until her death." I blinked while she babbled on nervously finally stopping when death suddenly entered the conversation.

Libeth rubbed her back soothingly, while I gazed at Eden confused at what I'd done. Eden shook his head unknowing, while Emery laughed behind the cover of his hand. "Gardener Denarii can be a bit intimidating at times as tall as she is."

"She resembles a Goddess tempting me into the desert with her beauty," Dahni murmured softly though we caught her words on the breeze. Emery turned away, laughing harder, not wishing to embarrass our new friend. Eden mimed tracing his hands along a curvy figure before blowing a kiss at me.

I raised my brow gazing down at my small chest and narrow hips before looking back at him and now he was also fighting to contain his laughter. I rolled my eyes at them both crossing my arms and awaiting the true start of the Tournament.

"I will be back; I wish to speak with my family before we start to reassure them I have found a good group." We all simultaneously raised our hands in fair well without actually speaking. Dahni shook her head at the anomaly before walking off to find her family in the stands.

"You two," Libeth pointed at Eden and Emery once Dahni was out of ear shot. "Are ridiculous." There was no true bite to her words, indeed she was laughing while she said it.

"And you," She turned to me shaking her head, "Stop…" Libeth waved her hand encompassing my entire form. "Stop being so…so Goddess like." That started Eden and Emery laughing again while Libeth sat there grinning like the evil wench she was.

"I asked but one question out of curiosity I did not for a moment expect that to happen…or to be compared to a Goddess." I furrowed my brow slightly.

Emery stroked his fingers along my cheek soothingly, "Our garden flower who fails to see her own worth, someone will be quite lucky to claim you some day." I blinked at the sincerity of his words.

"What he said," Eden offered with a grin of approval, Libeth simply hugged me close resting her head against my arm unable to reach my shoulder.

"You are all entirely too silly, to belong to someone so regal and well respected as I." We all turned to find Rosen standing behind us smiling good naturedly.

"Rosen," Libeth moved from me to her latching on like a leech.

Rosen laughed hugging her back. "I have a title you know."

"Not with us old woman," Emery deadpanned making her laugh again.

"I should bend you over my knee for such blatant disrespect." Her eyes continued to sparkle with mirth despite the seriousness of her tone.

Emery winked suggestively, "Mmmm, I'd love to see you try."

Rosen blushed to the gray tipped roots of her hair before turning away to compose herself. We all smiled but no one dared laugh regardless of the amusement we found. There were many forms of respect after all and though Rosen spoke to us as equals she was of a level with the Queen and you did not laugh in the face of the Queen's embarrassment. "I wanted to wish you all good fortune personally," she said once she'd found her composure.

"We appreciate it Head Gardener, truly we do." Libeth said pulling away from her after one final squeeze.

Rosen left us then, hurrying towards the stands, she held a seat beside the Queen. I wondered how many Councilors were jealous of her power. "Do you all have room for one more?" I shifted my gaze settling on a man more beautiful than handsome, almost prettier than Emery I could tell just by looking that he wasn't here for the Princess. A lover of men through and through.

Libeth smiled, "Indeed we do, what pray tell is your name?"

"Tailaan," He pronounced it Tay-lon, "I hail from Erangi, my parents wished me to settle down with a beautiful man and get married, find a third and have children. They shoved me on a ship to Angileri and it just so happens that the Queen's Tournament was scheduled to start perhaps a week after my arrival. Imagine my surprise at the opportunity."

Emery offered his hand in greeting, "Gardener Randel, I was born in Erangi, are the men still beautiful?"

Tailaan clasped Emery's hand in his smiling brightly, "Are the buildings still master pieces?" He countered not unkindly.

Emery laughed, truly happy in finding someone so far from home as he was, "Of course they are." They finished together. Tailaan dropped his hand.

"You are looking for a partner and a third?" Libeth asked curiously, Emery had explained both terms to us. A partner being whomever you wished to marry regardless of gender and a third being a person, if both partners were of the same sex, who would aid them in conception. A trio being what you were once you came together, the third was usually a really close friend who helped raised the child but was not truly in the relationship. Not to say that it couldn't happen, just to say it usually didn't.

"Yes, though I have a third in mind back home, I've known her since birth and she is backward in her love affairs as I am but wishes to have children. We agreed to raise them together regardless if she weds first or I do." Tailaan turned to Emery. "You wouldn't happen to be…"

Emery laughed blushing slightly, "I'm flattered to be asked, but I enjoy the love of a woman more often than not."

Tailaan sighed good naturedly brushing his hair from his face with delicately scarred hands. "I knew it was too good to be true."

"You dodged an arrow with this one," Libeth said teasingly.

Emery scoffed, "I am a true catch."

"If you say it often enough," Eden inserted. "It might become true."

We all laughed before settling down. We watched as Princess Mariel once more took the stand. I'm sure not a one person standing on the Training Fields had actually thought to eat during the break. Everyone grew still as she began explaining the rules. "There are twelve placements on the firing line, two groups will fire simultaneously, you have four arrows, one of which to practice with, you may fire at your own pace. A royal guard will raise a flag once everyone has finished firing, everyone will be scored based on which rings your arrows land in, there are four rings, the dot in the center is worth ten points, two inner circles are eight and sixth respectively and the two outer ringers are four and two. Your arrows are marked, the one fletched in white feathers is for practice, the others hold rings of green, one for the first arrow, two for the second and three for the third. Since there are five groups of six the last group will simply fill half of the firing line. Once this portion ends we will move on to long range firing and then firing at moving targets where the same rules will apply adding an arrow for each new phase of the competition and so you will have two practice arrows for long range firing and three practice arrows for firing on moving targets, if you are confident you may exchange practice arrows for green ringed arrows in an attempt to gain more points." A murmuring started with that added incentive, though it quickly died so that Her Highness could finishing speaking.

"Those that fail to have any arrows land within the rings on the targets will be removed from the Queen's Tournament, if you use magic that can be seen or detected by the naked eye, you will be removed from the Tournament. If you fail to reach a certain number of points by the end of this phase, you will be removed from the Tournament... Are there any questions?" There were no questions.

"Until your group is called, there is a place for you just inside the fence nearer to the stables, go there now and take your seats." Dahni found us as we took a seat on the green grass feeling more like children than adults as we waited watching those that preceded us.

"How good are you at the bow?" I asked both Dahni and Tailaan simultaneously, gazing back and forth between them.

Tailaan answered first, "I can for sure make it through the first round, I might perhaps hit a few of the long range targets. I will spectacularly fail the final round of moving targets a hunter I am not." He finished with a forlorn sigh.

"I grew up in a small wood on the border of Rahshi, I know a thing or two about hunting, standing targets should not be much of a problem if I have the right bow. Which is hard to find when you're as small as I am." I nodded watching the competition those of which more often than not failed at actually hitting the target.

Libeth nudged me in the side, "This might be easier than I first thought," just as she spoke I heard a whisper of assistance from the wood of an arrow and then the clearly struck note of a plant serving its purpose. Libeth sat up straighter, "Perhaps I spoke too soon." I heard the whispering and then the clarity of that note three more times, slowly but surely Emery and then Eden fell silent having each heard it in their own way. There was a plant mage on the line and they weren't playing fair.

"They must really be horrible at archery," Emery murmured as the next group of twelve were called. It seemed our group would be last.

"Sadly it wasn't detectable by the naked eye," I heaved out trying to find the mage among the group of men and woman standing off to the side, some saddened at their performance some excited and overly confident.

"Perhaps they're half blind," Libeth supplied brow furrowed. "I have never met a plant mage who couldn't hit a target from when first they picked up a bow."

Dahni and Tailaan looked right confused at the seemingly random conversation. "Many apologies," I said drawing their attention. "Her Highness said no discernable magic, meaning if you cannot see it you can still use it. Giving those with a gift an unfair advantage in my opinion not that anyone would know unless you shared that gift of course," I splayed my hand encompassing my fellow Gardeners and I. "We are the Queen's Gardeners, and be it plant mages to the masses, or garden mages to those who understand a little more, each of our gifts are powerful in their own right. We know the life of the green, and we can feel, hear or see in some cases, magic in use. Someone out there," I tipped my head towards the firing line. "Just used magic to aid them and we're discussing that now."

"How did they use it?" Dahni asked brow furrowed. "I am a water mage and I kind of cox the water from the land, she burbles and giggles and really just does what she wants half the time but sometimes when I need her, she listens to me." Before anyone could think to ask Dahni explained the female pronouns, "I say she because water to me is just one voice found in many places."

"I cannot explain the how of another mage but for me it's like…" Libeth sat for a moment, "It's like touching the stars, bright lights at the heart of each flower, a glow to every blade of grass and every leaf and I just see the pattern to reach my desired goal. That's where I place my magic, seeing other mages magic at work is a light show to me, whoever fired those arrows, their magic blazed, a forest fire in the center of a field, completely obvious. They either have little training, little power or…" Her expression turned thoughtful. "They wanted us to see it."

Eden interjected, "It felt too rushed to be planned, I'm more akin to believe they simply are a horrible archer despite their gift."

"Perhaps…" Everyone turned to me then, "Perhaps they are but average, after all every plant mage can fire an arrow and hit a target on their first try but not every plant mage is a great archer. Not every plant mage can hit the center of the target every single time or near to it to make them seem more skillful." They all thought on my words. "This is a competition of points, the goal being to get as many as you can so that you may advance passed the first day. It wouldn't do to fail here if you planned on making alliances yes."

Tailaan nodded his understanding, face twisted by a grimace of disdain, "I do hate politics."

Dahni laughed, "Yes, Angileri is so different then Raleli, but not bad different. There are many very accepting people, though not as many hereabout as tan as you or I." She said motioning towards me. "Many backwards in their love lives, it is refreshing actually to see such an open people. Though I feel a bit misplaced, seemingly everyone has a title." She blushed finding herself lacking.

"A title is but a word, some are more respectful than others, if you feel uncomfortable we may drop them in your company." I offered with a smile, causing Dahni to blush, Libeth stared at me, while Eden and Emery gazed on mouth agape at the high regard I'd just bestowed upon them.

"Tis alright, I find it fitting Gardener Denarii, the title suits you perfectly, donned in green as you are, with skin akin to the earth and hair as black as a raven's wing. You are of the land Gardener and you carry it everywhere you go." I tipped my head acknowledging her compliment.

"Stop making people fall in love with you," Libeth murmured just soft enough for me to hear as we stood proceeding to the firing line.

I shook my head as we approached the rack lined with bows. "You may choose a different bow for every round of arrows." A recruit explained as Tailaan hesitated over one bow or another. I traced my fingers over one a little smaller than I, the wood sang softly I blinked gazing on the ancient spirit it had once been a part of, she still lived towering and eternal somewhere in the heart of the forest. I grabbed the bow before following Emery down the line leaving him at his target. I walked a little further before gazing down the field at mine.

A recruit approached me with my arrows, "Would you like to exchange your practice arrow for one ringed with green?" He asked after a moment of silence where I stood gazing at the target the spirit of an ancient ash tree standing beside me.

"Yes." He offered me an arrow before standing back allowing me to fire unhindered. I notched the arrow allowing the world to fade away. I did not use my magic instead I allowed the ancient to guide me, I hefted the bow up, lighter than I thought it'd be for its size. The arrow sang softly long before I raised it to the bow, ready. The wind blew around me trying and failing to tug my hair free of the thong I'd tied it with. Gazing down a path of green all I could see was that small dot at the heart of the target. It's all I allowed myself to see. I took a deep breath notching the arrow and pulling it back to my shoulder. The faint song it sang grew louder, different but no less beautiful than the song of the bow. I released the arrow their joined melody climbing towards a crescendo. I notched another arrow allowing the ancient to guide me once more, until the song of the bow serving its purpose twinned once more with the arrow's, a continuous song as I fired my remaining bolts.

I lowered my bow once the song died, the spirit of the ash tree fading away as the canopy of the crowd grew louder. I looked up to see everyone on the firing line gazing at the target I'd struck. I glanced down range and stared, every arrow I'd fired had struck the same spot, shattering the one before it.

Libeth ran towards me laughing softly eyes sparkling with joyous excitement, "Amazing Rhyme, that was amazing to see. There was…there was this light behind you, a being of pure light, it was just there and somehow you felt it without actually using your magic and it was just so beautiful with each arrow you fired that light grew brighter until I could almost see someone standing there. A woman with hair made of leaves and skin a pale brown of a tree beneath the bark and flowers blooming all over like a gown and her eyes two orange orbs like the heart of some rare gem. It was…" Libeth sighed softly holding me tightly in her excitement. "It was memorable."

I chuckled pulling myself from Libeth's grasp arms aching slightly from her excitement. "Come, they're setting up the long range targets and it is no longer our turn."

I ushered Libeth over to our waiting group. "Can I marry you and bring you back to the desert with me?" Dahni asked once we were in ear shout.

"I hardly know you," I countered not unkindly laughing softly as she bounced on her heels just as excited as Libeth at my performance.

"I did not know you were so good at the bow," Emery said chuckling, "Though you're second only to Rosen among us so I should have guessed."

"Sometimes I wonder if you are the Head Gardener's equal," Eden murmured thoughtfully as the long range portion of the competition began. It was far worse than the first round.

"Goodness, I'd hate to be in an army with half these suitors surely they'd kill us all long before we reached battle." Tailaan grumbled wincing slightly as a tall man nearly shot himself in the foot.

"That, or we'd kill them to avoid our own death," I interjected as another suitor was carried from the field shot in the leg by the person beside him and I was hard pressed to call that an accident.

We all stilled as one when the whispering began and then that perfectly struck note rang true twice, wavered slightly on the third shot and then rang true again. "Weak indeed." Emery murmured once the second group moved to fire.

"The light fluttered as if they were struggling…" Libeth's brow furrowed, "Struggling to control their magic or the green, can't they see the pattern."

"Perhaps it's a feeling like with me, a feeling of rightness inside, maybe they just aren't feeling it." Emery offered up.

"Or it's a knowing, what to do when. Maybe they fail to know…" Eden supplied.

"I think they're trying to force it." I finished. "And we all know that bending nature is always harder than simply allowing it to be."

Dahni nodded her agreement. "Has anyone been able to figure out exactly who it is?" We all looked at each other but no one had a clear answer.

"I know that it's a woman, Rosen told me that the King of Dangilere brought a plant mage with him, and that she was his daughter. Now all we have to do is figure out what she looks like." Once more we stood to take the line going to pick our bows.

"Yes, sadly nearly half the suitors are women," Emery dead panned picking the bow I'd picked last time.

"We'll manage," I countered as I picked a smaller bow, one carved from the heart of an oak long gone now though the spirit lingered in the wood finding a purpose there. I traced my fingers along the thicker twine that would be more difficult to draw. The spirit of the oak soothed me, it knew its purpose, it trusted my strength. I took a deep breath as I gazed down range the target no larger than my palm so far was it from where I stood.

"Would you like to exchange your arrows Gardener?" the same recruit asked more sure of himself this time.

"Yes," he offered me the first arrow once more standing back. I notched the arrow raising it to a level with my eyes watching pale fingers trace my shirt sleeve, I knew that she existed to my eyes alone. That I could not truly feel her touch, perhaps it was my magic responding to the green but the path she traced along my arm left a trail of warmth. Those long fingers trailed down my arm, along my fingers to the bow and then the arrow beyond. Eyes burning dark green gazed at me, a sense that she was ready…that we were ready growing inside me. Together, or so it seemed, we drew back the arrow, softly at first the arrow began to sing, I released it slicing my fingers in the process, ignoring the slight pain in favor of listening to a different but no less beautiful song. I took the next arrow firing one after the other listening to the song as it rose and fell depending on where I struck the target. Once done I handed the recruit my bow and moved to join my group blood dripping from my fingertips.

"Not the same spot but still the center me thinks," Libeth said as I plopped down beside them, pulling gauze from the pouch at my hip. "Why are you bleeding?!" She exclaimed taking hold of my hand.

"The bow string was quite taunt; I wasn't sure I could even draw it. It cut me on each release." I grimaced as she wrapped my hand shaking her head.

"You're insane," Emery muttered having caught sight of the gashes lining the meaty part of my fingers.

"Why didn't you pick a different bow?" Eden asked once Libeth had finished Dahni and Tailaan looking on not knowing what to say.

I smiled softly tracing my finger along the blood that now stained my sleeve, "It was all she had," the only song that she would ever sing and she sang it so rarely, trapped inside a bow that no one was willing to use. "It was beautiful and completely worth it." I clenched my hand into a fist blood already showing through the white fabric of my bandage.

"Insane," Emery muttered at my barely adequate explanation.

Eden covered my hand with his, "Will you be able to finish the final round of archery?"

I smiled touched by his concern, "Yes, it aches some but I can fire six more arrows."

"You're going to the healers right after," Libeth said in a no nonsense tone.

I chuckled softly as Eden released my hand, "I will be sure to go to the infirmary afterwards if it makes you feel better, even though I myself am a healer."

"Just...shut up." Libeth said after a moment unable to find something more suitable, breaking the tension that had settled between us. "Don't be so reckless yeah? Not even for a beautiful song as you say..." She stroked my cheek waiting for me to respond, concern darkening her eyes.

"Many apologize...I'll be more careful promise." Emery breathed a sigh of relief leaning back on his hands.

"Good, I would hate to lose the only person who hates events such as these nearly as much if not more than I do." I chuckled softly as Libeth shoved him over.

"Way to show your concern Em, why not just shove her off a cliff," she grumbled while he righted himself and Dahni and Tailaan tried to hide their amusement at our strange dynamic.

Eden shushed them both as the whispering started not as strong as before, the note that rang out muddled every single time, fading quickly towards the end. "I have no idea how to explain what they're doing wrong." Eden said with a shake of his head. "If you're using your gift to aid you in archery, it shouldn't require so much energy, it's as if they used it all for this one event."

I nodded in agreement, but chose not to comment, after all this portion of the competition was over for them and we were none the wiser as to who it actually was. I could tell just by watching that we'd lost at least five suitors simply because they couldn't keep their arrows out of the ground.

"I do not feel so bad about my skills with the bow watching others fail so much worse than I ever dreamed I could," Tailaan spoke softly as we stood for the final time heading towards the rack of bows. This time I chose a bow that once belonged to an elm tree, strong wood that wouldn't falter the bow was made for my hand. The spirit that remained but a whisper in my ear having found a home in the earth somewhere else once more starting it's cycle anew.

I smiled softly, walking to my spot on the range watching the targets weave back and forth. There were three of them in a line disappearing as they crossed each other's path before appearing again. "Would you..."

"Yes," I answered before he could finish the question allowing him to place an arrow in my hand, I fired without listening for the song, grabbed another arrow without looking and fired again. I paused briefly watching the targets dance before firing two more. I paused one final time head cocked slightly listening, before firing my last two arrows smiling softly as a song so light as to not even exist was carried on the breeze for probably the last time. If I used my magic of course the spirit would answer but otherwise all I held was a lifeless piece of wood in my hands. I sighed heart heavy and yet light at the same time as I handed the recruit my bow hand on fire as I walked passed my group.

"I'm going to the infirmary," I said by way of explanation without ever hearing my score, I didn't need to, I knew when it was called that it would be perfect. The fading song of the elm had told me so...

Chapter 9
Sounds Like Fear

I sat beneath the great oak in the ball room examining my hand with a warm bowl of water, a rag, clean bandages and a premade salve laid out beside me. I hadn't wanted to go to the infirmary and have to explain my recklessness to people who sometimes looked to me for answers. As I'd said to Libeth I was a healer and any other day I'd have healed myself, but after what I'd done for Rosen the thought alone made me tired. With a grimace of pain, I scrubbed the small lacerations clean before slathering my hand in an anesthetic salve that would help me to heal more quickly. I sighed softly leaning back against the rough bark, the pain though bearable, was draining. I couldn't bring myself to struggle with the bandage, I closed my eyes willing myself to action. The fingers of my good had twitched, I didn't bother to open my eyes. Instead I dozed for a time feeling warm and safe beneath the glowing canopy of the great oak I'd grown.

The sound of the double doors, only a Gardener or her Majesty could open, closing caused me to flinch fully awake. I sheathed the blade I'd drawn in the moment between wakefulness and slumber, once I caught sight of who approached. "I didn't know anyone save the Queen and her Gardeners knew how to open those doors."

Her Highness started, turning to find me resting as I was beneath the glow of the great oak's lights, while she stood in mostly darkness. The sun had set some time ago and I hadn't fully activated the magic in the shards resting somewhere high overhead. I didn't want to be found after all. I supposed her Highness hadn't wanted to be found either, walking through a place not many entered, especially not the way she'd come. "My mother told me the secret of that door before I had enough magic to actually open it. Not because she knew that I would follow in her footsteps but because she knew I loved the gardens and would find that bit of magic enchanting…" She moved closer allowing me to see her eyes in the darkness. "I still do."

"Did she ever tell you the story?" I asked softly listening to the plants of the palace as they murmured about the goings on that day, people's reactions to the Tournament were foremost in their minds.

"About how those doors were made by the very first Gardener, how he cut down the trees and crafted the wood and put them up with the aid of the Queen and the dragons so only they knew the secret of how it worked." She smiled softly half turned away from me. "Yes I've heard the story many times, it was one of my favorites as a child. I had thought the Gardener seemed more befitting the Queen than her husband I recall…"

I chuckled softly at that, "There's was a marriage of politics, it was needed at the time and they loved each other…eventually."

"I really don't want eventually Denarii…" Her Highness murmured softly bowing her head.

I felt my laughter slip away as the reason for Adri's absence from her own Tournament reached me, the voices of the plants fading, ever present but not as all-consuming as they'd been but a moment before. "Have faith Highness, your Prince…Princess or commoner will come…someone will come for you." I said unwilling to believe otherwise.

The Princess tipped her head in acknowledgement of my words catching sight of the bowel of water now pink with blood, the rag now permanently stained, the salve practically gone and the bandages some soiled, some fresh, still neatly rolled. Her Highness stepped into the light without hesitation coming to kneel beside me taking my hand in hers gently afraid to cause me more pain. "What happened? Who hurt you?"

I gazed into the fierce twilight inferno that had become her eyes and felt those saplings once more taking root in the pit of my stomach. "I can protect myself Highness," I grumbled gently but firmly pulling my hand away.

"Yes but you belong to the Queen and… I will one day be Queen." I think that was the first time she said those words with conviction.

I smiled softly as she took my hand back examining how I'd expertly salved the lacerations. "In essence you're saying that one day I'll belong to you?"

Adri flushed refusing to turn away, "Yes."

I raised my good hand to trace the large bruise encompassing the left side of her face, "I was careless in the archery competition…"

"You shouldn't be," Her Highness rebuked gently, frowning. Concern softening the fierceness in her eyes.

"I know…but," emotion formed a lump in my throat. "The song she sang Highness; it was beautiful…they all are in their own way."

"Why are you so…different Denarii?" Adri voice full of more than curiosity, I found in her words a need, an unobtrusive need. Not an order or a demand, but simply a question.

My lips curled in amusement at the fact that I couldn't help but ruin this moment between us, "Well you know Highness I wasn't born here…"

She rolled her eyes dropping my hand, "Idiot," the insult was muttered so softly I wasn't actually sure if I heard it or not.

"Highness who hurt you?" I cupped her chin turning her face to more fully examine the blue, black, purple mass spanning literally

the entire lower half of the left side of her face. The Princess took a seat in front of me sighing softly.

"The ground," I raised my brow waiting for an explanation.

"Well a recruit…he was really large and well I kind of overstepped a bit, got overconfident and he slammed me." She hissed no doubt remembering the pain, "Into the ground, I wasn't ready, I didn't brace and so really it's my own fault. The healers told me as much and gave me some medicine to relieve the pain. I threatened to have them executed for not healing me fully outright and they laughed of course. Quoting my own policy on how we do not reward stupidity." Adri huffed blowing her hair from her face. "The nerve." Her eyes sparkled with mirth despite the fact that she'd truly been frustrated at the time.

"Not even the Heir?" I wondered aloud.

"Well I'm sure they would have, but…" She leaned forward as if we were in a crowded room instead of alone and whispered. "I didn't really feel up to going to the Tournament."

I laughed softly, "You used your injury to your advantage?"

Adri nodded smiling softly, "Pure genius I know."

I stroked her cheek again, "Surely it must hurt?"

"Yeah but it was worth it for a day of being left alone, no suitors, no Councilors just me enjoying the Gardens alone."

I continued to stroke her cheek watching the bruise slowly fade away as I used my magic to heal her, "You're just full of the brightest smiles Highness," I murmured once she was fully healed gazing at me curiously raising her hand to stroke her cheek.

"You healed me…Thank you." I caught my breath feeling overly warm at her gratitude.

I turned away, "It was nothing."

The Princess took my hand while I watched raising it to her lips. She pressed a kiss to my one of my wounds, then another, then another. "What are you…" I tried to pull away but she held fast.

"Trust me?" I relaxed my hand watching as she kissed each and every one of my lacerations, salve and blood staining her lips. I watched in fascination as her lips formed a small oh and she breathed fire, flickering flames of red gold flowing over my fingertips spreading down along my palm and falling over the edge of my hand. I felt warmth and I felt heat, but no pain. My hand was engulfed in flames but I was not burned…

After a moment Adri pulled away and the flames flickered out leaving my hand pink and tender, the lacerations that had once adorned my flesh gone without so much as a scar. I flexed my fingers. "You just…"

Her Highness smiled, "Yeah."

"That was pretty amazing." I offered softly, stroking the blood and salve from her lips with my thumb, heart thundering in my chest from the excitement of what had just occurred.

"It really was," Her Highness stroked her fingers through my hair bunching it slightly as she leaned closer pressing her brow to mine, "You keep telling me to find my Prince, my Princess, my commoner but what if that's not what I want. What if I want a Gardener?"

"I would tell you that Eden loves men, even if he's too shy to admit it and the Emery despite his girlish features loves a little bit of pain though he'd love you with a fierceness like no other. I'd say that Libeth would bring you the most joy, she's very vibrant, the way she sees the world. Rosen…is perhaps a little older than your mother and that would be awkward to explain." I furrowed my brow just thinking about it.

"My mother is actually Rosen's senior; she was not yet the Head Gardener when my mother became Queen. She gained the title a few years thereafter. She actually didn't want it in the beginning, she really did not want it when my mother brought on four children still aching for their homelands. Rosen is like a second mother to me…I cannot even imagine wanting her in that way." We shuddered simultaneously.

"What about you Denarii, what if I wanted you?" I chuckled softly unable to move away due to her fingers twinned in my hair.

"You don't want me Highness, I'm bluntly honest… to a fault actually, my temper when aroused can be…frightening. I tend to care about my gardens more than actual people…I shy away from any form of real responsibility or power. Tis not my place to stand beside someone so grand as you." I shook my head suddenly feeling uncomfortable with this line of conversation.

"Bluntly honest and yet perfectly respectful even when being disrespectful, a frightening temper, and yet you're the calmest person I've ever met. You care about your gardens yes, but no one that knows you has said you care about them any less than your gardens. I think those you love are equal to your plants in that respect. You never fail to get your brother out of trouble and everyone…save you thinks of you as Rosen's Second, her protégé, her Heir in that regard. You will one day take her place…" I pulled myself away from the Princess, untwining her fingers from my hair.

"I do not want it…" I countered as I stood leaning back against the great oak taking comfort in its quiet murmurs as I tried to catch my breath. "I never have…I don't think I ever will. I did not ask to come here..."

Adri stood, not the Princess, not the Heir or Her Highness in that moment just Adri. A woman who loved her gardens, who wished to make one of her own and explore it with the person she loved. "And yet here you are." Her words were bittersweet, "You did not ask for it and yet you are as I am, the Heir to power you do not truly want, you can refuse yes?" Her eyes were full of pain, her words husky with unshed tears. For the first time, I looked away unable to meet her gaze. "You can refuse but where would that leave your people…your gardens that you love so much? What then Gardener Denarii, do you hope that someone, anyone can do a better job than you because you were afraid…"

"I am not afraid." I countered watching the tears fall unbidden.

"Yes you are!" I flinched. "You're afraid of your power, afraid of taking Rosen's place and letting people down because what…because your different, because you don't think you're good enough?" She shoved me against the tree clenching her hands in the fabric of my shirt.

I stood motionless taking the abuse, "Afraid to accept my feelings…because I will one day be Queen. You tell me I will be great, that I will be happy one day, that I will be good for the people and yet we have the same fears. I am afraid, the only difference." Adri loosened her hands from my tunic stepping away from me and wiping her tears. "The only difference is that you can say no. Perhaps in another life I could have done the same, but I did not want to hope someone could do a better, I want to do better." She gazed at me and I saw a Queen in full glory, the spitting image of her mother despite the fact they looked nothing alike, it was the pose, the strength and the unwavering conviction in her eyes. "I may hate the position I find myself in, I may hate my title, for all the fact that it is but a word. I carry the weight of my entire people on my shoulders and I do it because I love them."

I watched as she took a step backward, and then another, "And I was wrong about you," her lip quivered with emotion, she bit it firmly shaking her head as she turned away.

I caught her hand, she glanced over her shoulder waiting for me to speak. "I am not afraid…I just do not want to deal with the strife that power brings. I do not want to be used for the power I hold…"

Adri pulled her hand free of mine, "That sounds a lot like fear to me."

"I'm sorry…" I couldn't even explain why I was apologizing.

"For what Gardener?" More tears streamed Adri's face as she walked away without waiting for a reply. I did not have one to give.

I stood there leaning against the great oak for a long time after that, for the first time in forever I felt no peace despite the comforting embrace of the ever present green. What I felt could not so easily be absolved.

*****

I stood preparing my mare, Carina, for the hunt that would take place that day. My fellow Gardeners and our new friends Dahni and Tailaan looked on me with concern. I hadn't said a word since I joined them that morning.

At last Libeth found her courage first, touching me gently on the arm, "Are you well?"

My lips twitched in the imitation of a smile I felt no desire to give, "Tired from my healing yesterday."

"You healed yourself then? I spoke with the Healers you did not at all even attempt to approach the infirmary. You promised." I turned away from the reproach in her eyes.

"That I would be more careful and I will be. A fri…someone I know healed me. I will be well. Just tired today is all." I stroked Carina's mane while she nipped playfully at my tunic searching for treats.

Princess Mariel took the stand waiting for silence. Libeth opened her mouth to speak but thought better of it. "Yesterday we lost ten, more than we thought we would, and so today's challenge is no longer a group activity." My fellow Gardeners and I shared a look but not one of us dared speak. "There are fifteen Royal Guards hiding in the forest and twenty of you, each of you will be given an orb." She held up a small ball of glowing light. "Inside it is the guard that you must find, it will change if someone else finds them first. You will all be blindfolded and drugged, so that you may sleep while you are placed by our recruits at your starting point. You must make it back here with your guard by nightfall."

She smiled softly, "None of them will come willingly once found. The rules of the challenge are such, if you find your guard in another's hands you may challenge their captor for them, the winner of said challenge wins the guard, you may use whatever magic or skills you have to aid you, you may not, maim, kill or permanently scar any of your fellow suitors. Those that fail to make it back to the Training Fields by nightfall will be removed from the Queen's Tournament, those that attempt to maim or kill their fellow suitors will be removed from the Tournament.

Those that return with a guard will gain ten points, there is no team work, one person claims one guard. You may aid each other in returning to the Training Fields, you will not be removed from the Tournament for failing to bring back a guard, not everyone is a warrior after all. This phase tests your survival skills, your sense of direction, and how you act under pressure. The orbs you carry will track your progress. A marker on a map in case you find yourself lost and need help returning, toss it in the air and gently request Guidance. Does anyone have any questions?"

"Is there a perk for extra points like in the last challenge?" Someone asked from behind us, I did not turn to look curious as to the answer.

Her Highness' eyes sparkled with mirth, "I am glad you asked. The Heir has agreed to participate in this challenge, she is out there hiding as well, hidden better than all the other guards combined. If you find her you may choose to pass any portion of the

Tournament you wish and of course you will still gain your points, this incentive is for those out there who are horrible fighters, or horrible at some form of politics or another. The catch…she must come willingly, if you ask and she refuses that is it. You will have gained the points for finding her, give her your orb and she will in turn give them to me so that your effort is not in vain, but you will not gain the pass. You may not challenge for the Heir if found in another's possession." Princess Mariel tipped her head to us.

"Good fortune to you all." As she finished those words and stepped down weakness overcame me. I watched in slow motion as Libeth fell to her knees eyes rolling back in her skull. I had time to think that it must be magic as my legs buckled beneath me, because if it had been a plant I'd have known to avoid it. Darkness bled in and stole my awareness of the world. I did not feel the softness of the grass pillowing my cheek, by then all I knew were the shadows of my own mind.

I woke with a start in the center of the forest a pack of supplies beside me, Carina's reins looped around a tree branch. A blindfold hung from my neck I pulled it free as I pushed myself into a seated position stuffing it into my pocket, the orb holding an image of my guard sitting in my lap. I rubbed my face gazing up at the positon of the sun now high in the sky. I had little more than half a day to find a Royal Guard or the Heir respectively.

I opened my pack examining what I'd been given. Inside I found a map and a compass I did not need, a water skin, some jerky, I could not tell what kind by looking and some dry biscuits, as well there were bandages and medicine to clot the blood and relieve pain. There was a cloak in case it rained and a small written note for luck. I closed the pack after putting the orb inside, slowly pushing myself to my feet, the slight headache I'd felt had faded as I'd become more aware of my surroundings.

"What should I do Carina?" I asked my horse gently stroking her muzzle, "I am not the best at politics, my honesty often gets in the way. Should I seek out Her Highness despite the fact that she will likely refuse my request?" Carina softly butted me in the chest with her head. "It is worth the risk is that what you're telling me?" I questioned laughing softly as her large head bobbed up and down her dark mane falling to cover her eyes. "My brother has trained you well in our language I do wish I could understand you half as well as he does."

Carina nipped at my hair affectionately while I wrapped my arms around her thick neck in a hug, we were at a height with each other Carina and I. Which is why I think my brother chose her for me. I needed a companion that stood as my equal he said, someone who would not have a problem looking me in the eyes. Carina had yet to fail as staring match, it made me laugh to even remotely try.

"They should not have said that we may use our gifts Carina," I murmured tying my pack to her saddle before taking hold of her reins. Checking to make sure I still held my blade and my pouch hidden by the fall of my tunic. "I may not have planted these trees, but I have walked these paths often enough to know every trail." I smiled softly listening to the slow drawl of the ancients, different but no less soothing than the constant chattering of my garden flowers. "Every lake, every stream, I know it all Carina. I learned patience in this forest, when I was young and missing my home." I moved quietly deeper into the Griffin Forest, named for the fact that you had to be as intelligent as a griffin to actually get anywhere without a map. "I learned patience through the trees, older than you or I Carina. Ancients I call them, they have survived the rise and the fall of many nations. They have been named by more monarchs than I care to remember."

Carina followed in my footsteps each of us silent in our movements. "They know every living thing that exists in their presence, magic or no magic. They know the ants, the wolves, the bears. They even know the fish can you believe it Carina; how can a tree know fish?" I chuckled as my mare rolled her eyes at me, she did not care much for my babbling, though she understood my words it meant nothing to her. I had not once mentioned food after all.

"Yes they know the fish, because all trees need water and fish exist in the water do they not? They know the squirrels, the rabbits and every rodent you can think of, as well they know the birds, all predators and all prey. They know us Carina…they know the footsteps of man. Each individually unique and yet achingly similar. The Ancients know it all," We came to a clearing. A small field full of tall grass where several deer grazed, the sun had passed its midpoint in the sky, the sky was free of clouds and a breeze blew cooling the sweat that had formed on my brow from our journey, the day was hot despite the breeze.

I sighed softly releasing the reins and untying my pack from Carina's saddle. "Why am I annoying you with all this useless babbling when all you really want is sweet grass?" I smiled softly stroking the line of her strong jaw. "Well Carina the ancients know all and I can understand them and so the conclusion to all my seemingly senseless chatter is that I know exactly where the Princess is hiding despite magic." I listened to the ancients speak of such wonders, slow to communicate but still fascinated by the magic of man. I saw in my mind's eye the river by which her Highness hid peeking out from a small grove formed by the lapping of water against an ancient that knew the river as a lover would and I smiled whistling softly as I once more disappeared into the forest. Glancing only once more at the sun slowly sinking towards the horizon. Regardless of the Princess' answer to my request, I would be back long before nightfall. After all I knew this forest. I knew exactly where to go to get to where I wished to be. It was sad really, to think that the Heir never even stood a chance. Rosen did not call me her better for nothing after all…

Chapter 10
The Hunt

I came upon the tree her Highness hid within, taller than any tree I'd seen before it, its circumference perhaps tripled my height, its canopy too high to see with human eyes alone it, could be nothing but a giant's spine, planted when the world was young and giants roamed as we do. I traced my fingers along its bark shivering in awe at his age. The spirit was undeniably male, not because he revealed himself to me, his slumber was too deep for that but because I could feel him and I just knew. I patted the tree gently before sliding down the slopping bank to a river that had no name.

The water raged, the river swollen with the new come spring, I drank deeply from my water skin before braiding my hair in one long plait. While the plants and trees of the forest would not offer hindrance I wasn't foolish enough to believe the water would do the same. That was not where my gift lay after all. I gazed at where the river rushed the trees' base, swirling and lapping furiously creating a little alcove cloaked in darkness, I watched the water rush through the trees creating its own path across the land and I began to remove my boots deciding that I did not want to drown.

I pulled off my tunic and then the pouch of useful seeds and vials, followed by my sheathed blade I wrapped both in the fabric of my tunic which I tucked into the Water proof pack. I tossed my boots and my pack higher up the bank not wanting to take the chance that the water would drag it away and then I plunged into the river diving deep beneath the root that formed an arch just beneath the water before surfacing on the other side. Thankful that the water though chilled wasn't freezing I swam towards the dark little nook pausing in my paddling when the river surged not wanting to find myself bashed against the base of said tree before I reached my destination. Once close enough I clung to the tough bark of exposed roots pulling myself along until I could crawl into more shallow water.

"Highness?!" I called breathless shivering as a breeze passed over my wet skin. "Princess?!" I called when I gained no response crawling closer to the darkness.

"You promised not to be reckless and here you are diving into a raging river," strong hands pulled me further into the darkness.

"How else was I to get in here?" I questioned tossing my braid over my shoulder.

"There's a small tunnel in the back!" she cried furiously.

I rubbed my hand over my face gazing at the light leaking through the man sized tunnel, no doubt made in preparation for this moment. "Highness, I'm sorry." I shifted so that I could see her more clearly, she was completely dry. Goddess I wished I'd thought to look for another way in, I wished I'd thought to ask. "Not for diving into the river, I was in no real danger. I'm sorry for yesterday…"

"Gardener just ask your question…"

"So you can refuse me," I shook my head. "I don't think so. I did not dive into a raging river for nothing."

"Calm but reckless, powerful and yet afraid…" The Princess mocked, "How do you live?"

"You don't understand," I breathed goose flesh stealing over my skin as the air grew chill without the heat of the sun to warm it.

"I understand perfectly…"

"You understand nothing!" I snapped in my anger. "You have lived under the protection of your mother's wing for the whole of your life Highness. You can go anywhere you wish to go; you can study anything your heart desires. You can marry who you love all with your mother's blessing. I do not want any title she can think to give me; she has already taken so much." I breathed shaking my head.

"She gave you a life," Adri countered a daughter defending her mother.

"She stole my life!" I cried heart aching. "I was happy, Kantari may seem like a backwards, island nation, but we were happy. I was to be a healer, because I knew the plants. My mother would teach me all the things she knew and Reason was to be a warrior, though my mother wanted that path for me since I was the eldest. I did not want to go, my mother, my family they loved me. Your mother took me against my will, perhaps she had my parents blessing because every parent wants a better life for their children but I did not want to come.

Everything was different, alien, the words, not as soothing to the ear, the gestures seeming unnecessary and I learned it. I learned it all, while aching for a home that would no longer be mine. All that reminds me of the jungle, lies in the garden. That is the only reason that I bare the title Gardener because it is the only place in this entire land that I feel at home." I sighed softly gazing at the steady stream of light shining down through the tunnel. "All I have is my pouch of seeds given by my mother, and the blade of viper's wrath, my father spent his life's saving on. That's all I have, that and the unwavering knowledge that my parents loved me, to remember them. I have long since forgotten their faces." Tears streamed my face, hidden by the shadows, mixing with the water still trailing along my skin. "I have forgotten my father's laugh and my mother's soothing scent, the way each of them called my name, I have lost my friends and all my plants. All of it gone from me, stolen by the passage of time.

"I can forgive her for taking me, because I am older now but I will not serve my jailor beyond the title I stepped off that ship carrying because I am trapped here." Adri opened her mouth to counter but I silenced her with a question. "Where can I go when all others know my title, know my worth to the Queen of Angileri? Where can I go and truly find peace...?"

Her Highness stared at me unable to find words, I tipped my head in acknowledgement of her silence. "You will be Queen one day, and I will be yours. Perhaps then I will feel differently, after all you are not your mother."

"You hide a lot within you Gardener…" she hesitated. "I understand a bit now of why you do not wish to take Rosen's place but I cannot help but think there is more."

I leaned back on my hands sighing as my fingers burrowed through decaying leaves and moist soil, it was warm. "I will not argue that I am Rosen's equal, her second or her better. I truly do not care…Rosen is where she belongs, she is a good politician. I can perhaps be good if I try, despite my penchant for blunt honesty but," I bobbed my head back and forth in a thoughtful gesture, "I do not care to try. As I have said I do not want any title your mother can give me, as well I do not want any title I have not earned. Being Head Gardener is more than being the most powerful after all and it took years for Rosen to reach this point, long after she herself gained the title actually." I chuckled at the thought. "Truly though my biggest reason is that I rather enjoy being anonymous, oh they know the brown skinned foreigner that works in the gardens, but no one ever truly makes the connection. People rarely if ever actually see me, I am good at living my life in the shadows. I rather enjoy the peace of it…"

I flinched startled as Adri threw something at me falling backwards onto damp soil and rotten leaves. I wiped decaying leaves from my brow realizing that she'd hit me with mud. "What was that for?" I mumbled curiously watching her crawl towards the tunnel hips swaying in an enticing manor as she moved.

"One of the smartest people I've ever met and you're still an idiot…" I scrambled to my feet following after her, pausing shortly at the tunnel waiting for her to clear it before quickly pulling myself out.

"Why am I an idiot?" I questioned brow furrowed trying to wipe as much soil from my body as possible, to no avail. I was simply smearing it around.

The Princess turned back to look at me face a mask of frustration, "Am I ugly? Is that what it is? Or am I truly as fat as everyone claims I am?" She traced her hands over her stomach self-consciously. I followed the path of her hands distracted by the motion. "I try so hard, I train with the guards, I run with them, I ride my horse and I still do not know for sure if I ever will enjoy being that high off the ground. I eat healthy and my body is as slim as it will ever be, I know because I've asked the healers and yet here I am." She waved her hands, "The second day of the Queen's Tournament standing in the middle of Griffin Forest with one of my mother's Gardeners who compliments me but does not truly **see** me."

"Highness you are standing right there…" I winced as she growled before marching off in the other direction. "Highness!" I raced back down the river bank grabbing my pack and my boots before sprinting after her. "Highness I haven't asked my question."

"The answer is no!" I easily caught up and kept stride my legs being longer than hers.

"I haven't asked." I sighed exasperated.

We walked in silence for a long time after that, me trailing in her footsteps barefoot and without a shirt, covered in mud while I carried my things wondering what exactly I'd done wrong. "Gardener…"

I glanced up gazing at the Princess' wary expression. "Yes?"

"Do you like me?" I blinked at the simple and yet earnest question.

"Well… Yes, Highness, we are friends…and I will one day serve you." I answered slowly sure that this was important even if I really did not understand the need to ask.

Adri made a strangling gesture too short to actually reach my throat. I watched smiling softly brow furrowed slightly at her frustration. "Are you purposely ignoring my feelings in an attempt to not hurt me?" She asked after a moment of thought.

"I would never…"

Do you ever want to kiss me?!" She exclaimed face reddening.

"Ahhh…" I murmured finally realizing what she was asking me, I scratched my head understanding why she'd called me an idiot. The chill had reached my brain surely that was the reason it'd taken this long for me to understand her ranting. "I have never actually contemplated the thought…one does not simply just kiss the Princess after all." I replied truthfully those saplings taking root and growing like crazy in the pit of my stomach. I felt as if I might be sick.

Her Highness stepped closer gazing up at me as she rested her hands lightly on my hips, "I want you to want to kiss me Denarii…"

I gazed down into the twilight of her eyes and I struggled to draw air, suddenly feeling warm all over. "I will make you a wager." Adri stepped back eyes sparkling anew. "If you can carry me all the way back to the Training Fields you will have earned your pass and I will have earned a kiss for having said yes when I have already twice told you no."

"I never asked," I murmured feeling a little dazed from her close proximity.

"True, but that makes no matter now… so do we have a deal Gardener or am I as fat as everyone says?" Her words were joking but, I could see the pain in her eyes. I wonder if she expected me to refuse…she underestimated how badly I wanted that pass…and perhaps a small part ached to feel her lips pressed against mine.

I opened my pack and pulled on my tunic, pouch and blade settled at each hip respectively before I pulled on my boots tying them quickly. I gave the Princess my pack before turning and kneeling on the ground, glancing over my shoulder at her Highness now watching me curiously. "You have yourself a deal Highness." Adri laughed before hopping on my back.

I stood turning towards a path that only I could see, the Princess wasn't light, she was fit more muscle than fat but she wasn't overly heavy either. Nowhere near as heavy as my brother, warmth suffused my face as she wrapped her legs firmly around my waist and nuzzled her face against my neck thankfully having moved my braid aside before climbing on. "Let's go Gardener, the day grows old."

I gazed at the position of the sun sweat beading on my brow from the heat slowly waning before continuing on the path I'd taken to get here. If fortune was with us, we'd make it back to the Training Fields a little before the sun reached the horizon. Goddess I breathed muscles burning with the added strain of extra weight I hoped fortune was with us…

"Are you tired?" Adri asked for about the tenth time since we'd started.

I grunted sweat trickling down my face as I gazed at the position of the sun, "No just hot." I murmured truthfully as we entered the clearing where I'd left Carina to graze. I set her Highness down greeting my mare with a heartfelt hug. "Did you miss me girl?" I asked chuckling as she butted me in the chest causing me to stumble.

"I've seen her before but never thought to ask how exactly you came across a horse from your homeland, wild horses from the jungle are hard to find and even harder to tame if you do…" I stroked Carina's muzzle smiling softly.

"A gift to my brother from one of the soldiers for saving his life, he'd said. Though my brother has never set foot on a battle

field, by his own choice, he's aided many a soldier in surviving with his training on horseback. I don't know how he got her, though I heard it was something to do with a drunken bet. Reason in turn gifted her to me…another reminder of home he told me and we have loved each other dearly ever since."

I beckoned Carina over to the Princess and watched as she nipped at her hair while Adri laughed stroking Carina's jaw and neck while murmuring words of praise. "Will we ride your horse now?" Her Highness asked raising her brow, her expression stating that this wasn't part of the deal.

I chuckled at the fact that I could read her expression so easily, "No Highness, Carina knows her way home I simply wished to unburden us of my pack." I hooked it onto my saddle before tying it so that it remained secure.

I clicked my tongue several times before watching Carina trot away, she'd probably stop and enjoy a bit of sweet grass along the way, but I wouldn't fault her for it. "The Training Fields are about a slither of the sun's span from here." I turned kneeling so that she could climb onto my back pulling my braid over my shoulder. "Let us finish this journey Highness. I grow hungry for more than jerky and dry biscuits."

"Mmmm, Gardener and we haven't even kissed." I wavered as I stood nearly falling over at the Princess' husky tone and suggestive words murmured so close to my ear.

I took a deep breath while she laughed softly apologizing, "You're going to be the death of me Highness." I mumbled marching across the small clearing avoiding the paths that others had taken, ignoring the guards sulking around the forest trying to remain undetected.

"Many apologizes Gardener; you are just so unflappable I could not help myself." Her lips passed over my jaw in what might have been considered a kiss if I were paying attention. I'd realize that later, but in that moment I stood motionless heart racing at the profound silence that had stolen over the forest…no not the forest, the green, all of the plants, all of the trees they were silent. The noise that never ceased, never stopped, the constant chatter in the back of my mind was gone. Slowly I allowed her Highness to slide down my back to the ground gazing up into the tree tops searching for any form of danger. "Gardener…" I silenced the Princess with the raise of my hand shifting so that I could see her from the corner of my eyes.

"What monsters exist in the Griffin Forest…" sure that her knowledge was greater than mine. "What monsters exist that hold magic of their own?"

Adri took in my tone sobering quickly as she gazed around, as I did using her eyes to scan the canopy above and behind me while I in turn gazed at the forest beyond her. "Anything that had once been a danger in this forest should be long gone Denarii, my mother wouldn't send a group of untried and half trained suitors into this forest if there was danger."

"As well I have walked nearly the entirety of these grounds and found no predator magical or otherwise that has ever truly been a danger so long as I've avoided them, they've avoided me."

I nodded to make sure reaching out to the trees, none would speak to me. My heart skipped a beat, I stepped closer to the Princess. "Can you feel it?" I asked mouth going dry as I fingered my blade.

The birds chirped, the wind blew, animals scurried in the underbrush but there was danger in the air, undetected by nature, purely unnatural in its presence.

"I don't know what I'm searching for?" Adri said honestly glancing at me before glancing away still searching. I loosened the draw string on my pouch pulling forth a hand full of thorns, muscles tensing as the silence grew slowly but surely spreading to the animals, first the rodents, then the birds and finally the air stilled until her Highness pressed her back to mine crouching low. "Where's the orb?" Her Highness questioned voice quivering with nerves.

"In the pack I tied to Carina's saddle…I never thought for a moment I'd need it. Many apologizes." I murmured voice suddenly loud in the silence.

"Why are you apologizing…"

"For the danger I suppose…" Before I could elaborate the silence was shattered by shadows raining from the trees. I blinked as they rushed towards us, flickering darkness that had no true form. I tossed the thorns into the air magic surging forth with a whispered command. Thorn covered vines sprang to life around us grabbing at the shadows.

Adri drew the short sword given to her for protection, while I ducked the swipe of wispy claws, flipping backward out of reach while the beast gave chase, landing on my toes several feet away. I slashed at the darkness with my blade as it came near, crimson liquid splattered across my shirt. The shadowy form cried out, a distinctly human sound of pain as it drew back numbness setting in. Magic… I had time to think as I kicked the shadow in what I supposed was its face and watched it fall to the ground shadows constantly shifting despite its motionless form. Before I had time to breathe several more converged in its place, all the while vines stretched taught continuing to grow in a shield around the Princess.

I twirled among them braid whipping behind me, the air filled with blooming flowers and glowing magic that created a distraction allowing me to disappear. I raced up the side of an ancient, the rough bark clutching at the soles of my boots pushing me higher into its leafy canopy. Roots freed themselves from the ground, tripping my pursuers as they realized where I'd gone. I watched as the bark shed from the trees like the dead skin of a snake as they attempted to climb after me. I dropped a large bud and saw one fall prey to child's slumber, blooming as it drifted towards the ground. Several remained caught in my web of vines surrounding the Princess, thinking to attack her once the raptor vines had stopped moving only to find themselves pulled into their restricting embrace. Her Highness stood in low guard sword at the ready, if any should get past my defense.

I leapt onto one of the remaining shadows my height and weight instantly knocking them unconscious as I rode them to the ground. The last I caught in the face with a well-timed flick of my blade causing the shadows to vanish revealing a man slowly drifting towards the afterlife.

The pocket of quiet that had existed vanished with his death, the green once more murmuring in the background of my mind always there, their silence warning me of a threat I couldn't see. I sunk to my knees breathing heavily as I clutched at the earth gazing on the unfamiliar face of the man I'd just killed. Her Highness slipped from the small space in the vines open to her, sheathing her sword as she came to me.

"Gardener…" she gazed at the enemies I'd managed to defeat in a matter of moments. "What else are you hiding from us…" Her Highness stood staring at the web of vines still moving, shifting with each attempt of a shadow's escape, the vines burrowed into the ground, stretched high into the canopy of the surrounding trees, wrapped around tree limbs and bodies alike. With an empty center where she had once been.

I wiped my blade on the dead man's tunic, not the shimmering gray of a shade, but similar enough to be disconcerting. Someone wanted people to believe that even the Shades were against Adri's succession. "Are these Shades?" Adri asked as I sheathed my blade, watching the shadows as they grew motionless in my web of vines strangled into unconsciousness, the magic hiding the fact that they were human still active proving that all but one still lived.

"No." I ripped open the man's shirt to find his chest scarred but bare of the Royal crest lost in shadows, their mantra inscribed beneath it. "They carry shadow magic, perhaps they are even mages of high caliber…not a one had lost their cloak of shadows despite the fact that they're unconscious, but they aren't Shades. All Shades carry the Royal crest of an Alia rose lost in shadows tattooed onto their breast, with a short mantra, written in the first language of Angileri which means to serve the Queen, even in death. His chest is bare." I released the tatters of his tunic allowing it to fall closed. I gazed at the position of the sun.

"Are we to leave them here?" The Princess stared at the few others lying unconscious on the forest floor, I pushed to my feet collecting the small husk of Child's Slumber lying beside one of them. "What is that?"

I tucked the seed into my pouch, watching as the vines sagged, once vibrantly green slowly darkening. I moved forward grabbing hold of the now stronger plant as the shadow men fell unceremoniously to the ground. Her Highness gave me a look but did not comment on the rough treatment. "We'll leave them here," I began tying one of the shadow men up, "None will escape without help." Once done with him I moved to the next, "As for the little pod I tucked into my pouch, it was the seed of Child's Slumber, a flower known for inducing sleep, they only produce one seed at a time unlike other plant's. It can knock out a room full of people depending on the phase of its blossoming."

Adri helped me drag the few stragglers closer to the rest, tying their hands and feet separately and then roping them together behind their backs. When they woke they'd all find themselves painfully unconformable, because neither of us was much forgiving in our positioning. "What else are you hiding in that little pouch of yours?" The Princess asked as I stripped one of the greener vines of thorns tucking them into my pouch. "And how do you separate everything in there?"

"I don't," I offered answering the latter of her two questions.

"You don't what…separate them? Then how do you know what you're pulling out of there, how did you happen upon of a handful of thorns instead of a mishmash of seeds?" Adri gazed at me with wide eyes while I searched the dead man for anything identifying him and finding nothing as I'd expected, but it did no harm in looking.

My lips curled slightly, we'd just been attacked and she stood here before me while I searched a dead man asking about the how of my pouch instead of cowering in fear. Moments ago she'd been crouched, eyes burning, sword raised ready to do battle. This woman was greater than anyone gave her credit for. I closed my pouch pushing to my feet chuckling as she stood waiting for an answer. I understood now more than ever why the guards and soldiers alike would give their lives to see her on the throne. "It's a part of my gift Highness, I have spent many a day practicing what I draw out of this pouch by feel alone."

"So when you stab your fingers…"

"Not feeling with my hands Highness, feeling with my magic, calling the seeds, calling the thorns into my hand until there came a point where I could just…" I offered her a twilight peony. "Know exactly what I held in my hand and use it to my advantage."

"How…" she took the peony tracing her finger along each blue petal speckled with lavender. "How did you do that? I didn't see you reach for anything…"

"Sleight of hand and magic," I chuckled slyly tracing my finger along my nose in a mischievous gesture. "And that's all you'll hear from me on the matter." I turned kneeling so that she could climb on my back. "Now come so that we can hopefully make it back before night fall, I have a wager to win."

Adri climbed on my back arms hanging low across my collarbone as she wrapped her thighs around my waist. "Every time I think I know a little bit more about you Gardener you reveal more mysteries." Her Highness sighed softly as I stood strolling out of the clearing as if we'd stopped for a small rest and nothing more.

"I am who I am Highness and if you happen to find me mysterious then that is your perception." I countered gazing at the sun now quite low on the horizon, if we made it to the Training Fields before nightfall it would be by the Goddess' will alone.

"Says the woman who just single handedly took down perhaps ten shadowy apparitions all by herself." Adri huffed likely rolling her eyes.

I chuckled but chose not to comment, she was right after all.

"You were very brave for a Princess," I mocked good naturedly. "I had half expected you to cower in fear." I continued trying to fill the silence.

Her Highness snorted indignant, "You do realize that unlike my brother on my sixteenth summer of life I actually went on campaign with the Guard Captain…men died in my honor. This small ambush was nothing to be afraid of, I knew we could handle ourselves." She sighed against my neck nuzzling the skin there and…breathing in my scent though I could have been mistaken I did not question it not wanting to embarrass her. "What of you Gardener, do you regret killing a man, were you afraid we might not survive?"

I thought on that moment before everything began when we stood back to back, muscles tense, I remembered the silence that had begun with the voices of the trees and slowly spreading from there, to the rodents, to the birds, and to the very air itself. The silence had been deafening, startling in its clarity, everything had been so sharp allowing me to act without hindrance. Was I afraid… "In the brief moment before everything began when I thought some monster out of legend had come upon us I was a little afraid." Adri chuckled at my admittance, "After I discovered they were but men hiding behind the cloak of their magic I grew more confident. I felt no remorse for the dead man, after all he tried to kill me first. And in case you were wondering not once did I fear for you, as you once told me you can protect yourself..."

"And yet your first action was to protect me." She murmured softly lips tracing over my jaw in a kiss, I stumbled nearly falling before catching myself.

"You're my friend," I husked tugging lightly at my shirt as if that were the problem.

"Perhaps one day you will look at me as more." Adri murmured softly against my skin.

I tipped my head in acknowledgement of her words. "Perhaps one day..." We traveled in silence the rest of the way to the Training Fields trying to win a race against the sun before it set over the horizon. Fortune must have been with us despite our encounter because we topped a hill and stood gazing out across the palace grounds just as the sun began to set. Libeth pointed towards us whooping her excitement at my accomplishment. I ran towards my fellow Gardeners and our new friends laughing gaily, the Princess still firmly latched onto my back laughing with me.

Chapter 11
Adri's Shade

Emery patted me on the back grinning, "For a moment there I thought we were gonna lose you. I should have known if anyone was likely to go for the Princess it would be you." He shook his head in disbelief.

We gazed at the Heir now talking with the Queen and her sister Princess Mariel, Prince Sorel hovering near by, curious as to what had happened.

"Lose me on the second day, in a forest no less." I smiled softly, "Not a chance Em not a chance."

Libeth hugged me bouncing with excitement, "I can't believe you managed to find the Princess…You're doing a really bad job of hiding how powerful you are." She added as an afterthought just low enough for me to hear.

I thought back to the web of vines, the bark shedding like dead skin from the trees… "I know." I murmured softly ending the conversation.

"Are you sure you do not wish to marry me, I believe my parents will be very proud if I bring a Goddess home with me, despite the fact that I've only ever been interested in men before," Dahni said hugging my other arm the flush to her cheeks telling me she was only half joking.

"Dahni I'm not going to marry you." I replied chuckling softly before dropping a kiss to her brow.

"Don't encourage her," Libeth warned. "Or you'll find yourself on your horse traveling across the desert with no one the wiser." Dahni stuttered her protest while Libeth laughed at her justified indignation.

I slipped free of them both, smiling at Eden who tipped his head in greeting but did not comment on all that had transpired. "How did everyone do?" I asked, after a moment, curious.

"Well..." Libeth gazed around the small group and then beyond before grinning, a spark of mischief shining in her eyes. "The Princess told us we could only bring back one guard; she did not say that we could not help each other capture guards." I gazed at the sly looks on everyone's faces, Dahni and Tailaan included.

"How did you all manage to pull it off?" I questioned resisting the urge to laugh at their genius, when I was so thoroughly impressed.

"First," Eden broke the silence. "Emery, Libeth and I found each other and then we found Dahni and Tailaan, it was easy work after that to capture the guards with the child's slumber seeds you gave to each of us...though we did manage to knock out Dahni by an accident she woke just before we approached the Training Fields." Libeth's sheepish look told me exactly who was at fault for that.

Dahni smiled shrugging slightly, "Things happen, all is well."

"We planned it like this before we left," Emery stated. "We were waiting to see if the rules countered our plan before we told you...not for a moment did we think that we'd be rendered unconscious the moment the Princess stepped down from speaking."

"It's alright," I smiled. "I'm proud of your planning. I'm glad we'll all be progressing to the third day of the Tournament. Do we know how many we've lost?"

Libeth shook her head, "We won't know for sure until the dawn of tomorrow when the next challenge starts."

"Gardener Denarii!" I glanced up to see her Majesty beckoning me over.

"Stay out of trouble," Libeth warned as I walked away glancing back at her to show that I'd heard and acknowledged her words.

I bowed slightly more from tiredness than anything else, if I went any lower I wasn't sure I'd be able to stand back up. Rosen sensing this took hold of my arm supporting me. The day was catching up to me. "Majesty?"

"Do you recall where exactly you left the impersonators?" Her words were quiet, her expression serene, you'd have never guessed she was talking about a possible kidnapping or at worst an assassination attempt.

"Yes," the Queen bowed her head in a nod while Princess Mariel offered me an orb.

Think of the path you took, remember as best you can and then push with your mind," She said guiding me. I did as she instructed, the Princess nodded gazing into the orb before taking it back from me. "Thank you." Mariel disappeared before I could so much as tip my head. The Queen followed not far behind leaving Rosen, Adri and I standing alone.

"That was quick…" I murmured rubbing my face tiredly to find that I was still covered in dried mud. No one had said a thing. I glanced towards the Princess to see her hiding a grin of amusement.

Rosen rubbed clumps of dried mud and grass from my neck, "I have no idea what you did to find yourself such a mess child but…" she snorted. "You are in great need of a bath."

"I'm well aware." I mumbled wryly, as she pulled random blades of grass from my tunic.

"Come Gardener, we must discuss our deal," Adri ushered me away. "You can bathe after." I allowed her to take my arm pulling me away from Rosen and towards the gardens we both loved so much.

We walked in silence that despite my nerves was comfortable, we entered the Queen's Garden and I believe we sighed simultaneously both finding peace. "I've missed this," Adri pulled away moving towards the fountain trailing her fingers through the water. "The only place on palace grounds I can just be without Royal Guards trailing in my wake."

I raised my brow, "Every time I've seen you there have been no guards anywhere in sight Princess." I joined her beside the fountain.

Adri chuckled softly, "I am good at losing them."

"That's not the safest thing to be doing at a time such as this," I offered wryly remembering her penchant for calling me reckless. "Especially after what just occurred."

"I can protect myself…"

"Only so far," I rebuked. "You are after all only one person and the Heir besides. You protecting yourself should be the last resort, not the first." The Princess stared at me eyes sparking with defiance but she didn't argue. "You fail to understand that you are the Heir now, not just some token Princess who can do as she wishes. The people need you Highness, the land is restless, our enemies planning, the Void slowly but surely growing not towards us but other lands." I waved my hands encompassing the gardens and beyond. "This is your safe haven but it is not the only place in this world, there are more suitors here for alliances than anything else, have you ever thought to ask why? A water mage!" I exclaimed, "A water mage, a highly sought after individual has come from Raleli and I've never met a water mage from the desert. They're needed too heavily to leave, that's like one of the Queen's Garden mages going to investigate the Void…something major has happened for her to have the blessing no less of her Head Councilor to come to us.

"Your brother is angry, a poisonous snake ready to bite when you turn your back, he has the Council against you and you haven't even taken the crown, Prince Eris is trying to take your hand by any means necessary and the Queen can do nothing without the support of her people. People are trying to kill you…the cards are stacked against you Highness and you stand here before me claiming you can protect yourself." I shook my head, "Now is not the time for pride, pride will get you killed and it would be a foolish death besides leaving your people bereft a ruler that they sorely need regardless if they believe it or not."

"I am not my mother…"

I took Adri by the shoulders gently halting her argument, "No one wants you to be." I spoke softly. "We want the Gardener that lies in your heart, the woman who will nurture this land until it grows to new heights. The woman who will make this land her garden, and let it thrive as nature should, who is loving and kind. The woman who forgives her brother his grievance despite the fact that his actions are unjust, who practices with her guards and makes them laugh when she falls, who threatens to behead her healers and shakes her head when they laugh in her face. A woman the people do not fear but respect and love because of who she is, not because of the title she carries. Your mother is a great Queen, but she will never be you Adri and I would serve you…"

My heart stopped when she kissed me, the saplings in my stomach growing to full grown trees as my eyes fluttered closed, her lips were soft, achingly soft against mine. Her strong hands wrapped around my arms to keep me in place as her mouth moved gently capturing and then recapturing my lips, stealing every thought from my mind until all I could hear was the gentle flow of our breathing and the green growing things, murmuring in the background, trying to be quiet for my sake. I shivered as she traced her hands up my arms to my neck and into the short hairs that graced the back of my neck. I thought briefly she must be standing on her toes because surely she hadn't grown in the last few moments. When she pulled away I stood wide eyed as she settled back on her feet, she had been standing on her toes, crossed my mind as my heart thumped a startled rabbit in my chest and I struggled to remember the process of drawing air into my lungs.

"I hadn't specified where I would kiss you," Adri murmured after a moment of silence, "I had thought to kiss you on the cheek, but…" Her Highness shook her head. "You are so good with words Gardener and then you said my name." She smiled and it was a smile I'd never seen from her before, as bright as the sun and as beautiful as any flower I'd ever seen, it was a smile meant just for me and once more my heart stuttered in my chest.

"Sister!" Princess Mariel strolled into the Queen's Garden wearing the guards practice uniform, we turned as one to face her. "You have a scheduled meeting with the Horse Master?"

Adri tipped her head in acknowledgement, "I enjoyed our talk Gardener…" She hesitated before continuing. "Rhyme. Thank you for your words." The Heir bowed slightly, Mariel's brows disappeared somewhere in the curling waves of her hair but she didn't comment. I stepped back startled at the show of respect. She stood gracing me with one more smile before turning to walk towards her sister. The Queen's third child gave me a curious look but refrained from commenting until they were far beyond the reach of the Queen's Garden. I'd have known if she'd spoken, the flowers would have told me so.

I sagged onto the fountain rubbing my hand gently across my chest, face warm, "Goddess," I murmured reaching up to touch my lips still tingling from her kiss. "I said her name…" I sat with my fingers on my lips. "She said my name," I breathed rubbing my hand along my neck. It felt nothing like the trail of heat her fingers had left in their wake. I brushed my bangs from my face, slipping free in spite of the plait I'd had my hair in all day. "Goddess…"

"Are you praying child?" I glanced up as a familiar voice drifted towards me in the growing darkness.

"If I am I don't know what is it I'm praying for." I shifted sideways allowing Rosen to take a seat beside me on the fountain.

"Peace perhaps…we could all use a little peace in our lives. Happiness…I know you try so hard to appear happy despite the fact that even now as old as you are you still miss your home." Rosen smiled at me bumping me lightly with her shoulder. "I know you are not praying for power you already have enough to surpass my own."

"Perhaps…" I turned to Rosen beseechingly. "I pray for guidance."

"Guidance in what? I believe you've forgiven her Majesty as much as you ever will which is more than most in your place. Your brother's story is so very different than yours despite that you're are twins."

"He was so excited to come here, to a new land, a new place to explore, once he'd learned of the horses. Once he found that he could make something of himself without having to ride my coat tails. He was such a man…even then." I murmured softly lips curling in a bittersweet smile. "I do not begrudge him the place he's found here; the niche he's carved for himself. His men respect him, he has the title he deserves. Reason is happy." I finished slowly unbraiding my hair.

Rosen placed her hand comfortingly on my shoulder, "The difference Rhyme is that he is happy with his horses and without them…can you say the same about your gardens."

I raised my hand holding hers to my shoulder lightly squeezing her fingertips as I thought of twilight eyes and satin soft lips. "No…but perhaps one day I will be."

Rosen smiled leaning forward to rest her brow against mine, I closed my eyes taking comfort in her closeness. She wrapped her arms around me and suddenly I felt as I had so long ago when I'd first arrived here, a child gazing up into the eyes of a woman who grew up in this land but still understood what it meant to be different, except now I was gazing down and the light in Rosen's eyes was respect, not the sympathy I'd seen years ago. I hugged her close squeezing her smaller frame, "Thank you." I murmured breathing in her scent of earthy soil and sunlight.

"For what?" She asked rubbing my back.

"For helping to make me into the woman I am today, for being the mother I thought I'd lost once I got on that ship…for being the guidance I did not know I needed for so long and giving me love. Thank you for being exactly who you are, Rosen Len, thank you from the bottom of my heart." The Head Gardener held me tighter then, breathing deeply through the emotion that blocked her throat.

"I could not have asked for a better student…or daughter to offer my guidance to Rhyme Denarii." I laughed softly thinking about all the mischief I'd gotten up to when I felt particularly wronged or angered in my youth.

"Are we thinking about the same Rhyme?" I questioned finally pulling away.

Rosen brushed my hair back from my face before pressing a tender kiss to my brow, "The one who sits before me now, more powerful than I, but respects my wisdom none the less. The woman honest in all things, who is reckless in pursuit of the green's song because to her plants have spirits too. The same one who has pretended all these years to be happy, for her brother's sake, the one who despite the fact that she dislikes violence has become a warrior for her mother's sake and a healer for her own…Friend to the Heir and perhaps one day more, be it Head Gardener or simply confident." She stroked my cheek smiling softly. "That's the Rhyme that I speak of, the one who even now continues to grow stronger in her gift. Not the child who grew up long before her time, but the woman that she's become in spite of it."

I blinked tears streaming my face at the fact that she saw all that in me, this woman who I respected more than all else, this woman who had nurtured me and mothered me when I'd needed it. I hugged her close again. "I love you Rosen." I murmured the first time I'd said those words to someone besides my brother since I'd left Kantari. "I love you so much." I murmured heart aching.

"I know." She murmured into the raven black waves of my hair, "I've known you loved me since the day you ran to find me in the Queen's Garden showing me your pouch and how you had finally learned to separate the seeds."

"I was so excited," I murmured remembering that day. "I'd been practicing the entire year, every day and I could not think of anyone who would appreciate it more than you."

"Not even your brother?" Rosen questioned curious as to the why she'd been first.

"Not like you would." I offered knowing it for the truth, Reason did not quite appreciate all that I could do, they would always just be pretty plants and parlor tricks to him.

"I love you too." I felt the firm press of her lips against my hair and I sighed content. "You still need a bath." Rosen said after a long moment of silence in which I had begun to drift off to sleep.

I sat up allowing her arms to fall away, "Thank you for the reminder," I stood stretching small bits of dirt flaking away from my clothes and skin to fall to the ground. I grimaced at the grimy feeling.

"You're welcome," the Head Gardener stood as well walking with me as I left the Queen's Garden parting on our walk towards the palace. Likely headed to speak with the Queen.

I strolled along the path leading to the palace, passing by the Training Fields catching sight of Reason and the Heir talking together, while several skilled soldiers put their horses through their paces demonstrating the skills my brother had taught them. I raised my hand in greeting as I passed, Reason returned the greeting recognizing the long sweep of my dark hair despite the distance no doubt.

Deciding that the servant's bathes would probably be full and not wanting to go back to my room just yet I went to the youngest of the Queen's Gardens, the one that often struggled to thrive. I circled the palace and entered the Griffin Forest following a stone laid path until I came upon Katina Lake named after the Queen's great grandmother, I stood on the sandy shore and gazed at the floating foliage at its center. I stripped myself bare tossing my clothes into the water before racing in, and diving once I reached the cliff's edge hidden beneath the surface of the water.

I swam deep, hair streaming behind me, I'd forgotten to braid it before I'd entered the water. I reached the center mass of greenery where I'd found, many of the fish liked to hide and pushed towards the surface. I breathed deep gazing on an arrangement of water lilies and lily pads, arrowhead and cattails all glowing softly in the light of the moon. I fell backward turning so that I lay floating among the plants. Once a small cliff that fell off into a deep valley, Katina Lake had been one of the elder of the Queen's Gardens. Until a child had died falling from the cliff's edge, her sister's child. Unable to bear the sight of it any longer, the Queen's grandmother had water mages come from every corner of the world and with her Garden mages had reshaped the land and made a lake. Now at the heart of the lake rests the largest Alia rose in existence glowing softly with magic that never dies in honor of a royal life that by rights should never have been lost.

Every child who came to live at the palace learned to swim, I closed my eyes remembering the story as told that day I'd first stepped into the water, thinking of how sad and yet beautiful it had been and still was. When I opened my eyes I lay resting on the Alia rose skin glowing softly. I smiled as the spirit of the rose stroked my hair not having many willing to risk death by entanglement in the plants just to get so close. She was beautiful, more human in appearance than most of the spirits I'd seen. I could not help but think that she looked a lot like Queen Katina's lost niece. I sighed softly rolling from the strong petals back into the water sinking briefly among the green before it swayed parting for me, slower to move with the hindrance of the water. I swam through the path created back towards the shore grabbing my clothes as I moved stumbling as I stood feeling heavier outside of the water.

I rung out my clothes as best I could, shivering in the evening chill as I pulled them on over wet skin. I cocked my head listening to the forest gazing into the shadowy canopies above. Someone was watching me…I pulled on my boots, checking to make sure my blade and pouch still rested against each hip hidden, though not so well anymore with my water laden clothes, by the fall of my tunic.

I moved towards the tree line whistling softly, the same song I'd sung with Rosen several days prior about Shades and how they came in the night. I stepped into the underbrush and ducked aside as someone fell from the shadows. I tackled them into the moonlight, and we struggled for a time rolling across the sand, Goddess I'd just gotten clean too. I pulled my blade free touching it to their throat, the shadows shifting around them, their form still distinctly human though of course I couldn't tell the gender. "One more move and it'll be your last." I warned face a mask of stone.

They lay motionless breathing heavily while I held my blade to their throat unwaveringly. I felt for the fabric of their shirt ignoring the feel of soft breasts, with the flick of my wrist I reversed the blade and sliced her shirt open while she cried out startled shadows faltering long enough for me to catch sight of the tattoo I was looking for. Before I could ask questions a fist shot out of the shadows catching me in the jaw, I fell sideways catching myself as they slide from beneath me shoving me with a firm foot to the side.

I rolled over pushing to my feet only to be knocked back down, "You know," I murmured warm blood trickling from the small cut above my brow as I caught her foot, not wanting to be kicked again, I dragged her back to the ground. "I never thought the Queen would sink so low." I grunted as we wrestled across the sand once more. I growled after being punched in the face several times unable to see the blows coming beneath the cloak of shadows.

Goddess those amateurs in the forest had been a cake walk compared to this stubborn Shade.

"What…" A familiar voice breathed recognizable even through the gravely cloak of her magic. I smirked sprinkling flower petals across her body watching as the shadows slowly dissipated revealing the Queen's third child, Princess Mariel startled to find her magic fading so swiftly.

"Low enough to make her own daughter a spy, a shadow mage of the highest order. A Shade…" I finished sitting back on my heels.

"It was my choice." The Princess murmured all fight gone out of her. I watched as she raised the soft petals to her face, blood red in color. "Succubus?" She questioned catching my eyes.

"Yes. Illegal in Angileri after a series of kidnappings made possible because the flower's petals neutralize all magic." The Princess tried to strike me again only to find her hands trapped in a nest of vines. "All magic except mine that is." I finished as she glared up at me.

"You are so much more than what you appear to be," Her Highness huffed trying to free her hands to no avail.

"And yet no more than I ever said I was." I murmured wondering how my shirt had become so torn. "Does your sister know that you watch over her?" I asked gazing at the thorny vines spiraling just above my heart.

"Does she know you're more than just a Gardener?" Mariel countered observing my tattoo with more understanding than anyone who had seen it before. "Does she know that you can speak with the dragons as she does?" She questioned proving once and for all that she was more than the pretty face everyone thought her to be.

My lips curled slightly, as I leaned over her gazing into the bright blue orbs that were her eyes, "You are a good actor Princess, hiding behind your frivolous, ditzy façade, playing the spoiled little royal, but really you're the most dangerous of your siblings aren't you." It wasn't a question, I stroked my finger along her cheek gazing into eyes that showed wisdom beyond her years. "The Queen's Spy Master, her confident in all things, her observer of hidden meetings and the protector of her most important asset; the Heir to the throne and your own beloved sister. Everyone thought if Adri stepped down you would take her place, but you've had your magic for a long time yes. You knew the outcome as your mother did, a daughter with shadow magic." I shook my head. "What if your sister had said no, what if she hadn't passed the Trials? A Shade cannot take the throne, a Shade cannot rule, nameless and faceless, all Shades remain in the shadows."

"The dragons told my mother…before I took the oath. They told her that Sorel would fail because of his arrogance and that I would hold no true title beyond Princess because of my magic. It was too strong, I wouldn't properly bond…despite Adri's love for the gardens a gift for the plants did not develop and so she went through the Trials and now here we are. I am where I want to be and she is where she has always belonged regardless of what she thinks." I tipped my head in understanding releasing her hands and shifting backwards allowing her to sit up gently rubbing her wrists.

"You're a good sister." I murmured finding my feet dusting sand from my trousers before going to retrieve my blade.

"How did you know I was near? How did you sense me in the darkness?" She called out scrambling to her feet, holding her shirt closed as crimson petals drifted down around her.

I smirked turning to face her as I sheathed my blade. "You're asking a plant mage how she sensed you in the forest…"

"None of the other Gardeners would have," Mariel countered walking towards me. "None of them ever have before. Not even Rosen, not truly. Though when I was young in my magic she came close a few times."

"You never thought to follow me before?" I raised my brow curious.

"You disappear often, and you're hard to find let alone keep track of. I saw no need when I knew you were harmless." Her Highness replied falling into step beside me as we entered the forest, trying and failing to summon her magic.

"What changed your mind?" I ducked beneath a low hanging branch and watched amused as the Princess walked right into it growling softly as she rubbed her face.

"You did that on purpose." I chuckled softly brow raised.

"What exactly did I do save duck Highness?" I questioned while she glared at me.

"You're stronger than my mother gave you credit for, stronger than Rosen has thought to admit though I'm sure that was purposeful on her part," She offered drolly as we continued on our way with her paying more attention to the forest around her least another low hanging branch smack her in the face.

"Why Princess, I have no idea what you're talking about." I said voice dripping with feigned innocence.

Princess Mariel shoved me back against a tree, while I wondered where exactly the Queen's daughters hid their strength. "You are dangerous Gardener Denarii, dangerous and powerful and yet my sister trusts you." She ripped open my shirt tracing her fingers along the tattoo on my chest pausing at the belt clenching my trousers shut before sliding her hand down to cup me firmly between the thighs. "The dragons for all intents and purposes trust you." Her hand tightened on sensitive flesh while we gazed into each other's eyes.

"If you like it rough Princess Gardener Rendell is your man, despite his pretty façade his is very forward in his love affairs." She clenched me tighter pinching my little bud, on purpose no less. "I'm more for gentle love making." I finished as if she weren't trying to tear out my womanhood.

"Funny…" She leaned forward sinking her teeth into the juncture of my throat, I clenched my teeth, jerking as she broke skin, the metallic scent of blood filling the air as she pulled away shadows slowly obscuring her features. She stepped away from me a triumphant smile gracing her lips. "The only person immune to the succubus flower's effects. Hmm good to know Gardener." I watched as she drifted along the ground leaving no foot prints. "As for the love making…perhaps another time. Just know for now that you have my trust…Let it not be taken lightly or lost. Bad things will happen if you cross me." I blinked and she was gone leaving me with an aching sex and a bloody mark on my neck. Not how I imagined my night would end. Not at all.

I raised my hand to my neck wincing slightly, who knew such a pretty woman could bite so hard, I wondered using my other hand to cup my sex. Who knew such a small woman could be so strong…Goddess not I. I stared at the blood now staining my hands, certainly not I.

Chapter 12
It Was Worth It

"What in the Gods' name happened to you?" Libeth asked the following morning as we stood on the Training Fields waiting for someone to announce the final stage of the first part of the Queen's Tournament. I took a drink of my favorite tea, near black in color, but anyone who'd ever made it would say it was crimson, so dark a red as to be almost black. I sipped my tea, red like the petals of the succubus flower, illegal unless used to make tea and you could only be found with the petals not the full grown plant itself.

I breathed deeply, "I'd lie and say I fell if I thought for even a moment that you'd believe me." Emery snorted turning to cover his amusement at my nonchalance about my battered appearance while Libeth glared at his turned back.

"Who dared to harm my Goddess?" Dahni asked completely serious, and all the more adorable because of it.

"She's not a Goddess…" Emery countered.

"She's an idiot." Libeth supplied fuming.

I took another sip of my tea, throat aching slightly with each swallow. Though I'd healed the bruises that had blossomed on my face I still retained the cut above my brow now stitched closed and the bite mark on my neck startling in how obvious it was. I could count every tooth mark. "Why am I an idiot?" I asked calmly brow raised curiously.

"You let someone do this to you!" Libeth exclaimed waving at my face and neck.

"Trust me," I countered. "I fought every step of the way…except the bite. That took me completely by surprise…" I rubbed my neck. "I wasn't expecting her to bite me." I murmured softly.

"I did not know you were into violence," Emery sounded betrayed as if I should come to him first with such a thing, which I would have if I were.

"I'm not…"

"The vicious bite mark on your neck says otherwise." Eden countered before I could even finish speaking.

I gave him a stern look causing him to raise his hands in surrender. "I'm not into to violence," I turned to Emery. "I do not enjoy pain. I am still very unbroken…"

"Goodness Rhyme, you bedded someone and they didn't get the opportunity to even touch you intimately."

"I bedded no one." I growled. "I got into an altercation, she hit me repeatedly in the face, split my brow open and bit me."

"What did you do to her? Surely she looks the worse for wear?" Dahni questioned curiously.

I took another drink from my cup watching Princess Mariel conversing with her sister, "Hmm, I'd never harm a lady without probable cause." Was all I said on the matter. Libeth, Emery and Eden shared looks between them. While Dahni looked on with a furrowed brow, Tailaan stood a little off to the side watching the other suitors.

"Does that mean you los…"

Before Dahni could finish her sentence her Majesty took the stand announcing those that we had lost the day prior, only three. A surprise in itself, I suppose we weren't the only ones that thought to aid each other. I glanced at Prince Eris and the smug look on his face, I had never hated anyone in my life, not even now, but he did make me feel close to such a point.

We were down to seventeen an odd number but it was no matter, one lucky suitor would get to spar twice. My lips twitched at that announcement, two times the chance to lose. I hoped it wasn't one of us. There would be nine matches, one person would spar twice, the winner of each individual match would proceed to the next phase of the Queen's Tournament, the rules were very simple. For this challenge you had to incapacitate your opponent, in this you would show how you would defend the Heir if trouble ever arose. The suitor who chose to spar twice, would be rewarded if and only if they won their second match as well as the first. They would be able to exclude them self from another part of the coming Tournament. If they lost said challenge, they would of course lose the reward, as well as their previously won spot, it was a double edged sword and the choice of course was yours. That person would not be chosen until eight matched were fought and won. We all had time to think.

"Why do I get the feeling," Emery said taking note of my expression, "That you're going to take that challenge."

"I would," I conceded, "But this isn't about me or what I would do in different circumstances, this is about the four of us, sticking together for as long as possible. After all there is always the possibility that I'd lose."

"I find that unlikely," I turned to find Arely standing close behind me, I was unsurprised that she'd sidled up close to us while we remained unaware. She wasn't the Sol-Lea for nothing after all. "Once upon a time we sparred together and I always found myself hard pressed to win against you and that was without your gift involved."

"Well it has been a few years…"

"I have a feeling your skills have only improved since then." Arely countered not unkindly.

"With all due respect Sol-Lea," I stepped forward. "You don't know me any longer. Don't presume to."

"Gardener Denarii will always be a Healer first." Libeth stated sensing the tension.

"And yet you make an amazing warrior…"

Eden stepped between us causing us each to step back least he shove us aside with his bulk. Emery stepped up beside him on my other side. "Perhaps you should leave Sol-Lea. With all due respect." He glanced at the blank expression on my face. "You aren't welcome here."

"Rhym…"

"My title," I stated firmly raising my chin, back straight. "Is Gardener and to you my name, is Denarii. Any other privileges were lost long ago." I finished throat aching with the emotion just seeing her face caused, so familiar and yet so very different, so much harder than it once was and yet slightly softer in my presence. The only difference now is that I was hard too and much like the ancient by the river I would not be moved and unlike the river, Arely could not carve a nook for herself in my heart, not any longer.

Arely cleared her throat, "I wish you good fortune Gardener, perhaps someday we can spar again if that day is not today." She turned and walked away still the strong woman I knew her to be, but, perhaps it was my imagination, it looked as if she had tears in her eyes. I turned to my friends smiling my gratitude sure that I would always be something she'd regret. I'd long since learned that it was her loss not mine.

"Thank you." I said sincerely giving Libeth a hug.

Emery smirked, "Hey you're our fearless leader second to Rosen of course and we'll always have your back. I can recall on more than one occasion as children that you had ours."

Dahni hugged me as well just because she could I think, and Eden laughed as I tried to peel her off of me. "One step closer to being done with this thing."

"Yes but the question is will we all make it?" Libeth asked brow furrowed, Emery hadn't lied when he said that we weren't all warriors.

"Let us just pray to the Goddess that if we don't all make it that it's enough to help her Highness in the long run." I murmured when Dahni went over to figure out what had Tailaan so occupied.

Eden gave a solemn nod while the recruits etched glowing rings of magic into the ground, four spanning the entirety Training Fields.

"The match ends when someone can no longer continue, no killing, no crippling, you may use your gift and all other skills you have to win these matches. Your opponent will be selected at random." The Queen held up one of the glowing orbs we'd used in the previous day's challenge. "Each of you will be given one, within it holds the image of your opponent and a number, that's when you'll be called into a ring. Good Fortune to you all."

Not long after her Majesty finished speaking the same recruit who'd handed me my arrows, who's name I believe was Donta, the Guard Captain's son, tossed each of us an orb. I gazed at the familiar face of my friend, rocks settling in the pit of my stomach. Number 17 and 18 we would go last. I glanced up into Libeth's somber eyes, "If you go easy on me. I will never forgive you."

She cracked a smile that didn't completely reach her eyes. "Of course it would come down to one of us fighting each other." I pulled her against my side allowing her to rest her head on my arm, while Eden and Emery looked on speechless. "I wanted so badly for all of us to make it to the end."

"I know." I rested my head atop hers sighing softly.

"Just promise me that no matter who wins, no matter what tricks we use, no matter the magic that we toss around this ring, that at the end of the day we'll still be friends when the dust clears?" I stirred my tea while Eden gave me a strange look, Emery was focused on fixing his hair and Libeth couldn't see my other side. I offered her my cup of tea absorbing her words.

She took it without hesitation, taking a sip of the dangerous brew, and sighing softly as it burned its way down her throat singing softly the entire way. "I promise, that no matter the outcome we'll still be friends."

Libeth squeezed my waist softly as Emery left us one of the first to fight and against Tailaan none the less. "Good fortune Rhyme."

"Same to you Libeth." She pulled away from me before walking off somewhere perhaps to plan out how she'd best me. Libeth would give her all, much like me she never did anything half way. I sheathed my blade. Eden didn't ask any questions and Dahni was clueless as to what might be wrong. I drank the remainder of my tea before handing the cup to a passing recruit who walked off brow furrowed in confusion.

"Are you two going to be alright?" I glanced down at Dahni, smiling softly.

"Yeah," I murmured. "If any of us could make it through fighting each other it would be Libeth and I. She's been a good friend for a long time."

Eden jabbed me lightly in the shoulder, "Good fortune to both of you. I promise I won't let Emery place bets. Libeth would never forgive him."

"Not unless he placed bets on the two of us." I countered thinking it out.

"I'll be sure to tell him you said that." Eden chuckled as I tried to sputter my way out of approval I hadn't meant to give.

Dahni left us next, a match was already over and she was fifth. I watched the matches from our place on the sidelines, ignoring the cheering of the crowd at our backs. "You two are last…if it goes for more than a few moments there's no way that you'll be able to hide your skill." Eden said once he was sure no one lingered around us.

Eden was only perhaps a smidge shorter than I was, and even so his bulky stature made him appear taller, the point I was trying to make is that, it allowed me to look him in the eye without ducking my head. "I feel that's the point." I gazed up into the stands where the Royal Family sat observing the festivities below, Royal Guards standing at several points around them. "I cannot hide forever, as much as I wish I could."

"Are you finally willing to admit that you are equal to Rosen?" Eden asked curious.

I smiled softly as I gazed into kind eyes, "I don't think I ever will." I admitted sighing softly.

"If it's any consolation, neither do I." He placed his hand on my shoulder. "You respect her too much, but it doesn't stop others from seeing as much. Even though Rosen hasn't announced her successor," Eden made a face that said he didn't believe his own words, "least we all start fighting amongst ourselves, we all know it's you. You're the best choice honestly and not just because you're the strongest." He countered before I could argue. "When it becomes official, we'll all be very happy Rhyme you deserve it…"

"And yet…" I don't want it went unsaid because at that moment we felt it… plant magic. Eden and I turned nearly as one to see a woman of about average height fighting against Dahni white petals making a vortex around her. "She has two…" I heard the petals singing a song for the wind but I couldn't hear the reply.

"Two gifts," Eden breathed as we watched Dahni trying to use her magic like a whip to escape, but the water lost form as she swayed eyes fluttering as she struggled to remain conscious to no

avail. Whatever sleeping agent found in those petals was made more prevalent as the wind whipped it around her. "What flower is that?" Eden asked curiously as the woman using the aid of her magic slowly lowered Dahni's slumbering form. She looked so peaceful and for that I was grateful, though I would miss her presence among us I was glad that she hadn't suffered overly much.

"Blue Bell," I murmured softly watching the spirit dance in the wind, "It's much like child's slumber but less potent, you'd have to breathe more heavily or ingest the plant for it to be effective in putting you to sleep as well you won't sleep as deeply or as long. Indeed, I'm sure Dahni will wake up in just a few moments. It was a good trick…"

"You could recognize the flower from this distance?" Eden sounded impressed.

"I can hardly see the colors of the petals as they settle, no I recognized the flower's song and the spirit now fading into the wind."

Emery joined us, limping slightly and holding an ice pack to his cheek but that seemed to be the extent of his injuries. "Always more than just a pretty face." I smiled softly as he brushed his hair from his face knuckles red but unbroken.

"I'd have lost if not for my gift, I'm not much of a fighter." He proclaimed sighing softly. "These matches are ending pretty quickly. Prince Eris won his…and the Sol-Lea hers, in less than a minute no less. Dahni…"

"Lost," I finished for him.

Eden shook his head, "She did not stand a chance."

"As well we know who the plant mage is, but we still don't have a name." I offered as the remaining fights came to a close.

Eden left us to fight his match, "I missed the plant mage?" Emery asked as Eden stepped into a ring with a man far smaller than he was, I could see him quivering from here and I knew that Eden would win without even having to see him throw a punch.

"Yes…" I turned from the fight, "She's a hybrid…" I hesitated thinking about the short hair cut in such a specific way. "I think…"

My orb glowed gently and I sighed softly, only two matches remained. I left Emery by himself, Eden passing me as I moved to enter one of the glowing rings. I stood breathing deeply waiting for my opponent, my friend. Libeth entered the ring just as the only remaining match ended leaving us the center of attention. The crowd grew silent.

I unbound my hair tucking the leather thong in my pocket. Libeth smiled at me unbuttoning her shirt and tossing it aside, the magic allowing the fabric to pass through. "No one will leave this circle as long one of you is still able to fight," Donta said from the sidelines trying to remain serious. "You may surrender if you feel you are unable to go on. Do either of you have any questions?" He glanced back and forth between us, neither of us offered up a question. "The match begins once you each toss your orb into the air, they'll vanish creating a show of light once it fades the match begins. Toss your orbs." The recruit walked from the circle as we tossed our orbs into the air.

My heart raced in my chest as my ears rang with a beautiful melody, I felt as if I were moving in slow motion as I ducked vines shooting through the remaining magic, twisting and turning to avoid being captured. A whisper of my magic caused the vines to wither and die, I'd fallen for the distraction. Libeth leapt through the slowly dying web of vines and kicked me in the chest. I flew off my feet as the crowd began to cheer. I rolled across the ground chest aching as I pushed to my feet catching her leg before she could kick me again. "Good kick," I grunted as she used the leverage I'd given her to jump up and kick me in the face freeing her other leg and leaving me slightly dazed.

She smirked looking a little blurry in my vision, "Thanks," I chuckled as she struggled to release her feet from the grass now growing to wrap around her ankles smirk vanishing as I repaid her kick to the chest with one of my own, that sent her flying. I pulled the pouch from my belt as she struggled to her feet smiling softly while she watched me warily.

"Are you ready?" vines grew in my hair twinning with the dark strands while I watched her, ensuring that it wouldn't get in my way. I gently tossed the pouch of surprises in the air catching it again and again while she looked on slowly widening her stance.

"If you throw that, I can use it too." Libeth warned taking a deep breath as she readied herself.

I bowed my head in acknowledgement, "You will finally discover all the things I hide in here." I murmured softly smile growing. "Or some of the things anyway."

Libeth grinned eyes sparking with challenge, she flicked her locks from her face only to have them fall back to cover her right eye. "Do it."

Needing no more prompting I threw my pouch high into the air, vines, thick, thin, thorny, smooth vines mashed all together grew wild in the sky, creating an obstacle course of the ring they could not escape. Libeth laughed as she slid beneath the vines the grass pulling her along as she swept my feet from under me.

I should have jumped. "Is that all you got?" I questioned poison coating my skin as I was unable to keep myself from falling into a small patch of hornets' nest, a small bramble like vine that when touched made you feel as if you'd been stung by hornets. I caught child's slumber and threw it towards her moving form, watching it bloom as it smacked her in the face.

She froze where she stood, as still as any ancient, holding her breath while I cut a path through the vines magic causing them to shift aside to make room for me. I caught her in the jaw with my fist before she had time to blink. Libeth grabbed hold of my arm before I could pull it back, Goddess I felt so slow, all the while the vines shifted around us our magic struggling against each other while we exchanged blows in the center of it all. I grunted as she elbowed me in the throat, the wound from last night smarting. Thorny vines snagged at my clothing as I lost my focus.

I purposely fell into their embrace before she could strike me again, allowing them to drag me away as petals began to flutter on the wind around us, they resembled tiny flickering flames caught on the breeze. I rolled over panting softly as Libeth looked on eyes widening slowly at the trap she found herself in. She turned and leapt through a small hole in the vines as I took a deep breath and blew my magic touching on those petals creating a burst of fire. Dragon's breath. The fire swept through the vines in a wide arch chasing her as she ran. Only fading once she'd climbed upwards towards the top of the dome of magic now surrounding us. A wide swatch of the ring laid bare but not for long, vines grew to replace the ones lost while I pushed myself to my feet shirt torn to shreds, arms aching and swollen from the thorns stuck there, little droplets of blood beading on my skin.

I blinked gazing at the spirits waging a battle all around me, the air filled with their song, crimson petals drifting on the breeze. Succubus I thought as I felt my magic wanting to fade, it remained steadfast where it belonged deep inside me. I listened to the green unable to see Libeth where I was on the ground. I saw her through the plants and couldn't help but smirk softly as she tried to catch her breath hand quivering as she held her opposite arm now numb from coming in contact with a plant called Limp Limb in her mad dash trying to escape the fire. A moss like plant that could grow just about anywhere even on other plants and vines, just the slightest brush against it could cause an arm or leg to go completely limp for seeming no reason at all. You could still feel it, you just couldn't move it, a very frustrating occurrence for sure. A few unsuspecting travelers had nearly died before it was discovered.

"Are you hiding Libeth?" I called magic touching on every vine, every petal, every bloom, echoing through the spirits of the green and becoming amplified by their song. Despite the confinement we found ourselves in I did not doubt that everyone in the stands heard my voice.

A path opened before me, her magic not mine, revealing Libeth seated on a platform of shifting vines. "You're so bright Rhyme…"

"Your songs are some of the most beautiful I've ever heard." I countered softly listening to the soothing melody we created together. It was beautiful…and destructive. I watched impressed as Libeth took a breath and blew imitating the trick I'd used just moment ago, a ball of fire heading straight towards me. "You just learn that from me?" I asked curious watching the fire approach.

"Yes…" I closed my eyes as the fire washed over me allowing the spirit to embrace me, I felt warmth, all-encompassing heat as it licked at my face, crawled over my skin and inside my clothing but it did not burn me. Slowly but surely the flames faded away. "That didn't work half as well as I planned it to." Libeth tsked as she took in my form completely unscathed.

"Why don't you come down here so we can finish this?" I asked beckoning her forward.

A stairway of moss and vines formed before me, "Why don't you meet me halfway?"

I tipped my head in acknowledgement placing my foot on the first step, "You tired yet Libeth?" I asked moving from a walk to a jog the vines pushing me upward as they forced her down, until we were racing towards each other our magic once more clashing.

"I've never used this much magic in a fight before." She admitted voice weary.

We met in the middle, she blocked my fist, I ducked her punch, vines wrapping around my arm as she struck me in the throat for the second time that day. I gasped pulling my limb free, vines snaking up my arm, thorns biting into my flesh. "Low blow," I rasped as more vines grabbed hold.

"I never said I'd play fair." Libeth chirped before punching me in the face rocking my head back. I struggled eyes rolling as the world faded around me. Her fist struck my face again, and again darkness closed in as the green sang a beautiful song…

I felt her fingers in my hair, saw child's slumber blooming in the palm of her hand. I held my breath while she waited, my throat burned, my lungs ached. I would need to breathe soon. I blinked watching twilight peonies blooming on the breeze, the signal I'd been waiting for, Libeth gazed at them curiously loosening her grip.

The vines around us loosened their hold, the flower in her hand falling from numb fingers, Libeth turned back to me shocked as she lost her grip on my hair and we tumbled to the ground together as our magic lessened in the vines. I hardly felt the pain of striking the ground. Libeth grunted.

"What did you do?" She choked out crawling towards me as the spirits slowly began to fade, faeries bursting from the flowers to settle all around us.

"Vipers wrath is very potent;" I murmured finally able to relax. "it can numb just about anything. I have a blade made of it actually…"

"You didn't cut me," she grumbled laying down beside me.

"No," I smirked, "But I dipped my blade in my tea while you weren't looking. It takes longer but still just as effective."

"You drank it too," Libeth murmured resting her head on my shoulder as she lost the remaining use of her limbs.

"Yeah…I drank the whole cup really…"

"How were you able to fight me at all?" Libeth questioned softly as the numbness fully set in.

My eyes sparkled with mirth, "Sheer will and determination." I choked out through numb lips, I could no longer feel the pain in my throat or anywhere else for that matter.

"Why…" The last word she could speak, her throat likely going numb thereafter.

"Tied…we'll stay together." Her body shook with laughter she couldn't release I closed my eyes smiling on the inside. It could have gone so many ways, I could have won before the numbness set in, it could have hit me first which it did and she could have won. Stalling had been the hardest part listening for that soft barely distinguishable song. And then just when I thought I couldn't struggle through the growing numbness Libeth had felt it too. The twilight peonies my little signal to myself that I could stop fighting it.

One sip to my entire cup, it was perhaps the hardest sparring match I'd ever fought. Hardly able to control my magic or movements, taking a beating I would usually be able to easily avoid. All for what, for the sake of friendship I suppose. Though Libeth wouldn't have held it against me if I'd won, she wanted us to stay together and now whether we go on or not she'll have gotten what she wanted and I was okay with that.

I felt the gentle brush of warmth on my cheek and opened my eyes, the only thing I could still control on my body, to find Adri hovering above me in all her glory. She looked as beautiful as always. Right now she was shaking her head at me mirth sparkling in the depths of her twilight orbs, turning the lavender flakes into shinning stars. "Idiot," She murmured softly my lips might have twitched but I couldn't tell before I closed my eyes again. For once I didn't argue, it had been a very stupid thing to do, but it was worth it and for the rest of my life regardless of what any one said against it. I would remember the mirth and happiness in Libeth's eyes sacrifice and reply that it was worth it, because to me it was and that's all that mattered.

Chapter 13
If You Let Me

I woke to find my right arm completely numb and my throat aching worse than it had been the night before. I raised my hand to my throat and closed my eyes as the warmth of my magic filled me. In my mind's eye I could see magic in the shape of glowing vines pushing the blood along ridding me of the bruise and then reinforcing the skin and muscle making it stronger, speeding up the healing process until the burning pain faded to nearly nothing just a small twinge gone by the time I dropped my hand and opened my eyes. I looked towards my numb arm to find Adri curled against me, head resting on my chest bare save for the band I wore to cover my breasts. Her arm lay slung across my waist hand curling over my hip. I was surprised I hadn't noticed the weight of her before, reinforcing the fact that in my mind she wasn't as heavy as she thought or others claimed her to be.

She looked younger asleep, her face free of stress, her wise eyes hidden beneath the cover of her eyelids, her body lax. Safe…the Princess felt safe, I stroked my fingers through the earth and sand strands that curled around her face, she did not so much as twitch. Hesitantly I pressed a gentle kiss to her brow stiffening slightly when she shifted before relaxing again, sighing softly in her sleep, a breath of cool air gusting across the heated skin of my chest. I relaxed heart slowing as I finally took in the fact that we were not in the infirmary, or my room for that matter. The walls were murals green things growing across the expanse of them, vines, trees, flowers any flower, any bloom, any tree you could think to name was there on the walls, on the ceiling all growing together in harmony. Some of the flowers held fairies, the glowing shadows of small bodies hidden within buds near ready to bloom, some were already free, fluttering around the trees looking splendidly happy and carefree.

There were centaurs, their coats coming in every shade one could find on a horse, from black to silver, from dapple to roan, chestnut, bay and any other one could think of. Their human halves just as varied. I saw a female that resembled the healers of my people, with brown skin and short hair cut in a specific way, her eyes were silver like my mother's her ears pointed and tipped with fur the color of her coat, she wore a vest for modesty and it was uniquely designed to mold over her chest. It was said that none had ever seen a centaur in Angileri because they hid behind human skins and at times I wondered why something so magical would ever wish to appear human. No I felt perhaps they had left us, like the giants or hid from us as the older Fae do. There stood a giant, hiding behind an ancient giant's spine all you could see was the bristles of a beard on his jaw, the edge of his nose and the glint of his eye and perhaps his hair near about mixing with the canopy of the tree he stood behind. A dragon flew across the ceiling shimmering blue and green like the sea, flying beside a griffin every red a human could dare name and perhaps a few one couldn't. A moon shown on part of these fanciful images and the sun shown on others. The longer I looked the more that I could see, but the most prominent theme was green, the setting a forest that resembled paradise to me. I could probably stare all day and never grow tired.

The furniture in the room was a golden cream color so that it stood out, the wooden floorboards near about black in color, a small table sat on either side of the bed. The one to my right holding the Heir's crown, the one closest to me holding a change of clothing, a pitcher of water and an empty glass. There was a window directly across from me, open now, revealing the lightening sky, I could hear birds chirping as they woke with the dawn. Another window on the opposite side of the room remained closed, curtains drawn to keep out the light. The door was a distance past the end of the bed beyond a little sitting area with a couch a few comfy chairs and a coffee table that held a chess set, one of the finest I'd ever seen, all of the

pieces set up so that one could play at any moment. The door like the floor was made of a dark wood, intricate vines carved into its face.

Much thought had gone into this rooms' construction, my gaze once more fell on the Princess, sleeping peacefully in my arms. I twitched the fingers of my right hand grimacing at the feel of pins and needles prickling along my arm as blood flowed. I tried to free my arm only to have her Highness burrow more snuggly against me murmuring incoherently against the skin resting above my heart. I chuckled softly realizing that I would be going nowhere unless I decided to wake her. I gazed out the window just beginning to brighten with the dawn of a new day, before closing my eyes shifting until I could at least feel my arm before drifting off to sleep with the Princess' scent filling my lungs bringing peace to my dreams.

The feel of someone's fingers trailing along my throat startled me into wakefulness, causing me to act before I even opened my eyes. I shot up catching hold of their hand before flipping them onto their back ignoring the startled yelp as I pinned them firmly to the bed beneath me. Too late I realized that I no longer had my blade and that the only person that could have touched me, unless someone had entered the room while we slept, which I'd have heard not used to this unfamiliar setting, would be the Princess. I opened my eyes now fully awake to find Adri flushed and breathless now thoroughly pinned beneath me. "My apologizes Highness I had not expected someone to touch me while I slept."

The Princess flushed a deeper shade of red, "Your throat was bruised last night, I woke to find it healed and I was curious. I did not think and so I apologize." She murmured sheepishly.

"No harm done…" I replied still holding her arms pinned above her head feeling overly warm as I gazed at her breasts now straining against the fabric of her shirt with each breath she took. Her breathing grew more erratic as I held her, heat pooling low in my gut.

"Gardener." My eyes snapped to her face, she shuddered beneath me, eyes heavy lidded and dark with…desire? "You can release me now."

I blinked freeing her hands slowly as I took a deep breath coming back to myself, I shifted off of her ignoring the heat in my loins and how good she felt beneath me. Goddess I rubbed my hand over my face before stroking my fingers through my hair to find vines still intermingled with dark strands. No wonder it hadn't fallen into my face or gotten in the way in the past few hours. I pulled them free, calling them to my hands with my magic before wrapping them around each other in a little ball. I placed the mass of green on the bedside table dark strands drifting into my face now free of vines.

"I…" I didn't know what to say.

"You were just waking," Her Highness placed a soothing hand on my shoulder causing me to look up into her smiling face, we were the same height sitting down. "All is well between us."

I sighed nodding my head, not wanting to explain that I'd been wide awake since I'd felt her fingers drifting across my throat. "Where am I?" I asked shifting until I could rest my back against the headboard. The loose green trousers I wore weren't mine, I poured myself a glass of water drinking slowly closing my eyes as the cool water soothed my dry throat now free of pain.

"These are my private quarters, my real ones…They once belonged to my father." She finished a little reminiscent of time long past. "The consort is given a room before the wedding to uphold tradition," Her Highness explained. "The monarch and consort are not allowed to lie with each other until the wedding." Adri chuckled at the look on my face. "It's just tradition…Rhyme." She hesitated before speaking my name, smiling bashfully. "They do share bodies beforehand to make sure the chemistry is true, just not beds a week prior to the wedding." The Princess shifted closer leaning forward until her lips rested warm and wet against my ear. I held my breath, "I have heard from the servants that it makes the wedding night all

the more pleasurable." I shivered at the tingling sensation her words trailed along the shell of my ear pulling away to collect myself.

"Whose trousers am I wearing…where is my blade and my pouch?" I asked after a moment of charged silence. The Princess sighed, shifting until the space between us was larger, allowing me to relax.

"The trousers are your brother's he insisted you would be more comfortable in them, he brought a change of clothing for you as well and beneath your shirt lay your pouch and your blade. My mother did not think it safe to leave you in the infirmary or your rooms after the small party of seasoned soldiers found the Shades we left in the forest all dead." I snapped to attention gazing into the shadowy pools of now somber eyes.

"I killed but one." I breathed as if she did not already know.

"I recall," She countered wryly. "Their throats were slit, every last one…even the one you'd already killed, to be sure no doubt."

"Someone knew…" I murmured thoughtfully.

"Or someone was waiting for us to leave." Adri countered.

"I would have heard…" I furrowed my brow while she looked on curiously waiting for an explanation. "The green…the plants. They speak to me. Always. I would have heard if someone were hiding unless they hid far beyond my reach. Far beyond the confines of the forest."

"Perhaps they were cloaked with magic as our attackers were?" The Princess offered tone thoughtful.

"I would have known." I found my eyes straying from her face to the thin fabric still covering her chest. "Their magic means nothing, it is not natural to the forest and so I would have known." I pulled my gaze back to her face. "The forest goes silent when there are predators about, whether visible or not I would have known." I finished remembering how quiet the green had become in my mind. How alone I'd felt...I did not quite understand how others could live with such profound silence. How very lonely it must be for them.

"And so we must conclude that...?" She gazed at me curiously waiting to see if I had anything to say on the matter.

"That someone in the palace played a hand in this, and they did not want to take the chance that someone would talk. Someone in the Tournament perhaps...it could be anyone. It truly is the perfect time to try for a kidnapping or assassination." I finished quietly.

"The Queen thinks it's a culmination of things coming together, that more than one enemy is at large here. The land is restless..." The Princess rubbed her face tiredly.

"It has been restless since your father died and grew more so when your brother failed his Trials. You have passed yours and for that I am grateful but there are so many others in power who do not see this for the blessing that it is." I shook my head. "Many who wish that your brother had been Heir or your sister. Those that have their own agendas." I huffed disgusted at the greedy nature often found in man.

"Sounds like politics," Adri commented seemingly unfazed by it all. "There is always someone trying to twist the system to their liking. More than one Councilor has been accused of such things...all men I might add, chosen before my mother came to power."

"Chosen by your grandmother? Who still lives, some say, with the dragons...I remember meeting her in my youth a very stern woman. I cannot see her appointing men so caught up in their greed." Her Highness shook her head smiling softly.

"Power corrupts people..."

"Yes and some would say that absolute power corrupts absolutely," I countered. "And yet all the women I have met in your family are what I expect royalty to be. Loyal to their people, just in the face of evil, generous when the land is failing…Royalty in some places is dictated by birth and in Angileri it is that but at the same time you have to pass your Trials. It makes for great rulers…"

"Not always," Adri countered smiling softly.

I chuckled, "Name one that wasn't." She shrugged unable think of a Queen that hadn't been great in their own way since taking the throne. "Exactly."

"You are quite the smart…" I cleared my throat giving her a look for daring to speak such vulgar language. The Princess laughed. "Every time I find myself about to curse, you stop me. Is there a reason for this Gardener?" She asked curiously shifting closer.

"I feel it wouldn't sound right coming from someone quite as articulate as yourself, you're to be Queen, no need to shock the masses with profanity." I spoke softly staring at the wall instead of her face or lower.

Her Highness cupped my cheek turning my face until my eyes met hers. "I would not dare speak such language where others could hear, but we are alone and I feel comfortable enough to say such things in your company. I have only just reached my twenty-first year after all. Sometimes I would like to act my own age, say what I want. Make my own mistakes without the Queendom being involved." Adri stroked her fingers along my jaw before trailing them down my neck causing me to shiver slightly.

"I really don't think…"

"Gardener…?" I gazed into her eyes waiting for her to speak. "Stop thinking." Goddess, she kissed me again and this time was better than the first. Deeper somehow, I wrapped my arms around her waist practically pulling her into my lap as our mouths moved together in a sensual dance. The Princess tugged playfully at my hair causing me to moan softly tightening my hold on her. She pulled away slightly not knowing if I moaned in pleasure or pain. "Did I hurt you?"

"No." I pressed her down on the bed devouring her lips slowly while she arched against me, clutching firmly at my back. I felt dizzy listening to her moaning for me, the way her breath feathered across my face. The feel of her hands trailing fire along my back, her soft ample breasts pressing against mine, the thump of her heart beating wildly against my chest. I rubbed my hands up and down her sides teasingly as we kissed lost in the taste of each other.

Goddess knows how far we'd have gotten if the green hadn't begun to clamor in my mind. I pulled away distracted just as a knock sounded on the door. "Adri love, it's your mother." The Princess sat up so abruptly that I fell to the floor. I scrambled to my feet while she fixed her hair and straightened her clothes. Her cheeks were still flushed, her lips bruised and her eyes dark. I cupped her face in my hands tracing my thumb lightly along her lips as my hands glowed with my magic.

When the Queen stepped into the room I was straightening my shirt sipping lightly from a glass of water standing beside the bedside table, if my hair looked a little mussed that could be contributed to the fact that I'd just slept on it without having braided it. The Princess smiled softly at her mother, breathing normally despite her breathlessness. If the Queen was at all suspicious she didn't show it and for that I was grateful, my heart was racing faster than it ever had before.

"It is good to see you heathy and whole after such a display of power and prowess, truly my daughter would be lucky to have someone such as you in her bed." I coughed choking on my water while the Princess blushed a shade of red I'd only seen in roses before burying her face in her hands.

"Mother!" She exclaimed exasperated while I tried to catch my breath.

Her Majesty smiled at our reactions to her statement. "I am looking out for my daughter's best interest." She waved her hand in my direction while facing the Princess excluding me from the conversation despite the fact that I could hear every word. "I know this woman would love you, she would cherish you in and outside of the bedroom, she would protect you." The Queen looked at me then eyes full of mirth. "I do not know how much you know of my daughter's feelings Gardener but she would not allow your head to rest anywhere short of her bed. Not even your brother could tell her different. It was quite interesting to see my daughter put her brother in his place for the first time in her life…"

"A sight I wish I had been awake to see." I added brow raised slightly.

Her Majesty laughed softly. "I will remember it for the rest of my life," She stroked her fingers through Adri's hair. "I did not want her wasting her time with telling you, so I did. Now you can recuperate or you can remain friends and she can move on. A Queen does not pine…"

"Mother I am not Queen." Adri murmured softly resting against her mother's side as she stroked her hair soothingly.

"Yet," Her Majesty and I spoke as one, causing a smile to appear on her Highness' face.

"I am not Queen yet," she added with exasperation.

"I will not insert myself further into your relationship whatever it may be at this time, friends or more. That is not why I came." Her Majesty sobered more Queen than mother, Adri sat up straight expression no doubt as sober as my own.

"The Shade impersonators were found dead, every last one and sadly with all the commotion that day, many suitors trampling through the forest we could find no leads. Indeed, the killer planned their escape well. All the Royal Guards are on high alert, the suitors are being watched more carefully by the soldiers and the Sol-Lea is leading the investigation. I wish we could end the Tournament now, but there are too many Leaders here, and we cannot be seen as weak." The Queen sighed. "I have heard that the Void is spreading on top of it all and the Council is divided unwilling to believe that Adri has passed her Trials without proof of her gift."

"Why would she lie?" I questioned blood boiling at the audacity of men.

"After you're Trials something is different, a small sign to prove you've made it, that you've survived and will forever be changed. My eyes were once brown…before my Trials." Her Majesty stroked her fingers through her daughter's hair, earth and sand. "Though many in the court think it a fashion statement Adri's hair will grow earth brown and a blond so pale it could almost be white until the day she dies. The blond streaks her proof that she passed the Trials." The Queen turned to me, "That's how I knew without her ever having to speak a word after she stumbled out of that portal pale as a sheet and shaking like a leaf. It is not a well know thing. Truly only a Queen knows, a Queen and the daughter that succeeds her so that she too may know when her child steps through the portal if they have passed or failed. You cannot lie. As well I have seen her powers." The Queen shook her head. "My son has gone too far in his hatred, he has poisoned the Council small bits at a time, and now I no longer have the power to be rid of them. He is weakening our Queendom and dividing my people and I do not know how it has gotten this far. Where men ask proof of their future Queen instead of trusting in her loyalty to the people."

"They see what your son wishes them to see Majesty and nothing more, they see the power that he has promised them. Your son has chosen his path and it grows darker the longer we allow him to walk it unhindered." I added solemnly.

"He will not outgrow this…"

"Not without help and very good thorough beating, your son needs to be brought low Majesty and I would be glad to do it for you." I offered expression a mask of indifference.

"You think you can change him, a man full grown now set in his ways?" The Queen asked sounding just a bit skeptical.

"He is hurting, he is spoiled, a brat having a tantrum, wanting something he thinks should be his. He gets others to do what he cannot, he is a poisonous snake that has yet to truly bite. His hands are soft, and unmarred, if he has struck a woman other than me I would be surprised. For now, he is all talk, Prince Eris...he could change that. He could make your son truly dangerous.

"I will fight him and beat him, without remorse, you will offer no aid, you will say his punishment is just for what he has done. The Council will learn, the men who challenged you will be cowed, in good faith you will give them their proof and then you will get rid of the ones strongest in their displeasure of your daughter and you will replace them with people you trust. None will question you in this, and you will have killed two birds with but one stone."

Her Majesty and her daughter stared at me as if they were truly seeing me for the first time, the silence stretched long between us before the Queen spoke, "What of my son?"

"I know someone who will love him well Majesty and they will not ever let him get away with such injustices again." I spoke softly voice sincere.

The Queen turned to her daughter and a look passed between them, before she turned back to me. "Will this be a public display or a private one?"

"As Sorel often says, he is still a Prince, I will not shame him before his people, only those that matter to him. Call your Council, a few select noblemen who you know for sure are on your side, bring forth all your Gardeners and but a few servants you can trust, when word spreads because it will we want it to be the right version of events. We will turn your son into a garden snake, harmless to us, but dangerous to rodents that lurk in the garden." Once I had finished the Queen once more turned to her daughter.

"Keep this one in your life, not many see the world as she does through unbiased eyes. She will offer good Council." The Queen said once more speaking as if I were not there.

Adri chuckled, "I will do my best mother."

"When should this punishment take place?" Her Majesty asked coming back to the matter at hand.

"You are Queen whenever you decide." I said not unkindly.

"How are you feeling?" She asked randomly.

"I am a bit tired still." I offered honestly.

"Eat, rest…cuddle and speak with my daughter," Adri buried her face in her hands again. "Tonight I will enact punishment on my son for all the trouble he has caused and I want you to be as strong as you possibly can. Tomorrow the Queen's Tournament continues." Her Majesty left us then without further hints or instructions.

"Your mother is not a subtle woman when it comes to affairs of the heart," I said after I was sure the Queen would not hear me.

"I suppose she got tired of hearing me talk about you," Adri offered cheeks flushed with embarrassment.

"How often did you speak of me?" I questioned climbing onto the bed.

"Often enough for my mother to take matters into her own hands," Her Highness said wryly shaking her head.

I chuckled softly, "She approves of me?"

"Could you not tell?" Her voice was filled with exasperation, "Love matters more to my mother than politics."

"You love me?" I spoke softly feeling a little breathless.

"I would not go that far," I relaxed slightly. "But I could in time...if you let me." I leaned forward and placed a kiss on the tip of her nose.

"Perhaps we should lay here and cuddle for a while?" I questioned patting the bed softly before laying down.

Her Highness laid down beside me snuggling close against my chest, I wrapped my arms around her enjoying the way her softness molded against mine. "This is nice."

I laid a kiss on her brow sighing softly in content, "I would not mind this."

"What do you mean?" Adri asked murmuring against my chest.

"Spending every morning of my life just like this..."

"Why Gardener we haven't even shared bodies and you're already proposing marriage who knew I was that good. Was it the feel of my tongue in your mouth...or the slight tugging of your hair? I didn't know you were into pain." Her Highness countered playfully making me laugh until tears streamed from my eyes.

"Goddess Adri that's not what I meant." She pushed up on her arms gazing down at me with a serious expression.

"What?" I questioned sobering quickly.

"You said my name again." I relaxed smiling softly.

"Is that a problem, should I not have done that?" I asked a bit unsure of myself.

"No," Adri stroked her fingers through my hair. "No it's fine. I like the way you say my name. It's different."

"Is it?" I murmured curiously eyes drifting closed as she continued to stroke her fingers through my hair.

"Yes, you say it with a bit of an accent. I enjoy hearing you speak my name." I wrapped my arm around her pulling her down to rest against me once more while she continued to play with my hair.

"Adri…" I murmured softly rubbing her back as my eyes grew heavy.

"Yes?" I opened my eyes to find myself lost in the twilight orbs that belonged to her.

"I could fall in love with you too…if you let me." The Princess smiled the brightest smile I had ever had the pleasure of seeing.

"I might just let you Gardener…if you try hard enough." I chuckled softly before allowing my eyes to close once more. Though I fought it, sleep claimed me soon after.

Chapter 14
Lialey's Gift

I left Adri curled into the warmth I left behind, exiting her quarters to find two Guards manning the door. I tipped my head in respect before going off to find one of my fellow Gardeners. I found myself not surprised at all when Libeth happened upon me first. She never could resist a bite to eat.

"You're awake?" She exclaimed dropping the pastry in her hand in favor of giving me a hug.

I hugged her back just as firmly resting my head atop hers chuckling softly as she hummed against me. "Yes I woke earlier but still felt drained so I slept a bit more. When did you wake up?"

Libeth pulled away gently tracing her finger over the stitches still marring my brow, when she pulled away the little bit of cloth holding my skin together came too and I sighed as the small ache that I hadn't even realized I'd felt until it was gone, left me. "It has been bothering me since yesterday morning." Libeth explained with a shrug. "And I woke not too long ago, well rested and ravenous."

"I'd forgotten about it to be honest or else I'd have healed it myself, and I'm glad I found you even if you weren't the Gardener I was looking for you'll be able to help me find him much quicker seeing as you two are together more often than not…"

"You're looking for Eden?" She questioned before I even had the chance to supply his name.

I smiled, it was no wonder people often mistook them for a couple, they knew each other like the back of their own hand. "Yes her Majesty will be having a…meeting of sorts this evening and I need to talk to him before hand to iron out some key details."

"I get the feeling you're not telling me everything," Libeth chuckled, "But that's nothing new. You'll tell me in time or I'll figure it out on my own. I haven't seen Eden around the palace. Rosen has issued a day of rest for the lot of us…it makes me a little antsy to think that not a one of us are in the gardens, but she's the boss." She tried to shrug off her unease, "I'd think since he's not on the palace grounds that he's out in the city of Anear either frequenting the Green Sprout catching up with old friends or at Lialey's Inn entertaining the children of passing merchants." Libeth slapped me on the shoulder before picking up her pastry. "Either way you're headed into Anear without me sadly I've been ordered to not leave the palace…Not that I'm complaining." She hummed her delight at the delicious sweet while I shook my head and went in search of my brother… I'd need my horse and no one took a horse from Reason's stables without his say so not even the Queen. It was a security precaution that no one minded at all. How could you if even the Queen abided by the rules.

After a small argument about my wellbeing Reason let me take Carina for a ride in the city, though he grumbled about stubbornness as I rode out I ignored him. If I hadn't needed to find Eden I'd have stayed in the palace, the city of Anear was a big place and I had never much enjoyed exploring. I checked the Green Sprout first, if you were a plant mage and needed some help, information or just wanted to see a friendly face this was the place to go. I had hoped that I would find Eden there, ending my search for the big lug but I had no such luck.

I took a deep breath before mounting my horse, "Carina," I murmured leaning against her strong neck stomach aching suddenly as nerves set in. "Do you think she remembers?" I breathed heavily closing my eyes as nervous sweat beaded on my brow. "It's been five years; I was young perhaps she's forgotten my face." I mumbled into her mane trying to convince myself more than anything else.

Lialey... I hoped it wasn't the same woman I remembered, more than one woman carried that name surely it was just a strange coincidence. I grimaced thinking it very unlikely, I had learned that more often than not fortune was not with me. Goddess why did the past have to catch up with me now? I received no answer, but I hadn't expected one.

I found Eden in the common room sitting by the fireplace glowing softly with magic and not warmth, helping to illuminate the room but not causing unnecessary heat. A blessing, because it was scorching outside, Angileri's growing seasons were hot and long, and humid more often than not. Surrounding him were several children, I inched closer sticking to the shadows while I looked for a feminine face that I'd tried for the last five years to forget. I'd blame Arely, I would truly but though I was hurting the decision was mine, at the time though I couldn't think...I didn't think. She'd asked me to do something and I had, I'd acted without thought of my actions.

And now...now I gazed on a child's face so familiar it was almost startling. I took a deep breath struggling to draw air, I rushed from the building ignoring Eden's startled look as I made my escape. I leaned against Carina trying to catch my breath as my heart raced, my hands quivering as I clutched at her mane. What had I done...what had I done that night so long ago...

"Rhyme..." I started turning to find Eden behind me hands raised as if he were trying to sooth a frightened horse. I took a breath trying to calm myself as I leaned against my mare taking comfort in her presence.

"I had wanted to speak to you..."

"When were you going to tell us?" For once I could not look him in the eyes.

"Tell you what?" I questioned hair escaping from the leather thong, I could never seem to tie right, to fall into my face.

"You had a child…" I shook my head brushing my hair from my face so that I could meet his accusations dead on.

"I didn't…" He stared at me for a long time trying to piece it together without any of the proper information.

"Your brother…" I shook my head.

"Explain…" He stepped closer gazing at me beseechingly. "Please? For once explain a part of your life so that I can understand, because you have said many times you are unbroken, but that girl…that girl in there looks so much like you as a child that it's uncanny."

"I was…I had come to the city just days after the Sol-Lea had left me without a goodbye. I was hurting and I wasn't thinking straight…"

"You slept with someone…" I shook my head again.

"No…" the memories came rushing back. "I did what I do best Eden. I healed someone." Eden stared at me confused and so I explained to him everything that had transpired that day a small eternity in the past.

*****

I was sitting at an Inn, the name of which I could not remember, some unsavory place of which I had no business I'm sure, but I hadn't wanted to be found or disturbed and I suppose my reputation was enough that no one had bothered me. I hadn't thought about it at the time. I was not drunk, my heart was hurting and I drank I'm sure I drank my fair share, but I had never had an ale or wine that actually effected my system one of the perks of being a plant mage of such high caliber so I cannot in good conscious use that as my excuse.

No I was hurting and I wasn't really thinking straight…I'd been enjoying dinner. Well I was eating though everything seemed pretty tasteless, I couldn't say if the food was bland or if my emotional state didn't allow me to taste the food. Probably a bit of both, I was eating my meal when a commotion started. A man came racing down the stairs, shouting, "I need a Healer! Someone…Anyone call a Healer!" He rushed towards the Inn keeper, near hysterical still shouting. "My sister…I came to visit her…I found her room broken into someone…someone hurt her. She's pregnant and there's so much blood." He gripped the man by the front of his shirt.

"If she dies so do you!" He growled threateningly, the Inn keeper took his threat very seriously, as well he should have, he didn't look to be joking, he beckoned his son forward and sent him in search of a Healer. He told him to run as fast as he could.

I did not finish my meal, instead when the man raced back up the stairs I followed him at a more sedate pace. It was not hard to find the room in which his sister had been staying the door was wide open, and several other guests lingered about no small hint of concern written on their faces. I stepped into the room and of course I was noticed, my height and my coloring ensured it. The man, Zayez I'd later find out, kneeled beside his sister clutching her hand between his begging her to keep fighting. She was pale, her face bruised, her brow drenched in sweat. She squeezed his hand weakly while I took in the blood soaking through her dress. I knew even if she lived the baby would not, she wasn't far enough along for it to even have a chance outside the womb.

I stepped forward and Zayez stood, "I am a Healer," I murmured softly. He shook my hand firmly and told me his name, sharing his sister's as well before pulling me forward.

"Surely you can save her?" I could hear the hope in his voice, and the desperation.

I glanced down at the woman slowly bleeding out before us, "I can save her…but the child will be lost…"

"No…" a murmured word had never sounded so loud. I stroked Lialey's hair from her face hands glowing softly with magic, slowly the bruises marring her appearance faded away. She sighed softly relaxing beneath my ministrations.

"Leave us?" I turned to her brother. "I will do all I can for your sister."

Zayez took my hands in his, "Thank you." He spoke softly before leaving the room and closing the door behind him.

I took a seat on the bed beside her resting my hands over her belly, I closed my eyes and sat still for a moment exploring the damage done to her body with my gift. A short time later I opened my eyes and gazed down at Lialey to find her gazing back at me. "Your child is gone…"

She shook her head tears in her eyes, "No…"

I tried to explain further but she would not let me and time was of the essence. I felt so helpless. "Do something…you're a Healer do something anything to save my baby."

"Your child is gone…"

"Do something…please…" She passed out soon after from blood loss, tears staining her cheeks, pulse weak, sweat cooling. I am no Goddess despite what others may say at times. I cannot bring back the dead. I am a Healer and a plant mage and so I did what I did best I healed her. I healed her and I sat looking on her rosy cheeks thinking about the child she'd lost…I thought of her accusations, I was a Healer and I had saved her but I'm sure when she woke she would not be grateful. I traced my hands over her abdomen before closing my eyes, I took a piece of my magic and I pressed it into her skin.

After all I could use nothing else, I am a plant mage after all and I help things grow and so twice over I did what I was good at. Once finished I stood tracing my hands over my mouth as I'd realized what I'd done. The level of mastery that I must have for it to be possible…I stepped away from the bed with shaking hands. Before turning and walking to the door, I opened it to find her brother siting on the floor opposite of the door quickly waking from a light doze.

He scrambled to his feet realizing who it was that stood before him. "Is she well?"

I bowed my head in a nod, "As well as can be expected for someone who has suffered much in such a short span of time."

"And the baby…"

I took a deep breath heart thundering in my chest. "I cannot say. Only time will tell." I left him then accepting his heartfelt thanks before proceeding down the stairs. I walked passed the common room in a daze standing in front of the Inn gazing out into the night without actually seeing anything. Once I'd come back to myself I found my horse in the small stable used for guests and rode her straight through the night back to the palace. I had acted without thought and I did not at first know it would work but I had heard what I would consider a seed…I had heard it sing softly to me as well I had healed others before of much worse injuries and none had left me quite so drained as what I'd done that night. I spent the next few years trying to forget…it did not work half as well as I wished it to.

*****

Eden stared at me for a long time after I'd finished, his expression completely blank, he opened his mouth to speak but no words came out and truly I did not blame him. I stood waiting for him to find his voice. "What you did… Rhyme… the level of skill to do what I think you've done. Rosen could not match it if she tried a million times. You did what birthing healers do and still you walked out of that room as if you'd done nothing at all. How…"

"Healing others is not as draining as healing myself, the body wants to be healed after all and I just help speed up the process. As for how I did what I did…I just thought of it in terms of plants Eden and I did not for a moment think it would work but at the end of the day I could have told myself I tried and slept well at night. I sped up her cycle…and then I used my gift and whispered to the egg…the seed inside of her. It was so simple to ask it to grow, like any seed that is its purpose and it sang to me Eden." I gazed back at him heart aching tears streaming my face, "She sang to me and it was the most beautiful song I've ever had the pleasuring of hearing in my life."

"What you've done…is it against the law?" He asked after a brief moment of silence.

I shook my head, "No, I could have done nothing without her consent, her body was willing. I have been taught many times an unwilling host will not bear fruit, she wanted a child and so her body allowed me to aid in the process. Her words though spoken in desperation were a formality and they were enough if viewed in any form of the law."

"Does your brother know…does the Queen?"

"I saw no reason to tell either, though I aided in the process the child is not mine but hers." I offered softly.

"Have you known this whole time?" I sighed softly once more tying my hair back, needing to do something with my hands. I pushed from Carina giving her a solid pat before moving from her side.

"She speaks to me…as the plants do. Like so many of them I helped her grow and she will always carry a small bit of my magic inside her."

"Will she grow to be as strong as you?" Eden ask voice full of curiosity.

"Her mother's ancestors are of the trees, the closest to nature you can get, I cannot say for sure what her gift will be, but she'll have a bit of plant magic in her no matter what path her gift takes."

"Lialey's ancestors are tree sprites?" He questioned incredulous…

I gave him a look I usually reserved for my brother that adeptly questioned his intelligence. "You come to the Inn often enough to have seen the woman yes? Or are you blind to her altogether foreign appearance?"

"I honestly thought the moss-like color of her hair was a fashion statement and a lovely one besides…Does it…" He hesitated for a moment before committing to his question. "Does it feel like moss as well?"

I thought back to that night, soothingly stroking her hair from her face while she lay on the brink of death and I answered in a voice so soft as to almost not be heard. "No…" I met his eyes for a time and he looked away first. "It doesn't feel like moss at all, though it is soft. As soft as the down on a new born chick."

Eden ran his fingers through his hair, "How have you kept this from us all these years…"

"Simple. I never went looking for the past." Eden stared at me then.

"Weren't you at all curious, aren't you now?" He inquired voice raised slightly.

I huffed bowing my head smiling wryly. "Of course I'm curious, who wouldn't be. I have heard her voice, I have seen her from a distance and I have done all that I can to ensure that they both have a good life, but that's all I'll ever do Eden. It's not my place to do more."

She's your child…"

"No." I said firmly. "She's not. If any other had did what I had done it would be no different, the fact the child looks like me and carries my magic changes nothing…"

Eden gripped me by the shoulders startling me into silence.

"Rhyme it changes everything…normally when a Healer aids in the conception process the child comes out resembling their mother, very rarely does the child hold characteristics of the Healer aiding in said conception. That girl, is a perfect blend of each of you." He shook me slightly, "You feel her Rhyme, you're standing here telling me about her song, about her voice that I'm sure never ceases and at the same time you're telling me she isn't yours but she is. You know she is…"

"I have no right…"

"You have every right and I'm sure if you just spoke with Lialey, whom I've come to know as a lovely woman, that she'd understand and be thankful for the gift you've given her. As well as the opportunity because I know even if she's unaware of where it's coming from that you probably have money sent to her every now and again, a fund she can draw from in her name because that's the type of person you are." I pulled away sighing softly gazing back at the Inn.

"What will I say Eden?" I chuckled shaking my head. "It's been five years…I hardly know the woman."

"And yet you still remember the feel of her hair." My fingers twitched slightly at his words.

"I don't think I'll ever forget it." Eden squeezed my shoulders gently before releasing me.

"If not Lialey than at least speak with the girl…truly Rhyme the resemblance." He shook his head.

I walked beside him back towards the Inn leaving Carina tied to a post beside several other horses. I would not be staying long enough to pay for a stall in the stable. "I will speak with her shortly but afterwards I need you to come with me. It's growing late and there's a small meeting with the Queen we must attend in which I need your help."

"Has something happened at the palace in the short time I've been missing?" He pulled up an extra seat setting it beside his by the fire.

I sat down slowly gazing into the magical flames that carried no heat but illuminated each of us equally. I watched the children approach no doubt interested in continuing whatever story Eden had left off on when he'd gotten up to follow me out. "It can wait until after you've appeased your audience," I offered chuckling softly watching amused as the children stole his attention.

Eden was so gentle and loving despite his size, I don't know how anyone could look him in the eyes and be afraid. More often than not he put you at ease, he made you feel safe. I placed my elbows on my knees before resting my chin in my hands listening attentively to his story while gazing on the face of the child that must be mine.

Her skin was brown, only slightly lighter than mine, she had my face, my expressive brows and cute little nose, the bow that made up her lips and the sharp cheekbones that made her stand out. Her hair though was all Lialey, a dark forest green, that shimmered with lighter strands the color of moss in the fire light. It made it appear as if she were growing a small tree out of her head that fell in swooping waves down to her shoulders. Her eyes were golden brown with an extra ring around the iris that glowed softly in the fire light. Another trait she'd taken from Lialey.

She looked about how I did at the age of five, too tall for my own good and awkward besides. It took me years to grow into my height because every time I thought I was done growing I would sprout up another inch or two. I swear it seemed to me Reason had grown all at once not having to suffer constantly as I did.

What we'd created together was beautiful, I smiled softly when she turned to look at me no doubt sensing my gaze upon her. She stared at me for a long time before blinking…the voices of the plants barely loud enough to hear in the city so far from the green grew a bit louder. One grew focused I recognized it instantly. *Hello…?*

I smiled more fully, *Hello.* I offered back softly not sure if she could hear me. I'd only ever spoken to the plants in such a way.

She smiled, a bright and glorious smile that I will never forget as long as I live. *Mommy has told me so much about you.*

Her voice though young, was clear. I could understand every word and I wondered if perhaps she could articulate so well because we were communicating through our magic and our thoughts and not aloud. I wondered if her voice would sound the same. *Has she?* I questioned curious to know what she meant.

The girl nodded firmly and I chuckled at her enthusiasm, glancing at Eden briefly to see that he was still engrossed in his story. *She says a kind woman saved her…and that I was a gift she left behind in her tummy…* She hesitated briefly expression sad, *because the baby before me could not survive…*

I gasped softly in surprise at her knowledge, while she gazed at me face a solemn mask. No older than four summers I could not fathom where she learned such an expression. *Mommy says you have done many great things to help people and that it kept you so busy you could not come to see us.* I felt tears warm my eyes at such innocence. *Mommy says when I see you…not if because she said eventually you'd come.* I laughed softly at the exasperation so clearly visible on her young face. *She says to tell you thank you. For the gift…for me.* She flashed me that bright smile again, full of joy and exuberance.

I felt tears stream my face and I let them fall. *Tell your Mommy I said your welcome.* She nodded firmly still beaming at me.

I will. Though I think you should... I bit my lip softly considering her words.

How about you tell me your name so when I talk to her it all comes out proper can't keep calling you "the gift" now can I? She giggled softly at that.

My name is Reah, but Mommy calls me Sprout because I refuse to stop growing. I smiled once more at her obvious exasperation.

The double meaning to her nickname was not lost on me. *It was nice meeting you Reah.*

She smiled at me. *It was nice meeting you too. Please talk with Mommy?*

I will. I bowed my head slightly in acknowledgement of her words. Reah turned from me then her voice fading away like all the others, barely an understandable whisper in the back of my mind.

Eden finished his story not soon after and the children wandered off as he stood, bemoaning the fact that story time was over. Reah ran to me quickly wrapping her arms around my waist as I stood. "Thank you…"

I rested my hand lightly on her back while stroking my fingers gently through her hair, just as soft as her mothers. Her voice was softer out loud, her speech a little harder to understand as if her thoughts had shaped themselves into words I understood but perhaps she could not yet say. I had not heard enough from her to tell. "You're welcome Little One." She pulled away shooting me one last beaming smile before running off to play with the other children.

Eden came to stand by my side, "Why do I feel like you did more than listen to me tell stories for the last hour or so?"

I shrugged lips curling slightly, "I have no clue what gave you that idea."

He looked at me as Libeth does when she knows I'm hiding something. "Really now, so Reah just ran up and hugged you for no good reason?"

I rubbed my chin feigning thoughtfulness. "That does appear to be what happened."

Eden raised his hands as if he might strangle the answers out of me while I struggled not to laugh stepping out of his reach…

"Gardener Eden you know I don't abide violence here." I stiffened at the sound of a voice I hadn't heard in over five years.

Eden dropped his hands, expression softening as he glanced at the near panic on my face before turning his attention to the woman behind me. "My apologizes Inn Keeper my companion can be a bit trying at times. I don't believe you two have met."

He took hold of my shoulder turning me gently around, "This is…"

"Gardener Denarii." Lialey supplied before he had a chance to even begin introductions. "We've met before. She saved my life and gave me a gift I have no chance of ever repaying."

"No payment is necessary…I did what I could." She stepped forward taking my hands in hers. I have no idea where Eden got off to so quickly.

"You did more than enough and I will be forever grateful for Reah, as well as the fund you set up to support us, without it I would be in a far different place and for that I'm eternally grateful." Lialey cupped my face in her hands and before I could remotely think to stop her she kissed me, my eyes widened slightly as her lips moved against mine…it was so gentle and sweet. I don't think I could have moved if I tried. When she pulled away I stood motionless not knowing what to do with myself. "I hope I see you again Gardener,

you have no need to fear me I blame you for nothing." She pecked my cheek one final time before walking away talking briefly with all the guests she came in contact with.

"I was not expecting that in the least." Eden murmured as he appeared beside me. I'd have flinched in fright but I did not wish to give him the satisfaction of scaring me a second time.

"Neither was I." I breathed still trying to figure out exactly what had happened.

"She forgave you, claimed you're blameless, thanked you for everything, told you to visit and kissed you all in one breath..." Eden gazed at me a hint of awe in his voice. "Sometimes I wonder if you really aren't the Goddess others claim you be."

I glanced at him unsure of what to say while he tapped his chin thoughtfully. "Not to disrupt your daze or anything but how quick do you think that kiss will get back to her Highness probably growing with the telling besides...?"

I came back to myself so quick I feared for a moment I might faint, "Let us hope it never does." I said as I marched towards the door.

"You do realize keeping this a secret from her will surely not end well, she's bound to find out and then jump to conclusions." Eden speed up trying to keep pace with me. I untied Carina's reins from the post I'd left her near. She butted me in the chest gently welcoming me back.

"I will tell her...though tonight isn't the night for soul bearing. Tonight is the night the Prince pays for all the wrongs he has wrought." I climbed into the saddle before offering Eden my hand.

"What have you gotten yourself into now?" Eden questioned taking my hand, I pulled him up behind me.

I smiled softly as he settled himself wrapping his arms gently around my waist. "The explanation will come later. Her Majesty will tell it best, for now just know that we have a meeting of sorts and before it starts I need you to agree to a favor."

"Sometimes I think you enjoy being mysterious." Eden grumbled softly.

I chuckled softly nudging Carina into a ground eating trot, "Perhaps just a bit." Eden laughed with me. Taking pity, I filled him in on what I needed of him as we rode towards the palace. As I knew he would he agreed to help whole heartedly. I wasn't the only one half in love with royalty after all.

Chapter 15
The Queen's Justice

We all stood gathered around the dais none willing to stand above her Majesty now seated on her throne. It was a rare sight for a Gardener to see the Queen in all her regal glory, despite the fact that our titles equated to that of noblemen, we were not required to attend court. Thank the Goddess for small mercies, Rosen's recap of certain events made it sound quite tedious, time consuming and at times completely unnecessary. On her left on a slightly smaller but no less grand throne sat the Heir, and two her right sat Princess Mariel, the seat beside her empty.

Across from us stood several noble men and women, Lady and Lord something or other, among them I could see several Councilmen, Libeth had brought with her several servants now offering food and drinks to our small party. I shook my head at the offer of wine, it would do nothing to soothe my nerves. Emery and Libeth toasted each other while Eden and I shared a look all too sober. The Prince was announced into the room, Prince Eris beside him, Sir Zeron trailing in their wake. I took a deep breath standing a little straighter.

Princess Mariel stood, stepping down the dais meeting her brother as he came forward, the room grew silent, even the green spoke softly and for that I was grateful. "Brother…you come before the court…" Her voice rang out, he flinched startled as she spanned her hand encompassing us all. "Accused of treason. How do you plead?" Her face was stoic, expressionless and I wondered how I ever mistook her for anything less than she was.

"I plead…" Her Majesty stood and I have never felt so small, she stood above us, of course she did, she stood on a platform, but the feeling that she was so much more than we could ever be had never been stronger than in that moment. Wine dribbled down Emery's chin and he did nothing to stop it. My heart raced in my chest as we all waited with baited breath for our Queen to speak. This…was royalty.

"You come before the court accused of treason and you stand as if you are untouchable, your choices are few. Very few, because regardless of what you say evidence is stacked against you." Slowly, the Queen descended her dais, coming to stand before her son, no one moved a muscle. "Bow before your Queen Sorel, she is not feeling gracious." Her voice, filled the throne room, thunder on a silent night, I hugged myself as he dropped to his knees before the woman he called mother, but at this moment, that woman was nowhere in sight. Libeth drew closer to me, the nobles held tight to their flutes of wine, the servants had suddenly become scarce and I had never seen so many guards appear out of thin air.

"You have undermined your sister's power, the Council questions her claims to rule, they question her word." She paced away from him, looking into the eyes of each and every one of her Council members. Every one of them turned their gaze away. "They question MY WORD?!" I think the entire room flinched, Libeth completely spilt her wine, Sorel smartly remained silent watching the Queen, face pale as he knelt waiting for justice. I did not doubt that it would come.

"They question their Queen, they believe that the Trials have chosen wrong, that it should have been you or your younger sister. You encourage these thoughts…this sense of power, the privilege. Claiming all will be different once a man once more sits the throne." Her rage was palpable. Goddess I was glad I had never had such righteous fury directed at me. "What could you give them Sorel? What have you promised my people, that has corrupted them so? What promises have you made to make men commit such atrocious acts. Willing to believe the word of a foreign Prince over the Heir

herself." There were several gasps of shock, more than one Council member looked away in shame, all of them men.

"I will tell you what you could give them, if by some stretch of the imagination you became King." She gazed out across her nobles, before turning back to her son. "Nothing… you know nothing about the land or the people, you have worked for no one. Not once have you apprenticed yourself, you know no trades, you play no instruments. You cannot even hold a sword or throw a proper punch. All that you are is because of me and though you were born with your title. It is but a word…" Her Majesty glanced at me when she said those words. "A word I can easily take away."

The Queen beckoned Rosen forward, she stepped up beside her, "Prince Sorel of Angileri…" She scoffed at his lack of other titles. "I hereby strip you of your title and your crown. Like a servant you will have to earn it back." I blinked not having expected that in the least. Rosen took his circlet from his head and while we watched vines mangled it beyond repair. Her Majesty turned from him then, walking back up her dais and taking a seat, Rosen held up the ball that had once been his crown, waiting. Adri descended in her mother's place, looking larger than life. A near perfect imitation of her mother, she took the ball of mangled silver and held it in her hands.

And then as she had just a few days prior she breathed fire, while everyone watched burning metal dripped through her fingers sizzling once it hit the marble floor. When she gazed out at her people her eyes glowed two slitted orbs… dragon eyes. Adri breathed fire until his crown was nothing more than a searing puddle cooling on the floor. Once done, she stepped back and without speaking a word she climbed the dais and took her seat at her mother's side.

"Proof for those unwilling to believe my word," The Queen explained smiling wryly.

"Sorel, I present to you two choices and you are lucky that you have a choice at all." Her Majesty growled, he gazed up at her pale faced, shaken to his core. "The first is exile, you may leave here, with the clothes on your back and nothing else, without horse, or carriage with a pack of dried biscuits and jerky and what you become from that point is up to you. Seeing as you have no trade, or any real skill I would hesitate in making this decision. Anyone found aiding you will be imprisoned their crime, treason and their punishment far worse than yours." Several nobles and Council members alike shrunk in the crowd. I took note of them and I'm sure the Queen and her daughters did too.

"Your second and final choice is to fight one of my Gardeners, I have heard of your disrespect and I thought it fitting that if you're to fight for your honor why not fight the woman you dishonored the most... After your future Queen that is...be glad that your sister holds such a forgiving heart. Death was my choice." Adri gazed at her mother shocked and even Princess Mariel raised her brow at her mother's harshness, I heard murmuring among the noblemen. I shook my head at how well her Majesty had set this up in such a short span of time.

"What do you choose Sorel?" She said after a moment of silence where everyone absorbed and contemplated the magnitude of his next few words.

"I choose..." His voice broke. It looked as if he might cry. "I choose to fight your Gardener your Majesty."

The Queen tipped her head in acknowledgement of his words, and if I hadn't been watching her every move I'd have missed the inhuman flash of her eyes before she clapped her hands together and with a small concussion of pure power that blew my hair back a fighting ring appeared etched into the stone fire flickering along its edges. If any had ever questioned that the Queen was not powerful that rumor died in that room when nearly fifty people witnessed her create a ring of magic without so much as a verbal command. "Gods..." Libeth breathed and I had to agree.

"Gardener Denarii, Champion on behalf of the Heir, Second to the Head Gardener, Healer of All, Beloved Sister of Horse Master Reason, Renowned Warrior of the Queen's Army and Suitor in the Queen's Tournament please step forward and mete out punishment. Bring honor to the crown in your actions." I bowed low heart swelling with pride and a grin breaking out across my face as I struggled not to laugh. Her Majesty had shattered the foundation her son stood on with words alone and for that. For that I could do nothing less than bow for her, I gazed at my shoes for a brief moment, purposely holding a bow she had not requested and I had no reason to give, purely to show my respect.

I stood slowly, stripping off my tunic and offering it to Libeth, next I removed my knife and untied my pouch full of my valuable seeds. I unbound my hair letting it settle about me. I moved forward, "I am a firm believer that titles are just words, the difference between you and I Sorel." I smiled softly as I stepped into the ring, "I earned every last one of mine. I have worked in the kitchens, I have scrubbed floors as punishments, I've washed my clothes. I have fought and bled with the Queen's men and I have suffered through training under my brother's hand on one of his horses. I have been apprenticed to the Head Healer and I have learned as much as I can about everything I put my hands to." I held up my hands scarred and calloused, "I call you soft handed because truly it is the most accurate insult I can call you. Sorel, you stand before me no longer a prince and you have nothing left to offer the world. If I ever so happen to lose mine, I can offer so much more than you can ever dream of."

The Guards pulled him to his feet, creating a path for him to walk through, he had no choice but to come join me. The Guard Captain stripped him of his shirt before pushing him forward, Sorel stumbled slightly, pausing in his steps. I raised my hand and beckoned him to advance. "Come Sorel, come face your punishment like the man that perhaps you will one day be and claim back a bit of your honor…because as of now you have none."

He walked forward head held high, face pale, fists clenched until he stood across from me, trapped as I was until one of us could fight no longer. We both knew who the victor would be, the question was not who would win, but of how long he would suffer. I breathed deeply before moving forward hair whipping behind me as I raced towards him. I snapped my leg up, hearing the sharp whipping sound of fabric being stretched taught quite suddenly, and turned adjusting my aim so that I caught him in the side instead of the head. He gasped breathless, I pivoted on the heel of my foot, hair falling into my face as I turned and kicked him square in the chest causing him to fly back into the barrier keeping us contained.

Sorel dropped to his knees, heaving slightly, saliva dripping from his chin while I watched. "Stand up." Her Majesty ordered without mercy. Her son climbed to his feet shakily raising his fists slightly not truly knowing what to do with them.

I moved towards him again, catching him in the chin with an uppercut that lifted him from his feet it was so powerful, his eyes rolled. I wrapped my arms around his body before he could fall and slammed him with all the power I had in me cushioning his head with my hands easily ignoring the stinging pain it left behind. I stepped back watching him slowly roll over wheezing softly. Bruises had already begun to form. "Stand up." Her Majesty ordered once more, and Goddess save him if he failed to obey.

Sorel lay on the ground for a time before pushing to his hands and knees and then climbing to his feet. After a deep breath he turned to face me, "Hit me Sorel." I offered my cheek watching him through the shifting strands of my hair. He raised his fist and swung, I grabbed his arm and pulled him close, dealing him several body shots before throwing him over my hip. He slammed into the ground again groaning in pain.

"This is not justice…" A Councilor proclaimed. "He's a Prince…"

"He's a man Councilor, a man who has committed treason, anyone else would be exiled or dead for said crime. He is my son, and that is the only thing saving his life, let it not be forfeit because of you." Silence reined, no one else dared to speak. "Get up Sorel. Now!" She growled when he remained on the ground too long for her liking.

He stood again, I punched him, I kicked him, I threw him every which way, my knuckles grew red from striking him repeatedly. My skin became slick with sweat and blood. I beat him all around that ring and each time he stood up it took longer than the last. Tears streamed his face and he begged me for mercy, but I could do nothing but fight as the Queen commanded and so I did. I hit him again and again and again… He lay at the foot of the Queen's mercy and I would beat him until he could no longer stand when she ordered it, until her words rang throughout the throne room and were met with silent defeat. Her son…Sorel of no title would not walk from that ring of his own power.

Tired of beating a broken man I skipped forward as he moved to stand and snapped out my foot watching his neck strain as his head flew back blood spraying from his mouth a he crumpled to the ground unmoving. "Stand up." The Queen ordered and it was a formality, I took a deep breath pulling a leather thong from my pocket. "Stand up Sorel." He remained motionless on the floor as I pushed my hair back from my face tying it up, a stray tendril still managing to escape. Nothing new. "Climb to your feet if you have the power to do so…" Her Majesty spoke again her voice softer not more a request than a demand. I moved forward and kneeled beside him assuring myself that he still lived. I righted his body gazing on all the damage I had done before standing and backing away. "Has your honor been appeased Gardener has the Heir's?" Her Majesty asked of me magic dissipating freeing us from her ring.

I gazed on the man that had once been a Prince who now lay defeated in every sense of the word before I bowed only slightly. "Yes your Majesty." She tipped her head in acknowledgement before two guards came forward to take him away. I glanced at Eden who intercepted them. The Queen caught my eye before motioning them away remembering what we'd agreed on. Eden hefted Sorel into his arms as if he weighed no more than a child, which is what he appeared to be battered and broken cradled in his arms. I watched as he left, escorted out by a team of guards, the same guards that had ushered the former Prince into the ring.

"Are there any objections to the justice dealt here today?" I honesty did not think anyone would be foolish enough to speak. I was wrong.

"How could you beat your own…"

"Councilor Renold I hereby strip you of your titles and all your lands. Everything that you had, everything that you were now belongs to your wife if you have one and your children if you birthed any. If you have neither it will go back to the crown. You are exiled from Angileri, you make take the clothes on your back and whatever happens to be filling your pockets at this time. A pack of dried biscuits and jerky will be supplied to you and a water skin if you're lucky. Soldiers will escort you to the Void, from there you are on your own. The guards will see you out." Several guards took him away while he stood pale faced unable to find words.

Her Majesty gazed at the gathered members of her Council searing them with her gaze. "Does anyone else question the justice dealt today? Does anyone question my mercy for a crime claimed as treason…Any one?" No one else spoke. The Queen bowed her head gently, breathing deeply before continuing to speak. "My daughter, your Highness Adri will sit the throne. Does anyone dispute this?" Another member hesitated but a moment, "Councilor Tessen, you are stripped of your title." He gapped like a fish. "Though you may remain in Angileri, you have a week to find a new title. You may start now." Several more guards ushered him out. "Anyone else question any of the decisions made today?" I honestly think at that moment everyone held their breath and tried to remain as still as

possible least they too be found guilty losing their titles and their lands.

If you cannot be loved than fear will do as they say, the Queen stood when no one dared to speak. "This private court is adjourned, Councilors to me, noble men and women alike thank you for bearing witness. Prince Eris, Sir Zeron, sorry for the harsh display," and just like that the Queen was gone the Councilors scrambling to keep their titles followed the Queen like good obedient children and the nobles disbanded a few smiling as they left at the justice dealt by their Majesty.

Princess Mariel had disappeared without anyone noticing and I couldn't have said when or to where. Rosen took Emery to check the gardens and Libeth was assigned to bed rest. I watched her go a little dazed, glass of wine half full in her hand. Adri strode from the dais standing before me with my tunic in her hands. She offered it to me without speaking a word, "Thank you." I murmured softly pulling my tunic over my head, freeing my hair and tying the laces baring my chest to the world.

"I have never seen such harshness from my mother…"

"And I don't think you ever will. That was not your mother punishing her son, that was the Queen of the realm punishing a subject who committed treason. She showed him a great mercy by offering him a choice, at all. And neither of his choices was death, lucky indeed. His body will heal, if fortune is with him and works hard, in time he will regain his title. By then he will be a different man…" I took my knife buckling it to my belt and then my pouch tying it just so. "Hopefully he will be a better man."

"Thank you for ending it." Adri said after a moment of silence where we stood gazing at each other.

"I do not enjoy beating a man who cannot defend himself…I do not enjoy beating a broken man, he needed it. I will not claim otherwise, and I understand why her Majesty did as she did, but I did not enjoy it and I am glad that it is done. I have never seen justice dealt so accurately. I hope next time I do not have to play a part." Her Highness took my hands in hers examining the broken and bleeding skin of my knuckles.

"You did not falter once; you did not hesitate in your actions. Your strikes were swift, your words though true held no harshness. I have never met a more fitting person to be my Champion and gain back my honor." She pressed tender kisses to my fingers gazing up at me as she did so but not once did she tried to heal them. "You have earned every title presented to you this day, and every scar that will grow on the bleeding knuckles of your hands Rhyme. Wear them proudly because they were spoken with pride." She kissed my hands one final time, "Your scars gained redeeming the honor of your future Queen. Look back on this moment and think not of beating a broken man but of healing a Princess' honor…"

I cupped her face in my hands swollen and aching from the fighting I had done and I leaned down pressing a kiss not to her lips but her brow allowing my eyes to drift closed as I enjoyed the soothing scent of her of skin, the softness of her brow beneath my lips. The gusting of her breath on my throat and the strength of her arms as she wrapped them around me. "Thank you…" I murmured against her skin tears slowly streaming my face. "Thank you." She did not ask what I thanked her for and I did not say. I had become a warrior for my mother, but I was a healer first and there was a vast difference between killing a man trying to end your life and beating a man who can hardly throw a punch while he lay battered on his knees begging you for mercy. She did not ask what I thanked her for…no I'm sure she already knew.

"How can you exist?" Adri asked stroking the tears from my face.

I chuckled softly brow furrowed as I opened my eyes to gaze down at her, "I resist the urge to die?" She laughed with me shaking her head.

"That's not what I meant silly. I meant…" She cupped my face in her hands as I found myself twinning my fingers in her hair unseating her circlet. It now sat on her head precariously close to falling, though neither of us paid it any mind. "How are you real…?" Her Highness questioned as she drew me closer pressing a tender kiss to my lips easily stealing my reply. I pressed my mouth more firmly against hers, heart racing in my chest. No kiss had ever felt quite like this. Like breathing fresh air for the first time, like breaking the surface of the water after you thought you would drown, like… coming home after you thought you would never see home again.

Our mouths moved in harmony neither of us completely dominating the other, back and forth we'd go, give and take. Over and over her lips danced against mine, a sinful waltz that I couldn't resist… The clattering of her circlet hitting the ground startled us into parting. I lay my brow against hers struggling to catch my breath, while she fought to do the same.

"We should…"

I pulled away slightly, "Yes we should…" We stood wrapped in each other's arms unmoving despite the fact that we knew we should move apart.

"Maybe just one more…" She offered pulling me down to meet her.

"Just one..." I murmured in agreement before our lips met again, just as good if not better than the last. I'd never met someone that tasted so good. Adri flicked her tongue into my mouth and despite my strength and all my power I felt my knees weaken beneath me.

The sound of someone clearing their throat caused us to break away from each other, each of us looking up startled to find the Queen lounging on her throne, legs thrown over the arm, elbow resting on the other, chin pressed against her knuckles as she watched us eyes twinkling with mirth. A smile slowly spread across her lips. "The highlight of my day for sure." She said breaking the silence, she crossed her legs, her robes parting to reveal trouser clad legs, ending in a pair of the finest boots I'd ever seen.

Adri picked up her circlet, trying and failing to fix her hair without a mirror. I took her crown stroking my fingers gently through her hair before placing it back on her head. "Thank you…" she breathed softly face a lovely shade of red. "How long have you been sitting there?" Her Highness asked crossing her arms, head held high.

I ran my fingers through my hair, wondering where my leather thong had gotten to, subtly I glanced at the floor, before catching sight of it now wrapped around the Princess' wrist. I decided I wasn't likely to get it back at that moment in time. "Long enough to confirm that Gardener Denarii returns your feelings. You don't after all kiss your friends like that." Adri covered her face while I gazed back and forth between them.

Her Majesty swung her legs down and quickly found her feet before tipping her head, "You have my blessing Gardener." She offered, expression now completely sober as she moved to exit the throne room, pausing briefly at the entrance meant specifically for the royal family. "Don't…" She warned. "Break her heart." And with that she was gone as if she'd never appeared in the first place.

"Do you think she saw everything?" Adri questioned after her mother had gone.

"It's very likely…" I replied without hesitation.

"I'm glad…." I gazed down at her brow raised.

"That your mother watched us while we…"

"No…I'm glad that she gave you her blessing. She likes you." I did not fight her as she pulled me closer twining her fingers in my hair.

"I cannot fathom why." We stood arms wrapped around each other gazing into each other's eyes while she played with my hair.

"You're smart, honest, strong, honorable and kind. What's not to like?" I pressed one final kiss to her brow careful not to unseat her circlet.

"We shall agree to disagree." I murmured before pulling away. "I have to speak with Eden."

"Will you…will you find me later? In the Queen's Garden?" Her Highness asked hesitantly gazing up at me with the twilight orbs that even now stole my breath away.

"I will try…but I can make no promises." Adri bowed her head in acknowledgement of my words before pushing up on her toes and pressing one final kiss to my cheek.

"Think before you act." Were her parting words before she too disappeared up the dais and around the thrones meant for the royal family. No doubt using the same entrance her mother had used to exit.

I gazed after her for a long moment before realizing that she hadn't once offered to give me back my leather thong, I chuckled softly brushing my hair back from my face as I moved to make my own exit.

Chapter 16
Enchantment

I never found Eden that night though I suppose I hadn't really expected to. He was probably comforting Sorel teaching him the ways of being a man or something of that nature. Despite his feelings he'd never take advantage of him, which is why I felt he was perfect for the job.

Free for the night I found myself wandering into the Queen's Garden, I took a seat by the fountain trailing my fingers lightly through the rippling pool, watching the spirits dance upon the water as their blossoms drifted across its surface. "Gardener..." I stood from where I sat smiling softly as the Princess approached.

Though my smile slowly faded when I caught sight of the turbulent storm brewing in her eyes. She advanced towards me and I stepped back, she looked near about as fearsome as the Queen had just hours prior. When she slapped me my head snapped to the side with the force of her blow and I hadn't even seen her raise her hand. "Goddess." I gasped raising my hand to my now stinging cheek.

"That was for allowing me to find out from one of my servants," She shoved me backward until I fell into the fountain. I sprang from the water coughing, in my shock, I'd gotten water in my nose. I took a few deep breaths wiping water from my eyes. "That was in case of the small chance that you might be using me." Adri pulled out a dagger, from where I couldn't tell you, twirling it easily in her hand. "Now you have never lied to me, and I don't think you're foolish enough to start now. I want to know if this woman is your lover?"

"No." I watched her blade remembering Reason telling me a story about how once the Princess had pinned a man to a wall with throwing knives, without nicking flesh, from a distance, while he struggled. I had no delusions that she'd miss now.

"Is the child yours?" She raised her hand before I could answer. "Never mind, I know she is. More importantly how did it happen…and when?"

And so dripping wet, still standing motionless in the fountain I told her Highness the same story I'd told Eden, adding the events of that day at the end. "She forgave me and then she kissed me and I was so shocked about the former I thought nothing of the latter and I should have told you…but honestly I did not think the news would have reached you by nightfall Highness and there were other things on my mind." I said honestly breathing easier once the dagger disappeared back to where it had come from.

"That at least I understand," Adri gave me a once over lips curling in amusement. "You did not actually think I would hurt you?"

I stepped from the fountain brushing my laden hair back from my face, she'd yet to give me my leather thong. I wasn't about to ask for it. "It is said you once pinned a man to a wall with throwing knives…that weren't even yours. I wasn't willing to take chances."

The Princess laughed softly, "That was a rumor…one I haven't heard for quite some time actually."

"And yet you haven't disputed it. Ever…"

"How would you know?" She questioned stepping closer.

I gazed down at her sweeping my hand out across the Queen's Garden without ever turning my gaze from hers. "I hear things."

Adri chuckled tracing her hands over the front of my tunic, now molded to my body. "I'm still angry."

"I'd gathered as much. There's a reason I'm not touching you." I murmured softly as she settled her hands on my hips.

"There's another woman who bears your child, and you are not lovers but I'm sure she wishes you to be...I have so much to offer but it's nothing that you want, she has everything. A simple life, the chance to be something other than the Queen's Garden Mage... yes I know about that little quirk of titles."

I raised my brow curious, "What do you know?"

"I know that you aren't just a lowly plant mage, no you're a garden mage through and through able to cultivate an entire field for a week and be able to harvest from it on the eve of the seventh day..." Adri gazed up at me lips curling slightly. "I distinctly remember one special garden mage bragging once or twice that the Queen had the best of the best."

"Oh Yeah," I murmured shaking my head sheepishly.

"Do I even remotely stand a chance?" The Princess asked suddenly bringing us back to the matter at hand.

Hesitantly I raised my hands to cup her face, gazing down into the star filled sky residing within the glimmering orbs of her eyes, Goddess I had never seen such beautiful eyes. Eyes that drew you in and held you captive for small bouts of eternity while you stood staring not caring at all. There were galaxies in her eyes, endless constellations of stars that you could map out if you just gazed on them long enough... and yet it seemed I never had enough time before I was drawn back. "Rhyme..." Back to reality. I blinked feeling a little dazed and wondered how long I'd stood gazing down at her.

"Lialey and I share a child...we will always be connected, but the only kisses I find myself thinking about are yours Highness." I placed a kiss on her brow not wishing to be slapped, she had said she was still angry after all. "I will do whatever you ask of me Adri to make up for my horrendous mistake."

"Anything?" She questioned mind already working no doubt.

"Within reason," I countered not liking the mischievous glint in her eyes.

"Anything within reason…" I watched her think for a little longer before coming to a conclusion that I wasn't altogether sure I was going to like. "Tomorrow is the first challenge of the political phase of the Queen's Tournament and it's so easy the only way anyone could fail is if they're an idiot. You need to book an Inn under a different name, trying not to be recognized and get the room for a cheap as possible. There's a set amount for everyone depending on the place. This is a test of subterfuge ensuring that if the need ever arises for me to hide my identity my Consort will know exactly what to do…"

"Who comes up with these tests?" I wondered out loud brow furrowed slightly.

"There's a book actually, the last test though is always a surprise." I opened my mouth but Adri was shaking her head. "No I will not tell you. I shouldn't have told you about this one but I knew you'd pass with or without the information. I needed you to know for what I wish to say." She cleared her throat and though I couldn't see clearly, by the way she bowed her head gazing in the vicinity of our boots I'd say she was blushing.

"If you allow me to mark you…and deliberately go to…Lialey's Inn. I will consider your mistake made up for." She murmured softly while I struggled to hear.

"Mark as in?" I questioned, I wasn't about to willingly let her stab me.

"A passion mark. Here." She traced her fingers along the curve of my neck.

"You want it to be visible. So that she can see I belong to someone…" I felt my lips curling slightly. "Why Princess I know that you own me as Queen after all I will be your mage but I never considered you owning me like that."

Adri flushed, "You don't have to say yes Gardener." She countered stiffly.

"But you'd like me to." I countered softly far more serious. She gazed at the fountain unwilling to answer.

"I will say yes," I took several steps backwards pulling her with me until we stood closer to the fountain. "If you sit on my lap while you do it and get all nice and wet…" She sputtered indignantly while I watched her confused before finally realizing how that came out. I found my face warming as well. "Not like that…I just meant because of my clothing being soaked and you'll be sitting on me…it." I stopped talking not wanting to make it worse.

"I understand." I tipped my head in acknowledgement of her words before sitting on the edge of the fountain pulling her down onto my lap. She hesitated to press her full weight upon me.

"I'll crush you." Adri protested as I pulled her more firmly on top of me, heart beginning to race as her curves molded against mine. I settled my hands at the small of her back holding her steady so that she wouldn't fall.

"You're lighter than you think you are, now stop struggling and mark me…" I shivered as those words crossed my lips and it had nothing to do with the chill and everything to do with…other things.

"I feel like I'm not the only one who wants this." Adri murmured softly cupping my jaw in her hand gently turning my head to the side exposing the expanse of my neck. I didn't argue, the heat pooling in the pit of my stomach would have been proof of my lie. I felt her lips first, soft and warm. The press of them against my skin made me breathless, my eyes fluttered as I clutched at her back. She kissed me several times, my pulse leaping beneath her mouth, a startled jackrabbit on the run. The flick of her tongue along damp flesh caused my hips to buck gently beneath her. I felt heat rush to

my face as she paused clutching at my shoulders waiting to make sure I had settled. "Stretching?" Adri questioned giving me an out.

I cleared my throat glad that she couldn't tell I was blushing heavily in the darkness. "I felt a cramp, but it was no fault of yours." I replied lying smoothly. She bowed her head in a nod before pressing several tender kisses along my neck, I braced myself as she paused before I felt the swirl of her tongue. I clenched my hands in her shirt eyes squeezed shut as I struggled to remain still. Goddess, it was so hard to breathe... her tongue left a burning trail of pleasure that sang through my blood and struck me directly in the groin.

"Highness..." I growled softly voice sounding gruffer than I meant, if she kept that up I would come undone without ever having felt her hands upon me, and that would surely be a sin of some kind. Who knew a mouth could be so skilled?

"My apologizes...I got distracted." I choked on my sound of amusement as she sucked at my pulse, each pull a bolt of pleasure to my sex. I never thought for a moment when I agreed to this that it would be so hard to control myself. She sucked at my skin and swirled her tongue along aching flesh for what seemed like hours, nipping at tender flesh while I fought the urge to squirm beneath her. Just when I thought that she'd finished, Adri bit me, hard. I moaned softly in pleasure as well as pain, it hurt Goddess did it hurt but only for a moment before she once more soothed it with her tongue. She pulled back tracing her thumb lightly over the tender flesh of my neck. "I think that'll do." I allowed her to stand from my lap, letting my hands fall to rest on my knees. I fought to catch my breath while trying to appear as if I weren't doing so.

My legs...I rubbed my thighs not sure if I could stand without falling. Adri leaned down and pressed a tender kiss to my cheek. "Thank you...for allowing me to mark you. I know it seems childish but still thank you."

I pulled her back to kiss me properly, enjoying the feel of her lips moving gently against mine. "I don't mind Adri if this is what it takes to soothe your mind, then I don't mind at all."

She smiled softly kissing me again before taking hold of my hands and tugging me to my feet. "Come Gardener let's get you out of those wet clothes and into bed."

I raised my brow allowing her to pull me along. "So soon Princess, I thought you said you were angry with me?"

Adri laughed shaking her head in exasperation, "Not like that Rhyme."

I laughed along with her wrapping my arms around her waist soaking her straight through while she screamed and tried to escape. "Should not have pushed me in the fountain Adri." I murmured before she broke away.

"Stay…" She warned while I crept closer. "Gardener don't…" I chased her all around the Queen's Garden the sound of our laughter causing the spirits to dance in merriment. It was such a beautiful sight. I wished, not for the first time that others could see them as I did…

*****

As the Princess had said the challenge was an easy one, the Queen had of course explained everything in far more detail and truly as Adri had claimed I could not for the world of me think of a reason that anyone should fail this challenge. Not with other magicks available once you set foot in the city.

"Who's idea was it to use transformative enchantments?" Emery questioned in a soft feminine voice, Eden had bought the charms and to be fair had thrown them in a pouch and had us pick at

random. Emery was a woman of average height and striking features. More than once a man had taken a chance on him only to be shot down quite firmly. Libeth found it highly amusing. She was older, near about the Queen's and Rosen's age, her hair was dandelion fluff upon her head and she was tiny, not bent with age just short and adorable. She took her role as our elder very seriously and had chastised Emery more than once for his rudeness to others.

"Considering how well we're known; I do not think we had much of a choice." I rumbled voice a deep but gentle timbre. Like Emery I had lucked out and drawn the opposite gender and I could completely understand his discomfort. These enchantments were very thorough and it disturbed me no small bit to have something hanging awkwardly between my legs where once there was nothing at all. I wasn't enjoying this in the least, and though I understood the need we could have each stuck to our own gender.

"Who's idea was it to pick at random instead of stick to men being men and women being women?" He countered growling.

No one answered though we all looked at Eden who appeared as a boy perhaps just entering his sixteenth summer. For all intents and purposes. As we were normally so we were still a ragtag group of individuals that just so happen to fall together. Libeth of whom we called Gran, was our leader. A Healer of high regard from Kantari, my home, her tan skin and short though fluffy hair gave our story credibility. She'd come upon me first in Angileri helping to heal the sick with small medicines and salves I'd made with my own hand and had taken me under her wing. I went by Rhy and I'd protect her from anything and everything if I could. Gran had found Erie next dying of a wasting sickness and had saved her life. Deciding she had no family left and nothing better to do she'd thought why not and had joined up with us.

Little Den had come last, an awkward but kind boy he admired Rhy and found a calling in the art of healing and so when asked if he felt up to an apprenticeship away from his small town bordering a forest most didn't even know about he'd jumped at the chance.

We were in Anear to learn of the Queen's Tournament so that we could pass the news along to smaller towns and villages we might pass through on our journey of life and healing. Gran was no Lord or Lady but she wasn't a peasant either, she had money, that she didn't speak of often. More often than not she preferred to live off the land to Den's and Erie's dismay. Rhy had long since grown used to her ways, which is why when push came to shove Gran consulted him first.

We'd spent the better part of the morning concocting a story that was simple and yet believable that none of us would forget. The rest of the day we had to explore the city, to which we had never been. Ask questions about things we'd never heard of before, try our best to stay on track without growing distracted by all the splendor, find an Inn that wouldn't cheat us and heal those that came to be healed. I hefted my bag of dried leaves, medicines and salves on my shoulder, wishing the day already over so that I could return my pouch and my blade to where they belonged.

Libeth...Gran wacked Erie with her walking stick, that she didn't need for walking. I was sure she kept it just to hit people with. Emery...Erie glared back at her. "Watch it old woman or you might find yourself strung up by your..."

I glared her down, "Emery," I rumbled breaking character, I stopped allowing Den to ooh and ah at some magic trick happening on the corner. Several people flowed between us, I waited until they were gone. "Relax, I know you're uncomfortable..." I gazed down at my body shuddering slightly. "Trust me I am too, but it's only a few more hours. Once we've booked the rooms the challenge is over and we can take off these rings and dissipate these enchantments, but until then you're Erie and I'm Rhy just deal with it. Okay?"

He grumbled a little more before sighing softly. "Yeah…Okay." He nudged my shoulder slightly. "How does it feel to be a man?"

I shifted my trousers slightly, "Right uncomfortable." I admitted not unkindly.

"I feel the exact same way. I hope this ends before I have to go to the bathroom." I gave him a look of justified horror as Den and Gran came back to us laughing softly.

"You and I both Emery, you and I both." Once they reached us Erie apologized for her dour mood and we moved on in search of a good afternoon meal unable to decide if we wanted to eat on the go at one of the many street vendors or sit in one of the restaurants where it was cool and shaded.

Den decided for us finding a good vendor that made unique pastries mixing meat and sweet fruit jelly to make an interestingly delicious salty and sweet concoction that was filling besides. Gran bought several more and had them sent back to the palace via a runner. Cook would be very pleased to try something new.

Gods above can we just pick an Inn?!" Erie exclaimed clenching her legs together as she fought the urge to control her bladder.

"But we're having such fun." Den replied racing towards the heart of the city.

Erie and I shared a look before chasing after him while Gran of course followed more leisurely behind us.

"I'm going to kill him for making us suffer on purpose." Erie growled furiously as we searched through the crowd now filling the Center Market. Goddess fifth day through seventh day were always hell at the Center Market. People came from all over to sell their wares and I had never questioned it as it wasn't my place but I was sure more than half of the things sold were illegal.

Just when I was ready to agree to murder Den came racing out of the mass of people face pale, eyes wide. "Rhy…" He murmured taking hold of my arm, staying in character despite his distress. I was glad we'd chosen to use the shortened versions of our names. I don't think he'd have managed it otherwise. "You have to see this."

Erie and I shared a look before following without hesitation or comment. The crowd parted several feet ahead of us to reveal a man standing at a table piled high with cages. I stared at the small Fae resting within. There were faeries, and was that a dragon…or a lizard? I blinked unsure if what I saw was a baby griffin or an animal that appeared to look very much like it. I hoped it was the latter, but I couldn't be sure. "I am most positive this is illegal." Erie hissed from beside me and I had to agree that it must have been on some level and yet here he sat unmolested selling mythical beings as if it were an everyday occurrence. Though certainly I had never seen him before.

"We should inform her…" I touched Erie gently on the shoulder halting her words. "We will."

Den tugged on my hand, "How much coin did you bring?" He questioned gazing off to the side of the table.

I followed his line of sight and stared at the very human appearing creature seated in a too small cage. "Holy hell." Erie murmured covering her mouth and I had to agree.

"Hopefully enough to buy a person." I replied before stepping away from my companions and up to the table. "Kind sir?" He turned from a man interested in a lackluster faerie to take me in. I smiled as kindly as I could. "I was interested in the…slave you have in the larger cage."

He snorted glancing in the general direction, "Oh her…you wouldn't want her she's quite nasty. Tends to bite the hand that feeds her if you know what I mean." I fought the urge to grimace as he leered suggestively. I did not blame her in the least.

"I can handle nasty." I stated not unkindly. We stared at each other for what seemed a small eternity before he snorted turning away first. "Well I suppose there's no harm in letting you have a look. Just let me finish with this gentleman first."

I tipped my head in acknowledgement before moving to get a closer look at the being I planned on buying with any luck. Her eyes were dark brown, ringed with honey making them glow eerily despite the afternoon sun. Her hair was reddish brown, streaked with blond, that shown even while matted and dirty. Her cheeks were sharp, a little like mine in that regard, her skin tan from the sun and covered in dirt making it hard to distinguish what color she actually was. Her ears…her ears gave me pause for they identified her as what she truly was. Sticking up past her hair narrowing to gentle points, her ears were tipped with fur now black with grime. She was a Marr, a cousin to the centaur, Marr appeared human, save for their distinctive eyes and ears. I'd heard stories about a tail but I couldn't see one hiding in the shadows of her cage. Marr were usually found on the plains of Erangi or the deep forests of Angileri and sometimes upon the deserts of Raleli. They were mentioned widely in tales of lore but like all the other mythical creatures of old rarely ever seen. She was beautiful and frightening, the power of a horse twice the size of a man placed inside a small fragile seeming package. I'm surprised she hadn't managed to kill her master with all the rage I saw brewing in her eyes.

"Would you like me to take her from the cage?" I glanced away from the cage to find the vendor now standing beside me.

"I would like that sir…" I waited for him to supply a name.

He did not disappoint. "Santi," he offered his hand, "and I'm no Sir." I shook it firmly as he snorted again. When my brother snorted I found it a bit endearing because it seemed very much like something he picked from his horses. Santi doing it just made me want to punch him in the face until he stopped moving…violent I know, but he undoubtedly deserved it.

"I would like that Santi. Thank you." I stood back as he pulled a key from his belt mumbling some small enchantment before placing it in the lock and opening the cage.

"Now as I said she can be a bit nasty, the collar on her neck." He tapped the band of supple leather cleaner than anything else on her actually. "It keeps her from harming herself and whoever happens to own her at that moment in time. A beautiful bit of magic and likely very expensive." He grunted forlornly, which I didn't know was possible until that moment. "Sadly she was wearing it long before she came to be in my care and I haven't yet found a way to remove it, harder for the fact that I couldn't possibly name the caster." Gripping her arm, firmly but not harshly, he turned her for me.

"She's a bit on the thin side, though she can't harm herself she can refuse to eat and her teeth are too sharp for me to force her…well not sharp but certainly powerful. It hurts her to hurt me but by the Gods she's managed to suffer through the pain of it more than once." He brushed her hair back from her face, "I'd call her a beauty but not everyone would. She talks sometimes, and she knows several languages most of which I don't." He shared a glance with me. "I'm sure that's the point of it. Great with horses, loves them to death, though I wouldn't let her near your mount unless you want to find yourself without one the following morning."

He sighed softly stepping back, "I'd call her a hard worker if she were willing to work, but she's not. Warming your bed is also not smart, she managed to kill an owner that way and despite her beauty I never tried." My estimation of him rose slightly. "Really I've just been waiting for someone to take her off my hands, she has a lot of rage in her and I don't want to die." He stroked his chin gazing on my blank expression before turning once more to the Marr.

"Really you'd be doing me a great service if you bought her, so I'll sell her for half the price I got her two gold, two silver and a copper and if it's not marked with the Queen I ain't taking it."

I whistled softly, "You want my hard earned crowns," I shook my head as I took a small well-worn money pouch from the bag I was carrying. "If it weren't such a bargain I'd be a little more upset." I grumbled and that was the honest truth I thought he'd ask for much more, but either his fear or his compassion was greater than I'd first thought.

Santi laughed softly. "You look like someone who will take care, I'm a gruff man through and through. Raised rough, and I know it." I offered him the money, he took it before shaking my hand giving me back one of my gold coins. I pocketed it without saying a word. If his trade weren't so…wrong, I'd almost have called him a good man. I'd have to say in spite of it that he was still a decent one. I took in the scars on his hands sure that he had been quite literal when he'd first mentioned her biting the hand that fed her.

"Would you like me to cast a small sleeping charm to make things a bit easier on you?" He asked as we finished up our business.

"Yes…I'd like that very much." He tipped his head softly before mumbling under his breath for a brief moment. When she fainted I caught her easily and lifted her into my arms.

"Before I leave you I find myself curious…what exactly is her name?" I questioned over my shoulder before I could get too far away.

"Ahh I completely forgot, her name is on her collar. I never could read it so I just called her Girl. Maybe you'll have better luck." I bowed my head in a small show of thanks before I disappeared into the crowd of people.

I found Erie and Den exactly where I'd left them, with Gran now keeping them company. Den grinned upon seeing me, while Gran gaped. "You did it!" He exclaimed cheerily.

"I'm so happy." Erie, said lowly. "Really I am, but I can hardly hold it any longer can we please find an Inn so I can drop this disturbing enchantment and go to the bathroom?" We all shared a quick look before nodding in agreement.

"I'm sorry we made you walk around all day when I knew the Inn we'd choose from the start." Erie stared at me in disbelief as we walked at a steady clip through the city taking several back alleys to avoid the crowded streets.

"Which Inn were we going to choose?" Erie asked shaking her head hands clenched over her abdomen.

Den smiled softly casting his gaze my way before proceeding to answer for me. "Why Lialey's of course."

"Son of a…" Erie cursed damn near the whole way there without any of us offering a form of protest. She was completely justified after all.

Den had spoken all of one sentence before Lialey had figured out the ragtag bunch of Healers standing before her were actually the Queen's Gardeners though she didn't say as much until we had booked our rooms and for that we were all thankful. After exchanging money for our keys Erie…Emery took off his ring and tossed it in the fire before racing up the stairs in search of a bathroom.

I took mine off next shuddering slightly as I settled back into myself doing the same with mine. "I never want to do that again." I offered in a voice I was glad to hear again.

Libeth took hers off next chuckling softly. "I had fun and I'm surprised Emery doesn't know that Lialey has a bath room for guests right behind the bar through the door right before you reach the kitchen."

I gave her a look, "Fun for you, at least you remained the right gender. It just felt wrong for the both of us and you likely only know about that bathroom because you're always trying to get a bit

of extra food." Eden nodded his agreement without ever saying a word.

"I see your lover didn't agree with our shared kiss." I turned back to Lialey to find her smiling good naturedly, eyes sparkling softly with mirth. "I should have thought to ask and for that I apologize. I hope you didn't get into too much trouble."

I traced my fingers lightly along the passion mark on my neck, the teeth more prominent than the last time I'd been bitten. "Not too much trouble, but I wouldn't recommend doing it again."

Lialey chuckled softly taking in the ring of teeth clearly visible despite the bruising. "I won't and I really am sorry. Of course you're still welcome to see Rhea and I would love it if we could be friends."

"I would love that." She bowed her head before giving me a gentle hug that I returned without hesitation.

We stepped away and she moved onto another customer, "I'm trying to figure out how I'm just now noticing that vicious bite mark on your neck." Libeth said cradling our newly acquired charge against her chest. The Marr was covered in a cloak and if anyone asked, the only one so far being Lialey, we said she was the niece of one of the maids we'd let tag along with us. It hadn't gone further than that. "When we didn't acquire our enchantments until we entered the city."

"Lack of true observation skill…" I offered causing Eden to laugh as we made our way up the stairs in search of our rooms.

"Ah you're so funny…I bet you won't be laughing when whoever gave you that bite mark figures out you bought a woman from a shady vendor at Center Market." Libeth countered as I identified our rooms at the end of the hall, we'd gotten two. They stood across from each other. I paused before opening our door with a sigh allowing Libeth to step past me into our shared room.

Eden stood at the door smiling softly as he shook his head. "She has you their Rhyme. Her Highness won't be pleased but she'll understand…probably." He paused for a moment taking in the look of frustration growing on my face at this new found predicament. "At least she's not a sex slave…" I slammed the door in his face before he could say something to make it worse.

Chapter 17
A Weightless Crown

"Ow!" I glanced up from listening to Rhea excitedly telling me about her day to see Libeth sucking on her fingertips.

"Should avoid teeth," Rhea murmured softly biting air to demonstrate the danger.

"I agree with you." I replied chuckling as I stroked my fingers playfully through her hair. "What else did you do today, any magic?"

She shook her sighing softly, "None yet." I pulled her close placing a tender kiss on her brow. "You'll get there Little One."

"I know." I smiled at her optimism and confidence at such a young age.

"Ow!" Libeth exclaimed for what seemed like the hundredth time since she'd started.

Rhea pulled me down so that she could whisper in my ear, "Not smart, avoid teeth." I chuckled at her opinion of Libeth and her struggles to feed the Marr.

"I'm sure she's trying very hard." I whispered back, as we gazed at Libeth briefly watching her raise a spoon filled with stew quite warily to the Marr's mouth her fingers red and tender.

"Not enough." Rhea shook her head as Libeth growled her frustration. By this point she was probably wearing more of the stew than she'd managed to actually feed to the woman.

"You know what." She stood from her seat across from the Marr, she hadn't let anyone get close enough to remotely try to find the writing on her collar, let alone read it. Libeth came over to me and set the bowl in my lap. "You feed her while I seat here with your daughter and we mumble how horrible you're doing."

"I said nothing of the sort, I just agreed with Rhea's assessment of avoiding her teeth." Libeth gave me a dead panned expression. I sighed softly and stood from my seat allowing her to take my place.

"Good luck Rhym," Rhea offered as Libeth sat down beside her grumbling about her sore fingers.

I smiled down at her once more stroking her hair, "Thank you Little One." She hadn't yet managed to pronounce any of our names correctly but we didn't mind.

I moved towards the Marr and took the seat across from her, her hands and feet were bound Santi hadn't offered to unshackle her and I hadn't asked. She was quite dangerous after all. I held the bowl of stew in my hands breathing in its scent. "I don't know how much Libeth actually managed to get into you or if you've really tasted it, but it's good." I took a bite humming as small chucks of meat and potatoes near about melted on my tongue. "I know if I feed you bread you'll bite me, and if I offer you stew somehow I'll end up wearing it and really I don't want that." I took another bite of her stew. It really was delicious and I'd had my fair share but I didn't at all mind eating a little more.

"Now we're not trying to hurt you, we're here for a bit of rest and then we'll be heading back to the palace. Her Majesty is already aware of your predicament and she will do everything in her power to free you of your collar, and give you the best life she can if you wish to stay or the means to make it where ever you want to go if you don't, but I need you to eat. I need you to not bite me when I feed you and I need you to cooperate as much as you are able. If you agree I will free your hands and feet and hope that you do not try to harm anyone in this room because if you do…I won't be quite so nice as I'm being right now." We stared at each other for a long time

before I offered her a bite of stew. She took it hesitantly while watching me for trickery all the while. I fed her the remainder of the bowl with bits of warm bread intermixed and a nice cup of watered down wine.

I took her hands gently in mine, gazing on the thick metal cuffs, "You aren't by chance carrying the key to these are you…" She gave me a dour look that told me she understood even if I hadn't been sure before. I chuckled softly, "I didn't think so but it doesn't hurt to ask." I took two seeds from my pouch turning the cuffs until I could see where the key would be inserted before dropping one into each. "Don't be frightened I warned," before listening for the little seeds coaxing them to grow. The Marr gasped as leafy stems sprung from the key holes a small click issued from each before the cuffs opened freeing her hands. I used the same plant to open the cuffs on her ankles and then gathered the small plant placing it in the cup once filled with wine. It glowed with my magic still growing slowly. When it was finished it would be similar but not the same as the vines growing from my window sill back at the palace.

The Marr rubbed her wrists eyes brimming with curiosity, "Are you going to tell me your name or am I go to have to try and read it from your collar?" I questioned not unkindly.

She grimaced slightly, "My people call me Renkari, but you will call me Renka." Her voice was scratchy with disuse and she carried an accent, though her words were easily understandable this was not her first language.

I tipped my head in acknowledgement, "Renka, you may call me Denarii. Gardener Denarii, you may not understand the true meaning of those words as yet, but you will. Try to get a bit of rest, a few recruits from the Queen's army will come with mounts for us in just a few hours."

"I will not ride an enslaved horse." Her eyes flashed and her jaw clenched with anger.

"Do not pass judgment on her Majesty's horses until you've met them."

I stood from my seat and moved to usher Libeth from the room picking Rhea up and holding her in my arms. "I too heavy." Rhea grumped trying to get down.

"Nonsense," I countered holding her against me as we tromped down the stairs. "You're as light as moss."

She giggled at my comparison, "It my hair," I fluffed my fingers through it as I weighed her in my arms.

"You might just be right Little One." I set her down as we reached the bottom of the stairs getting a big hug and a kiss before I allowed her to run to her mother who easily picked her up and spun her around once more filling her with laughter.

"I suppose you'll be leaving soon?" Lialey said drawing closer, more of a question than a statement, Rhea wrapped in her arms head resting on her shoulder as she played with her mother's hair so much like her own.

"Yes, the Queen's Tournament isn't yet over and we made our promises to protect the Princess as best we could until the end." I stroked Rhea's hair, sure that she would be sleep soon. "I had fun with her, she's quite smart for her age."

"I'm sure she gets it from you," Lialey chuckled softly. "I was the devil at her age, always getting into trouble. Rhea is the complete opposite."

I thought about the girl I was before I left home and smiled softly. "I was a sweetheart…Reason on the other hand." Rhea snuggled against her mother smiling while Lialey laughed at what I implied.

"As I said she gets it from you." I gave her a hug with Rhea pressed lightly between us.

"Sweet dreams Little One." I murmured pressing a lingering kiss to her head before Lialey took her off to bed.

"Are the horses here yet?!" Libeth cried racing down the stairs with Emery trailing not far behind.

I turned brow furrowed about to answer when a recruit walked through the door gazing around curiously. I recognized him instantly. "Donta?" He looked up and I beckoned him over meeting me as Libeth and Emery approached.

"Your mounts are ready Gardeners; I was instructed to bring one extra though I was not specifically told why. Simply that you have a guest..." Donta gazed at each of us waiting for a more in-depth answer that none of us were willing to give. He bowed slightly in respect, before stepping back, "Whenever you're ready." He made an about face before marching off to watch the horses no doubt.

"What has you so riled?" I questioned once Donta was gone and everyone went back to enjoying their evening meal and conversation.

"She's annoying me." Libeth whispered furiously. "Staring at me and snapping her teeth."

Emery chuckled softly, "That's not so annoying."

"Her teeth are powerful and the room is otherwise silent I swear it sounds like the crack of thunder every time." Libeth countered shaking her head.

"Well the mounts are here, we just need to gather up Eden and Renka...the Marr," I added by way of explanation. "And we'll be on our way."

Eden came tromping down the stairs as I finished speaking, Renka trailing reluctantly in his wake. "She has very strong teeth..." He grumped tracing his fingers soothingly over a growing bruise on the back of his hand. "And she's faster than she looks." Eden nudged her slightly until she stood beside me, both Emery and Libeth took a step back.

"I haven't been bitten yet and I don't plan to be," Emery said before walking away.

"I've been bitten enough for a life time." Libeth shook her head following after him.

"I am so glad you bought her, making her your responsibility." Eden murmured proceeding to disappear as well and thus leaving me alone with the Marr.

I gave her a once over, she was near about a height with me, but not quite. "If you bite me…" I left it at that.

Renka gave me a once over staring for a brief moment at the mark on my neck. "You seem to enjoy being bitten." She snapped her teeth at me for emphasis and so loud was the sound of her teeth crashing together I could not help but wonder if it hurt. Libeth hadn't been exaggerating when she compared the noise to thunder.

"I enjoy the pleasure that comes before the bite, the pleasure forms the bruise. The bite I guess you could say is to ensure no one misses the mark. I wear it proudly but I don't enjoy being bitten and neither, I'm sure, do you." I raised my brow and waited for an answer that didn't come, but it was of no matter her silence was answer enough.

"Don't bite me Renka…just don't." I warned once more before ushering her towards the door.

She snorted sounding so much like a horse that I did a double take to ensure a mount hadn't appeared behind me. "You are interesting Gardener I'll give you that much."

"I do my best," I tossed over my shoulder as we exited the back of the Inn and headed towards our companions now waiting just outside the stable.

Carina met me with a head butt to the chest. I chuckled softly ignoring the ache it left behind as I wrapped my arms around her neck and rested my head firmly against hers. "I see you missed my penchant for rambling." I murmured softly nuzzling my cheek against hers. I may not have had my brother's gift, but there wasn't a being on this earth that understood me quite as well as my horse.

"Are you going to introduce us?" I glanced up to find Renka watching us curiously, I stroked my fingers lightly through Carina's mane while all around us everyone mounted up.

"Carina this is Renka of the Horse People…" I nudged Carina's head with my own and it budged not at all. I chuckled softly at her stubbornness. "The Horse People are the Marr if you remember all my childhood stories and Renka…" I turned beckoning her closer taking her hand and setting it upon Carina's muzzle allowing her to get acquainted "this is Carina, my mare and some might say the only friend who can't tell me to shut up…" Carina lightly placed her hoof on my boot, enough pressure for it to be uncomfortable but not yet painful. I glanced down. "Well not with words anyway." I finished wryly Carina gave a little whinny, her version of a laugh before removing her hoof from my foot inspecting Renka more thoroughly.

Donta came up beside me and I lent him my ear while Renka conversed with my horse in a language I could not hope to understand. "We're ready Gardener, I've been informed that all other suitors have returned to the palace." He hesitated before adding with a small smile. "Sadly none have failed."

I sighed hearing the news but I'd expected nothing less, "We'll be ready shortly." He bowed slightly before moving away going to talk to Libeth and Emery and then Eden respectively giving them the news.

When I turned back around Renka was hugging Carina cheek to cheek while gazing at me, eyes glowing softly as she gently stroked her finger through Carina's mane. "Your mare is a lovely creature…" She hesitated for a moment. "If I were ever to willingly ride a horse it would be yours. As well she tells me she remembers all of your stories." Renka smiled softly hiding her mirth against Carina's strong neck. "They're all so very detailed, a tree would have trouble forgetting and we all know how dense trees can be…" Her gazed flickered to me. "Her words not mine." She finished with a shrug.

I laughed good naturedly, "Trees actually have very long memories." I scolded coming to gently scratch behind her ears right where she enjoyed it most. "And thank you that means a lot coming from one of your kind." Renka flicked her ears at me but otherwise didn't respond simply watching the playful interaction between me and my horse. "How will you get to the palace if not by riding?" I questioned after a brief bout of silence. I knew everyone was waiting on us, though I would not rush her, she'd been through enough.

Her lips quirked and as I watched reddish brown fur began to grow on her face, "I said I wouldn't ride a horse…" Carina shied away charging forward and pushing me with her, while where we once stood Renka shifted, like water, fluid and natural from one form to the next.

"I suppose we won't be needing the extra mount…" Donta breathed as we took in the magnificent beast now standing before us. Renka was taller than every horse in the stable, massive but trim a beast made for speed, but easily filled with strength. Her muscles practically rippled beneath her coat of reddish brown, tarnished by grime. Like her hair her mane and tail were a mixture of red, brown and white. The fact that it was matted took away from its splendor. Her eyes now much larger glowed beautifully in the afternoon sun, she looked like something straight out of legend itself. After a small bout of gawking I climbed into the saddle. Renka butted her head lightly against Carina's mirth sparkling in her eyes.

"A warning would have been nice." I said watching her ears flick in my direction. She rolled her eyes at me and I laughed softly. I glanced around to be sure that everyone was ready before I spurred

Carina into a trot, Renka falling in beside me and my fellow Gardeners behind while the recruits fanned out around us practicing their guarding skills. Truly I had to admit it was the perfect little exercise.

*****

Everyone had grown used to Renka turning into a horse by the time we approached the palace gates, the trouble started when the stable hands not having seen her turn into a horse tried to take control of her by grabbing hold of the leather collar around her neck, it had grown as she had. Quite a handy bit of magic that. One went flying before anyone had a chance to react and then of course all hell broke loose as more hands came to subdue her. Just about everyone loss control of their mounts, I was smart enough to leap from Carina before Renka's distress affected her. Despite my caution she remained the calmest of the bunch.

Guards came, there were ropes and men shouting trying to gain control of the situation. I got tired of all the commotion, gently I rubbed my brow in frustration while Renka took out several guards. The infirmary would be filled that night; I could just tell. "How long do you think this will last?" Donta asked slowly sidling up beside me weighed down by several of the saddle bags he'd managed to rescue from getting trampled.

I took the bag I'd been carrying around throughout our trip through the city and opened it digging inside until I found the two items I was looking for. My blade and more importantly, my pouch. "Not much longer." I took a few familiar seeds from my pouch before chucking them into the fray, with a frustrated huff of air I released my magic and watched as everyone grew more distressed before growing still as raptor vines tangled them in their embrace, stopping all form of movement.

Renka, eyes rolling, breathing heavily muzzle twinned shut stood at the center of it all trying to calm herself. "What the Gods is going on here!" Reason exclaimed racing into the courtyard with several more guards trailing in his wake.

"I am so glad you managed to subdue everyone before your brother arrived Gardener." Donta murmured shaking his head at the pandemonium his presence would have caused among his stable hands and the guards. I was in full agreement.

Libeth squirmed her way free of vines no doubt using her magic to loosen them, before answering. "Your men are all fools, they thought to capture our guest." She motioned towards Renka who now appeared much calmer.

"The giant wild horse in the heart of this mess?!" Reason questioned incredulous.

"Not a horse…" I supplied. "One of the Horse People." My brother stared at me confused just as Renka changed back, her transition just as seamless as before. She shed the vines meant for a much larger creature before slowly working her way free of the mess finding her way to my side.

"Your men are fools." She grumbled to my brother crossing her arms, while he and everyone who hadn't seen her change gapped in amazement at the spectacle that had just occurred before them.

"I see our guest has arrived." Everyone turned to find the Queen standing idly by smiling softly at the scene before her. Everyone who was able save Renka and I bowed low in respect.

I bowed slightly, standing quickly. "Majesty this is Renka, of the Horse People. Renka this is her Majesty Servasli Averell…" I quirked my lips in amusement before finishing. "Of many titles I do not care to name." I could see Reason covering his face in embarrassment out of the corner of my eye. Donta cleared his throat covering his amusement and her Majesty laughed out right as she approached us.

"I cannot wait until you take Rosen's place...or accept an open seat on the Council whichever comes first. You'll certainly stir things up." The Queen gazed around her courtyard as if to emphasize her point. "Renka of the Horse People." Her Majesty took her hands in her own, bowing slightly to place a kiss upon her hands. "It is an honor to meet you. I hope you find comfort in my palace while we work to free you." She traced her fingers over the leather collar circling her neck. "I assure you the man who thought it wise to sell you in my market will be brought to justice. Come let us get you settled." I watched as Princess Mariel appeared out of nowhere. Literally, I saw the smoky shadow of her magic briefly before she appeared as if walking from around the corner, joining her mother in ushering away the Marr.

"Gardener..." The Queen turned back to me once more taking in the complicated scene of stable hands, horses and guards all wrapped together in taunt vines. "Clean up this mess."

My lips twitched in amusement, "Of course Your Majesty." She tipped her head in acknowledgement of my words before turning away a small bit of mirth still glittering in her eyes.

"Brother clean up this mess." I snapped my fingers for effect more than anything and the vines withered, dying quickly as they settled upon the hard packed earth, small wild flowers blooming wherever they landed. Freeing beast and man alike from their bounds. Once done I turned and walked away my fellow Gardeners falling in beside me while the recruits gazed after us with no little bit of awe in their eyes.

"I thought you were trying to hide your gift?" Libeth questioned laughing softly as we walked away the sun setting behind us.

I smiled softly, "What's the point in hiding something I've learned that nearly everyone knows." I countered with a shrug.

Eden slapped me lightly on the back while Emery shook his head smiling, "Our fearless leader."

"Second to Rosen." I added without hesitation.

"That's up for debate you know?" Libeth added as we entered the palace. I shook my head refusing to ask how. I'd had enough excitement for one day and I still had a Princess to find. My smile faded slightly, the flowers told me all I needed to know. Though I'd have known exactly where to find her without it. The Queen's Garden...it was our place.

I left my fellow Gardeners in the kitchen and went in search of the future Queen of Angileri pausing briefly in the Heart Garden in my attempt to remain hidden from the guards patrolling the palace. I swear they questioned me full well knowing who I was besides.

I found her Highness leaning against the wall surrounded by glowing Were Lilies, I glanced at the sky in surprise, the moon was only half full. I supposed they'd bloomed from magic alone with the coming of night. She sat with her head resting against her knees gazing down at the glowing flowers, her circlet sparkled on the ground beside her, though the sight was not as shocking as the tears shimmering on her cheeks.

I approached slowly taking a seat beside her against the wall, close but with a small space between us. "What brings you to tears Highness?" I asked softly setting the gift I'd made off to the side.

We sat in silence for a long time with her gazing down upon the flowers while I gazed at her heart aching softly for her pain. "Can I tell you a story?" Adri asked abruptly still gazing at the ground.

I bowed my head gently in a nod of approval. "Of course."

She took a deep breath before she began voice quivering with emotion, "Long ago...when the Queen was young she gave birth to a beautiful baby girl, everyone thought she would grow to be as lovely as her mother and grow she did... Into an equally lovely little girl. With an imagination out of this world, different than her peers and

with more power besides the girl often found herself alone in her mother's garden day dreaming about the day that some prince would come take her away from it all… A Prince worthy of her… as the girl grew older and learned more about her mother's gardens and thus more about her mother's Gardeners the day dreams changed. Just a bit, the Prince was more normal seeming, less flashy, humbler… A man willing to get his hands dirty, a man willing to walk and play and work the garden with the girl. A man perhaps like her mother's Gardeners…" The Princess paused for a time before continuing her story, "The girl fell in love with the idea, so much so that she got to know each and every one of the Queen's Gardener's by interacting with them, as well as listening to the stories told by others. It reached a point years later, where the girl now a young woman knew them each by heart, near about as well as her mother did.

"An accomplishment indeed to know the little intricacies of their craft, what colors the flowers bloomed when and by whom the gardens were worked. Her sister called it a gift and her brother a waste of her precious time. It was a knowledge gained not all at once but over an expanse of time little by little. Of course the young woman did not just stop at her mother's Gardeners though they were her main focus. She knew everyone in the palace, their names, their families and even some of their hopes and dreams. She knew everyone except the Gardener she wished to know most. The one who hid from her most skillfully. The Gardener that seemed in her opinion so much better than the rest, though strangely not as well known. You know the Prince became more and more like that Gardener every day and perhaps she fell in love with the idea more than she should have…"

I met her gaze fully as she turned to me finishing her story. "When she met that Gardener still so full of mysteries, she could not have been more shocked at how easily such a normal seeming person could change her idea of what a Prince should be."

"Adri…" I took her hands in mine moving closer. "That Gardener has spent the better part of the last ten years watching that little girl battle the faeries that she couldn't see, pulling the weeds from around the fountain so that it could look more beautiful and getting scolded besides when she returned to the Queen covered in grime." Adri chuckled softly bowing her head at that little tidbit. "She watched that girl grow into a beautiful young woman that she admired above all else…and if that Gardener had once thought for a moment that she could love that woman the way she knew she deserved to be loved. If she had thought for a moment that it was worth it she'd have revealed herself long ago." I cupped her face in my hands stroking her tears away. "You are an amazing individual Princess and despite the fact that you're young you've done more for your country than most men can claim in their entire lives. You cause saplings to take root in my stomach and Goddess if I don't find myself lost in the endless twilight of your eyes every time I look at you. I love you…" I smiled softly. "And it happened not all at once like in the fairytales, nor was it over the last few weeks of spending time together but over an expanse of time little by little." Adri laughed softly at me stealing the words from her story eyes sparkling with mirth.

"You aren't just saying that…" I gave her the look that question deserved and she laughed harder resting her brow against mine as she twinned her fingers in my hair. "You know when you asked me if I loved you…after you fought Libeth I lied… I was already in love with you."

I chuckled softly. "I was afraid you'd say it then when I was still trying to figure it all out…Crazy the difference a few days can make."

Adri sighed. "Has it only been a few days it feels like a small eternity."

"Doesn't it though." I agreed as we sat brow to brow, eyes closed as we held each other.

"Are you falling asleep?" Adri asked softly after a long bout of silence fingers gently rubbing along my scalp.

I opened my eyes, "No…I'm fully awake."

"So you can repeat exactly what I just said?" Her Highness questioned brow raised curiously.

I smiled sheepishly, "I may have drifted off for a bit."

"As I thought, I asked what you had there." She tipped her head towards the gift wrapped in a satin cloth tied lightly with green ribbon.

I pulled it from behind me and offered it to her, "A gift I made for you." Adri took it gently, gazing at me briefly. "Open it." She smiled softly before pulling the ribbon watching it come undone before unwrapping the satin.

"You made me a crown." She lifted it from the cloth gazing at in wonder, formed from vines and supple braches intertwined with flowers. It was beautiful the wood if you looked closely held small images of dancing faeries, the vines if you watched long enough shifted so that it was always stable and the flowers glowed softly, they'd change color with the seasons. It was perhaps more intricate than the circlet of silver she often wore around the palace. "It's so light." Adri murmured tears once more streaming her face.

"I thought perhaps when the weight of your Queendom became too much you could come here…to our Garden and wear this crown, or perhaps if you wish when you become Queen you will have your new crown cast in this image so that you may always carry a bit of your Garden with you…"

Adri pulled me close pressing a tender kiss to my lips, "You made me a crown. Light so that I could bare the weight more easily when it all became too much." She laughed softly. "Goddess how could I not love you…" She kissed me again, more deeply this time and I found myself lost in the taste of her.

I pressed her down onto the ground the Were Lilies glowing all around us, while beneath us the grass grew suddenly thicker, now softer than grass had a right to be. I settled between her thighs as we kissed our tongues waging war with each other neither winning fully before growing distracted. I trailed my hands down her sides playing lightly with the hem of her tunic while she scratched her nails lightly along my scalp causing warm tingles to shoot through my body.

I moaned softly as she nibbled playfully at my bottom lip, "Perhaps we should stop…"

Adri tightened her hold on me pulling me more firmly against her as she devoured my mouth with hers causing me to forget what I'd been trying to do as I melted against her heat pooling low in my belly. "I think we should stay…" She traced kisses along my neck causing me to arch against her. "Mmmm, is that another cramp Gardener?" I felt my face warming slightly now caught in the lie I'd told last night.

"No comment." I husked tightening my hold on her as she continued to trace kisses along my neck. "We should stop…" I murmured again slipping my hands beneath her tunic tracing my fingers along her warm soft skin.

"I'll stop…" Adri murmured softly, flipping us over until I lay pinned beneath her, hands gently but firmly held above my head as I panted softly skin flushed with desire, sex aching with need. My heart raced in my chest as she gazed down at me, eyes full of love and desire. After a moment of gazing into each other's eyes she leaned close nipping lightly at my ear before finishing her sentence. "When you scream my name…."

Chapter 18
I Love You

"You know Princess," I murmured softly as we lay spent after our love making. "I'm not altogether sure you haven't done this before

Adri chuckled softly tracing her fingers lightly over the swirling green stems traveling across the expanse of my skin. "What can I say Gardener, something about you motivates me to do my best."

I moaned softly as her hand once more traveled south, catching it before it could reach my tender sex. "You're insatiable." I shivered voice growing huskier as she nibbled at a sensitive spot on my neck.

"And yet you're the one that unwittingly used your magic to grow us this lovely cocoon of foliage hiding us away from the world." She slipped inside me gently eyes sparkling with mirth as my breathing grew more erratic.

"What does that have to do with…" I arched against her hand, her pace slow and measured not wishing to make the tenderness worse. "Your appetite…?" I questioned once I remembered what we were talking about.

Adri gazed at the vines twinning together over our heads growing thicker as we moved together, smiling softly as glowing flowers bloomed around us. "You've made a little alcove against the wall formed completely from plants and you're asking about my appetite…"

I pulled her closer capturing her lips with mine as I grew closer to the edge, with a soft cry against her lips I came undone wrapped around her fingers the stars filling her eyes blinding me to anything else. I melted into the soft grass, that felt more like a bed the longer we lay on it. "If you touch me again, I'll…"

"Enjoy every moment of it?" Adri questioned cheekily before snuggling against my side chuckling softly.

"Shut up…"

"Mmmm, you're too tired to make me." I grumbled softly at that assessment but didn't argue.

We sat in silence for a while as she traced her fingers along my skin, "Where did you get these tattoos?" Adri questioned curiously propping her elbow on the ground cheek resting on her hand so that she could more easily look me in the eyes.

I raised my hand to brush her hair out of her face, curlier than it had been due to our love making. "I suppose… you could say I lost a bet." I offered remembering the day I'd met the former Queen of Angileri, a stern woman for sure.

Adri chuckled softly, "Am I ever going to get a straight answer out of you concerning anything important?"

I pulled her down for a kiss tracing my hands soothingly along the warm expanse of her back, "Eventually," I replied cheekily. She bit my lip a little harder than usual before soothing the small ache with her tongue.

"No games Rhyme." I sighed softly.

"A bet I lost to an old woman once…she told me if I could use my gift to touch her that she would help me get home. Then she provided me with the seeds and stood absolutely still for me. I can't tell you if she'd have kept her promise because I never got the chance to find out. Despite all my efforts I couldn't touch her once…she gave me this tattoo the price for being unable to do as she

asked and I've had it ever since. I've had it long before the Sol-Lea who never got to see me naked…"

"Her loss," Adri countered softly causing me to laugh.

"So possessive." I chuckled softly as she lay against me.

"There are quite a few women that wish to claim your heart, I have every right to feel as I do." I did not argue; she spoke nothing but the truth after all.

I stroked my fingers lightly through her hair taking in the beauty of the spirits happy but subdued as they sat crowded around us sheltering us from prying eyes. I spoke not a word of it to the Princess, I doubt she would have appreciated the spectacle half as much as I.

"I wish that we could just cancel the Queen's Tournament and get rid of all the foreign monarchs so I could have you to myself for a little while." Adri sighed resting her hand over bundle of stems circling my heart easily drawing my attention away from the spirits.

"It's almost over, two more political challenges and the then surprise challenge. Three more days, four at most." I offered as I stroked her hair.

"Three more days if all goes well…" I gazed at the moon through the green no longer growing above our heads. "I hate the political portion, at least one of the challenges is more difficult than all the other challenges combined."

I furrowed my brow. "More difficult than fighting or capturing guards?" I questioned curiously.

Adri placed a tender kiss upon my shoulder. "It's politics, deception and intrigue go hand and hand. It's often dangerous and tiring. I read the book of challenges and more than once a suitor has died in this portion of the Tournament." I stilled my fingers in her hair.

"How? And why do we still hold this portion if it's so dangerous?" I asked curiosity growing.

"It's always been an accident, it's not often enough for it to be common knowledge and we hold it because, if you're no good at politics you won't last long as consort…" Like her father went unsaid between us.

"The challenge is about fear Rhyme, if you're afraid you won't make it, it makes you vulnerable, gifts are useless. The challenge is about over coming vulnerability and making it to the end despite your fear…" Adri gazed down at me expression somber. "Rhyme if this challenge comes tomorrow I want you to skip it?"

"How will I know?" I questioned unwilling to argue with the fear I saw lurking in her eyes.

"A feeling I suppose, there are many choices and this challenge is chosen at random. I won't be there to tell you, my mother is holding Council trying to find replacements for the members lost and I must be there." Adri stroked her fingers lightly over my cheek. "I know all the challenges are supposed to be a secret but I'd hate for something to happen to you if I could help you avoid it."

"I'll do as you ask." I replied without hesitation.

"Thank you." She relaxed visibly before once more snuggling against my side, pressing a kiss to my cheek. "I'd hate to lose you after just truly finding you..."

I rolled us over causing Adri to squeal is surprise laughing softly as I pinned her beneath me. "I plan to stick around for a long…" I leaned down to kiss her savoring the taste of her before pulling away, "long…" she pulled me back to her flicking her tongue against my lips requesting entrance. I allowed it growing lost in the feeling of her body pressed against mine while her tongue gently explored my mouth. A small eternity later I pulled away to catch my breath finally able to finish my sentence. "Time…"

Adri smiled softly once she realized what I'd said, "Is that a promise?"

I nuzzled my cheek against hers breathing in her scent, "Undoubtedly."

"Good," Adri breathed tracing her hands up and down my back while I lay resting on top of her each of us gazing into each other's eyes. I stroked my fingers lightly over her stomach watching the muscles dance beneath my fingertips. Slowly I began tracing my fingers lower smiling as I felt her reacting to me. She caught my hand and held it against her abdomen. We sat there for a while with her holding my hand close against her, taking in the peaceful silence that filled the night broken by the burbling of the fountain and all the nightly creatures that always seemed to find their way into the Queen's Garden. "Is it possible..." Adri hesitated for a moment. "Is it possible for us to have children together?" Her words were so soft I had to fight to hear her.

I twitched my fingers and she released my hand, once more I traced my fingers along her abdomen more purposeful now. I closed my eyes and felt inside of her with my magic, waiting for a response...I laughed softly opening my eyes at the ticklish sensation touching her induced. I cupped her face in my hands and kissed her deeply. "Is that a yes...?" Adri questioned breathlessly once she pulled away.

"Yes..." I traced my fingers along her skin chuckling softly in delight upon hearing all the new voices. "Goddess..." I breathed as we watched my fingers glowing softly against her skin.

"What is it?" Adri asked tracing her fingers lightly over my smiling lips, amused by the mirth she no doubt shinning in my eyes. "What do you feel...what do you hear?"

I gently traced my fingers lightly over her skin above where I knew each ovary to rest, another breathy laugh escaping me, before I could answer. "It's like I'm holding my pouch of seeds and they're clamoring to be chosen bumping and prodding against my magic. It tickles…As well I can hear them, all together and yet at the same time separately unique. Some are louder than others…but all of them are beautiful. All of them holding their own potential." I settled my hands more firmly against her skin, letting my magic fade away. "I imagine if every mother felt what I'd felt they'd either have many children or none at all…because how can you choose…"

"You have so many gifts Rhyme…what some Healers study years to be able to accomplish you do by an accident. Those Healers are rare and scattered far and wide. Not even my mother has one in her care…though I'm sure several reside in Angileri they are valuable. And it's easy to understand why. The world is a dangerous place for a woman of your many talents. The Queen's Gardener, Second to her Head Gardener, an amazing Healer, strong enough to heal yourself even, with the ability to fertilize an egg with your magic and aid in conception of those who can't conceive on their own… many would kill for a mage of your caliber. I see more clearly why you wished to hide the power that you possess." I smiled softly as she cupped my face in her hands.

"In the words of a very stubborn Princess I know…I can protect myself." Adri chuckled pulling me close for a brief but tender kiss.

"And in the words of a very wise mysterious Gardener I know…you shouldn't have to." We shared another kiss, which lead to several others…which of course lead to other more amorous things. "We have to stop," Adri moaned softly. "Otherwise I'll have to explain why I'm overly tired and walking funny tomorrow…" She gasped softly as I traced my thumb firmly over her little bud.

"As I recall I said that several hours ago and your response was and I quote… I'll stop when you scream my name." Adri moaned softly chuckling against my lips as she held me close and enjoyed everything I had to give. I had the pleasure of hearing her scream my name several times.

*****

We stood before the second challenge in the second phase of the Queen's Tournament, a maze made entirely of plants. "I know some of you might think this challenge a bit unfair considering half of the suitors are plant mages." Her Highness Mariel said from her place by the entrance. The Shade Princess looked as if she would commit murder with her eyes whenever I so much as glanced in her direction…I would not all be surprised if she knew exactly what had kept her sister so busy the previous night. "You would be wrong." I tried to pay very close attention, but continuously found my mind wandering…

Libeth nudged me gently drawing my attention. "Are you alright?" I traced my fingers over my neck where Adri had marked me, I could not seem to get the woman out of my head. "Rhyme…" I met her concerned gaze smiling softly to show I was well.

I caught the tail end of the Mariel's explanation… "Depending on how many make it through the maze this will be the final challenge of phase two. You may choose to step out of this challenge if you've won the right or continue. You'll have five minutes to decide. After those five minutes you will enter in groups of three or four and from there I must say good fortune to you all."

I gazed on the maze wondering how they'd managed to hide this from me, I'd been through every part of Griffin Forest…or so I'd thought until this moment gazing on the leafy walls parted before us. I wished that I'd been paying attention when the Princess had spoken about this challenge truly I had no idea what I was getting myself into. I traced my hands over the beacon orb I now held assured at least that if anything were to go wrong I need only toss it into the air and aid would come for me.

"The goal is to try to stick together yeah?" Libeth questioned drawing Emery and Eden closer to us.

Emery gazed towards the entrance to the labyrinth made entirely of green. "The Princess said we have no advantage here…am I the only one wondering why?" We all shared a look none of us holding an answer. I wondered briefly if this was the challenge that Adri had warned me about. My stomach felt twisted but I could not discern the reason why.

"The time to enter is now!" Her Majesty shouted drawing our attention.

"Whatever you do…" Libeth said standing close to me. "Make sure you stick close together." Eden squeezed my shoulder in reassurance, while Emery tossed me a wink. I bowed my head in a silent promise as we all surged forward as one.

We walked through the arching wall of greenery and suddenly everything went silent, I stopped in my tracks head cocked in confusion. I turned to ask Libeth a question to find myself suddenly standing alone. "Where did…" I turned around to find a wall of plant life where once the entrance had been. "How did…"

I reached out with my gift to find an impenetrable wall, I touched the hedge with my hand only to pull back sharply hissing in pain gazing down at my hand now scorched and bleeding. I now understood Adri's warning, why the Shade Princess said that no plant mage would have an advantage here.

The maze was alive, and it would not allow me to communicate with it. I clenched my hand, flinching at a sudden snapping sound to my left. I turned to see several vines stretched taunt between two leafy walls. As I watched more snapped into place slowly advancing towards me stabbing through the hedge before growing out from there. I stepped back seeing how sharp each tip was. I turned as the vines seemed to snap faster and faster quickly advancing towards me. I ran having no choice but to let the maze guide me wherever it wished…

I stopped to take a breath making sure that I wasn't in danger, the corner I'd just turned had faded as if it had never been and I found myself given only two options. Once more I reached for my gift feeling nothing, the voices in my head gone as if they had never been. The silence they left behind deafening in itself, so used to hearing the voices of the green as I was. I could go forward or back, my options a straight line. After catching my breath, I slowly began to jog forward hoping against hope to find an end to this hell.

I found nothing of the sort, I jogged and jogged and then I walked but I never seemed to grow closer to any end, nor despite all my trying did I grow closer to my gift. As requested I'd left my blade and my pouch back in my rooms, for this challenge you came without any form of aid or weapons. Goddess I wished I'd kept them both. I would not feel quite so vulnerable as I did in that moment wandering around lost in a place where I should have thrived. I stood still for a moment, just taking a few deep breathes to calm myself. When I opened my eyes I found myself at an intersection that had literally appeared out of nowhere. I had three choices. Left right or straight.

I went right and found myself immersed in a dizzying array of twists and turns there after, all the while the walls grew closer and closer until they closed in on me, sparking against my skin as I fought to escape. I ran as fast as I could, hissing in pain every time bare skin seared against a wall that by all rights should not have burned and just when I thought I would be another statistic in Adri's suitors' challenge book an opening appeared and I burst forth falling to my knees in a small little clearing.

I sat there breathing heavily as I took in my wounds, I had several tears in my tunic, where I'd rolled up my sleeves, I could see steaks of blood where I'd lost skin to the walls. I leaned back on my hands one aching from earlier, how long had I been lost here trying to find my way… I gazed at the position of the sun unsure if it had moved at all. I reached into my pocket searching for the orb I'd been given for if I found myself in distress…My brow furrowed in confusion as I searched my other pocket. I turned each inside out finding nothing despite the fact that I remembered placing the orb in my pocket. I flopped down on the hard packed earth and closed my eyes for a brief moment of rest, not only was I unable to use my gift but as well I'd lost the only thing that could save me if I found myself in dire need of attention. I prayed to the Goddess that I'd make it through this in one piece, otherwise Adri would never forgive me…

I flipped to my feet at the sound of footsteps approaching. When I opened my eyes to find Prince Eris strolling towards me I was justly suspicious. "The old woman wasn't lying when she told me I'd find you here. All the more reason to keep her around I suppose."

He stopped several feet away out of striking distance, "You know when I first arrived I tried for a brief time to take this little forest nation the old fashion way…"

"Drugging and then raping the future heir is the old fashioned way?" I questioned skeptically.

He tipped his head back and forth thoughtfully a smirk slowly spreading across his face. "I suppose not but I've never been all that conventional."

"Why are you here?" I was tired of seeing his face already.

"To gloat…after all despite your many gifts you never once saw this coming. You never saw me as a threat after you beat me up in the Princess fake rooms, never even contemplated I could do more. Oh you bested the Shades that weren't really Shades but never discovered where they came from despite the fact that the Sol-Lea is back…seemingly from the dead I might add. You are so unpredictable and at every turn that I tried to subdue you, you chose a different path and I'm just quite tired of your face Gardener." His smirk vanished as if it had never been.

"I've come to break you Denarii… to destroy everything you hold dear and make you question all the things you thought you

knew. Though before I do that I'll give you one more chance to come to my side. How about it?"

I glared at him stomach twisting into knots, I reached for my gift and once more found nothing. "I don't know what game you're playing but I wouldn't join your side even if my life depended on it…"

"Funny that you should say that," Eris countered raising his hand. "Because it kinda does…" I cried out as a vine sharper than any blade I've ever felt pierced through my left shoulder. I stared at the blood glistening on the sharpened tip struggling to stay conscious. Pain spiked through my thigh as my knees sagged and I found myself gazing down to realize that another had pierced my right thigh simultaneously.

"Now that I don't have to worry about you trying to hurt me, let me take a little time to destroy your world." I watched him wave a very familiar blade in front of my face while I breathed heavily sweat beading on my skin as I tried to fight through the shock.

"The Sol-Lea you know and love…is dead. She died when she ran head long into the Void thinking she could destroy it. Which is probably why our plot to get you to fall in love with her again didn't work too well. Though I'm sure the fact that a small piece of the old her still lurks in the heart of the new also played a part. She really did love you." Eris traced the blade lightly under my chin while I struggled to stay up right on one quivering leg.

"Go on ask me what I'm talking about I know you're curious…" I tipped my head away from the blade I knew to be mine ignoring the blood now dripping from my chin.

"What…do you mean?" I growled out as pain sparked through my body whenever I so much as twitched.

"The Void, the horrible thing spawned from some war centuries before our ancestors were even a thought in their parents' eyes, is growing…" I shook my head.

"No…it stopped. It's grown no further than its current borders." I countered knowing this for fact.

"It's growing not across the land, tired of being pushed back by plant mages, but inside of people and it is magnificent." He laughed gleefully as he traced his finger along the vine sticking out of my body gently tweaking the bloody tip.

"The Sol-Lea is a prime example of that…and your Princess. Who better to be taken by darkness than one who lives in the shadows. How else do you think I set this up…getting you to come to a place where your gift did not work, getting you to give up your weapons without question. All this time you thought Prince Sorel was the threat, but he was just a pawn used to distract you from the bigger picture. Mariel has always been the real danger…what piece on the board holds more power than the Queen…" He waited for an answer that I had no strength or willingness to give. I flinched as he traced my blade down my cheek causing pain and numbing flesh in an instant. "None but the hand that wields the Queen…is strongest of all and who among her children is closest to the Queen Denarii? Who is her right hand, who goes to every meeting ever held, who stands behind her shoulder…who guides the Queen."

"You're lying." I choked out blood dripping from the cut on my face. "Mariel would never betray her mother."

"No…she wouldn't I give you that. The Princess is so loyal it hurts…but I've been here for little over a month and the Sol-Lea has spent much time with the Queen's youngest daughter and that little piece of the Void within her has been slowly growing to fruition. As I stand here regaling on and on about how much you've truly failed the Queen is being murdered and cold blood by her daughter who just can't seem to stop herself. Tragic really."

"The beauty of it being that no one will ever know it was her with so many foreign monarchs' gathered in one place… It could be anyone. The Heir of course has died with her mother and the Prince is no longer a Prince. I'll slither my way into Mariel's heart and

we'll stop all those plant mages from attacking the Void so that it can spread as it wishes while I gain power and riches beyond my imagining. A win all around for me. I have to say the best part about it all as that I could have done nothing without the Head Gardener. What was her name…." He tapped his chin thoughtfully.

"Rosen…" He glanced over his shoulder while I fought to look up. I felt my heart shattering into a million pieces.

"Ahh, yes here she is. The woman to whom I owe all my success." She came forward and all the fight drained from me as she cupped my face in her hands.

"Tell me…tell me he's lying?" I begged tears warming my eyes. "Please…"

"I did what I had to do…" she pressed a gentle kiss to my brow before stepping aside.

"It hurts doesn't it?" He breathed deeply. "I knew I would love this moment, the broken look on your face I will cherish it truly I will, but like all memories it will fade in time." He stroked his fingers through my hair wrapping it gently around his arm while I gazed at the ground slowly growing numb. "You know what doesn't fade…souvenirs." I shuddered as he slashed the blade through my hair sagging against the vines as I lost everything that had ever meant anything to me. A lock of hair fell across my face…short like the healers of my people.

Eris held my long locks in his hands grinning gleefully, "So long and beautiful and now it's all mine. It really does feel amazing…better than I ever thought it would." He sighed. "I must be going Gardener…I do hope the rest of your short existence is as horrible as I could have hoped to make it." He left me then handing my blade to Rosen murmuring a few quiet words before exiting where he'd appeared.

Rosen stepped close tracing her fingers through the now much shorter strands of my hair. Her face was impassive, a mask as she held me close for a brief moment. "I love you." Were the last words she spoke to me before plunging my blade straight through my chest and just missing my heart. I shuddered gently in pain grimacing slightly. Goddess it hurt…but nothing hurt more than her betrayal. Not even, I found, my own approaching death. "Just remember that I love you…" were the last words I heard uttered as she stroked her fingers across my eyes and warm darkness swallowed me whole.

Chapter 19
The Value of Dirt

I dreamed of Rosen… of words she'd spoken to me once after I'd asked her why she'd tried to poison me. "Rhyme no plant can harm you unless you let it. I have fed you countless poisons and none have done a thing. For a long time, you didn't even know. Plants…or should I say the spirits of the plants find something in you and they choose to do no harm. All you need is a seed and you can accomplish anything you set your mind to… I'm just trying to make you realize that and I wasn't going to manage it by taking the nice approach. Just remember no matter what I do or how much it hurts that I'll always care about you…"

I woke all at once gasping softly to find myself still alive and in a great amount of pain as I hung limply from two vines my blade still protruding from my chest. I blinked at the soft whispering I could hear in my mind before gazing down at the blade to see a small stem wrapped around its base. The stem had grown while I slept holding the wound closed around the blade so that I wouldn't bleed out. I raised my good hand and stroked the small green shoot allowing my magic to flow freely. With no small effort I pushed the vines out of my body patching them with the raptor vines I'd grown from the small stem as I lay on the ground trying to catch my breath. "Goddess…" I grunted as I gazed on the spirit that sat upon my window sill. "That hurt."

While I lay there on the ground suffering I fought to heal myself to no avail, I had to get out of the maze. Or else despite my best efforts I would die… with the aid of the little magic that I could use thanks to the plant that I'm sure Rosen had provided I made myself something of a walking stick, several vines wrapped firmly together, and I slowly but surely ambled my way forward. Not wishing to struggle all the way to an end I might never reach I used the vines to create holes in the walls walking through one after another until I found myself free crumpling to my knees as the voices came back to me, the magic in my chest near to bursting with the need to be released. I lay resting against an ancient with my eyes closed while my body fought to heal itself. It hurt nearly as much as sustaining the wounds had and still the blade protruded from my chest.

I rubbed my shoulder assuring myself that it was whole and my thigh to be sure of the same before gripping the blade sticking out of my chest. I took a deep breath heart racing with nerves before wrenching it from my breast crying out at the spurt of blood, fighting the wave of dizziness before my magic set in and I healed myself. Once done I lay gasping against cool bark thinking of all the ways that could have gone wrong.

I gazed on the familiar spirit that in many ways had saved my life, "Thank you." I murmured softly raptor vines still draped across my torso.

"Well that was interesting…" I started grimacing as my body still ached with the pain of my wounds. I glanced up to find Renka creeping out of the shadows.

"If you're here to kill me do it quickly. I'm too tired of feeling pain." I husked too fatigued to offer up a fight.

"I can't say you've done anything in the short time I've known you to deserve my wrath." She countered crouching down beside me. "I was exploring the forest when all hell broke loose at the palace. I couldn't tell you who's responsible or if the Queen still lives. I hope she does…she was different than the other monarch's I've met." Renka tugged lightly at the hair that fell across my brow eyes softening with sadness. "Your beautiful mane is gone."

"It'll grow back." I offered with a shrug as I fought to stand with her help.

"What happened in there...?" I allowed Renka to bear much of my weight as we trudged through Griffin Forest trying to get as far away from the maze as possible least guards be lurking about.

I huffed right leg aching each time I dared place weight on it despite that I'd healed it. The pain I knew, would linger for several hours, it took time for the body to fully accept such an extensive healing. Rest would have done me good. "The Void...has found a new way to spread. Not across the land as it's been doing seemingly forever, but now through people. It's inside the Sol-Lea, a foreign Prince who I think is behind it all and the Princess... the Queen's third child."

"From what I heard the Queen and the Heir are dead...and the Head Gardener played a hand in it all." We paused briefly while I fought to catch my breath.

Renka snorted, "I escaped my master only to find myself immersed in a war still bound," She tugged gently at her collar shaking her head. "Do you think it true?"

"That both the Queen and the Heir are gone...I don't know. I want to believe they still live, I want to believe that Rosen would never betray her Queen, but I am tired, hurting and quite disheartened to find that I did not see this coming. Right now I don't know what to believe." I answered honestly as we began to move again.

"It sounds a lot like you're giving up...and perhaps I know nothing. Nothing of this Queen or this land save through the eyes of a slave, but I have lived and I have survived despite many hardships simply by telling myself I must go on." We paused again, everything hurt, my heart most of all and I wanted to lay down surrounded by the green and just die. Instead I listened to her words and tried to find heart. "I came upon you when you burst through a wall of green that quickly put itself back together, you were bleeding heavily with a large blade sticking out of your chest. Now if I had seen that on the plains...I'd have said you were dead Gardener. If I had seen that anywhere I'd have said you were dead…I thought, I was about to watch you die. And then you did something miraculous, you healed yourself…"

"You healed yourself from wounds I thought unhealable. I have never heard of the Queen's Gardeners before coming here but I'm know now and I will never forget. Regardless if I stay or go after this collar is gone I will never forget you Denarii." I smiled softly at her words as she dragged me through the forest.

"I suppose that means you no longer want to bite me?" I questioned voice a little husky with lingering pain.

Renka chuckled softly, "I wouldn't go that far."

"Just thought I should ask is all." I replied shrugging gently least I cause myself more pain.

She bowed her head slightly in acknowledgement of my words but otherwise gave no answer, her brow was furrowed with concentration, her ears flicking every which way. No doubt listening for danger. We moved as fast as we were able with me still feeling the pain of my wounds now gone. It hurt…Goddess it felt as if I still had several holes in my body, each movement sending shockwaves of blazing fiery pain shooting along every nerve.

Sweat soaked my shirt and plastered my hair to my scalp, each breath was a struggle, each step a conscious effort. I had healed the wounds but my mind needed time to catch up and I had no time to give. Renka paused as frequently as she could, my body screamed that it wasn't frequent enough. A journey that once took just a slither of the sun's span suddenly took four times as long. I just wanted to stop moving…Goddess. "Gardener we have to keep moving." Renka muttered urgently gazing back the way we'd come, she'd been doing that more and more often as the sun marched its way across the sky.

I slumped down against a tree gazing at the light of the sun filtered through the leafy canopy above. I traced my fingers over the roots cradling me as I leaned heavily against strong bark. "How long

have they been following us?" I questioned softly as sweat trickled down my face and dripped off my chin.

Renka huffed nostrils flaring as her ears went back, "For several slithers of the sun…"

"Since I escaped the maze?" She gazed at me solemnly, her silence my answer.

"You should run." I breathed softly as I closed my eyes.

"We have to keep…"

"If I stay with you, they'll catch both of us. Go on Renka," I blinked up at her. "This isn't your war after all."

I watched her eyes flare before she took my arm in hers. "No, but your Queen gave me freedom despite the collar around my neck and this is my choice." Renka pulled me to my feet before using her strength to flip me into the air. The world slowed for a moment, I briefly glimpsed the beginning of fur on her face, the leaves sparkled with the light of the setting sun and oddly I felt really calm… and then suddenly time sped up.

I fell onto the back of a mare larger than any I'd ever seen before gasping as the pain I'd felt rocket through me as if it were fresh, darkness bled in as the ground rushed by beneath me. I fought the urge to be sick while clutching firmly to Renka's mane as she galloped head long into Griffin Forest moving faster than any mount I've ever ridden. After a small eternity she slowed and then stopped. I slipped from her back…

"Woah…" Strong hands clutched at my sides keeping me from hitting the ground. I opened my eyes to find Renka hovering over me sweat beading across her brow as she lowered me gently to the ground. "I have you. I have you." She soothed stroking her fingers lightly across my brow. I glanced around us sure that we were as close to the heart of the forest as we were going to get in my current state. I opened my mouth, but Renka shook her head. "We're safe Gardener…for now we're safe. Rest…heal. I'll guard you." She smiled softly, eyes bright and yet solemn. "My choice, remember?" Chuckling softly, I allowed my body to relax fighting sleep for all of a moment before it consumed me.

I woke in the night to find myself curled in Renka's lap, a fire burning brightly several feet away, while several fish lay baking in the ashes. I sat up gently rubbing my hand through my hair wondering why it felt so light...I paused when I found the end of the silky strands far quicker than I was used to. The events of the day came rushing back to me and I gasped softly heart aching a new. "How are your wounds?" Renka questioned drawing my attention from my inner turmoil.

I shifted slightly shrugging my shoulders, before pushing to my feet to find my leg easily able to support me. I sat back down beside her on the bed of leaves she'd laid out for us. I gazed around our small camp site guarded well by a circle of trees grown closely together. "You did well." I offered impressed.

Renka raised her brow at me, "All I did was build the fire and catch the fish, when you passed out the leaves beneath you grew lush and soft and the trees swayed close so that they may protect you from prying eyes." She shook her head, "So it is I that should be saying you did well." I gazed around our little cozy space, warm despite the chill of the night.

"Are you sure I did all this in my sleep..." I questioned curiously.

She snorted, more horse than human, "I haven't been sure of anything since you bought me from that merchant in Center Market."

"I'd apologize but I couldn't tell you what I'd be apologizing for." I'd said shaking my head softly.

Renka pulled the fish from the ashes and offered it to me on a large leaf. "Yes...apologize for freeing me from slavery." Renka gave me a look. "You don't owe me an apology Denarii..."

"Rhyme…" I offered taking the leaf from her out stretched hand. "My friends," I continued as she waited for an explanation. "They call me Rhyme and I can't really think of you as anything else if you were willing to risk your life to save mine despite that you know nothing of the situation."

Renka smiled softly eyes glowing softly in the fire light, "It's been a long time since I've been considered a friend."

"How does it feel?" I questioned taking a small bite of my fish mouth falling open to avoid scorching my tongue. "Ho…hot…"

Renka laughed softly at my theatrics being far more careful as she took her first bite. "Considering the fact that I literally just took it from the fire I would think so…and," she paused chewing slowly before swallowing. "It feels amazing; after all I've spent the last few years of my life being considered less than human and you sit here hardly knowing me at all, talking as if we are equals."

"You are just as much as a person as I am…" I countered, much more careful with my second bite. "I am not talking to you as if we were equals, that indicates that I think less of you…I am talking to you as an equal because that's what we are. You are a person and you change into a horse, but so what, I talk to plants and I am considered one of the most respected people in Angileri. It is all about perception… fancy titles be damned it is the way you look at the world and just as it is your choice to be here with me despite the danger. It's my choice to see the world as I do, an equal platform for all despite titles and power."

Renka smiled, gazing down at her fish. "I'm starting to understand why you are so favored by your Queen Gardener."

I choked a little on my fish in my amusement. "Perhaps you can explain it to me then."

Renka used her thumb to wipe a few scales off my cheek. "Not many with power such as yours view the world as you do." She pulled her hand away, "It's quite refreshing actually."

"Power such as mine?" I questioned softly sucking softly on my tinder fingers.

"You are a noble Rhyme…oh you don't carry the title of Lord or Lady but you are a noble, Gardener taking the place of the former. The Queen adores you, you live in the palace and socialize with soldiers and royal guards alike. You have more coin than most can dream of holding in their entire lifetime, you're educated…you probably know more than one language, you can defend yourself no doubt trained by your brother who holds the title Horse Master. You are a person of high regard and value, more so even than the Queen…she has an Heir sadly making her expendable. There is only one you." Renka finished off her fish popping the last piece into her mouth. "As I said you have much knowledge and much power, not factoring your gift…and yet you are kind and courteous. You treat a slave as your equal because I'm a person and that's enough." She shook her head, "Nothing about you is truly as it appears. You have so much and you value it…perhaps that's it. You actually value all that you have."

"My mother taught me the value of dirt Renka…now I know you're asking yourself how can dirt have value. As a child I asked myself the same thing." I tossed the bones of my meal into the fire before resting my elbows on my knees. "I will tell you what my mother told me and maybe that will make you understand a little more of why I am the way I am…"

Renka leaned forward as I brushed some leaves aside picking up a hand full of dirt in my hands holding it out before us, "Dirt is the beginning…of everything, from the smallest blade of grass to the greatest giant's spine. Everything that lives and breathes is blessed to walk upon this earth…we use it and abuse it without ever thinking about how important it really is. But if suddenly dirt disappeared where would we be…what would we have?" Renka's ears twitched as she watched enraptured as the moist soil grew dry and suddenly fell between my hands dry sand. "Nothing, we'd have nothing. No water, for where would it rest, where would it gather, how could it

rush across land that did not exist. No sustenance, no plants would grow, no prey would feed, no predators would hunt. No air to breathe just a wasteland where nothing can exist."

I picked up another handful of dirt, mixed with rocks and leaves and twigs, as well there were things harder to see, small little beings that fed on smaller littler beings. "Dirt is messy and gritty and sometimes just plain disgusting at times and most people think nothing of it, but ask any plant mage and you'll discover that in the blink of an eye with just a hand full of dirt…" I smiled softly as all the hidden seeds began to sprout causing my hand to glow softly with magic while green shoots grew, steadily twinning around my fingers. "They can create whole new worlds." I finished softly. "Now if you can find value in dirt. Something most do not even consider valuable than you should value what is truly valuable even more because as dirt can dry up and become a brittle wasteland like a desert so too can the things you value disappear. So value them as they should be valued and you'll never have any regrets."

"I grew up in a different place than this…and when my mother told me that story it was in reference to a doll I broke in my anger. A doll she had spent many nights knitting together, using materials it took her months to save up and buy. It was such a beautiful doll and I destroyed it…" I dug softly in the ground making a small hole before placing the bundle of plants I now held in their new home. "And now it's gone forever and I regretted it instantly, I still regret it because of the pain it caused my mother. I will never forget the look in her eyes as the doll came apart before us..." I sighed softly as I patted the soil gently before dusting off my hands. "Just as well I'll never forget the value of dirt and all the things I hold dear." I twirled my knife in my hand gently.

"I gather that dirt is a metaphor for the things we often take for granted…" Renka murmured softly placing her hand on mine causing me to stop the mindless twirling of my blade.

I placed my hand over hers, "She used words that a child and a growing plant mage would understand…and it stuck as you see I still know the story."

"I think everyone would be a lot better off if they understood the value of dirt as you do." Renka offered squeezing my hand gently. "Especially a few of those hard headed nobles." Renka and I both laughed at that.

"I agree whole heartedly," I murmured softly covering her hand with mine in silent thanks before allowing our hands to fall apart. Renka stuck the blade in the ground close to the fire away from our bed of leaves.

"We should sleep Gardener," She murmured with a yawn splaying out on the ground nuzzling into leaves that were far softer than they should be.

"You sleep, I'll stand guard. I'm not feeling very tired at the moment." Renka mumbled her agreement as I tossed several large twigs into the fire to keep it burning. When I glanced back at her, she was half buried in the plush foliage fast asleep. I chuckled softly as I gazed into the fire thinking of all that had transpired that day.

I traced my fingers through the shortened uneven strands of my hair before hesitantly pulling my blade from the ground remembering at the last moment that it was made from a plant and not steel despite its indestructibleness and would not hold my reflection. I listened to the green and asked a small request standing after a moment when I found what I sought. I glanced back once more to make sure that Renka still slept before slipping away from the campsite.

Not even half a slither of the moon's span away I found a small pond, I knelt before the water's edge and looked on my reflection. I looked haggard and defeated, my hair at varying lengths as if he'd tried to cut it all at once and failed miserably. My reflection wavered as if disturbed and I raised my hands to my face to find that I was crying. My shoulders shook softly, I covered my

mouth as if others might hear as I sobbed finally allowing the pain to catch up to me. Once done I used the fresh water to clean my face, he had taken everything from me. My love, my trust, my promise…I picked up my blade and held my hair in my hands tracing it along the silky strands dropping them into the water as they separated in my hand. I could sit here and wallow in self-pity at all that I had lost or… I could take it back. I'm sure you guessed exactly which I chose to do. I'd lost everything before, and I hadn't given up then. I wasn't about to start now and give that man the satisfaction.

I stood from the pond watching strands of my hair drift away as I ran my fingers through what remained, several locks falling to rest over my left eye. I tucked my blade into my belt missing my sheath, Prince Eris should have killed me himself, because he had no idea the wrath he'd unwittingly unleashed. I smiled softly at my reflection before returning to camp, I used a bit of my magic to ensure that the trees would wake me if the enemy came upon us and then I curled up close to Renka for warmth and promptly fell asleep more tired than I thought after such an eventful day…

The whispering of the green woke me long before I was ready as warm and comfortable as I had been buried in soft leaves, I shook Renka awake as the dawning sun began lightening the forest. "Renka…Renka wake up there are people coming towards us."

The Marr bolted up right squinting her eyes at me in confusion, "Gardener…your hair." She reached to touch it curiously, and I gently brushed her hand away.

"Later, we have to hide." I pulled her to her feet and motioned towards the tree we'd been sleeping under.

"We're climbing that?" She questioned incredulous.

"I promise not to let you fall." I pushed her forward and watched for anyone approaching while the bark of the tree grew rough where she placed her hands offering leverage while I pushed from behind.

"I will note that climbing a tree with no hand holds should be impossible and that this feeling of being pushed upward is very unsettling." She murmured becoming more aware the higher she climbed. I halted our climb when we came to a tree limb thick enough and long enough to bear our combined weight easily. "As well why didn't we do any of this yesterday?"

I sat quietly peeking through the leaves waiting, using my magic to subtly shift the position of the leaves where we slept, "I was disheartened and extremely fatigued yesterday and couldn't have done any of this if I tried. And when will you learn that where plants and I are concerned nothing is impossible."

Renka snorted as she leaned forward with me trying to see what I was doing as the enemy grew steadily closer. "What are we…"

"Gods!!!" We watched as someone flew through the air into the clearing swinging back and forth from a leafy vine that seemed to have appeared out of nowhere.

"How the hell…" Another person screamed before finding themselves hanging upside down swinging by their legs beside their companion. "How did you do that." The Marr asked once the only sound that could be heard was the soft bickering beneath us.

I turned to her wiggling my fingers gently as a smile spread across my face, "Why magic of course."

"Where did the vines come from, how did you get them to…to string them up like that." Renka rubbed her face. "Gods and Goddesses it's too early."

I chuckled softly pulling her closer and tracing a path with my fingers to a large tree hovering over the smaller trees beneath, this tree made the ones beneath look like saplings in comparison. It stood even larger than the tree in which we presided. "I call trees like that ancients…they're scattered around the forest, most heavily in the forest's heart. They all have vines hanging from them, don't ask me why but they do, no matter what tree it is they're generally littered with vines." I traced the path from the tree to the ground below. "The vines don't really reach the ground but I used my magic to aid in their growth so that they could fall just so pooling on the ground there, right where those two entered the clearing. I knew where they'd enter from the voices of the green and with a little whispered request..." I splayed my hand displaying our guests, "there they are hanging upside down trying to figure out what happened."

We watched them swing back and forth for a while, "I think one of them knows you," Renka said ears twitching softly.

"The one on the right claims it's the one on the left's fault and the one on the left is laughing a little saying she would find you and that she has, this is obviously your work after all. No magic has ever shown as brightly as yours. She says she could free them but it's best to just wait for you to come out and do it yourself." She finished gazing at me curiously.

I laughed softly knowing instantly who it was as soon as she started talking about how bright my magic was. "That's Libeth for sure...as for the other woman. I suppose we should go find out." I wrapped my arm around the Marr's waist and jumped from the tree before she realized what I had in mind and of course she screamed bloody murder all the way to the ground. We landed in the pile of leaves that had once been our bed no worse for wear, though of course Renka was a little breathless. "Are you well?" I asked dusting leaves from my tunic filled with holes and still covered with blood as if it were the most natural thing in the world.

"If you ever do that without warning again," Renka threatened nostrils flaring wide as her eyes sparked with her rage. "I will bite you."

I smiled cheekily, "But wasn't it you that said I enjoyed that sort of thing. Why reward me for bad behavior..."

"I think I liked you better a little disheartened, certainly less dangerous to my health…" I helped her pull leaves from her hair.

"You weren't in any danger I said I wouldn't let you fall." I countered softly.

"Yes but I certainly didn't think you'd jump either." She grumbled pouting cutely. I pinched her cheek and she smacked my hand glaring some more.

"Next time I'll warn you." I offered turning to take in the two women hanging in the middle of our camp.

"Goddess I hope there isn't a next time…" She mumbled softly behind my back before stepping up beside me.

"Endearing yourself to another woman I see," Libeth breathed brushing her hair out of her face. "Has she seen you naked yet? I'm waiting for the day for you to tell me that someone has finally broken you in…"

Renka wrapped her arms snuggly around my waist nuzzling softly at my neck, I leaned back against her sure that this would be interesting. "Well the day has finally come." Her voice was quite silky and seductive when she wanted it to be. And her accent was exquisite, thicker than normal. "Her body is that of a Goddess…" We watched as Libeth's mouth dropped open in speechlessness.

The Marr pulled away laughing loudly, "Thank you Rhyme for that moment truly…thank you." Renka shook her head walking away while Libeth flushed in embarrassment.

"The fact that you'd believe I'd sleep with a near stranger after knowing me as you do is a bit insulting." I raised my brow and with a whispered command Libeth fell to the ground groaning in pain. I watched her for a moment, "I'd say I was sorry but I'd be lying." I offered before turning to her companion.

She raised her hands in a defensive gesture, "Goddess please don't drop me like that." I gripped the vine holding her legs and lowered her gently to the ground.

"Where she deserved it, you do not." I helped her to her feet after freeing her legs while Renka helped Libeth.

"I'm sorry…" Libeth wheezed. "I wasn't thinking…what happened to your hair?" She asked concern filling her voice as she reached forward.

I brushed her hand away gazing curiously at the woman standing before me wearing a hair style quite similar to mine. "We were betrothed once?" I questioned taking in the brown of her skin and the look of her face, the two very different color of her eyes.

She laughed softly, "Yes as I recall you told my father and yours that if it was a choice between my pig of a brother and me you'd choose me every time despite the fact that I was quite shy then. It's good to see you again…"

I took her hand and pulled her close resting my cheek against hers and closing my eyes to enjoy a moment I never thought I'd have again, embracing one of my people as I once did on the island. "Taeli, you've grown so much." I murmured softly stroking her hair.

"As have you, your accent is nearly gone but I still hear it. Mine has faded as well, ever since the King of Dangilere adopted me I've been hard pressed to find other's from back home. I miss them." She sighed softly rubbing my back.

"As do I," I murmured before pulling away.

"Of course you two know each other," Libeth shook her head. "Kantari must be smaller than I thought."

"It's actually a very large and diverse continent, with small tribes and larger settlements scattered throughout. Many of the natives have tan skin as these two do, but as well some of the Horse People reside there and breed so there offspring turn out looking quite unique..." Renka interjected gently. "I have family that lives there," she added when we all looked at her curiously.

"As much as I would like to spend the next few hours reminiscing about how much we miss our home together that's not why we came to find you. The palace..."

"Has been taken." I finished for her.

"Yes and the Queen perhaps..."

"Killed," Renka supplied. The Marr and I shared a look before I turned back to our companions.

"Let me tell you the story of how I lost my hair..."

Chapter 20
Innocents

"Goddess that's devastating." Taeli stroked her fingers gently through my hair tears forming in her eyes.

"She can touch your hair but I can't…" Libeth grumbled softly behind her.

Taeli turned on her, "In Kantari our first greeting is that of touch," She pulled Libeth roughly against her. "We touch cheeks, we stroke each other's hair ensuring in our hearts and our minds that our friends are well." Taeli held Libeth's face against hers as she stroked her hair while explaining our customs. "Our culture is centered on touch and camaraderie. Regardless of the fact that we haven't seen each other since we were children it's second nature, it's an offer of comfort…" She shoved her away. "Not pity or a sick fascination to feel the difference. Do not question things you do not understand."

I held them apart, "Now's not the time to be at each other's throats for something so trivial." I argued looking at each of them in turn.

"She think she knows you…" Libeth countered.

"She does…" I murmured softly accent a little heavier than usual. "She knows my heart and my home she knows all the things I grew up with…but you do as well. You know the Gardener; all the struggles we've been through to learn new customs and a new language. You both know me, so how about instead of fighting over the things you think you know, learn about the things you don't and get over yourselves." I dropped my hands from between them. "Or I'll make you…" They shared a look at that ominous threat.

"Did you two bring a group of guards with you?" Renka questioned finally coming back into the conversation once all was said and done.

"No...why?" Taeli gazed at her brow furrowed slightly.

Renka gazed into the treetops ears going back slowly, "I was hoping that perhaps we were surrounded by friends." She offered softly.

I followed her gaze taking in the silence that had befallen us already sure of what I would find, shadows...shadows filled the treetops to overflowing darkening the lightening sky with their presence. More than I could think to count, I turned in a circle heart racing in my chest. "Goddess..." Taeli breathed drawing closer to me. "What are those?" her voice quivered slightly with fear.

"Shades." Libeth replied stepping closer as well. We stood in the center of our camp surrounded by Shades, the fire slowly dying beside us. I'm honestly surprised it had lasted through the night...magic might have played a part.

"Is running even an option?" Renka questioned fists clenched at her sides.

"Running will get us killed faster than fighting will." I replied trying to come up with a plan.

"Fighting will still likely get us killed." Taeli countered voice quivering.

"Can you even fight?" Libeth asked, and I waited for a reply needing to know if she'd be an asset or a hindrance in this coming battle.

Taeli snorted, "You think my father would have let me leave the island if I couldn't...but fighting several warriors with spears and swords is different than fighting something you're not even sure you can touch."

"They're still men…under all those billowing shadows they're still men. Fight them as if they are." I supplied as the air grew tense. "Libeth do you have your pouch?"

"No…" I glanced over my shoulder at the smile I heard in her voice. "I have yours." She hefted it in her hand as Shades rained down from the trees silent in their execution and just as several touched the ground she tossed it into the air.

Time slowed, my heart paused in its beat, I drew my blade, Renka transformed, Taeli…threw a tornado and Libeth used her magic to call forth the vines. After that I simply focused on keeping myself alive.

Vines danced, every now and again I could see Libeth using dragon's breath to blow fire, Renka trampled a shade that nearly took off Taeli's head and I twirled through the masses slashing every limb I could reach with my blade. It felt as if we fought forever, every Shade we defeated replaced by two more. I think one person even got set ablaze, falling into the campfire still slowly dying.

"Rhyme!" Libeth cried out, I turned to find her struggling on the ground with a Shade.

"Let…." I pulled down the vine that had once held Libeth watching it wither until the end held a narrow tip. "Her…" I flicked it outward catching the Shade around the throat. "GO!" I pulled backward flipping him over my head off into the distance while Libeth watched catching her breath.

"Remind me to never make you angry." I offered my hand and she took it allowing me to pull her to her feet.

"Maybe later," I replied punching a Shade in the face over Libeth's shoulder causing her to widen her eyes as they fell to the ground behind her.

"Nice punch…" She glanced at the whip I held in my hand brow raised. "Nice whip."

"How are you feeling?" I flicked my whip and Libeth and I watched another Shade go flying somewhere.

"Is that you, the vine or the magic?" Libeth asked curious at the effect. "And I'm okay I suppose, can't do this forever. My magic is waning…" She took my blade and threw it, I turned to watch it catch in a Shade where I supposed the throat would be, right before they could capture Renka.

I glanced at the vine whip before answering, "Probably a bit of all three. I'm not overly tired magic wise, but I'm still weak in body after healing myself and eventually someone will make a mistake. Did you find my pouch?"

"I caught it when it fell," she murmured guarding my back as she handed it to me.

With a quick glance inside I found exactly what I was looking for. "Make sure when we run you run for my blade…or I'll never forgive you."

Libeth bowed her head in understanding, before tossing several crimson petals at a group of Shades advancing towards us, the petals caught a tailwind from Taeli and whirled around them. The shadows melted away leaving them looking decidedly human and confused. Renka was easily able to handle them from there.

"Nice use of succubus." I murmured softly in appreciation.

Libeth shrugged lips curling slightly, "I try."

"You grab Taeli, I'll get Renka." I wrapped the vine whip around my shoulder as Libeth looked on curiously. I opened my palm and she stepped back as Child's Slumber began to bloom. "You should start running…" I tossed it into the dying embers. "Now…" Libeth paled and turned sprinting as fast as she could towards my childhood friend.

I glanced around spotting Renka and racing towards her shoving Shades aside as I moved not wanting to be in the vicinity when the sleeping agent permeated the air. Just before I reached her a Shade sprang towards me, I chopped them in the throat before flipping them over my shoulder and then leaped on the next using them as a stepping to stool before finding myself on the Marr's back. I leaned down closer to her ear, thighs clenched tight around her girth as she tried to unseat me. "Head for the open spaces Renka…beyond our campsite where the trees grew close together last night!" I cried breathlessly trying to get her to hear me through her panic.

She reared up trampling several Shades as she dropped down galloping towards the edge of our campsite. I glanced around us, catching sight of Libeth dragging Taeli in another direction grabbing my blade from the fallen Shade's throat as she passed exiting the circle of trees just before we did. I called forth my magic, actually able to feel the large draw in such as short span of time requesting that the trees embrace for me. Renka transformed catching me on her back as she turned gazing wide eyed as the ancients swayed their towering forms closer together and the younger trees beneath filled in their empty spaces. Creating an unescapable chamber.

Gods and Goddesses what…how…" Renka stood speechless for as long as it took Libeth and Taeli to circle around and find us.

"What did you do?" Taeli voiced the question Renka herself could not ask while she admired the beautiful sphere that had formed completely of trees, awing in itself, and the magnitude of power it took to create.

"We killed them…" Libeth answered for me wiping my blade along her pant leg before handing it back to me.

"How?" Renka questioned turning to face us brow furrowed in confusion.

"There is a plant, called child's slumber. Just a breath of its essence in full bloom can knock out a room full of people. At this stage that's all it will do…over time the flower withers and the sleeping agent draws inward growing more potent." Libeth traced her fingers through her hair as I tied my pouch to my waist heart heavy. She sighed softly fingers quivering as she held her hair back, eyes dark with emotion.

"It can be used as a way to ease a person's passing…if burned and left it makes a person sleep and never wake up. Rhyme easily made the flower reach that point and then she tossed it in the fire…" Libeth turned towards the chamber I had created to keep them from escaping. The death chamber.

"There were so many…" Renka breathed, ears back, eyes solemn.

Taeli wrapped her arm around my waist pulling me close, "We should go."

"We have to check to see if any of them are alive…we have to know if any of them are our people or imposters." I countered with a lump in my throat.

We all stood for a moment listening to the normal sounds of the forest as the dawn turned to day. I took a breath and stepped forward, two trees parted for me creating an opening big enough for a large man to pass through. I stepped into the clearing that had once been our campsite and covered my mouth tears streaming from my eyes. The fire had finally died all that remained smoking embers. I covered my nose with my shirt tears staining my bloody sleeve. There were no shadows…just men laid out falling wherever ever they'd stood when the scent reached them. Their cloaks of obscurity gone in death. I moved towards the closest man and crouched gripping at his shirt.

"What are you looking for?" Renka questioned standing in the entrance to this place wishing to come no further than that. I could see Libeth crouched low between her legs gazing at the ground fingers still held tightly in her hair. Taeli stood beside her a look of concern on her face as she clutched her shoulder offering words of comfort I couldn't hear.

I tore the man's shirt and bit my lip at what I found there…more tears burned my eyes as I stood, nose still covered so as not to breathe the harmful fumes. I backed away taking one last look around to assure myself that no one lived before stepping out of the clearing. I laid my hands upon the young trees as they slowly moved back together sealing shut with not so much as a whisper of sound. As silent as the tomb I had just created. "We should go…" I murmured softly after sending a silent prayer of forgiveness up to the Goddess.

"We just killed…"

"No." I turned wiping the tears from my eyes. "I killed them…"

"I didn't stop you." Libeth countered.

I didn't argue with her, instead I once more tucked my blade into my belt hefting the vine whip on my shoulder. "We should go."

Taeli gripped my shoulder, "Rhyme what you did…"

"What was necessary." Renka finished ears flickering softly. "And if we want it all to be for nothing we can sit here and let more find us."

Libeth stood, hair is disarray, "I knew that there would be death…after all he took our Queen…our Heir. I knew we would have to fight…but those were Shades Rhyme…not mere shadow mages, not imitations or imposters." Libeth shook her head. "I saw the sorrow on your face exiting that…that tomb."

"They're traitors…" Renka countered.

"They're innocent!" Libeth cried.

"Innocent save for the fact that they were in the wrong place at the wrong time infected by the Void they could not see; given orders they could not refuse. We are killing our own people all so that we may live because of that man!" Libeth wept silently while

Taeli held her close. "I came to this country thinking that I would have a better life." She turned to me anger in her eyes, "You should have killed him Rhyme…you should have killed him when you found him that night."

"I could have." I replied softly thinking of all the things we could have avoided. "But it's not who I am. I stroked a tear from Libeth's face smiling softly. "Hold onto that righteous anger, onto the sorrow at the death we had to bring upon all those innocents. We'll pay him back in kind."

Taeli opened her mouth to speak and I raised my hand, "I'm not saying revenge is the answer. I'm certain it won't erase this moment from our minds, nor will not ease our passage into sleep at night and I'm positive it won't make us feel better…"

Libeth snorted. "Speak for yourself…"

Renka turned chuckling slightly while I fought not to crack a smile. Libeth gazed at us curiously, eyes still red from her tears. "What…" I shook my head. "What's so funny?"

"It won't make us feel better but at least he'll be dead." I finished ignoring her question.

"Truly…" Renka inserted before Libeth could repeat herself. "We should get going…" She furrowed her brow gazing at our companions. "Where are we headed to exactly?"

I gazed up through the trees allowing the sun to shine on my face as I listened to the spirits of the green heart aching with sorrow. Despite the darkness I felt a smile spread across my face as Libeth answered Renka's question, "We're going to the heart of Griffin Forest."

"What lies at the heart of Griffin Forest?" I took a breath allowing my gaze to fall before marching forward following the spirits as they raced towards our destination in excitement.

"The largest ongoing project in Gardener history." Libeth offered before chasing after me before I got too far ahead.

"That tells me nothing?!" Renka cried following in our wake with Taeli in tow. "I didn't even know what a Gardener was before two days ago."

I laughed softly as the trees glowed with inner light and the earth itself moved beneath us to push us forward faster than we could ever dream of going. "Though I don't think I'll ever forget..."

I gazed at her smiling softly as the world moved along beside us in waves of shimmering green and brown. "Whatever you do…" I murmured voice echoing all around us. "Don't stop moving."

*****

"Can you do that?" Renka gazed at Libeth as the world slowed around us, coalescing back into trees of every shape and size, underbrush willing to trip the unwary at every turn and earth scattered with leaves and pine needles. I stopped moving, gazing around while listening to the green.

"I wouldn't be foolish enough to try." Libeth murmured her reply.

"You came in search of me together…but were there other's?" I questioned turning to face them brow furrowed softly.

Taeli and Libeth shared a brief look. "As many as we could safely find. Guards, recruits, soldiers, some servants, many of the suitors including Emery and Eden and several of the foreign monarchs and citizens, Tailaan and Dahni among them. All of Anear though…the city itself is at their mercy." Libeth offered with a grimace.

"I can hear their voices…" Renka raised an ear and everyone held their breath listening.

"I hear nothing and I am positive my hearing is far superior than yours." I chuckled softly as she snorted causing Taeli and Libeth to gaze at her with wide eyes.

"Not with my ears…I hear them through the green…" I closed my eyes. "I can see them too, waiting."

"Waiting for what…what is the project you speak of?" Taeli asked before Renka had the chance.

"When Angileri was young and the first Queen Alia sat the throne, she knew in her heart that others would challenge if not her then one of her daughters. She went to her first Gardener whom she loved with all her heart…some say even more than her own husband and she requested that he make a place where her family…where her country could be safe. That no man or beast may enter against his will not hers. May only my right hand, most trusted among my people and strongest of my Gardeners be allowed to enter and all others who wish entry follow in his wake. Even I. Were her words to him…" I opened my eyes. "Those words are inscribed on the ancients that guard the entrance to his creation. A haven large enough to house half of the Queen's army and most if not all of the city of Anear at this point. It's a Gardener paradise built in the treetops that did not exist before Alia came to power…in the heart of Griffin Forest."

"May my right hand, most trusted among my people and strongest of my Gardeners be allowed to enter and all others who wish entry follow in his wake. Even I…" Renka murmured ears dropping. "The Head Gardener…has betrayed us. She meant to kill you and surely she knows of this place."

"Rosen led us here as children." Libeth supplied playing with her hair and just making it worse at this point.

"She will come with her Shades and her soldiers infected by the Void and she will destroy us." Renka finished dejectedly.

I moved forward heading toward where I knew their camp to be, sure that I would know them when I saw them. "What hope do we have?" Taeli questioned receiving no answer, Libeth moved with me not wishing to be left behind.

"As I told Renka." I breathed walking past several guards who gazed on me with wide eyed recognition to stand before the Ancients. I gazed up craning my neck to take in their magnificence, their song ringing gently in my ears, their purpose easily fulfilled. Their spirits towered high above me, "It's all about perception..."

"You found her!" We turned as one to see Reason, Eden, Emery and another man racing towards us.

"Ahh I forgot to mention we found your brother." Libeth offered sheepishly when I gave her a look right before Reason swept me from the ground and into his arms.

"Gods you get heavier every time," He grunted setting me down and taking me in, cupping my face in his hands as he looked me over. "What happened to your hair, who's blood is this, why are your clothes torn?"

I brushed his hands away, "I'm not about to tell the story a million times, let's just say I came in contact with the man who did all this personally and move on." Reason pressed his cheek against mine stroking his fingers gently through my hair. "Praise the Goddess that you're alive." He murmured softly in Kantar a language I haven't heard since we were children.

"I would never leave you without saying goodbye." I replied in our home tongue squeezing him softly.

"Only you would counter with something like that as if you could fight the Goddess if she truly wished to call you home." He pulled away chucking softly at my confidence.

"I would fight her Rea, if it meant leaving you without goodbye. I would fight her." I replied honestly.

My brother pressed a kiss to my brow trailing his fingers through my hair one final time. "Never change Rhy Goddess, never change."

"I hadn't planned on it." I pressed a kiss to his cheek playing gently with his hair before pulling away.

"We should hold a meeting..." I turned staring for a moment at the man who was no longer a Prince.

"How is it that the Queen and Heir are possibly dead, and that Princess Mariel is infected with the Void but Sorel stands here before me beside the heart of Griffin Forest completely well and whole?" Eden pulled him closer to his large frame no doubt sensing my mounting anger and frustration.

"He's not so bad after you beat the arrogance out of him Rhyme and now's not the time for fighting. What he says has merit, we should hold a meeting or a small Council to discuss what's happened and plan for the future..." I gazed into Eden's eyes and sighed softly easily able to see how much he cared for the man who once would not have given him the time of day.

I glanced behind me deciding that the Ancients would go nowhere in our absence. "Call a meeting or, gather all those you think important...I'm going to get clean and then I'm going to eat." Reason shook his head but didn't fight me or call me back when I walked away.

I turned to find Renka trailing behind me, "Why are you following me?" I asked curiously heading for a river I knew to be close to here.

"You know this forest, better than anyone else and you can fight if something goes wrong. As well you treat me as an equal and if I have to choose someone to stick with among all these strangers why not let it be the one I know the most about." We stood on the back of the river while I slowly peeled off my clothes.

"You hardly know me at all," I countered pulling off my boots.

"That's still more than I know any of them." Renka leapt into the river ending our conversation. "Gods and Goddesses that's cold!" She exclaimed as she burst through the surface of the water.

I jumped in after her before I could give myself the chance to change my mind, agreeing whole heartedly with Renka's assessment. "Goddess…" I gasped swimming towards the river's edge easily able to find soap weed, I offered some to Renka before scrubbing myself furiously trying to work as fast as I could while shivering.

"You could have just asked me to warm the water you know." I glanced up to see Dani walking towards us smiling softly a large bundle of clothing held in her hands.

"I wasn't thinking." I offered honestly ducking beneath the water to clean my hair before coming up again. "Are those clothes for us?" I questioned wiping the water from my eyes.

"Are you going to marry me?" Dahni countered smile growing into a grin.

"I chuckled climbing from the water watching her eyes widen and her cheek redden as she took in my nakedness. "Not likely." I replied gently taking our clothing from her motionless fingers. "But you're welcome to enjoy the view…" I dried off as quickly as I could, before tossing Renka the towel. "So long as you don't touch." I smacked her hand as she reached for the curling tattoos along my torso. I pulled on my under things before hopping into my trousers. "Huh…" I slung my belt around my waist. "These are actually my trousers." I glanced at Dahni waiting for an explanation.

I watched her admiring my half naked form, eyes wandering, cheeks flushed. "She looks as if she means to devour you." Renka murmured softly coming to stand beside me.

"I'm letting her admire so long as she doesn't touch…" I replied still waiting for Dahni to catch up and answer my question. She didn't look as if she ever would. "Dahni…" I spoke her name loudly startling her slightly.

"Goddess." She breathed forcing her gaze to meet mine. "You're magnificent…" She held her hands to her warm cheeks. "As for the answer to your question, they are. Your brother, steadily refused that you were dead and brought much of your things with him when he escaped claiming that you would want them…it brought him comfort and no one was willing to fight the Horse Master of Angileri's army. We've heard stories of your men…and he helped train those men. Smarter not to chance it."

I silently agreed, "Thank you for bringing them to me…" I pulled on my tunic before tying on my pouch.

"He said you'd be missing this," she offered me my sheath. I took it gladly sheathing my blade before buckling it properly to my belt.

"My brother knows me well." I smiled softly picking up the vine I'd made into a whip and slinging it over my shoulder.

"Well… You guys are practically the spitting image of each other…the only difference being gender and now your hair. It looks lovely by the way." I smiled at Dahni's unassuming compliment.

"You're the first person to tell me so," we walked back towards the large camp that we could hear despite the distance, Renka falling into step beside us.

"I can't imagine why…it makes you look more dangerous." She hesitated for a moment before asking again. "Are you sure you do not wish to marry me?"

I laughed softly, while Renka shook her head. "I'm sure Dahni."

"Just making sure." I bowed my head in understanding smiling at her determination...

*****

"How many times did that girl ask you to marry her?" Renka requested once Dahni had left us. We sat inside a large tent a table before us covered by a map of Angileri and the surrounding countries the Void the division between them all except, Erangi land of beautiful men and Kantari my home both safe separated from the masses by a large ocean and for which I was grateful.

"Many times and I'm sure she will ask me many times more." I smiled at the thought resting my hand upon Kantari tracing my fingers gently along the jungle paths that no one understood better than a native.

"When you said it was all about perception what did you mean?" I blinked coming back to myself as Renka broke the lingering silence between us.

I opened my mouth to speak, paused and then went to speak again... Someone burst into the tent before I could find the words. We both stood ready for anything. "The meeting has been pushed back...Prince Eris sent us a message..." Emery left the tent and we followed quickly behind.

I pushed through the crowd of people gathered at the edge of our makeshift settlement until I came to the center Emery just ahead of me. "We haven't touched her...because..."

I paused shuddering at the feeling that touched me when I grew closer, just as I could see the spirits of the green so too could I see the wisps of shadowy Void seeping off of the person laid out in our midst. "She's infected with the Void." I finished for him, he bowed his head expression grave. "How did she get here, how did she find us?" I questioned as several soldiers pushed everyone back urging those who didn't need to be there back to their tasks. Most went without a backwards glance glad in the fact that others were handling it. Some lingered but not for long. The soldiers were good intimidation.

"She just stumbled into camp, I imagine she knows because Rosen told her or guided her somehow." Libeth offered crouching close to her body but not close enough to be touched if she were to suddenly spring awake.

"That means we have less time than I thought." Taeli crouched down as well shifting the woman's head with her sleeve so that we could more easily see her face. "They know exactly where we are, meaning they could come at any time and easily demolish us. There are not enough soldiers here to defend against this illness…" She pulled her hand back quickly gazing briefly at her fingers before shifting further away. "It's growing stronger. When it first began you could fight it and truly you could not have said if it existed in a person at all. This is blatant…" She stood moving closer to us. "I swear I can almost feel it…something that's just not right and if this is what we're up against…" She took a deep breath before continuing. "We'll lose. Waging a war against innocent people, infected before they realize what's going on, fighting without will or understanding. It'll destroy us, because who will want to fight?" No one answered and that was answer enough.

"We need to fix this…" Taeli murmured softly rubbing her hand over her mouth. "We need to fix it, to heal it and yet this blatant infection tells us we're running out of time to figure out how."

I moved closer to the body and crouched down beside Libeth wondering what held her so captivated startling slightly when I realized I knew her. I reached forward without thinking and gently

stroked Kiyen's hair back from her face. I glanced up to r
everyone gazed on me with baited breath...I stroked her
briefly watching the shadows cling to my hand. I shudder
feeling before quickly pulling my hand away. I gazed at my fingers
until the shadows faded breathing easier once they were gone. Kiyen
remained unconscious, "We'll enter the Last Garden...and hope that
in the time it takes to figure this out our entire nation is not
destroyed."

"We're just missing one very vital person." Reason breathed
pulling his hair back into a ponytail as he grew frustrated. "Goddess
I never thought my death would be at the hands of something created
thousands of years ago by men and women I can't even name."

"I have read the tree...the Queen trust lies in Head Gardener
Rosen above all else, she is her right hand in all things that her
youngest daughter is not. She sits the Council and holds the Queen's
ear. She holds her title because she is strongest and she has betrayed
us." My brother shook his head. "We're all going to die."

"I have explored every inch of Griffin Forest...I have even
been on the other side of the Ancients and you are right...but
perception is everything brother and if I'm right..." I ran my fingers
through my hair still able to hear the Ancients song ringing gently in
my ears. It's all I could hear this close to them, the other voices of
the forest were just white noise in the background, I was aware of
them but I couldn't understand a thing even if I tried. "If I'm right
then we don't need Rosen at all."

Chapter 21
Head Gardener

I gazed at the palace servant that was also my friend and felt older than my twenty-three years, when my mother forced me to come here for a better life I don't think she could have ever imagined something quite like this would happen.

"We need to move her..." Reason and Eden moved forward. "Without anyone touching her for an extended period of time." Taeli added quickly before they could touch Kiyen.

"Do we have a sling for injured?" Libeth asked after a moment of thoughtful silence.

"Yes actually," Reason added chuckling slightly before sending two guards to fetch it for us. "It was beneath your bed," he replied shrugging slightly as he gazed at me, "And I found myself thinking. Why not...?"

I smiled softly, "Thank you for believing in me Rea," he smiled at me before tousling my hair.

I shoved him away with a well-placed glare, "I'm going to enjoy being able to do that." He laughed softly while I fixed my hair. The guards returned just as I thought to retaliate.

We laid the sling as close as possible, without touching her. "Now how are we going to do this?" Libeth glanced around the circle of people waiting for ideas. While everyone stood around nervously gazing at each other waiting for someone else to volunteer I crouched low and slipped my arms beneath Kiyen's still frame and then with a small bit of effort lifted her from the ground shuddering slightly at the sickening feeling that overtook me.

I felt my eyes flutter, time slowed, it felt as if I gazed out at the world through a veil of shadows. I heard whispers, just beneath the song of the Ancients seductive voices nauseating in their intensity. I took a deep breath before setting her as gently as I could into the sling. I sat back on my heels ignoring the whispers and waiting for the wisps of the Void to disappear from my skin. "Goddess..." I breathed before glancing up to find everyone staring at me. "What?" I pushed myself to my feet. "You were all taking too long and I couldn't stand to see her lying on the ground anymore." I sighed softly. "She's my friend…"

"How do you feel?" Taeli asked carefully.

"That's a hard question to answer considering all that has happened in the last few days." I replied honestly.

"Is the Void inside you?" She tried again.

I gave her a look that questioned her intelligence. "If it were, do you really think I'd reply honestly?" I countered not unkindly.

Everyone relaxed, "That's definitely Rhy." Reason said rolling his eyes at my smart remark.

I gazed around the circle of people and saw that the only royalty before us was a Prince that no longer held his title. I furrowed my brow. "Where are the foreign monarchs…where are the people and their guards?" I questioned curious.

Emery answered, "They departed while Libeth and Taeli went in search of you…this is a war they cannot fight, something none came prepared for and many cannot afford to die or be infected when they have no one to replace them…it would be catastrophic. We did the best we could as Gardeners and not politicians to ensure that if they chose not to aid us, then at least they would not initiate war with us in this time of weakness because if we fall…surely the Void will come for them next." Emery turned to Taeli, "Your father, King Teaon of Dangilere leaves you in his steed as well as his most trusted guards, he promised to send half his army to aid us in whatever we may need. Several others volunteered food and Healers. We took what was offered graciously, the highest ranking military man here is the Captain of your father's guard detail and we were not willing to let him lead us." He glanced at the Prince. "There is no royalty, there are nobles and those suitors who wished to stay and aid us like Tailaan and Dahni. We have many of our soldiers and our guard and most if not all of the recruits…but as Taeli said they would destroy us if they came upon us now."

I glanced at my fellow Gardeners, at Tailaan, Dahni, the foreign Captain and the Prince that was not a Prince…these were the people that we had to save a nation. Who would we follow? "Who's in charge if not Captain…" I glanced at him waiting for a name.

He stepped forward and offered me his arm, I took it in a warrior clasp. "Captain Sowin at your service Gardener."

"I would say it's a pleasure but…" I shrugged and he nodded his understanding though a simple bow of his head would have sufficed I did not hold it against him.

"Who is in charge if not Captain Sowin? Guard Captain Neola is hopefully safe but nowhere to be found, the Sol-Lea is infected and the Head Gardener…" I took a deep breath heart aching. "Rosen…for all intents and purposes is a traitor."

"Perhaps your people should vote," Sowin offered not wishing to offend.

I glanced around the circle of people before me, "Are we to have our meeting here then…at the edge of camp?" I questioned.

"Why not…we are Gardeners not meant to be confined to stuffy tents," Eden sat upon the ground beginning the circle and everyone followed suit. The ground was lush covered in grass, it grew soft beneath me, Renka who sat beside me blinked in surprise before shifting away and then back again. She said nothing while I watched and chose not to explain herself once she was done.

"Where do we start?" Dahni asked curiously glancing around the circle.

"Let's start with what we know." Reason supplied, "And go from there."

"The Void has spread…"

"Where did it start?" I wondered aloud.

"The Void lies in the heart of all our joint nations…it is what keeps us from meeting. Angileri, Raleli, Dangilere and…" Dahni rubbed her head trying to supply the last nation that would touch ours if not for the Void.

"Samere." Taeli supplied, "Often forgotten considering how well they keep to themselves, across the water lies Erangi and Kantari and the ice nation Ierilo in the mountains. There are others but those are the big seven that truly hold power, all others exist at the will of kind monarchs that see no need to over throw them."

Dahni bowed her head, "Yes, it began their hundreds or thousands of years ago, long before us. Alia the Queen of Angileri was the first to fight it with her Gardeners…and others followed. It grew stagnant. Until two years ago. Those on the border were in danger and we did not know it. It spread slowly…" Dahni shook her head. "I came with permission from the Council hoping to find answers, but I did not make it as far as I'd hoped in the Tournament…and then it didn't matter anymore."

"As you well know I came with the same intention, hoping that Angileri, known for its forests and gardens would be able to stop it. The strongest plant mages in the world are found in Angileri…there's even a saying." I raised my brow at Taeli's words.

"There's a saying?" I could not help but ask.

Emery tipped his head catching my attention, "It is like beautiful men and architecture in Erangi. If you're looking for a plant mage you go looking in Angileri. There's a reason why the Green Sprout exists and it's not just because it's a good tavern." He finished with a shrug.

"The Void has begun spreading more quickly, taking root in all kinds of people, young, old, weak, strong, morals don't matter though I'm sure those with ill intent enjoy the power the Void brings to them, while those with kind hearts find themselves pushed to the back of their own minds an observer in their body." Taeli continued bringing us back on track.

"How do you know this?" Libeth inserted.

Taeli sighed, "my friend…tried to attack my father, the King. When he died he thanked us and struggled to put into words the horror he had experienced without being able to do anything about it. A fate worse than death…"

"The Queen and Heir may be dead, Mariel is infected and Rosen has betrayed us. Is there anything else we have not said aloud?" Eden added gazing around.

No one said a word, "Now we come to the two most important questions. Who's in charge and how do we stop it?

"Well we said we would vote on who's in charge," Reason supplied. "I suppose we should do that first; we'll all write it down on a scrap of paper and then Captain Sowin can tell us who has the majority. How does that sound?" He gazed around waiting for someone to object, when no one did a recruit on standby offered us each as bit of paper, I waved him away picking up a leaf cradling it in my hand, as I watched murmuring to it with my magic the veins within the leaf shifted to form several words. I curled it up and offered it to the recruit as he came back around.

Sowin took the small sheets of parchment waiting until he held all in his hand before reading each of them carefully, making note of them on a sheet of parchment of his own, raising his brow slightly when he came to my leaf. Reason snorted when he saw it shaking his head with a smile. "Well…it's unanimous," I leaned back on my hands dread settling in the pit of my stomach when he looked at me. "You did not vote for yourself… but" Sowin chuckled. "Your leaf says anyone who can do the job and you qualify."

I fell back onto the ground slinging my arm over my face as I groaned loudly. "Finally where we all thought you should be sister," Reason said a smile clear in his voice.

"Now Head Gardener Rhyme…what should we do to fix this?" Libeth asked using a title I'd hope I'd never hear in reference to me.

"Gods!" Someone exclaimed causing me to shoot up, heart racing, to find Kiyen pushing herself from the ground. She looked haggard but if I couldn't see the wisps of Void flickering with in her near taking on a form I understood, I'd have thought she was fine. The sick feeling that I'd felt while she was unconscious was gone as if it had never been.

"Gardener Rhyme?" She squinted at me before smiling warmly. "You're alive…he told us you were dead but I didn't believe him." She crawled towards me while the others watched in horror not knowing what to do, not knowing who was in control or if Kiyen was even aware of the Void lurking inside of her. I sat leaning back on my hands as she grew closer trying to remain calm. "I knew you of all people wouldn't die so easily." Tears formed in her eyes before trickling down her face, I twitched slightly when she touched me. "They sent me with a message…but never told me anything and Resli." Kiyen sobbed softly climbing into my lap. "Resli is still there, my brother in all but blood and he has him doing Gods know what."

I wrapped my arms around her pressing my hands lightly against her back, murmuring words of comfort as the Void clung to my skin, narrowing my perception of the world as those voices, similar to the green but more malevolent spoke to me. I found myself captivated by the voices that sounded almost familiar if not for the seductive power that lingered within them…

"Rhyme…Rhyme!" I woke with a gasp rolling over blinking in confusion to find myself laid out on the ground.

"What happened?" I groaned pushing myself up to find Kiyen once more unconscious on the sling in the center of our small gathering. Libeth and Eden were crouched beside me, Sowin now sitting a little closer to Kiyen his sword in hand.

"The Void played on your compassion…"

I shook my head. "No, she looked fine, her words were sincere…"

"That's what the Void does Head Gardener, it is not always a blatant attack with swords and knives or bows and arrows. The goal is not always to kill but to spread, like a fire, like a disease, like a…"

"Weed." I supplied without thought.

"Exactly, that is what makes it so dangerous, it exploits people, Kiyen's emotions are genuine, her remorse heartfelt and you love her so of course you wish to give comfort. The Void spreads through touch…can you imagine how many people have grown infected this way…" Taeli's words left me feeling hallow.

I moved forward and gently stroked Kiyen's hair before pulling back and pushing to my feet. "Goddess," I traced my fingers through my hair. "We need to fix this." I turned away walking back towards the Ancients, Renka and Libeth quick to follow.

I moved quickly through tents littering the forest and stopped once more before the Ancients towering side by side. The trees beside them forming a wall that literally separated this part of Griffin Forest from the rest. And if you rode as hard as you could in either direction, you might not realize it at first, but you'd find that the wall of trees kept going seemingly forever until several sun spans later when you arrived right back where you'd started.

"Explain how this is about perception?" Renka said waiting patiently while we gazed on the Ancients waiting for the others to catch up.

I sighed softly laying my hands gently upon the words etched into the wood, "Rosen told me that only one of the Queen's Gardeners could cause the Ancients to part, that at most times it was the Head Gardener. Trusted and respected above all else…she had never heard of their being two people because this is more than about strength and if you're found lacking you aren't just pushed away, you're drained of all your magic and if you don't die then well you'll wish you were. She told me once that if anyone could do it, it would be me because even though she's the Head Gardener we both know who's the stronger mage. I'm sure every Gardener has known for quite some time."

"The grass…it grew soft beneath you without you saying or doing anything. I shifted away and found the ground hard before shifting close to you again and finding it close enough to sleep on. The green as you call it…aids you without question." Renka said explaining what she'd been doing earlier.

Libeth placed her hand on my shoulder, "You can do this." She murmured softly as everyone else finally caught up.

I turned to Renka, "For once I agree with one of your friends." She supplied snorting softly.

I chuckled softly before leaning forward and resting my brow on sun warmed bark, "This could take a while I warned." Before closing my eyes and asking a request…my chest felt as if it were ripped opened as the Ancients drew heavily on my magic speaking slowly, words took decades to form while I stood before them trying to understand, to comprehend all that had come before me. Watching and absorbing as much as I could until I found myself kneeling before the very first Gardener, stripped bare of all my power. I could hardly breathe and truly in that moment I felt death would have been a blessing.

I gazed up at his glowing form, struggling to keep my head up so tired was I in that moment. I did not think I could stand; I did not even remotely think to try. His name I knew was Gal and he gazed down at me for centuries longer than it took the Ancients to tell me the story of this place. "Rhyme." He spoke my name and it was heart stopping in its beauty and simultaneously excruciatingly painful at the same time. I clutched at the ground feeling my nails dig into rough bark where my body truly existed. My head hung low as I fought the urge to scream, tears streamed from my eyes. Each breath I took was labored. I was so sure that I would die, that I would be drained of my magic and fall dead in a matter of moments or was it years, decades, centuries. Time held no meaning, I have never wanted anything to end so badly. Death in that moment would have been a blessing.

"Gardener Rhyme…" I gazed at him through the shortened strands of my hair, spittle dripping from my mouth now frozen in a silent scream. If I could have told him to shut the hell up I would have. "I see your pain, I have taken your magic and still you refuse to give in." My ears rung, blood dripped from my nose, my arms quivered. Goddess, I never thought it would be this hard. Head Gardener Gal stood in deep thought gazing off at something I could not see beyond the glowing light that surrounded us. I realized as he stood silent that I could no longer hear the voices of the green, I could not hear the song of the Ancients. All I could hear were the ringing of his words in my ears.

"You have come this far," He leaned down and cupped my jaw in his hands lifting my head with ease. "I suppose. I will take your measure…" I shuddered as his eyes pulled me in and dragged me under. Just as I had watched the birth of this place, the slow but steady rise of every bridge and building so too did it…did he, did the Ancients take me in, from my birth, through my childhood, past me being taken, to the woman I had become. The Ancients and through them this man, this place knew my worth. They knew me more thoroughly than anyone ever had and when he pulled away freeing me of his gaze I felt raw, worn thin and weak. I felt more defeated in that single moment than I had when Eris had shattered my world…one did not remotely compare to the other.

Head Gardener Gal stroked his chin while tears streamed steadily from my eyes, he bowed his head once before taking me in once more. Now quivering with the last bit of strength I held, fighting to stay on my hands and knees. Blood streaming from my eyes, my ears, my nose and my mouth, while I struggled to breathe.

"I have but one question." I closed my eyes at the pain his words caused. "Why was this haven formed?"

My eyes fluttered open and I answered with the first thing that came to mind, "To protect the woman and the people you love." I croaked unable to say more even if I tried. Head Gardener Gal smiled softly before reaching down and taking me gently by the shoulders. He pulled me to my feet and steadied me. "Rhyme, Gardener Rhyme, now Head Gardener Rhyme Denarii formally of Kantari now of Angileri, child born of the green, lover of the earth," he waved his hand before me. "I have measured your worth, I know you to be strong, the Queen trusts your judgement and the Princess has fallen for your personality. Enter the Last Garden, and may all those you love and wish to protect follow safely behind you. Lead them well Head Gardener and know that your predecessors are with you." He slapped me firmly on the back and the world instantly went black.

When I opened my eyes I found myself kneeling at the base of the Ancients hands curled into fists against strong bark. My heart raced, I moved my hand to clutch at my chest. I could feel that my magic lay where it should, near about gone but still there. The green sang my praise, the Ancients singing with them. I breathed a sigh of relief that I still lived with my magic intact, for a long time I kneeled there too weak to stand. I glanced up to see a new day had dawned, the sky slowly lightening. I did not know if it were but one or several, to me, it had felt like centuries. My throat was dry, my lips cracked, my face was streaked with tears. I touched at my nose, my ears and my mouth to ensure that I was not bleeding. After what seemed a slither of the sun's span I glanced around to find myself not alone.

The embers of a fire lay smoldering not ten feet behind me, around the dying embers lay Reason, Libeth and Taeli fast asleep. I could see Renka walking through the trees along the edge of camp slowly making her way back in this direction ears flicking every which way. I called on my magic trying to gain her attention and chuckled softly when a root shifted knocking her from her feet. She stood quickly, and glanced around before turning towards me. I raised my hand weakly when she narrowed her eyes dropping it as she came running towards me. "You're alive." She cried softly as she kneeled beside me, so as not to wake the others.

"Yeah…and I'm just as surprised as you are." I husked softly. The Marr quickly pulled a canteen from her hip and raised it to my lips helping me drink slowly. "How long was I…out." I questioned softly resting my head on her shoulder.

"Two seven days…Prince Eris has sent more infected and several dead." Renka offered holding me against her least I fall over. She turned towards the Ancients still firmly in place. "They have not parted…is your magic gone?"

"No…" I took a deep breath glad to find it free of pain. "I still have my magic."

"The trees…"

"Call them Ancients." I supplied trying with her help to push to my feet.

"The Ancients have not parted," Renka wrapped her arm around my waist holding me easily while I struggled to stay standing on legs riddled with cramps. I grimaced stretching as best I could with her help.

Once I was able to stand on my own I placed my hands upon the words etched by the very first Gardener. I listened to the Ancients song before closing my eyes and making a request. I stepped back as the ground shuddered waking the others sleeping by the remains of a fire, the first Head Gardener's voice rang in my head. *Enter the Last Garden, and may all those you love and wish to protect follow safely behind you.*

The Ancients shifted only slightly creating an opening large enough for a small dragon to climb through, easily passible for several men standing abreast. I stepped through the entrance with

Renka standing close behind to find myself met by a line of centaurs. "Gods…" Renka breathed in awe as they towered over us, with hair cascading in waves down their backs, kept at bay by the warrior bun I was used to seeing on my brother. They wore vests of green, with patterns of spiraling vines in gold and black. They held swords and bows alike and all held an air of power. A female came forward pawing at the ground with her hooves.

"Finally come into your own Rhy?" Her voice was strong, authoritative and yet familiar in its tenderness. I smiled softly as she leaned close resting her brow against mine.

"Fletcher," I breathed recognizing her scent and the softness of her hair from when I had first come through the Ancients. "It has been so long." She squeezed me softly before pulling away.

"I feel that you are not here to add to the Last Garden, but to finally put it to some use." She shifted her large girth until she stood beside me, her men parting to reveal a path winding up to the top of a hill. "I did not think it would happen in my lifetime, but I can't say I'm disappointed it did."

"You won't feel that way for long." I murmured softly leaning against her side.

"Who are your friends?" Fletcher questioned taking note of my words but choosing not to comment on them.

I glanced over my shoulder to see Renka, Reason and Taeli gapping like fools at the creatures before them. I chuckled at their fascination, we hadn't even topped the hill yet. Libeth came to greet Fletcher as I had, having met her before.

"You know Libeth," I waved my hand towards the other three. "The one who looks like my twin, is my twin Reason, Taeli comes from the same land we hail from and Renka." I clutched her shoulder squeezing softly. "Renka is one of the Marr."

"It is good to meet you, cousin." Fletcher said good naturedly as she bent down and pulled Renka into a bone crushing hug.

Renka hugged her back just as strongly completely ignorant of the fact that her feet no longer touched the ground. Fletcher set her down gently smiling softly at us all. "Fawlin will guide you and your Gardeners to where you belong while we take the others on a tour."

"There are many more," I warned as Fawlin pulled me to the side, I kept hold of Renka deciding it was best to keep her with me. Libeth came with us knowing all that lay instore for them.

Fletcher bowed her head in acknowledgement, "We will gather them Head Gardener, let Fawlin lead you to your place and we will handle the rest."

I tipped my head slightly in accent before moving with the smaller centaur, though she was no less grand than her leader. Libeth took Fawlin's offered hand leaping when she pulled her up and onto her back.

"Do you trust me?" I asked Renka softly as we walked up the hill.

"With my life, as crazy as that sounds." She offered back gazing all around her. The only difference thus far were the centaurs, perhaps the trees were greener but who could truly tell.

I murmured softly in her ear as two more centaurs broke off and came towards us no doubt about to offer us a ride. Before they reached us Renka broke into a slow jog and I smiled at her choice. I ran after her jumping when she bent low for a moment landing on her back, I twinned my fingers in her mane, her transformation happening smoothly from one breath to the next and suddenly we were galloping towards the crest of the hill with Fawlin and her fellow centaurs fighting to catch up. Renka gave a horsey laugh and I laughed with her as we topped the hill and raced across a bridge formed from a fallen Ancient the other side a paradise created from the dreams of a thousand Gardeners.

Chapter 22
Freedom

"How is this possible?" Renka and I stood on the edge of a pool confined to the inside of a massive tree truck towering hundreds of feet in the air, above it at an angle was the top of the tree also hallowed out though it's canopy still existed at the very top, branches lined with leaves formed in the shape of small grooves were fed water from a water fall high above and if you looked hard enough through the rushing water pouring down through the hallow trunk and into this pool, you could almost see it. "How is this tree still growing, when it's clearly been destroyed?" She walked along the edge of the artificial lake trying to get closer to the upper half of the trunk. "There are plants growing in there despite the rushing water…" She glanced down. "There are fish swimming in this pool, there are plants growing inside of this tree beneath water that's clearer than any water I've ever seen." She crouched down tracing her fingers lightly through the water, brows raised in surprise. "The water is warm and it doesn't over flow…Head Gardener." Renka stood and looked at me. "How…"

"Is this possible?" I finished for her, she nodded slowly waiting for an answer. I sat on the edge of the lake, a large band of smoothed wood, the inner rings of the tree clearly visible. I traced my fingers along its surface listening to its peaceful song, this ancient had found new purpose and a lovely purpose it was. "This pool…this lake was here long before me, before Rosen and perhaps even before the Head Gardener before her. Every generation of Gardeners adds something of their own. I would have never thought of something like this, perhaps this mage had two gifts one of the green and one of the water. As for how it's possible…magic exists Renka and that is the only explanation I can give. Magic and the determination to make this possible."

"This place…is amazing." Renka moved back to the bridge from which we'd come smaller than the one we'd first crossed but no less intricate, an ancient split in half paved smooth somehow, with plants shooting up on either side, green and beautiful. I knew that when darkness fell the adorable buds at the top of those plants would bloom and glow. As they would do every night forever without pause or interference, these plants would never die. They were called eternal fireflies. I watched her stroke one gently causing it to bob slightly back and forth. "Has anyone ever fallen?" She glanced down passed the bridge to see another beneath us, there were thousands connecting the upper workings of the trees and the building hard to discern in their canopies if you did not know where to look.

"Of that I am not sure, but when we were young and reckless my fellow Gardeners and I tested the failsafe and jumped. Goddess Rosen punished us right good for our stupidity but we know it works." I pushed to my feet and came to stand beside her. "You can't see it, but there are plants weaved together, to form a nest and I've never seen anything like it before and nor has Rosen as welled traveled as she is. Some plants only exist here. If you fall those seemingly loose growing plants grow taunt catching you in their embrace and tossing you back up and into this pool. Some cause you to slide down onto strategically placed platforms, but this we thought would be the most fun…" I hesitated for a moment smiling softly. "Do you trust me?"

Renka snorted, "I let you ride me, in a nonthreatening situation." I tipped my head in acknowledgement before wrapping her in a hug and tipping forward. She screamed almost as loudly as she did when I jumped out of a tree, almost but not quite. I laughed as we fell closing my eyes as I felt leaves brush against my face, relaxing completely when they embraced us slowing our descent. And then suddenly we were being flung into the air the green giggling gaily as we landed in the warm pool of water.

I pulled Renka to the surface before she could panic laughing softly as I burst through the water. The Marr shoved me back under with a growl of frustration. "I told you to warn me if you ever did something like that again!" She cried swimming for the water's edge.

I came back up sputtering before swimming after her, "I asked if you trusted me." I countered.

"Yes and like earlier I would have appreciated a small whispered explanation," I watched her struggle trying to pull herself out not realizing that the pool sat further down then it appeared when looking from above in certain areas. I followed the green arrows engraved into the dark wood and until I found the ones pointing down and stood on the small platform hidden beneath the water before climbing the gentle slope leading out.

"Rhyme!" I jogged around to where she sat treading water before leaning down offering my hand, pulling her out with a grunt of effort.

"If you had just moved a little further to the left or right you could have stepped out. There are four hidden platforms beneath the water and a slope leading out from there." I offered slicking my hair back.

"The water is clear, how is it that I don't see them?" She questioned as we made our way back to the bridge.

"The pool is fed constantly by the waterfall, which means the water ripples sometimes gently and sometimes not, but it distorts what lies beneath and the platforms are the same darkened wood as the surrounding walls. Which is why you follow the arrows." I crouched down pointing them out to her."

"Ahhh, I see." She shoved me back into the water. I came up sputtering once more nose burning from the unexpected plunge. "That's for the surprise. Do it again and I might bite something off."

I pulled myself out beside her while she watched confused. "Plant mage, giant tree that's still alive…" I slicked my hair back again. "Need I say more?"

Renka flickered her ears roughly in my direction, I blinked startled as it struck me in the face. "No. I got it."

"Do you feel better for having done that at least?" I asked referring to my second unintended plunge as she started across the bridge trailing behind least she feel the need to push me again.

"Not really." Her ears dropped as I caught up to her. I wrapped my arm around her waist steering her along a bridge that you'd walk by easily if you weren't aware of it.

"I accept your apology," I murmured, she shook her head butting her head gently against mine before pulling away.

"Where are we going now?" She questioned as we passed through the trunk of an ancient gazing at the intricate patterns carved into the wood arching above us glowing softly with moss. We passed through several other trunks such as these before coming to a tunnel created from a fallen ancient. I stepped onto the lip pausing when Renka clutched at my shoulder. "Is this tree still living as well?"

I listened carefully, able to hear the sleepy murmurs of the moss, the slow drawl of the ancients we'd passed through, and the Ancients singing softly in the background of it all. I furrowed my brow blinking before gazing on the fallen tree before us searching for its spirit while listening for its voice and hearing nothing. "No. It's dead." I blink away the spirits before pulling her along. "As for where we're going…" I smiled. "You'll see." I pulled her along.

"I'm starting to understand why you had that bite mark or your neck…it was out of frustration." I laughed softly at that semi-accurate description.

"We're almost there." I offered after half a slither of the sun's span spent traveling through trees, along thick limbs, beneath elaborate bridges, past countless fancifully built homes and shops that had no names or owners. I was sure that Renka hadn't seen any of them despite gazing at them with vision far sharper than mine, such was the nature of this place. Hidden in plain sight, it ensured that even if someone managed to get through the Ancients guarding the entrance that the city would never be found.

"Gods…this place is so green, full of life and yet empty. It's saddening to know that such a place exists and the only ones here to guard it all is a small troop of centaurs. Why create such a place if not to live here?" Renka wondered as we came to an archway, the sun shining brightly beyond it.

I paused in the archway thinking on her words, "I honestly don't know."

I stepped through with Renka trailing behind, she froze in her tracks as she took in the glory of what I had created. I watched as she moved to the center of the small grove, she tilted her head back letting the sun shine on her face for a brief moment before letting her head fall and gazed around. There were flowers blooming everywhere, if you could name it, it was there, flowers that only bloomed in winter, in fall, at night, in the spring, in summer, at dawn existed all at once in that moment, in that space. All my favorite trees lined the circumference of the space, a sapling giant's spine, standing beside a young ancient forming the archway leading into this space. An apple tree cast shade over a small area where lush grass grew, soft enough to lay on, half its canopy weighed down with luscious fruit, the other half raining down pink apple blossoms. Faeries fluttered from flower to flower playing tag, birds chirped nesting in the trees. A small pond sat off to one side fish regularly coming to the surface, a bridge formed from thickly twined raptor vines took you back up into the canopy of the ancients, though it was harder to find then my way had been. The sun shone down perfectly on everything it needed to touch so that it all grew as it should. "Is this yours?" Renka asked after a time turning to look at me.

I gazed around smiling softly proud at how it had all turned out. "Yeah…" I strolled forward and took a seat beneath my apple tree, picking up an apple that had fallen to the ground and rubbing it gently on my shirt. The lush grass had kept it from bruising. "After we'd been here for a few years and all knew the language well enough to speak properly Rosen rewarded us. She brought us here to the heart of Griffin Forest and opened the gate." I shivered at the pain I'd experienced. "The centaurs gave us a tour, Fletcher had been much younger then, her father had been in charge. We saw everything we could, but not as much as we'd hoped as children. We swam in the pool I first showed you, and jumped from the bridge there. We were scolded and punished for scaring a few years off her life."

I rolled the apple back and forth from one hand to the other as Renka took a seat beside me, "Rosen told us many stories about all the Gardeners that came before us, she instilled in us a sense of belonging. Of finally being a part of something greater than ourselves and then she told us to make something…anything we wanted, our part of this place that someone might find and explore generations from now and find amazing. She left us then for two seven days each of us had a centaur as guardian and we did what we wanted." I laid my hand on the ground, "We're actually sitting on a dead ancient, this space is how massive its trunk had been, it had fallen destroying several other trees, I healed them and hallowed this space out much like the pool we've been too."

"I filled it with soil…that was the first seven day, and I had lots of help from the plants, the second seven day was spent acquiring all the plants, seeds and saplings I needed to make what I'd wanted. I placed them strategically so that one plants growth would not stunt another's. I dung the hole for the pond and lined it with water repellent vines so that it would not just seep into the soil. I filled this place with as much magic as I could spare until the entire grove glowed softly with it and asked simply of the green to become what it willed and then I left and let nature take its course." I waved my hand to encompass all that we could see, "This is the result."

I took a bite of my apple, enjoying the way it sang across my taste buds. Renka picked up an apple nearly the size of her head and gazed at it curiously before rubbing it on her shirt. "I'd ask how it's possible to create such a place in perhaps ten years or less but I know what your answer will be."

I stared in fascination as she nearly bit the entire apple in half with just one bite. "How…" She gazed at me eyes glowing softly ears flicking in my direction. "Never mind." She smiled softly before taking a smaller more human seeming bite of her apple.

"It's annoying isn't it?" She questioned leaning back against the tree.

"Just a tad," I offered continuing to enjoy my apple, not realizing how hungry I'd been until that moment. Though Renka had stated I'd been gone…for two seven days I hadn't given it much thought.

I plucked a few blades of grass after finishing my apple and proceeded to eat them while Renka watched chewing slowly brow raised. "Why are you…" I wiggled my brows eating several more blades of grass. "Why in the Gods are you eating grass when there are countless apples littering the ground around you. If you reply magic I will bite off a chunk of your flesh." She warned pointing her apple core at me before eating it in two bites, though I'm sure she could have finished it in one.

"It's sweet grass, soft like a pillow and sweet enough to eat. They're greens really. Here try some." I twisted up a small bit and raised it to her mouth, she gazed at my fingers warily ears laid back. "I just ate it."

"One blade at a time not a small bundle of maybe disgusting." I chuckled softly before popping it into my mouth before offering her another small buddle.

"I will bite you..." I tipped my head in acknowledgement of her words before pushing the sweet grass into her mouth. She chewed slowly before swallowing, she gave me a narrowed eyed look before picking up another apple. "It's not bad, but I like the apples better."

"Hmm," I tossed an apple at her head that she caught easily in her mouth chomping it in half while I wrinkled my nose at how widely she stretched her jaw. "How the…"

"One of the Horse People," was her only explanation and really you shouldn't have needed more than that.

We sat for a time just enjoying the warm sun and the simple peace of being, while sating our bellies with apples and sweet grass. I traced my fingers through the damp strands of her hair as she lay dozing with her head on my shoulder, each of us leaning back against the strong trunk of the apple tree. I found myself trailing my fingers lightly over the collar wrapped around her neck, it was warm and supple, a light tan leather without scars or blemishes despite how long I'm sure she'd been wearing it. There were no seams, it was just one unbroken ring if I didn't know what it's purpose was I'd call it beautiful in its simplicity. "Does it hurt…" I questioned not sure if she was awake enough to answer, her breathing deep and evenly spaced.

The Marr sighed, the air gusting from her lungs, "No," she breathed. "On most days I hardly feel it at all. I've worn it for such a long time…"

"After this is all said and done we'll have it off you before you know it…"

Renka chuckled wryly, "You won't. There are only two ways to get it off, the enchanter ensured that by dying soon after the magic was cast."

"Well you can still travel freely…" She shook her head ears drooping.

"A slave that can travel far from their master can easily escape Head Gardener. I can travel no further than a hundred feet from the person who owns me. Otherwise it become uncomfortable…that or I find myself questioning why I left. It's maddening to know that if I just keep walking I'll be free but to suddenly find yourself turned around wandering back in the other direction. How do you think I came upon you when you came through the maze, why do you think I haven't left your side since?" I thought about how close we'd been since she'd found me.

"When I told you to go…?" I questioned.

"I'd not have let you die alone; I would have saved you regardless. I could have tried to escape, let you die and perhaps be free…though I doubt it. Someone always finds me. Which is the reason I only ever killed one man. He deserved it, but his death did not free me from my chains. I do not regret helping you, but my choices were quite limited."

"You said there were two ways to free you?" I stroked her ear smiling softly when it batted lightly against my fingers.

"We are free of all human limitations in death." I rolled my eyes at the cliché. "I'm not willing to die just yet, though there were times…" She grew silent for a moment.

I shrugged the shoulder her head lay against, "And the other?"

"Someone who cares for me has to agree to wear it freely…"

"They have to take your place?" Renka sat up, tracing her fingers lightly along her collar. I could see several words written in a language I could half understand. Her name no doubt, Santi hadn't lied about that.

"If you're asking if they're restricted to the same limitations then no, they could hurt me or even kill me if they wished without feeling a hint of pain, we could part and never see each other again and they would not feel compelled to return. No the only thing they would have to show that we'd known each other at all would be this collar, that would no longer bear my name." Renka shrugged at the look on my face.

"What's the catch?" I wondered aloud, deciding that it sounded too simple.

"They'd have to actually care about me and we'd have to share a kiss." I narrowed my eyes while she gazed off into the distance seeing something that I couldn't.

"It sounds almost too easy…"

"And yet here I am years later still enslaved." Renka spoke softly voice filled with bitterness. "You'd be surprised by how many people think less of you because of what you are, not who you are." She shook her head, "Different has never been good for me." Tears formed in her eyes larger than normal, though perfectly suited for one of the Horse people. Her lips quivered as she struggled not to cry.

"If a kiss is all it takes to free you and all I need do is wear a collar you hardly feel for the rest of my life then I'll do it." I offered without hesitation.

"Really…" The Marr choked on a sob eyes sparkling with hope, they were brighter than I'd first thought darkened by sadness and experience. The world could be a cold place and I'm sure she'd experienced more than her fair share.

I bowed my head gently cupping her face in my hands, "Hopefully I care enough yeah?"

Renka chuckled softly shifting closer, "You offered…no one else ever has."

"True." I murmured softly tracing the tears from her face as I leaned in heart racing in my chest as I pressed my lips against hers. Renka hesitated for a moment before kissing me back. She tasted of sweet grass and apples, of tears and sadness. Her lips were soft, and supple against mine. I could tell that perhaps she hadn't kissed many people in her life, her mouth hesitant, and a little unsure as it moved against mine.

Time slowed, the light of the sun flickered beyond my closed eyelids, my heart thumped strongly in my chest, I could feel hers beating just as strongly against mine. Her hair was soft though still a little damp as I twinned my fingers in it. I shivered slightly as she laced her fingers along my neck. A kiss that was meant to be short and sweet grew longer, more passionate. My lungs screamed for air and still we kissed…When we pulled away I gasped blinking spots out of my vision. I opened my eyes to find myself on the ground with Renka hovering above me. I was really starting to get tired of finding myself laid out on the ground…I thought briefly before raising my hand to trace along the smooth expanse of her neck.

"It worked?" I questioned hoarsely trying to catch my breath.

Renka gently traced her fingers along the collar circling my neck. "Only one way to find out. She leaned down before I could ask her what she was doing and bit me at the juncture where my neck met my shoulder. I arched from the ground crying out softly as pain sang along my nerves.

"Goddess…" I groaned when she pulled away wiping her mouth. I raised my hand to my neck fingers coming away damp with blood. "You bit me. I just freed you and the first thing you do is bite me?"

"Hmm," Her eyes glowed softly with mirth as she traced her thumb gently along the wound. I hissed pushing her hand away. "I think it looks good."

I rolled over pushing myself into a sitting position, blood dampening the neck of my shirt. "You broke the skin."

"I have very strong teeth…your skin is very soft. I bit you as gently as I could." I gazed at her over my shoulder in disbelief.

"That was gentle?!" She bowed her head solemnly. "Goddess I'd hate for you to have been angry and done that."

"That's how I killed that one owner…I wasn't gentle at all." I cupped my neck, able to feel the collar resting lightly against my fingertips. I hardly felt it at all so light was it around my neck.

"It looks different now," She reached forward tracing the supple leather. "There are vines, green vines, and a small flower where my name once was…" Renka smiled softly. "It's a flower from the plains, it signifies freedom to my people." I watched her as she wiped several more tears from her face.

"How does it feel to be free to do as you wish?" I asked dropping my hand ignoring the stinging burn every time I shifted my neck.

The Marr pressed her brow gently against mine twinning her fingers in my hair as she nuzzled my cheek softly in affection. "Like a dream come true…"

Chapter 23
Leaf

I chuckled softly resting my cheek against hers, "We should go before Fletcher sends out a search party, we've been gone for some time

Renka stood pulling me easily to my feet, "Aren't you going to heal yourself?" She questioned as I grimaced stretching my neck.

"Of such a simple wound?" I shook my head. "It'll heal on its own no point in wasting the magic for something only skin deep."

"You're truly one of a kind." Renka breathed following me along the vine bridge, shifting from side to side noticing how it didn't sway. "How…"

"Is this possible…" I finished for her chuckling softly as we moved upward. She rolled her eyes which caused me to smile. "Why magic of course." She groaned and resisted all urges to ask again knowing exactly the answer that she would receive.

We were about half way along the bridge when I heard my name, I paused in my tracks, head cocked listening carefully only to realize the voice was in my head, echoing through the green. I gripped Renka by the shoulder, "We have to head to the palace. Libeth is calling for me."

"I haven't heard anything…the palace…" She gazed at me brow furrowed. "This place has a palace?"

I nudged Renka forward jogging slowly making sure to keep hold as the world began to slide by in waves of shimmering green and brown, the green moving beneath us pushing us more quickly towards where we needed to go. "She spoke through the green," Renka jogged steadily beside me brow beading with sweat. "And this place is the equivalent of Anear. A city hidden in the trees."

"I couldn't tell you which way of travel is faster, but I can easily tell you which I prefer…" Renka gasped quickly transforming from one breath to the next, I twinned my fingers in her mane and leapt onto her back as the world slowed and we thundered across tree limbs large enough for carriages to ride along.

My heart raced with trepidation, "Hurry Renka…we have to hurry." I murmured as Libeth's voice continuously echoed through my mind growing more urgent with each passing second. I did not know what we would find when we got there, but the twisting of my stomach assured it wouldn't be good.

*****

"The palace is inside of a tree?" Renka shook her head in disbelief.

I gazed at her curiously, "You've seen this place, why would you expect anything else and it's inside several connecting trees actually and it would be more accurate to call them ancients as large and as old as they are. This is the oldest part of the forest, the very heart of the Last Garden. It makes sense for it to be here."

"I didn't even notice until we were practically standing right on top of it." Renka murmured taking in the canopy of mixed leaves overhead shading us from the sun.

"That's the point, completely hidden in plain sight." I replied entering a wall formed of smoothed bark. Renka traced her fingers along it as we passed. As we walked through the corridors that smelled of apple, pine, cherries, oak…a mixture of scents that blended together to form something heavenly and calming. The walls held carvings, intricate designs from every nation a Gardener called home. Tapestries filled with fantastical creatures from legends you might have heard when you were a child. Giants raced down the corridors with pixies playing along the hills and valleys that made up their bodies, centaurs cavorted with the Marr and horses alike. There were shadow figures at every juncture we took with vines and leaves sprouting behind them and names carved skillfully into the wood beneath.

"There were trees…ancients…" Renka corrected herself as she leaned closed to read the name of one of my predecessors, "Outside the palace, at varying heights, without canopies. Are they pools as well?"

I stopped in front of two double doors gazing on the only two images that were made of shadows. The Marr stared eyes wide with shock. I traced my fingers along my name heart aching slightly at what it took to get me here. "There are five in total…and they're filled with soil. One for each of the gardens that we tend."

"How…" Renka gazed at me and then the likeness of me, identical right down to the solemnness that now filled my eyes. "Is that possible?" Beside me stood the first Head Gardener Gal. We stood as guards to every room that would ever house the Queen. I knew from Rosen that if you held ill intent you could not enter…or you could. It would just be the most uncomfortable feeling of your life.

I laid my hands against cool wood pushing gently as I answered Renka's question, separating the first Head Gardener from the current Head Gardener. "Why magic of course." We entered the Council room to find everyone seated around the table, the centaurs stood of course and on the table, a literal map of the world lay a body. Libeth stood, having taken the seat of my Second, tears streamed her face. There wasn't a pair of dry eyes in the room.

"She's gone Rhyme…the Princess is gone." I stepped into the room heart lodge in my throat.

"Mariel?" I questioned knowing the answer but not wanting to believe it.

Libeth shook her head beckoning me forward, I came on weakened legs resting my hands atop the table as she took hold of the white shroud covering her form. "We've been receiving infected and dead for the last two seven days and each person brings with them a message. The infected speak and the dead have written messages. We have been trying to find some way to free them, to cure them, anything that would help so that when we fight we aren't fighting our friends." She pulled back the shroud to reveal Adri's pale face. "He's tired of waiting…and so today he took our hope from us."

My legs buckled as a sob tore through my chest, nothing in my life had prepared me for this, seeing the woman I loved wearing my crown woven of living green laid out before me. "No…" I murmured hoarsely unable to believe it. "No…no…no…no." I cupped her face in my hands resting my brow against hers. "It wasn't meant to end like this." I pressed a kiss to her cheek. "We were supposed to be happy, I would have taken it, all the strife, the power, whatever it took I'd have taken it on my shoulders and bore it gladly if it meant I could hold you in my arms at night." I pressed a kiss to her cold lips. "We were supposed to have children…two beautiful little girls…because you're a girl and I love you remember. Wake up Princess…Adri. Please…" I begged fingers locked in the fabric of her shirt. "Please wake up…"

Libeth clutched at my shoulder trying to pull me away. "Don't…" A chair reassembled itself into something closely resembling a knight standing between me and my friend. "Touch me." I warned.

Libeth stepped back gazing at the green warrior with wide eyes, flowers bloomed atop his head and truly he did not appear dangerous, he would harm no one. That wasn't his purpose, his purpose was to keep anyone from touching me. "Rhyme…she's dead." I shook my head unwilling to believe it.

Reason stood, "We should plan an attack before he comes with Rosen and the other Princess…once he's defeated perhaps Mariel can take her trials."

"We still haven't found a cure, we don't know how to stop this and he's likely taken the whole city by now." Tail countered from her seat further down the table more towards the center, half way between the centaurs and the Gardeners, Captain Sowin sat beside her.

"Without the Heir he's already won." Eden added dejectedly. "What are we fighting for."

"Our people," Libeth countered. "There are innocent people, dying day by day while we sit here twiddling our thumbs hoping to find answers. We need to do something…"

"But the answer is what," Captain Sowin finally spoke up. "How can we fight innocent people? We can't no one's heart is in it. And so we must find a cure, some end to this infection that spreads for the sake of spreading with a mad man at its mantle and for that we need time. Time that we no longer have because, your future and I must say ours as well lies before us on this table dead. We find ourselves in a vicious cycle of indecision."

I listened to their words gently tracing my fingers through Adri's hair as tears streamed my face. My fingers tangled slightly and I pulled them free to find my fingers wrapped around a plant. One I found intimately familiar. I'd eaten it once, though Rosen hadn't told me until much later. "How come she did not call on the dragons?" Dahni asked brow furrowed as she thought aloud.

I felt a small spark of hope, I answered her questioned leaning down as I did so listening for a heartbeat. "Would you really want a fire breathing dragon infected with the Void?" Her silence was answer enough. I might have been overly hopeful and so I beckoned Renka forward nudging my green knight aside. Emery traced his hands along a wooden arm slowly sprouting leaves. He was slowly going from dangerous to harmlessly adorable as we watched.

"Do you hear that?" I questioned holding my breath. She leaned close pressing a quivering ear against the Heir's still chest.

The Marr stood there for a long time, before pulling away brow furrowed.

"Her heart is beating...every now and again. She's alive but not for long." Renka offered eyes shimmering with unshed tears.

I pulled off my shirt and tossed it aside, before shedding my trousers, belt knife and all, nearly falling over as I struggled to kick off my boots. "Why are you getting naked?" Fletcher questioned arms crossed over her chest.

"Not that we mind," Fawlin added. "Just seems a bit inappropriate."

"When I was younger...I met the Queen's mother...she was a stern woman. She told me that if I could touch her with my magic that she would send me home...she gave me everything I needed and still I could not touch her. I didn't find out until later that she'd cheated." I pulled the shroud from Adri's body and tossed it on the floor before placing my hands on her chest. "She was a plant mage, not overly strong but skilled in deflection, the seeds she gave me, grown by her own hand, she could talk to them too and of course they obeyed her request. I lost our little wager and required I get this tattoo...except it's not a tattoo."

I took a deep breath closing my eyes as the green stems making swirling paths along my skin began to glow and dance beneath my skin. "Gods..." Renka breathed as the plants broke through skin bringing with it beads of blood leaving instant scars in their wake. "Their plants."

"A spell actually..." I breathed through the pain sharp but brief, as they moved from me to the Princess glowing brighter as they twinned around her form. "It can't heal death...only the Goddess or a God can do that, but it can help you cheat it by pulling you back from the brink. It was meant to save my life...but she said I could use it on another at the risk of dying myself."

"Only you would tell us that after it's too late to stop you." My brother said in exasperated alarm. Blood dripped onto the table as the green crawled across my body parting my skin neatly as it broke free.

I smiled softly, "Death's door is a dangerous poison and completely incurable…but if you're already dead people have been known to be revived with it. In theory." I added with a shrug.

"You're about to die and you're telling us something that might save you…in theory?!" Tailaan exclaimed, when I had nearly forgotten he was there.

"Does she do stuff like this all the time?" Captain Sowin asked when everyone else appeared to be far more calm than they should be in such a situation.

"She's quite reckless." Libeth replied.

"It would serve you right to die for your recklessness." Reason countered nostrils flaring.

"You don't mean that." He turned away tears in his eyes.

"You better not leave me. Goddess I just got you back and I just can't handle you being taken from me again." He said accent stronger due to emotion.

"I'm not ready to say goodbye." Reason bowed his head unwilling to look at me die before his eyes.

"When I…" I didn't want to say die. "When I pass out, someone anyone shove this plant," I tipped my head to the leaves lying on the table. "Down my throat by any means necessary. It should work…in theory." I could almost hear Adri calling me an idiot, I chuckled softly at the thought.

The last flower parted from my skin and I shuddered at the emptiness that overtook me, I thought death would be painful, I thought it would be endless…but it was peaceful. I took in the people rushing towards me, my friends, my family. My legs buckled, Adri took a deep breath face flushed with health and vitality. In that moment I saw all the struggles of my childhood, first in Kantari and then here in Angileri...I saw my life now another struggle, that I was currently losing and I think for a brief moment I glimpsed the future. Darkness stole me away from my happiness and I forgot all that I saw, but I'd heard two songs, that I hope to one day hear again...

Pain sang along the nerves in my cheek and I woke with a groan to find Adri glaring down at me, "Ouch..." I murmured softly instantly finding myself lost in the twilight of her eyes. "Not even a thank you Princess?" I questioned pushing myself to a sitting position to find myself sitting on a bed, the sheets were green, the comforter covered in a pattern of leaves. From the window, nearly taking up an entire wall, hung raptor vines, I smiled softly. The curtains were drawn letting in sunlight, the spirit lay along the window sill gazing out at the world. I had yet to figure out if it were the same one, or if they all just looked so similar it was impossible to tell, I mean it was the same mother plant after all.

"I'm angry with you for being reckless...but grateful that you figured out whatever it is that Rosen sent with me. I didn't think I'd ever wake up."

"I don't mind your anger...it means you're alive to feel angry." I raised my hand to stroke her cheek. She smiled reluctantly leaning into the touch. "You found my room, I slept here for two seven days as a child and of course I could not help but dub it mine. I even brought my raptor vines."

Adri chuckled, "Actually Fletcher...the centaur. An awe inspiring thing to wake up to by the way. Guided me here, I wanted you to rest and I didn't know where any of the bedrooms were. Though I figured it was yours when I saw the vines. They look exactly like the vines growing from your windowsill in Anear...though there's definitely more here. They're more vibrant and thicker too." She narrowed her eyes, "I even think they're growing up the wall. I haven't examined them that closely."

"Who saved me?" I asked curiously.

"Renka, she chewed that plant up so thoroughly I would have thought it were always a liquid if I hadn't seen Rosen tuck it into my hair." She chuckled slightly at that. "And then she kissed you…" Adri gave me a look. "Kinda like she'd done it before."

"She tastes like apples…" I offered honestly. Adri shook her head tracing her fingers lightly along the collar circling my neck.

"I want to be angry, but she told me why you did it." I felt her trace her fingers over the healing mark on my neck. "Hmm, she said she got you good. Punishment for being a smart…" I gave her a look and she chuckled. "I was gonna say aleck."

"Sure you were." I countered wryly.

"Shut up and kiss me." She demanded pulling me close.

I wrapped my arms around her waist leaning forward to kiss her tenderly, though it didn't stay that way for long. Adri twinned her fingers in my hair devouring my lips almost desperately. Her breath hitched between kisses and I could taste salt on her tongue, she may not have said it but I could feel how much she had feared for my life. She had almost lost me and if it had broken me to see her near death on the table I can imagine that she'd have felt the same. "If you ever do something so reckless again…without me there. I'll never forgive you." She murmured against my lips as we lay catching our breath.

"So long as you're there?" She traced her fingers along my naked torso, where there were once green stems, lay pale scars.

"I know that you will continue to be an idiot, it's something that I love about you. Your pursuit of answers, of the green's song as you call it, of justice…whatever you set your mind to, your drive and determination. It sometimes leads you to do reckless, brave, inventive things and to stop you would be taking a piece of who you are. I love all of you and that means that I'm going to have to let you be yourself, but if you're going to be an idiot I want to be there to help if things go wrong. If I'm not and I find out what you did…" She traced her fingers down along my torso playing along the band of my underwear. "I'll have to punish you."

My heart raced in my chest as my skin jumped beneath her fingertips, "How exactly would you do that?"

"Perhaps I should show you?" Her voice sent shivers of delight racing along my spine.

I bit my lip gently, "Perhaps you should." I croaked now aching for her to touch me.

Adri pulled her hand away kissing me tenderly on the cheek, "Later…now you need your rest because tomorrow, a war begins."

I watched her stand from the bed and walk to the door leaving me hot and bothered. "That's not fair."

The Princess winked at me, "The very definition of life." She countered before closing the door behind her. I groaned as I laid back on the bed wishing that she would come back and touch me, though of course she never did.

"Did she punish you?" I glanced up to see Renka peeking beyond the edge of the door.

"Yes. Yes, she did." I grumbled as she slipped into the room.

"How are you feeling?" She asking coming to sit on the edge of the bed pressing her brow gently against mine.

"Like I just took a nap." I offered smiling softly as she nuzzled my cheek.

"How long have I been out?" I wondered aloud hoping that it wasn't another two weeks.

"The rest of yesterday's sun's span and a bit of today's…it's about midmorning now." I laid my head on her shoulder as she climbed onto the bed resting beside me.

"I hear we go to war tomorrow and we still haven't found a cure for the people infected with the Void." I commented feeling torn about it all.

"The Dangilere soldiers have finally arrived, and with them more food than we can possibly eat and a small band of famous Healers. They came through for us, as for the war we don't have much of a choice. Prince Eris isn't giving us one, we either take it to him or he brings it to us and I don't want to see this place destroyed." I chuckled softly.

"They'd never make it passed the Ancients…"

"Perhaps that's true but the soldiers adapt at fighting in the forest are of Angileri, few though they may, be I know they're far more skilled than any others…even the recruits. You're Queen assured it, a woman of power in a world ruled mostly by men she had no choice." I agreed wholeheartedly. "Besides if anyone can find some way to stop this thing you can…even so we won't be able to save them all. I believe there are innocents, maybe even most of them are. But some of these people are traitors you have to remember that."

I stroked my fingers lightly along her neck while she traced her fingers over the pale scars on my back. "Did it hurt?" She asked after a moment of silence where I lay absorbing her words.

"Yes…but less than you'd expect it would be considering the magic leaving my body literally parting my skin along the way. It was as gentle as it could be and if I died it was the most peaceful death I ever could have felt." Renka butted her head gently against mine.

"Don't go getting any ideas, that plant I chewed up was no sweet grass let me tell you and I'd rather not have to do it again if I can help it." I chuckled at her wry tone resting my head on her chest.

"I hadn't planned on it…" I murmured softly finding it harder to string words together.

"I leave you alone for several hours and I come back to find you cuddled up with the Marr," I opened my eyes to find Adri standing in the doorway smiling softly eyes sparkling with mirth.

"I thought about making her our third," I mumbled softly closing my eyes. I felt Renka's fingers pause slightly before she continued to stroke my hair.

"I'm a Princess, of just about the most well known Queendom in the world, I've studied every one of the big seven in detail growing up, so if you think I don't know what that means you're mistaken." Adri said climbing into bed behind me and pressing me snuggly between the two. "Makes me wonder how surprised you'd be if I actually considered it and said yes. It's happened in the history of Angileri before."

"Mmmm, nothing surprises me anymore…" I slurred out once more drifting towards sleep no longer truly paying attention to her words.

You say that now…" Was the last thing I heard before slumber drug me away again.

I woke in the night to find myself still curled between the Princess and the Marr now fast asleep. I pushed up into a sitting position rubbing my eyes softly before climbing over Renka to much grumbling. I smiled softly at her protest as she snuggled back against the Princess, they looked adorable together. I glanced around the room, now glowing softly due to the eternal fireflies standing in each corner of the room, I found a bundle of fresh clothes in the arms of my little green knight I took them with a gentle thank you surprised he still existed. He definitely looked harmless now completely covered in small green shoots and flowers.

I pulled on my trousers and tunic quickly noting the softness of the fabric, both of them a dark green. It was softer than anything I owned in my closet and I knew that it must have been Adri's doing. I smiled softly at the thought before leaving the room on bare feet, not wishing to wake my bedmates looking for my pouch or my blade.

I found myself walking down an empty corridor smelling of apples stomach grumbling with hunger. I paused watching as a branch sprouted from dormant wood, an apple grew quickly before dropping into my hand. I paused in my first bite sensing the whispers of awe through the green and turned to find my little green knight trailing silently behind me.

"You can talk…" I murmured curiously tracing my fingers lightly over the soft leaves sprouting from his head shaped like an old fashioned knight helmet with the visor hiding his appearance. All I could see was his eyes two glowing orbs of burnt orange. They were soft, kind eyes.

He gazed at the wall, eyes flickering slightly in a blink? At the branch still easily visible. I felt the beginning of a question more a feeling than actual words. Another apple sprouted exactly like the first though smaller in size. I plucked it gently taking his wooden hand far more complex then I'd first realized setting it their gently. "It's my magic…" I explained. "How I created you. The green growing things, they understand me." I tapped my mind, "Without words." He gazed curiously at the apple before raising it to his mouth pressing it lightly against the visor. "Huh…can you actually eat that…" I watched with wide eyes as the apple grew into the visor where his mouth should be before disappearing. I heard a crunching sound for a few moments before I felt a humming in my mind and sensed happiness.

I took a bite of my apple while his eyes smiled up at me, "I have a feeling you aren't going anywhere any time soon." I murmured softly deciding that he needed a name. "I suppose I'll call you Leaf...how does that sound?" I felt that hum of happiness before smiling softly. "Yeah sounds good to me too, let's go I think I figured something out."

I proceeded on my search listening to the voices as the green as we moved through the palace. I topped the stairs leading down to the dungeons, made as a formality more than anything considering no one ever thought this place would see use. They were actually very cozy. "I honestly don't know why I didn't check here first, considering that it's probably the only place to properly contain those infected with the Void." I murmured as Leaf stood beside me gazing down into the darkness of the stairwell.

I felt a spark of curiosity, "How are we gonna see in the dark? We aren't..." I started walking down the stairs tracing my fingers along the walls waking the moss that grew their now glowing softly. Leaf raced down the rest of the stairs tracing his hand along the opposite wall completely fascinated by the magic his touch caused. I chuckled softly as I followed more slowly finding him waiting for me patiently at the bottom of the stairs.

It was cooler down here but no less welcoming than the rest of the palace, he tried that trick on the walls down here and found that it worked just the same. Where once we stood in darkness we now stood casting shadows in soft glowing green light. I gazed into each cell looking for familiar faces finding Kiyen and the Princess side by side towards the end. "We probably got both Princesses on the same day, one broken and infected, the other so close to death it shouldn't have mattered. I mean how can you fight when they're nothing to fight for..." Leaf traced his hands lightly along the cold steel, some of the small bit of metal that existed in this place.

"It's harder to break than wood, on that I suppose the Gardeners agreed though there are woods that exist that are impossible to break...they're just as impossible to form though. These locks are much like the locks that exist to the ballroom back at the palace in Anear. Impossible...unless you're a plant mage." I traced my hand lightly over the keyhole hand glowing softly with my magic. "This is so you can see it. Otherwise my requests I call them are voiceless and without effects." I felt a sense of gratitude for the display. "You're welcome."

I opened the cell and stepped inside. "I know you're awake…if anyone's aware of all the damage they've done it would be you. You're too stubborn to give up in my opinion." I spoke to the form lying comfortably on the bed beneath a large window that let the light of the moon into the spacious room. I could see the Void moving around inside her and once more I heard the familiar seductive whispering.

Mariel pushed herself into a sitting position leaning back against the wall with a heartfelt sigh. "What do you want Gardener…if you come any closer I'll attack. I won't be able to pass up the chance." She warned through gritted teeth.

I stood where I was, "Thanks for the warning."

"I try where I can." She huffed, "Not like it's worth anything."

"What does it feel like?" I asked curiously needing to know. "Is it like a slow spread, is it a complete change…what does it feel like to be taken over?"

"It's like…a seed. It begins with a seed that you can feel, though some people can see it. I couldn't. I thought it was just a bad feeling, but it grew and I felt unsure of my actions as if perhaps that weren't completely my own… The Prince came to me, told me what he planned to do…what I would do and I knew instantly that I should go to my mother but I couldn't. Something in me thought it was a great plan." I could see the glimmer of tears streaming her face and for the first time I thought she appeared exactly as she was. A young woman completely out of her depth. "I conspired against my mother…my sister. All this time I thought it was Sorel my mother had to worry about…I never for a moment that it would be me that betrayed them. I feel death would be a small mercy at this point for all that I've done."

"You might be more aware of your actions than most but it's still not you Princess…"

"I don't deserve that title." She countered bowing her head.

"You do. More than most actually." I stepped forward slowly. "I was going to try this with Kiyen. I didn't think Prince Eris would give us both Princesses at the same time, but he's angry and I guess baiting us to act. It worked we go to war tomorrow. As Renka said there are people not completely innocent…but I would like to be able to save as many as I can." I glanced at the position of the moon. "I have some time before my bed mates realize I've been gone for quite some time. I know if I get any closer you'll attack…but what if I give you permission to touch me."

Mariel glanced up at me with the glimmer of the Void in her eyes, "That works just as well…why are you doing this. Risking your sanity and freewill?"

"You said it's like a seed right, that it grows and just spreads, up until this point no one had truly gotten hurt. It was Prince Eris that changed the game. The Void is covered in vipers' wrath, a near indestructible bramble that grows in excess. The blade I have has no voice…no spirit, no purpose. Perhaps the spirit found a way to escape…to plant itself in people, to grow and spread?" The Princess gazed at me with a thoughtful expression. "What does a weed do?" I asked softly.

"It starts off small, but grows profusely, where once there was one you suddenly find yourself with ten. It spreads until it destroys a garden if you don't pull it, choking the life out of everything…" Mariel finished voice trailing off as she started to see my point.

"Perhaps it's just the way I see the world, in metaphors of green growing things and that which destroys them, maybe I'm wrong." I crouched on the floor just a few feet away, "But I can hear the voices Princess and if I can hear them than perhaps they can hear me…perhaps I can plant a little seed of my own and change its purpose?"

"I have nothing to lose if you're wrong." Mariel murmured softly sliding to the floor.

"But you have everything to gain if I'm right…" I offered my hands she took them without speaking face grim. I shuddered softly watching as the Void slowly began to spread trying to plant a seed inside me. I closed my eyes and listened to the voices.

Chapter 24
Promise

I burst into my room filled with excitement shirt soaked with sweat and feeling slightly drained but not overly so. Renka lay still fast asleep though Adri was nowhere in sight, Leaf trailed behind me practically vibrating with exhilaration even if he wasn't positively sure what had transpired. "Renka," I nudged the Marr gently. "Renka wake up…" I shook her a little more firmly.

"One more slither of the sun's span…" She groaned trying to bury her head beneath the bed covers. I shook her some more until she flicked an ear in my direction. "What?" She mumbled grumpily.

"I did it." I breathed climbing onto the bed.

I waited for her to uncover her head and take in my disheveled state. "What did you do?" Renka asked softly gazing up at me curiously.

"I went down to the dungeon…"

"Alone," The Marr protested.

"That's beside the point now," I waved it away and hoped she'd forget the recklessness of my actions. The frustrated glint in her eyes told me otherwise. "I talked to the Princess, the Queen's third child about the Void inside her. I already had an idea about it being similar to a weed but she helped me solidify it. I concluded that the Void is just the spirit of the vipers' wrath that spans its borders which means I could speak to it…and so I let her touch me."

Renka sat up, "You could have been…"

"Infected," I finished for her watching her nostrils flare, sure that she was angry now. "Yes I know but I wasn't." Between her and Adri I felt as if I couldn't do anything. "I convinced it to change Renka. I made it something beautiful, something bright, soft, and fading…" I sighed. "Fading in those who feel intruded upon and lingering in those who need it most. It's encouragement and confidence and all that's good. I got it to stop spreading I just have to make a place for it, where it can grow here in Angileri. Where all the green is…"

"I now understand what the Princess was talking about when she called you a reckless idiot. Admittedly I got a bit of that with the jumping from trees and off of bridges and risking your life. You could have been infected…" She raised her hand. "You weren't I got that and I'm happy that you figured this all out, but you literally died yesterday or nearly two sun spans ago now."

"Yes, but I didn't…" Renka shook her head.

"If that's your only argument it's not good enough." I sighed softly leaning back against the headboard.

"I can't change who I am…"

"No but you can take someone with you, there is nothing wrong with someone having your back. I don't care what you do, all this time I've been following you around have I said anything? No, because I was with you. Just next time wake me up, or the Princess." She laid back down. "How are you feeling after that? Tired at all?"

"A bit…and I knew I could handle myself." She snapped her teeth at me, like that first time in Lialey's Inn. "I realize that it's different now, that my position as Head Gardener calls for less recklessness, as well I have people that care for me and do not wish to see me hurt or dead. I understand that I do…but…"

"Your heart is just too big sometimes and you can't help yourself." Renka finished for me smiling softly, gently nudging her brow lightly against mine. She tugged playfully at my collar pressing a tender kiss to my lips. I felt my heart skip a beat, as she moved her mouth against mine. For a moment I sat motionless eyes fluttering closed as I hesitantly kissed her back. She tasted of apples, far better than any I'd ever eaten, which is saying something considering I could create a perfect fruit. Renka bit my lip gently near feather light, and yet it left a noticeable sting. I hissed softly remembering the power in those teeth and noting the control it must have taken not to break skin or even bite right through my lip. "Next time I won't be so gentle." She warned softly before snuggling back among the bed covers. "As well I'd lose those clothes and pretend you just went to the bathroom if you don't want the Princess to know right this moment…you're more likely to actually get sleep if she doesn't."

"What about the kiss?" I questioned brow furrowed as I stripped out of my clothes rubbing myself down before climbing back into bed, Leaf took them from me and tucked them in the closet sensing the need for secrecy.

Renka chuckled closing her eyes, "You should have stayed awake a little longer Head Gardener."

"Renka…Renka…" I whispered nudging her softly but I received no answer.

I gave up when Adri walked back into the room carrying a tray on which sat a pitcher of water and several beautifully designed wooden cups. "It took me forever to find the kitchens," She set the tray on the nightstand beside where she'd lain previously. "Cook would be so jealous if she were here…"

"Is she alive?" I asked as she trailed off lost in thought.

"I'm not sure, a lot of people fled, some did not, many were infected and more than I would have liked killed. The city…" Adri took a sip of water from her cup. I glanced down to see Renka's eyes wide open, ears quivering slightly as she listened. Leaf stood guard in the corner out of sight and out of mind. "It took generations to rebuild after the war with the dragons…and he destroyed it all in just about three seven days." The Princess took a deep breath, a single tear streaming down her cheek, eyes dark with pain. "I have never hated someone more than I hate that man."

I wrapped my arms around her from behind pulling her back against me, "We'll defeat him Adri…"

"We'll defeat him, but even then we've already lost so much." I pressed a tender kiss to her cheek while Renka soothingly rubbed her thigh.

"I was saying just over two sun spans ago I think it was, why not just live here…" Renka supplied tentatively. "Then it was just a thought, an idea, a dream. But perhaps it can become a reality. What would it take if we've already lost everything?"

We sat in silence for a while, allowing Adri to process her words, in the end without the presence of the Queen it was her call. The Princess sighed softly, "Let's just sleep and figure it all out after. No one knows what tomorrow will bring. Hopefully an end…one way or another."

I shifted Adri to the middle so that Renka and I could cuddle her from both sides… "There are rooms enough to house a thousand servants and at least a hundred royals. Why are we all sharing my room?" I asked curiously after a moment of thought.

Adri chuckled slightly, while Renka snorted reaching over to gently close my eyes. "Go to sleep Head Gardener. War is tiring and you need your rest." I grumbled softly but soon found myself drifting into slumber with Adri's scent filling my nose and Renka's taste lingering on my lips. It was one of the best sleeps I've ever had.

*****

War…I stood in the corner of Mariel's cell donned in armor made of finely carved wood, supple leather softening the side that lay snug against my body, thinking about war while I waited for her to wake up. "How long have you been standing there?" She husked pushing into a sitting position.

I blinked coming back to myself tracing my fingers lightly over my helmet, a large leaf curled at the brow making it more ornate, though I knew it was very effective protection. It would also hide me in the forest, just as the thin layer of moss would help shield my armor. "How are you feeling?" I asked softly avoiding her question. I could see the Void shinning softly within her, near about gone now.

"Like myself." Mariel rubbed her hand gently over her chest. "Is that what you wanted to hear?" She replied after a brief moment of silence.

I tossed her the coiled vine whip I'd never gotten rid of, "Would you like to stay here until it's all over? Or do you want to help guard this place?"

The Princess vanished in a small cloud of shimmering shadows, "Do you really need to ask?" I turned to find her standing outside her cell beside Leaf, whip slung over her shoulder. "Where do I get myself armor like that?" She questioned as I stepped out of the cell and closed the door behind me.

"Become a Gardener and I'll think about telling you." She snorted at my reply before trailing behind me up the stairs.

Leaf poked at her curiously trying to see if his hand would go through her I think. I could easily sense his curiosity. Mariel gazed down at him inquisitively, he'd finally stopped sprouting leaves and flowers but the overall effect of being covered in so much green is that he appeared harmless. The green that rode him remained silent…because it was all a part of him, it made sense. One voice for one being. "What is that?" The Princess asked leaning close as I lead her back to my rooms, I could see her eyes tracking every corridor, while she gazed at the murals on the walls with muted fascination. Not as obvious as Renka had been.

"It was a chair…" I glanced behind us as we passed through the corridor smelling of apples. Leaf stopped beneath the branch still sprouting from the wall, using a small bit of magic I caused an apple to grow. He raised his small hands and caught it easily before holding it to his visor. Mariel and I watched mesmerized as he ate. "Now his name is Leaf, a little green knight."

We waited for him to catch up before proceeding on our way, "What does he do?" Mariel lightly traced a flower blooming on his head pulling her hand away quickly when he glanced up.

I traced my fingers through my hair still not quite used to its short length, "I'm sure he fights considering his little wooden sword, but otherwise he just follows me around exploring new things. I'll be leaving him with you." The Princess bowed her head in a nod brow furrowed slightly.

"Can he die…" I gazed down at him curiously, staring at his plate armor that had once been the seat of a chair now covered in braided vines.

"I don't know." I answered honestly. "Treat him as if he can. Like a mythical being you've never seen before." I offered not wanting him to be sacrificed lightly. He was innocent, a child really and it would sadden me to see him destroyed unnecessarily.

"I'll defend him the best I can with just a whip…" She murmured wryly.

"I don't even think you know how to use that thing," I countered raising my brow as I took it back. "It was a test; I can defend against a whip made from plants. I didn't want to chance you attacking me with a sword." I pushed open the door to my room, now empty save for the spirit sitting on the windowsill. Someone had made the bed, Renka or Adri…perhaps both. The tray holding the pitcher of water and wooden cups was gone. I moved towards a section of the wall made of bamboo panels instead of smooth seamless wood and tucked my fingers into a little groove using it to slide open the closet.

"I thought that was a design…" Mariel glanced at the other parts of the wall with bamboo panels. "What are those two?" She pointed to the one opposite the closet on the other side of the room perpendicular to the long window, and then the one adjacent to the door.

"The one across the room is the bathroom, with a pool large enough for four to bath in comfortably, a toilet with constant running water and a basin to wash your hands. There are drying cloths for your body and hands as well as cloths and soap to wash your body. Most of the soaps are herbal in nature and therefore very relaxing. Just about every room in this wing has the same thing. The pools of water are all connected…don't ask me how. They run from a hot spring so they're always pretty hot even during the winter." I explained as I pulled out clothes that would fit her, glad that my brother had just about brought my whole wardrobe.

"The other is decoration so that all the walls save for the one with the window, match." I kneeled down and opened a bamboo panel inside the closet to reveal a space hiding two swords and another dagger. One sword was black similar to the color of the blade I carried on my hip but longer, a scimitar if I was guessing correctly by the shape. The other was pale and of a similar size and shape to the first.

"You have swords and daggers hidden in the floors?" Mariel questioned brows raised as I handed her a pile of clothing, the paler of the two swords and the dagger after sheathing them properly. The other sword I buckled to my hip beside my dagger of vipers' wrath.

"Those were there long before I discovered this room…but I figured it's better to use them than to let them go to waste sitting in this closet." I tipped my head towards the bathroom as I closed the door. "Bath, get clean. I'll send a guide to help you find the others. They'll lead you to the Ancients guarding the entrance. Every one there is at your disposal, from the royal guards and recruits, few though they are, to the soldiers lent to us by the King of Dangilere. As I said, you have Leaf and Eden will be staying here to help with your brother of course." I moved towards the window, turning in place, helmet tucked beneath my arm. "There are also centaurs…" I offered not wanting her to be shocked when she met her guide. "Good fortune Princess." I hesitated for a moment before adding. "Keep our people safe."

"I'll do as you ask…" Mariel bowed slightly, blue eyes sparking with fire. I pulled on my helmet. It fit snuggly covering my head fully, curving around my ears and over my brow so that I could still see and hear, before coming down on either side to protect the sides of my face without hindering my peripheral vision. Like my armor, soft leather lined the inside adding an extra layer of protection and comfort. I leaned my hands on the windowsill, breathing deeply as I gazed out at a world of green all of it whispering to me of wonder and life. "Gardener."

I glanced over my shoulder to see Mariel standing close beside me, Leaf stood close at hand holding her clothes and her weapons. She placed her hand gently on my shoulder and looked me in the eyes, expression softening. "Bring that man to his knees…and ensure our Queen makes it home."

I grasped her arm in a warrior clasp, bowing over our joined arms. "I'll do as you ask to the best of my ability." I promised. She tipped her head in respect before releasing my arm and disappearing in a cloud of shadowy darkness her clothing and her sword gone from Leaf's arms. He turned to me for guidance and I pointed towards the bathroom. "She's in there…protect her. She's more important than I am." I smiled softly as Leaf ran towards the door, warmed by the fact that in his eyes no one was more important than I.

For a moment I just stood observing it all, the sun shining down on the ancients filling this place, the birds flying through the sky and diving playfully through the trees. I could see one of the empty plots that perhaps would be a garden in time. Several people and centaurs strode across bridges made of trees and vines. It wasn't full by a long shot…we were missing more than half of the population of Anear. I could not say for sure if most had escaped, I knew not all had. I thanked the Goddess for my connection to Rhea, allowing me to hear her, to feel her in my mind. She was alive, healthy and whole. She and her mother had been among those able to escape before the Void truly spread and for that I was grateful. I breathed deeply enjoying all the fresh scents of the green that reached my nose. War…I leapt out the window catching a vine as I fell and swinging onto the massive bridge below. Fawlin raised her brow as I landed beside her but chose not to comment. It was not kind…

I stumbled as someone smacked me soundly on the back of the head, instantly pulled from my thoughts. I whirled around to find Fletcher standing behind me. She shrugged, "I was instructed by the Princess and our cousin of the Horse People that if you did anything reckless without someone about, to smack you soundly upside the head."

"I was perfectly safe," I argued without real heat lips twitching slightly as Fletcher gazed up at the distance from my window, which you could hardly see from this angle, to where we stood now.

She began trotting forward with Fawlin and I trailing behind, I jogged to keep up taking her offered hand before jumping as she pulled landing with a thump on her back. "Your idea of safe and mine differ greatly." She countered as I wrapped my arms around her waist clad in leather armor and firmly clenched my thighs about her girth as she moved from a trot to a gallop, Fawlin pulling up beside us easily keeping pace.

I snorted softly but otherwise gave no comment, "Did you grab what you needed?" Fawlin questioned referring to my need to go back while everyone moved forward and set up without us.

I glanced over my shoulder no longer able to see the palace hidden in plain sight among the green. "Yeah…I found it exactly where I knew it would be."

"Where's your little green knight?" Fletcher asked once she realized he'd not come with us.

"I left him behind, though I'm sure he'll catch up." Fletcher and Fawlin bowed their heads in understanding before falling silent. As we grew closer to the entrance of this place the atmosphere grew more tense with anticipation of what was to come. I took a deep breath and closed my eyes as the centaurs rode on. War…I thought briefly. We were going to wage a small war…

*****

I left the Queen's third child in charge of her brother, the few innocents that had escaped with us like Tailaan and Dahni, half the soldiers, the royal guards, the centaurs, the recruits and most of the Healers. My brother and Emery led the rest of the soldiers and the remainder of the healers through the city in search of small bands of the soldiers Prince Eris infected or managed to convince to commit treason. Renka, Libeth, Adri, Taeli and I traveled through the forest. The goal was to sneak in through the Pleasure Garden, while Reason lead the soldiers straight to the front of the palace, creating commotion and therefore a distraction. Hopefully giving us enough time to find her Majesty who with good fortune, was still alive and then apprehend Prince Eris. It was a simple plan, we prayed to the Goddess that it would work.

"Am I the only one that just realized that we have three very important people key to our nations continuation heading directly into the heart of something that will likely end badly?" Libeth questioned as we passed the tomb of trees I'd created a few seven days prior. It felt like a small eternity ago now.

Renka snorted, "A future Queen, a Princess from a foreign land and a Head Gardener who could probably level the city if she wished. No I'm sure we're all very aware of what we're walking into." She glanced at Libeth with glowing eyes. "We're all grown women here, we've made our choices. Now we just have to live with them…" She glanced over her shoulder at the chamber of death, eyes grave. "Or die by them…" The Marr finished softly before turning away.

"No one's dying if I can help it." Adri countered trying to recognize where we were in relations to the palace with no avail. I didn't hold it against her. It took years for me to figure it out.

"So long as no one dies we should be fine, considering we have two of the strongest Healers in Angileri among us." I offered softly tracing my fingers lightly over the bark of a newly dead tree brow furrowed. I pulled away when I heard the hint of seductive murmuring slowly fading into something encouraging…it would disappear in time and this tree would become something new. I gazed into the forest along the path that would lead us to the palace, my heart heavy in my chest as I listened closing my eyes and trying to see through the trees up ahead of us. It felt as if I were trying to gaze through sand, impossible.

I clenched my fist as I opened my eyes silent tears streaming down my face. Renka placed her hand on my shoulder as Adri stepped up beside me. "What's wrong?" They asked simultaneously concern in their voices, one light and sweet, the other lower, a bit deeper with the pain of living but no less lovely.

"The forest…past this point, is all weeds…The trees still stand, but they're just pretty shells holding the Void." I moved forward whipping my face as I looked for the spirits I'd once known and saw none, just the fading darkness, and growing light of the Void. One day…it would be something new, something beautiful but the spirits that I had known and loved were gone for good. It hurt to know that I would likely never see them again.

"Are we in danger?" Taeli questioned hesitating in moving any further beyond where we stood.

"No…the Void is changing, willing to plant roots and stand still. This is a good a place as any for it to flourish. I just wish…" I gazed around me for a brief moment before moving forward allowing Renka's hand to drop from my shoulder. "I just wish I could have said goodbye."

I stopped after a few steps head cocked slightly as I listened to the green, a shrill cry filled the air alerting us to the fact that my brother and his soldiers had reached the palace. "We have to hurry…" I held Adri back before she could run off.

"I have to do something first…it's important to me." I finished softly when they all turned to me.

Adri and Renka shared a look, "You go on ahead," Renka offered. "Your mother's in there and I know you're aching to save her. I'll go with the Head Gardener. We'll meet you."

"Promise?" Adri questioned conflict sparking in her eyes as she gazed at us, wanting to stay but in her heart needing to go.

"Promise." We spoke together before urging her on.

Libeth slapped me lightly on the back, "Resist the urge to die."

"I'll do my best." I replied wryly.

"That's all I ask." She raced after the Princess not wishing to lose her. Taeli pressed a kissed to my cheek and stroked her fingers through my hair before she too was gone.

"Just tell me what we're about to do won't make us break our promise." Renka said turning to me once they'd disappeared from view.

"What we're about to do won't make us break our promise." I said what she wished me to say as I started jogging towards the Queen's forth Garden, Katerina Lake.

"I feel like you're just repeating what I said." Renka countered catching up to me.

"I said exactly what you asked me to say," I heard the snapping of her teeth close to my ear and chuckled softly.

What are we doing?" We broke through the trees and found ourselves on a familiar sandy beach. Renka stopped me at the edge of the water, once a beautiful healthy blue, now a murky brackish green, waiting for an answer.

I pointed to the large dying, near dead mass of petals still floating in the center of the lake. "That's the only thing that survived." I gazed at her. "I don't need to go any further to know that all the Gardens I've once tended are long dead. He poisoned them…he poisoned the land knowing how long it would take to heal. Even if we defeat him…even if he dies. He'll never be forgotten, he ensured it." I moved towards the water only to be stopped again.

"There's something in the lake…" Renka murmured softly stepping out into shallow water. "A serpent I think." She gazed back at me, "I had thought it probably wasn't there before." I stepped into the water with her glancing down as if I could see to the very depths of the lake. "I didn't much know this Prince Eris before coming here…but I can honestly say I'm really starting to hate him now."

"I've disliked him since I met him and hated him since he attacked the Heir…now. Now I feel a simmering rage for all the things he's taken from me." I gazed at the distance between the shore and the dying Alia rose we needed to reach. "Can you tell how large it is by sound alone?"

Renka crouched down ear flicked toward the water. She sat there listening for a long time, brow furrowed in concertation. "Large enough to swallow us whole. I lost it…I think it's at the bottom." She stood, "I think I could reach the flower and retrieve what you want…but I won't make it back before it reaches the surface. As soon as I enter the water and start swimming, it'll be coming for me." I watched her nostrils flare in frustration. "How badly do you need what lies inside of there?" She turned to face me observing my face beneath my helmet. She wore the same armor the centaurs wore made mostly of leather. It was enchanted so that it would change when she transformed.

"It is the only thing that remains of all the Gardens I've tended for the whole of my life. The only green thing left uninfected and free of poison. Anear is uninhabitable…part of our forest dead. Our palace no doubt destroyed. If we leave here, and I'm sure we must. I want something good to remember." Renka bowed her head in understanding before stripping out of her armor.

"Just don't let me break our promise?" She tossed aside her shirt and pulled off her boots, slinging her braid over her shoulder.

I unwound the whip I'd gotten back from Mariel and moved to the lip of the cliff hidden beneath the water. "I won't." I promised speaking softly as if the serpent hiding in the depths of the lake could hear me. Renka pressed a quick tender kiss to my lips before diving into the water swimming for all she was worth towards the center of the lake.

I watched with my heart in my throat as Renka swam, pumping her arms and kicking her legs as quickly and efficiently as she could. I thought for sure she was safe, but just as she reached the dead plants blocking the dying rose the serpent broke the surface and my heart stopped. It looked like a dragon without wings, two large iridescent eyes glowed ominously tracking across the surface of the water with the precision of a predator. I snapped my whip drawing its attention. "Hey ugly?!"

I flicked the whip again as Renka pulled herself from the water reaching her hand into the heart of the large Alia rose. The serpent roared, I snapped my whip as it charged catching it around its thick neck. I pulled it taunt, the whip glowing with the strength of my magic. With a grunt of effort, I stepped backward pulling seeds from my pouch as I did so. Sweat beaded on my brow as vines grew quickly in my palm, falling past the edge of my hand into the water. I murmured a furious request as I slipped towards the lip of the cliff water splashing as I struggled to remain in control of a beast at least ten times my size. Once I was sure that the vines had done as I asked, I wrapped the vines around the whip and let go. I knew that the vines had burrowed into the cliff beneath the water with sharp tips, they would continue digging into earth made soft by the water until they couldn't burrow anymore. I poured my magic into the vines, into the whip now twinned with them, healing the plants as they tore. Trying to keep them together long enough for Renka to make it back to shore. All the while the serpent thrashed and roared trying to escape straining towards Renka as she dove back into the water.

I watched her progress, feeling time slow as, despite my magic, the vines broke with one great surge of strength from the serpent. Horror filled me as the serpent's maw stretched wide enough for a grown man to stand tall and it raised itself from the water before crashing down where Renka had been. The water lapped against my legs in wave. "Renka..." I pulled off my helmet and tossed it aside, quickly stripping out of my armor preparing to dive in after her despite the fact that the serpent had probably reached the depths of the lake. A deepness I would likely never reached before the need for air became too great, tears burned in my eyes as I tossed aside my breast plate.

Just as I prepared to do the impossible the water began to bubble, frothing red with blood. I sunk to my knees at the edge of the cliff bloody water staining my clothes. I flinched as a hand shot out of the water grasping the leather collar circling my neck. I pulled back out of self-preservation. Renka crawled from the water hand still wrapped around my collar before flopping down beside me bloody water streaming from her face. "Gods..." She gasped letting the shallow water pass over her. "I thought I was going to die."

I gazed at the water where the serpent lay dead floating upon its surface. "Why aren't you?" I asked curiously standing quickly, tucking my arms beneath her before pulling her completely from the water growing more bloody by the second. She lay on the sand breathing deeply fist clutched to her chest.

"I panicked…in its throat I think and transformed. The world exploded and I was free. I swam blind hoping that I was heading up, not down and just when I felt as if my lungs would burst I saw my collar as familiar to me as my own name." I brushed her hair back from her face leaning down to place a kiss on her brow. "You're so lucky I love you…I'd not have risked my life for seeds if it were anyone else."

I chuckled softly as she opened her fist revealing the seeds that had once lain at the heart of the Alia rose. I took them gently and tucked them safely into my pouch. "You love me?" I questioned after I was sure they weren't in danger of falling out.

"Maybe just a tad…" Renka murmured closing her eyes as I stroked her brow.

I smiled softly pressing another kiss to her brow, "We have to move now. We have a promise to keep remember?

Renka moaned softly before pushing herself into a sitting position and reaching for her armor. I did the same, feeling grateful that Renka wasn't normal by any means. If she was she'd be dead. I watched her as she shook as much sand from her clothing as she could, grumbling softly. My armor wrapped around me snuggly in an embrace. I pulled my helmet on my head after slicking my hair back. "Are we riding or running?" Renka asked once she'd finished.

"It's up to you…" Renka raced forward before I could finish my sentence and I raced after her jumping as she transformed. I landed on her back clutching at her mane chuckling softly as she tossed her head. I'd know the choice she'd make as soon as she asked, as fascinated as she was by my magic. She grew a bit sick by the world moving by us in shimmering waves. I didn't hold it against her, there were very few who could stand it for long. Rosen and Libeth chief among them.

Chapter 25
An End and a Beginning

We left the forest in what felt like just a few seconds and thundered across the Training Fields once familiar now completely foreign. The grassed once lush with life now darkened, brown near black from poison. The stable bursting with activity, lay destroyed a pile of ash, the horses long gone. The recruits and soldiers taken from this place, by necessity to survive or force, the silence was deafening without them. The stands I created were the only thing that remained of what once was…bringing to heart a sense of melancholy. If they lived I could not here them, I could not see their vibrant spirits as we passed. I clenched my fists in Renka's mane resting my cheek along her strong neck urging her forward. There was nothing for us here…not anymore.

Renka changed back when we came to the vipers' wrath, gazing at the mass of thorny brambles that spanned the entirety of the Pleasure Garden, beneath them no doubt lay dead flowers. The world had never seemed so dark and gray as it did in that moment coming into a land renowned for its greenery now barren of it. "It hurts me…" Renka murmured softly drawing my attention. Her eyes were full of sadness glowing slightly in the muted light from the sun, a day once bright was now made dull. "It hurts me to come to this place once full of activity, and people. Of green growing things and bright sunlight and see it destroyed. It hurts me…so I can only imagine how it must feel for you." She finished softly.

"Like my life has been taken from me all over again," I offered before proceeding forward, drawing my sword as we came to the double doors leading into the ballroom now wide open.

Renka trailed behind ears flickering attentively, "Your brother has made it into the palace…soldiers battle in the halls. They're too loud for me to hear anything else."

I tipped my head in acknowledgement of her words, "I suppose the best place to go would be the throne room." Renka moved first with me guiding her through the halls after all her hearing was better than mine, she'd sense an enemy long before I would. I glanced periodically behind us to ensure that we were safe on that front.

"Gods!" I spun around seeing Renka duck a sword that had appeared out of thin air. I opened my pouched and tossed a handful of succubus petals slashing the air furiously as a man began to appear. He fell at our feet now completely visible blood spurting from his chest. "Of course you would be as good with a sword as you are with a whip and dagger…is there any weapon you can't use?" Renka questioned drawing my attention from the fact that I'd just killed a man…it never got any easier.

I actually thought about her question as I wiped my sword free of blood on the dead man's tunic unwilling to look at his face for fear that I would find that I knew him. "I don't think I would do too well with an axe." I murmured softly.

Renka chuckled helping me to my feet and wiping a spot of blood from my cheek, "I suppose it's a good thing you're not carrying an axe then."

"A good thing indeed," I offered back as we continued on our way. "We're nearly there…" I pointed down the corridor with the tip of my sword. "Just around that corner where the tapestry of the first Queen of Angileri has been defaced…" I gazed at the tatters of something that had survived generations, now destroyed in a moment of rage or disgust. Renka placed her hand on my shoulder bringing me back to myself. "Lies the throne room…" I finished quietly not wishing to draw unnecessary attention.

"What do you think we'll find there…" Renka asked unwilling to move just yet.

I gazed down the hall sword pointed at the ground. "An end…whether if it's our own or his. We'll doubtfully find an end." I supplied solemnly. Renka gazed at me for a brief moment before we moved as one jogging towards the throne room.

She reached the doors first, transforming as she rammed into them bursting through the doors with me right behind hiding in her shadow. We found Prince Eris sitting on the throne smiling softly as if he'd expected our arrival. I glanced quickly around the room to find Adri off to the side cradling her mother to her chest, tears streaming down her face as she spoke to her motionless body is whispered words. Libeth lay crumpled beside a stone wall cracked from the impact of her body no doubt. Taeli I saw forced to her knees beside the throne by several guards, blood streamed from a cut above her brow. She breathed heavily grimacing in pain.

At once I blinked and a room once empty was now full of men, "Gods I'm tired of walking into ambushes." Renka grumbled as she changed back, shifting closer to me.

"You and me both…" I replied sword raised slightly.

"So glad of you to join us." Prince Eris smiled. "We've been waiting with baited breath for your arrival." He waved his hand towards the Princess. "As you can see the Heir holds her mother slowly dying in her arms. Your Gardener there is either dead or unconscious and…" He furrowed his brow at Taeli as guard wrenched her head back by her hair causing her to cry out. "I really have no idea who she is but she's pretty useless to you now. Hmm, your soldiers will eventually take the palace…but there's nothing for you here."

I shook my head, "What was the point…in ruling a Queendom you planned to destroy?"

"Regardless if I live or die I will always be known as the man who demolished the nation everyone thought untouchable." He shrugged the Queen's crown upon his brow glinted in the light from above. "Though I hadn't really planned on dying as you can see." He finished gazing around the room at how vastly out numbered we were. "If I live and I will live, I can rebuild or move on, and if I die, unlikely as that seems…there's nothing here for you. A win for me either way and ultimately a loss for you." I watched a grin of malicious glee spread across his face. "Taking everything you loved was also enjoyable. It was almost too easy to be honest."

I raised my sword pointing it at his chest steadily, "By my word I will watch the life drain from your eyes and when you're gone…" I met his gaze head on. "When you're gone I promise, that no one will remember your name."

His grin grew wider still as I slowly lowered my sword, "Promises, promises Denarii but did you forget you have to reach me first?"

"No…I just wanted you to be aware of what will happen when I do." I held my pouch of seeds in my hand firmly closed. I let it fall to the ground while he watched brow raised.

"I'm sure you'll need all the handy tricks in that pouch of yours if you hope to make it out of here alive." He countered condescendingly.

"I'm tired of handy tricks." I countered with a shrug allowing my magic to seep into the ground as the Shades attacked, normal soldiers hiding among them. I fought furiously with Renka at my back using brute strength to send Shades and soldiers alike flying in every direction. I slashed here and there, taking off limbs and ignoring screams as I cut a man in two before slitting another's throat. I danced through the shadows never staying in one spot too long least I find myself on the wrong end of someone else's blade. Renka remained at my back, always, guarding me from those who wished to sneak up behind.

"You'll grow tired eventually…and if not you. Your friend will." Eris called after I'd killed a number of traitors, that's how I had to look at them. Men and women who had betrayed their Queen for power, otherwise I'd never find sleep again…if I survived. I wasn't yet sure we'd survive.

"You tired?" I gasped breathlessly, when they'd paused briefly trying to find an opening in our defense. The Prince sat watching rubbing his hands together happily.

Renka's nostrils flared as she breathed deeply, her eyes flashing. "I hope you have a plan Head Gardener…because I'd really hate to die unbroken." I blinked startled at her sudden truth sharing a brief look before turning to face our adversaries.

"I have a plan…it'll just take a little longer to set up." I continued pouring my magic into the ground finding exactly what I'd aimed for…roots, deeply buried roots, dormant but not dead. Strong and thick and dangerous. I glanced up at Prince Eris judging the distance from the ground to the throne seated atop the dais. "Do you trust me?" I questioned as the Shades and soldiers began creeping forward.

Renka shook her head, huffing out a breath, "Sometimes more than I think I should…Why?" I ducked as she spun taking off a soldier's head with nothing but her fist and a whole lot of rage. She screamed a completely inhuman sound and in that moment of slight hesitation caused by fear of the unknown I took several more lives.

"When it happens transform…" I called softly.

Renka growled at my cryptic words but didn't argue, too distracted by trying to stay alive to speak. "Rhyme!" I turned to see a sword heading for my torso too quick for me to block or avoid. For a moment I saw my death and then just as quickly a dagger appeared in the soldier's neck blood splattering my face. I wiped my cheek as he raised his hand towards his neck in confusion blood dribbling from his mouth as he crumpled to the ground never completing his movement. I turned to find Libeth sitting up against the wall face pale, hand held firmly to her side the other falling from where she'd extended it to throw the dagger that had saved my life.

I impaled the person who thought to try the same thing showing no mercy as he fell to the ground. "Is it almost time?" Renka questioned as she kicked a man clear across the room, I heard his bones break as he struck the wall. He didn't move when he hit the ground instantly dead on impact.

The ground began to shake, I kept my feet as stone cracked, shattering completely as large roots from trees far older than I pushed from the ground catching soldiers and Shades alike by surprise. Renka ran towards me as I knocked a man aside clearing my line of sight to the man sitting on the dais. She transformed just as she reached me and I jumped letting her momentum carry me for a time, a root flicked upward curling slightly and I leaped using it as a foothold before jumping again raising my sword as it slammed down killing those not quick enough to get out the way. I took in the Prince watching the smile slowly fade from his eyes at last as he saw his death in mine. I screamed a sound of rage and anguish at all that he'd taken from me as I landed on the dais thrusting my sword straight through his chest.

I leaned forward twisting the blade to the side as I gazed him in the eyes, "I never break my promises." I hissed softly wrenching my sword from his body. He chuckled softly choking on his own blood as with grim finality the light faded from his eyes.

Someone touched my shoulder and I turned sword raised to find Rosen gazing at me with kind eyes. I gazed around confused to find bodies littering the ground...that I could see, the rest destroyed by raised roots that once again lay still, now covered in blood and yet still pulsing with the life of my magic. "You betray us..." I lowered my sword unable and unwilling to kill even one more person.

"No..." Rosen took my sword gently from limp fingers. "I ensured that you all made it out of the palace alive. It was I who struck you with the knife, not in the heart but beside it. As strong as you are I knew you could heal it. It was I who suggested poison to the Princess instead of killing her out right, I twinned the plant in her hair. I sent the Princesses together. I threw the dagger that just saved your life..." I watched as she wiped my blade free of blood on a dead man's sleeve. Nimbly plucking the Queen's crown from his head and offering each to me.

"I hate you…" I murmured softly tears blurring my vision. "I hate you more than words can say for what you put me through. For making me think even for a moment that you'd betrayed us."

"I love you too…for achieving all that I'd expected of you and more." I did not fight her as she pulled me into her arms and held me firmly against her chest despite the blood that coated every inch of me. I was so tired of fighting.

"The Queen…" I started as I pulled away using my magic briefly causing the roots to shift revealing a small alcove where Adri had dragged her mother. Libeth sat beside them leaning against the wall eyes closed hand clutched firmly against her side. Taeli crouched near at hand a bloody rag that looked as if it had once been a part of her shirt tied around her head. I leapt from the dais and raced towards them as Renka dragged herself from beneath a large root, legs bent oddly brow dripping with sweat.

Rosen broke away from me and moved towards the Marr alarmed by her injuries, "Gods…" I heard Renka say, voice breathy with pain as I dropped down beside the Princess sword clattering beside me. I'd forgotten I'd held it in my haste.

"How is she?" I asked softly noting the tears streaming Adri's face, as well as the blue tint to the Queen's lips and the waxy pallor of her skin.

"Tell me you can heal her Rhyme…tell me you can heal her like you healed me?" Adri pleaded softly cradling her mother in her arms.

I gazed down at the Queen not needing to feel for her pulse to know that she was long gone… She'd probably been dead before the battle had even begun. I checked anyway. I felt for her pulse at her neck, at her wrist, and even her thigh. I rested my head on her chest and listened carefully, I held my palm lightly above her mouth and nose on the off chance that perhaps I heard wrong. I pulsed my magic through her veins…only to have it bleed out finding no purchase. No pain that I could heal, no wound that I could close. I laid her crown respectfully upon her chest, before gently folding her hands over it. Adri sobbed softly as I looked at her with grief stricken eyes. "She's gone Adri…the Queen…is gone."

She broke completely then, Rosen appearing to take her in strong arms. "How…" The Princess cried… "How? She has no wounds; she looks like she's sleeping." Rosen and I shared a meaningful look but neither of us spoke. Neither of us wished to say poison, though I'm sure on some level Adri knew. "Mother…" Adri placed kisses all over the Queen's face. "Mother I need you…"

A grunt of effort drew my attention from Adri's pain and I turned to find Renka laying on the ground nostrils flaring in pained frustration. I allowed Rosen to comfort the Princess, drowning in my own emotions as I moved towards the Marr pulling off my helmet as I stepped over several bodies. I knelt beside her taking in the mangled mess of her legs. "I suppose you didn't move out of the way fast enough?" I questioned softly as she gazed up at me twitching with pain.

"This was me trusting you…" She grunted resting her cheek upon her hands sweat and blood dripping onto the stone floor still intact where she lay.

I traced my hands along her legs closing my eyes and aiding the healing process, watching muscles knitting together as bone reconnected and blood replenished itself pumping steadily through healthy veins as neurons fired sparking movement in limbs once paralyzed due to pain. "Gods…" Renka moaned in agony as it all caught up to her brain in an instant, before rolling over and pushing herself into a sitting position. "I'd thank you but some part of me blames you for it."

"You were too slow…" I countered playfully despite all that had transpired.

Renka snapped her teeth at me before pushing unsteadily to her feet, "At least he's dead…" She sighed as I caught her round the waist to keep her from falling on legs that no doubt didn't quite feel like her own. "Despite all that he's taken from us at least he's gone." The Marr finished gazing at the Heir as she cried her heart out against Rosen's chest. "Still smiling even in death…Gods I hate him."

"He's dead…the past tense would be hated." I offered without thinking. Renka snorted shaking her head as she moved towards the Princess with my aid, grimacing in pain despite the healing.

"How did you make it through the forest like this Head Gardener… I feel as if I'll be sick." Renka questioned as I lowered her down beside Libeth, feeling the pain of her broken bones despite the fact that she was healed. I knew from experience that she'd feel that way until she slept. All severe healings in a short span of time were like that.

"Necessity," Was the only answer I could think to give.

The sound of a lot of people in a crowded space reached us soon after and I breathed a sigh of relief as my brother burst through the doors of the throne room with Captain Sowin trailing not far behind. He looked as I felt, covered in blood and battle weary but whole. The Healers reached us first, but they could do no more than I could. After all you couldn't bring back the dead. Reason held me tightly when he reached me, rejoicing in the fact that I had lived. Once the Heir was all cried out, we formed a sling of a banana leaf and vines, Captain Sowin had found my pouch. Gently as if she might break we placed Adri's mother in the sling, as well as all those unable to walk, among them were Renka and Libeth.

Then as one we marched from the palace roots destroying what remained of the building we left behind. We were halfway across the Training Fields when a large bird soared overhead…a warm tingling filled my mind and I halted our procession just short of the Heir's own command. What I'd first thought was a bird grew into something unmistakably reptilian. Murmurs started as a dragon formed of emerald so dark it was near black landed gently before us. It's large slitted eyes far bluer than the Queen's had been. *Majesty...* When she spoke, her voice vibrated through my entire body. I shuddered softly as more tears streamed Adri's face. The dragon, Apora could be speaking of no one else. *We felt the loss of a Great Soul and thought to send aid...* She swung her head on a long sinuous neck taking in all that remained of what had been a beautiful place. *I see we've come too late. Is there anything we may offer you?* Her voice was full of grief, large eyes shining with sadness.

Adri turned gazing back at the ruins of the palace and beyond as if she could glimpse the city now deserted. "Burn it…finish what that man started and ensure that no one can live here for generations to come." She spoke for everyone's benefit, just as Apora could speak in her mind so too could she likely speak into hers.

Are you sure? The Heir…the Queen bowed her head in a firm sign of approval before marching on.

Apora and I gazed at each other for a long moment. *Cleanse it…so that when she feels ready the green may grow here again.* I added before marching after my Queen. I caught up to her easily, our soldiers marching steadily behind. I glanced over my shoulder when we reached the forest watching fire spread across what once was while we moved towards what would be. Rosen placed her hand on my shoulder turning me away and nudging me towards our future. I didn't look back again…

*****

One Year Later

I moaned shivering in frustrated delight as I watched Renka give pleasure to Adri from my position tied to the headboard by something easily escapable as vines. My punishment for disappearing for a seven day without notifying anyone. The guards had been in a panic thinking they'd lost one of the Queen's Consorts and no doubt thinking that it would be their heads. They were new, a gift from King Teaon of Dangilere presented by his daughter and ambassador Princess Taeli and did not truly understand the way things worked here. They'd understand in time. No one was punished for my actions…save me.

"I promise I won't run off again without letting you know now please let me free myself." I think that was the worst part of it, we all knew I could easily free myself if I wished, but we also knew I couldn't stand to see either of them upset with me for long and so would take my punishment willingly until one of them said otherwise.

"What do you think?" Renka husked pressing a tender kiss against Adri's thigh as she came back to herself twinning her fingers lovely through Renka's tricolored hair. It was nearly as long as mine had been once upon a time. "Has she suffered enough?"

Adri gazed at the frustration in my eyes, the sweat coating my skin, and my fists clenched tightly around the vines holding me in place before sighing softly. "You were doing so well Rhyme…where did you go?" Her Majesty questioned allowing me to free my hands.

"I know." I pulled my hands free vines once more becoming a part of the headboard as if they'd never left.

"We just held our joining ceremony a seven day ago. You remember the dragons, the royalty, the parade of soldiers…" Renka's nostrils flared just talking about it. I think she hated politics ten times more than I did.

I grimaced remembering it all in vivid detail, "I remember."

"You're no longer just the Head Gardener, a large title in itself, you're now the Queen's Consort and royalty in your own right. So knowing the danger…why did you disappear without a guard detail or allowing Renka or I to know where you'd gone?" Adri asked concern furrowing her brow. "We don't want to lose you."

"I know. I know and I'm sorry, truly honestly it'll never happen again. I just wanted to give you a gift of my own Dri." I clutched her hands in mine while Renka rubbed her back soothingly sensing her distress in a way only someone not fully human could.

"Rhyme you are a gift in yourself…what more could you possibly give me?" She asked softly eyes shining with all the love she felt for me.

I took a deep breath before speaking, "You're pregnant…Renka is as well. I told her on the night of our joining ceremony." I watched tears of joy shimmer in her eyes. "I also told Renka to trust me…before I left." I glared at the Marr who smiled sweetly. "You'd think she'd have mentioned that."

"You'd think by now, you know how much I hate you doing things without explanation and that I would of course adeptly punish you given the chance in the future after said request…" Renka offered nonchalantly when Adri gazed at her curiously.

"She has you there Rhy…" Adri used the shortened version of my name, signaling that I was no longer in her ill grace.

I relaxed pressing a tender kiss to her fingertips. "That she does Dri that she does. Now your gift…" I smiled softly thinking of the skill and divine intervention it had taken to achieve what I'd done. "You'll love it Majesty…and you'll finally forget that man who thought he took everything from you."

"Not everything…" Adri stroked my cheek gently while Renka butted her head playfully. "Just enough though…"

"Just enough." I agreed tracing my fingers along her tummy listening to the familiar song of our child. I relaxed more fully soothed beyond compare.

"I wish…I could hear him, her…can you tell at this point what they are?" Adri gazed at me with wonder in her eyes waiting for me to answer.

"They're both girls…" I smiled. "Two beautiful girls…" I made a small suggestion in my mind pushing it towards those two lovely songs I'd never forget as long as I live.

Renka's eyes widened first, "Gods", she breathed in awe as Adri brought her hands to her mouth tears falling more steadily now.

"They're so beautiful…how did you choose?" I leaned forward pressing a tender kiss to Adri's lips and then Renka's, the Marr gripped me by the collar and nipped my bottom lip as softly as she could, leaving behind an all too familiar stinging sensation that she soothed with her tongue. I thought briefly of the past…Adri's near death and me saving her…of almost dying myself and all the things I couldn't remember and the two beautiful songs that I could.

I pulled away smiling softly… "They sounded familiar." Adri chuckled wiping her face. "We should sleep…the faster we sleep the faster I get to show you your gift." I glanced between them, "Who's in the middle tonight?" I remembered that I'd been in the middle the night before but not who'd been there the night before that.

"It's Renka's turn," Adri nudged the Marr, and we all shifted until she lay pressed snuggly between us.

I playfully tried to catch her flickering ear in my mouth while Adri watched fighting laughter. Fed up after just a few moments Renka snorted her frustration and laid her ears flat, I continued nipping at her until she turned to face me. "I will bite you." She threated with no real heat.

I bared my throat heart racing with desire, "I can take you." Renka's eyes glowed in the dim light of the room lit by the eternal fireflies standing in every corner of the room. I could see Leaf inching towards the door not wanting to be traumatized by another bout of lovemaking. He'd been so quiet I'd forgotten he was there.

"I think she's challenging you Ren…" Adri murmured resting her chin on her upraised palm.

"You think a Gardener can take one of the Horse People?" Renka asked no one in particular.

"I think…" Adri watched the quick rise and fall of my chest as I tensed slightly waiting for Renka to move. "We're about to find out." Renka pounced and like always I lost, after all despite my magic, I was only human.

"Goddess," I breathed as she pressed me down against the mattress tracing firm hands along my body. I wrapped my legs around her waist as she slipped her hand between my thighs easily finding my need. "Don't stop…" I gasped when she slipped inside me. She didn't…not for a long time after that at least and by then I was long spent...

I woke slowly to the feel of warm fingers tracing the scars trailing along my back, I shifted slightly opening my eyes to see Adri sitting up in bed reading through several sheaves of parchment hands completely full. I shifted groaning when I felt the twinge of pain from the bite mark on my neck. Renka chuckled softly behind me while Adri smiled down at me reaching forward to trace her fingers through my hair now just a little shorter than shoulder length. "You're awake."

"When did you bite me?" I questioned brow furrowed as I tried to remember all that had transpired the night before. After the first three orgasms everything was a bit of a blur, I'm not surprised I don't remember it.

"Last orgasm, just before you passed out." She explained with Adri there to tip her head in full agreement.

"How'd I get in the middle?" I closed my eyes unwilling to move just yet, enjoying the comfort their joint presence brought me before I had to start the day.

"I had to use the bathroom in the middle of the night and didn't want to wake you." Renka pressed a tender kiss between my shoulder blades. "Do you want to show the Queen her gift now or later?" The Marr asked making me groan again, staying in bed all day sounded way too good right then.

"Rhyme you have to get up, Libeth has already come knocking and your brother not far behind her for Ren. We all have our duties and I don't really want to have my Chief Advisor and the previous Head Gardener to come looking for us...you remember what happened last time." I pushed up right, Renka already running for the closet while Adri laughed at our haste.

The "last time," Rosen had found us lounging in bed ignoring our duties she'd knocked us out with an enchantment, no doubt having Mariel's help in some way and we'd all woken up in the center of the city in nothing but our underthings. The Queen at least had been surrounded by guards, we'd not been joined yet and therefore weren't that lucky. It wasn't an experience we'd soon forget.

"What are you reading love?" I turned to face Adri realizing that she was already fully dressed wearing her mother's crown. On most days she wore the one cast in the image of the one I'd made of plants. When we were in the Gardens and she felt burdened she wore the one I'd crafted and when she was missing her mother, she wore her crown to remember her.

"A letter from the King of Ierilo, Sir Zeron made it home and recounted all that he remembered of what transpired before he escaped. The King sends his regards and denies all knowledge of his son's actions. He hopes this will not disrupt the peace between us..."

She glanced up at me. "Considering the fact that Prince Eris tried to kill his protector and that said protector didn't agree with his actions from the start. I'm inclined to agree that Prince Eris had his own agenda coming here that had nothing to do with his father. An old man now lacking an Heir...though I think he lucked out with that one."

Renka snorted drawing our attention, she'd just finished braiding her hair letting it go so that it could swing gently behind her. Somehow she'd woven a few strands over the circlet atop her head in several areas, to keep it from falling off when she went to train the horses. Reason trained the soldiers to ride the horses and Renka trained the horses to understand and care for the riders making my brother's job easier. They loved their work but sometimes...mostly always butted heads. "I fully agree."

I donned my circlet mostly silver with vines wrapped around it, they twinned in my hair ensuring that it wouldn't fall off if I did something crazy...I'd lost it several times the first day alone. Adri had not been pleased. "As do I," I pulled Adri to her feet pressing a kiss to her lips as I pulled the parchment from her hands. "Work later, I want to show you your gift."

"Alright, alright...but we have to be quick. I have a Council meeting later to introduce the new members." Adri smiled against my lips, "It's gonna be interesting."

"Indeed, who did you pick again. The Sol-Lea once infected by the Void...no one really knows how exactly she just reappeared after everything was said and done with seemingly no idea of what had happened for the past few years. Captain Sowin...not even a citizen of Angileri..."

"Neither are you." Adri countered.

Renka raised her hands, "Marriage counts for something," she argued. "Guard Captain Neola refused, Lialey refused enjoying the safeness of her anonymity. Ahh and I think the last one was…Cook's daughter. So a traitor, a foreigner, and a servant." The Marr laughed softly.

"I wish I were there to see the looks on their faces." I flicked her braid on my way to the door. "I'll be sure to tell you all about it." As the Head Gardener I had an automatic seat on the Council. The joy it brought to my life I thought with a grimace of distaste.

"I look forward to it," I opened the door and ushered them forward Leaf waiting on the other side to greet them with warm happiness that they couldn't feel. I smiled down at the green knight closing the door behind me, like always, unless I said otherwise, he trailed behind me ready to explore.

*****

Renka, I could tell knew exactly where we were going when we began our trek through several tree trunks, and tunnels made of long dead lumber, no doubt remembering it from all those months ago. She raised her brow at me curiously. I simply smiled and raised my finger to my lips, she smiled back and shook her head. Just as we reached the familiar archway with sunlight shinning beyond I halted them, "You have to close your eyes now." I spoke softly as if others might hear me. They shared a look but did as I'd asked. "No peeking." I tugged them forward each by an arm guiding them into the center of my own private garden.

I breathed a sigh of relief to find it just as I'd left it, so beautiful that it took my breath away. I asked a request of my children, still little more than mere seeds inside their mothers, and prayed to the Goddess that it would work. "You can look now."

Adri opened her eyes, widening slightly as she first took in the beauty of this place and then the large Alia rose floating in the center of the small pond, on the edge of the pond there were small green buds that when night fell regardless if the moon shown or not would bloom into were lilies. I still hadn't quite figured out how I'd done it without magic but here they were. I smiled softly as Adri gasped in shock and Renka choked on air finally seeing exactly what I saw through the magic of our daughters. On the edge of the pond sitting among the buds of the were lilies sat two spirits side by side, one in the striking image of a Queen's niece small and beautiful and the other resembling the former Queen of Angileri, Adri's mother.

Adri stepped forward hesitantly before gazing back at me… "Can I talk to her?"

"I'd not have brought you here otherwise." I nudge her forward gently. "Take as much time as you need." Adri moved forward on shaky legs crouching down beside the two spirits and speaking slowly. They turned to her listening attentively to all she had to say.

"Is that her…is that the former Queen of Angileri?" Renka asked coming to stand beside me.

"I'm not sure…I've never wondered where the spirits come from, I just know that they're there and that after I've seen them once I always see the same spirit associated with the same flower. Some flowers all have spirits of their own, small spirits like the faeries and some are like the former Queen, one large spirit for an entire group of blooms. I'd like to think it's her…"

"This is the best gift you could have given her, the chance to say goodbye." Renka laid her head on my shoulder while we watched Adri's face light up with laughter. "How long will this last? Being able to see what you see?"

"Until the girls are born I suppose and perhaps a little after depending on if the magic lingers." I wrapped my arm around her waist resting my head atop hers.

"She'll be here every day." Renka murmured chuckling softly.

"Do you really mind if it means she'll finally be able to move on and forget about that man?" I questioned.

Renka sighed softly, "No. No I don't." The Marr nuzzled my neck gently above my collar where she'd marked me. "She looks so happy Rhyme and you did that…"

"No we did it. Together." I squeezed her arm softly as we watched the Queen waving her hands about sharing all the crazy things that had happened in the past few months, all the people returning, the coronation, the wedding, my disappearing acts and the punishments as a result Adri shared it all while we stood watching from a distance remembering it all with her and laughing when it was appropriate.

The sun shone down brightly upon us, slowly creeping along the sky, eventually Renka and I found ourselves sitting beside Adri talking with the spirits. The spirit of the former Queen, for I was sure it was her now despite the green spouting from her hair and the emerald tint to her skin, turned to me winking playfully. I winked back before gazing back and forth between the two women I loved realizing in that moment that I'd found my home.

It had taken years of struggling and fighting a small war to reach it, but I wouldn't have it any other way and in the silence of my own mind I thanked Queen Servasli for giving me everything I never knew I wanted. After all it all began when she took me away…

Epilogue

Renka, Adri and I sat around a table in the center of Lialey's Inn, Eden was entertaining a group of small children with Rhea's help. I smiled as she weaved magic in the air for the children to see. She was a natural at it, Servali and Lasil sat off to the side entertaining themselves with a few seeds I'd given them when we'd arrived. Leaf watched as always fascinated by even the hint of magic. The girls looked exactly like their mothers'. Servali with her earth and sand hair and her striking twilight eyes. Lasil with my dark hair and features but Renka's ringed irises, I watched her ears flicker curiously as the seeds grew into different flowers one even sprouting a faerie while they watched. I could hear their oohing and ahhing from here. "They're beautiful, just like their mothers'." Lialey murmured pressing a kiss to my cheek, before winking playfully at Adri and Renka to show she meant no harm. She was gone as quick as she came, always busy.

"Who do you think will succeed whom?" Renka asked watching our children play, Rhea included in that question.

Adri stroked her cheek, "It seems a bit too obvious for me to really tell. I want to say that surely Rhea will follow in Rhyme's footsteps, but she has a passion for performing and I would not put it past her to become a bard. Servali has my features and so one would think perhaps she'd be the next Queen…but she has a gentle nature and enjoys the green nearly as much as if not more than Rhyme does." I chuckled thinking of all the messes we'd gotten into together. "And Lasil is of the Horse People obviously, she could go either way, she might wish to travel and then perhaps come back pass her trials and one day be Queen… and so perhaps it's not as obvious as one might think." Adri finished with a sigh. "Though we have years yet to figure it out, they've just reached their sixth summer and Rhea her tenth. No need to rush them into anything."

"I was simply curious is all Majesty, you're the one plotting it all out." Adri stuck her tongue out at Renka's teasing while I watched our children play.

"You're speaking as if it isn't possible for us to have more children," I countered as Lasil got tired of seeds and came racing towards us. She reached for the Queen, murmuring *up* in her mind unaware that unlike when she was in the womb, Adri could no longer hear her. "Use your words Sweetling," I offered gently stilling Adri's hands before she could pick her up. "She has to learn to speak…" I said in answer to Adri's questioning look. "Instead of using her thoughts."

Lasil went to flare her nostrils in frustration when Renka snapped her teeth like thunder in warning, not about to tolerate any sass. "Up Mama?" Lasil asked meekly.

"You're a bit old for this love," Adri said with a grunt of effort as she pulled our child onto her lap.

Servali came next offering me the flowers she'd gotten to bloom smiling softly. I stroked my fingers through her hair gently. "They look lovely Servali, would you like me to braid them into a crown on your head?" She nodded vigorously too delighted to speak. I turned her around and gently weaved the flowers into her hair, a skill I'd learned from watching Renka do it every day before we went to work.

"You're here!" Sorel rushed forward hugging his sister tightly. I stood accepting a hug of my own. The Prince that wasn't, had become more of a man than I'd ever thought he'd been so many years ago now.

"How was Dangilere?" Renka asked accepting a hug of her own as Eden finished his story telling and came to greet his husband with a kiss.

Rhea nudge me with her shoulder opening her palm to reveal an Alia rose, "Not bad Sprout not bad at all." I said in admiration. "Of course I could do better."

Rhea scoffed, eyes sparkling with mirth, "Not a chance." Servali giggled at our usual banter. I snapped my fingers for effect nothing more and sat back as the seeds I'd placed earlier came to life and like on the day I'd first met my royal wife. twilight peonies floated gently from above.

Adri shook her head catching one in her palm smiling softly as her face warmed, "Show off."

"One day I'm going to beat you." Rhea shook her head holding one of the peonies in her hand before bringing it to her face to breathe in its scent. "That day just isn't today."

"Dangilere was interesting, not as green that's for sure. Of course I missed my family the entire time, but finally got a few things straightened out. They're willing to work with us to push out the freedom for all law that encompasses mythical creatures and magical beings." Renka whooped softly clapping her hands together before butting her head against Sorel's in excitement.

He stumbled backwards in a daze, not expecting it. Thankfully Eden caught him before he could fall. The girls laughed softly, us adults covered it a bit better but we were all thoroughly amused by the display. "Did we miss it?" Libeth, Emery, Rosen and Mariel came rushing into Inn gazing at us as if we'd announced big news. Rhea gazed at me curiously a question tickling at my mind. I shook my head; she'd have to wait like everyone else.

Sorel shared his news again and of course there was more cheering, we all shared a glass of tea conscious of the children and not wanting them to feel left out of the festivities. Reason strolled in a little later with Taeli in tow and our table had grown from one, to two, to three before we knew it. People were gawking at so much royalty in one place, acting well, normal. I was sure it was probably a fascinating sight to behold. What happened next would probably stick in their minds for the rest of their lives. I enjoyed that thought immensely. "Seriously you guys, it's not a big deal and I'd not have done it without Taeli. Regardless I have no real weight and so the negations will have to be passed along to someone better able to represent the Queendom."

"So humble..." I murmured as I stood, everyone becoming silent. "A little over six years ago I never thought you would come this far, I never thought that you'd push past the bitterness of what you didn't have and finally appreciate all the things you did. You were stripped of your title and I thought it fitting because you didn't deserve it. I didn't even see you as a man...I saw you as less than." I smiled brightly. "I am happy to finally say you've proved me wrong. With our busy schedules none of were able to make ending the slavery of mythical creatures in different nations a priority and so you did. You went beyond our borders and met with foreign monarchs and ambassadors alike, you did what none of us could do. You dedicated your time and effort to a just cause and finally, you're seeing the fruits of your labor. The first nation willing to agree to an end to slavery and one of the big seven, no less. It's no small accomplishment and now you're saying that you're willing to pass the torch so to speak because you don't carry the weight you need to really get things done."

I glanced briefly at Adri asking permission with my eyes, she bowed her head in a sign of approval, smiling behind the cover of her hand. "I don't think anyone can go forward and keep pushing this quite as firmly as you have with such sheer determination and a passion that never seems to die. Which is why your Queen is willing to bestow upon you the title Prince, and all the lands and money that comes with it to aid you in your endeavor." I raised my glass to him and everyone raised there's with me while the man that had once more become a Prince gazed at me in shock. "Congratulations Prince Sorel," I bowed slightly. "You've finally earned your title, and with it my respect."

Mariel came from behind him placing a circlet crafted from silver upon his brow, a flower from the plains where Renka had grown up was most prominent in the piece. It signified the freedom he would bring about while representing the Queen of Angileri. "You've done well brother." She placed a kiss to his cheek after settling the crown properly on his head.

Everyone cheered, even those surrounding us, seeing history in the making. Sorel stood as I took my seat, everyone quieted again. Rhea hugged me from behind smiling against my cheek, Servali stood leaning on the table beside me and Lasil had drifted off against Adri's chest. We waited for him to speak. "I don't know what to say...thank you just doesn't seem to be enough, but thank you none the less. I have so many thoughts racing through my mind, but chief among them being that I wouldn't be here without you Head Gardener. It all began when you disrespected me, ready and willing to prove that a title meant nothing without actions to uphold the honor of it. You broke me, but you were not cruel, and you gave me the love of my life who I didn't even know I was searching for." Eden smiled softly as Sorel tipped his glass in his honor.

"Everything I have, is because of you..." He raised his glass high and we joined him in a toast. "To titles well-earned and beatings that are never forgotten."

Everyone laughed before we drank our juice, I glanced up at the single were lily sprouting from a beam overhead. The spirit of the former Queen gazed down at us face lit joyously. She winked at me and I winked back before enjoying the rest of the evening spent with family. Life had never been so good.

54855831R00221

Made in the USA
Lexington, KY
30 August 2016